The Heavenly Surrender

Center Point
Large Print

Also by Marcia Lynn McClure and available from Center Point Large Print:

Dusty Britches
Weathered Too Young
The Windswept Flame
The Visions of Ransom Lake

**This Large Print Book carries the
Seal of Approval of N.A.V.H.**

The Heavenly Surrender

Marcia Lynn McClure

CENTER POINT LARGE PRINT
THORNDIKE, MAINE

This Center Point Large Print edition
is published in the year 2017 by arrangement with
Distractions Ink.

The text of this Large Print edition is unabridged.
In other aspects, this book may vary
from the original edition.
Printed in the United States of America
on permanent paper.
Set in 16-point Times New Roman type.

ISBN: 978-1-68324-380-9

Library of Congress Cataloging-in-Publication Data

Names: McClure, Marcia Lynn, author.
Title: The heavenly surrender / Marcia Lynn McClure.
Description: Center Point Large Print edition. | Thorndike, Maine :
Center Point Large Print, 2017.
Identifiers: LCCN 2017004025 | ISBN 9781683243809
    (hardcover : alk. paper)
Subjects: LCSH: Large type books. | Domestic fiction. | GSAFD: Love
stories.
Classification: LCC PS3613.C36 H43 2017 | DDC 813/.6—dc23
LC record available at https://lccn.loc.gov/2017004025

To My Faithful Friends . . .
Who have read loyally
and enjoyed thoroughly . . .
from the beginning!

And
To Karen . . .
Because after all . . . this is still your book!

The Heavenly Surrender

Chapter One

"Ya're loose in the head, Brevan McLean! Loose, I tell ya," Brenna scolded her brother.

Brevan looked down at his younger sister standing next to the wagon. She glared up at him—furiously.

"It's me own business, it is, Brenna. And none of it yars," he reminded.

"Ha!" she exclaimed. "None of me business, is it? Well, let me tell ya a thing or two," she began, pointing a dainty index finger at the man—wagging it with chiding. It was an Irish accent that deepened noticeably as Brenna's emotions heightened—still, her dark hair and blue eyes somewhat belied her ancestry. "I'll not be havin' it! Do ya hear me? I'll not be havin' ya runnin' off and marryin' some old, wrinkled-up raisin of a woman!"

"And what makes ya be so certain she be old and wrinkled up?" Brevan asked.

He was amused at his sister's near hysteria. Brevan McLean's even darker hair and even bluer eyes were more deceiving yet. It seemed the people in the North American West perceived Irishmen to be always green eyed, red haired, and quick tempered. Thick accent and quick temperament were the only obvious physical attributes possessed by the McLeans—who were in fact native Irishmen now settled in the eastern Colorado territory.

"Why else would she be havin' to answer advertisements to find a husband then? Hmm? Tell me that? She's either wrinkled up and old . . . or larger than any ship you and I ever set our eyes upon! I tell ya, Brevan . . . ya're mad! Don't do it." Brenna sighed. She knew that no amount of scolding could convince her brother to abandon his current course.

"Now, Brenna," Brevan began. "Ya've got the steam a blowin' from yar ears like a lunatic woman. I've explained this to ya 'til me throat is raw from explainin'—you and our little brat of a brother, Brian, have married and begun to settle onto yar own lands. That be well and fine, and I'm happy for the both of ya, I am . . . but Father left me this land, he did . . . these orchards, the fields. I'll not let him down by losin' them or lessenin' their worth . . . and I cannot do it alone. I'm man enough to admit it, I am. And it's time I settled as well. Ya know that I've not the patience, nor the time, to waste on courtin' some silly young lass who'll be worthless when it comes to hard work." He raised a hand to silence his sister—her mouth falling open with the intent of arguing again. "This Genieva Bankmans sounds to be a hard-workin', serious-minded woman. Ya've read the letters she's written to me, haven't ya now?"

Brenna dropped a guilty gaze to the ground for a moment but looked up quickly when Brevan chuckled before continuing. "It's me own decision . . . none but mine. I've set me mind to this, Brenna." Taking the lines of his team in hand, he added, "I'm off now to pick up me new wife at the train station. I'm sure ya'll be here to meet her . . . a starin' and a gawkin' like ya just seen one of the little people dancin' a jig on yar knee." Brevan snapped the leather at the backs of the team of horses, and the wagon lurched forward.

"Ya're lost in the mind, Brevan McLean! And ya're too daft to know it!" Brenna cried after him. Turning on her heels, she stormed off in the direction of the farm and orchard owned by her new husband and bordering Brevan's lands to the west. "Father and Mother are sure as rollin' over in their coffins at seein' this," she muttered, shaking her head with severe disapproval.

Undaunted by his sister's nagging, the uncommonly handsome Brevan McLean drove toward town with renewed determination—toward town and whatever the train steaming from the east would leave there.

"I know me own needs," he grumbled to himself. Taking the paper from his shirt pocket, he once more read the most recent letter he'd received from the as yet unseen Miss Genieva Bankmans. Again he noted the neat and immaculately straight-lined penmanship as he read:

Dear Mr. McLean,

I feel, as you do, that this arrangement will be beneficial and satisfactory for both of us. I agree that we, having committed to follow through with the previously corresponded terms, will legally marry upon my arrival next week. I expect nothing from you, save a place of residence, the required necessities of living, hard work to keep my mind and physical being occupied, and respect. I, in turn, will assist you in whatever is required to sustain and maintain your land and crops, while providing meals, doing mending, and fulfilling other non-intimate duties commonly performed by a man's legal wife.

I will arrive in Blue Springs on the 10:00 a.m. train, April 3rd. And finally, to answer your rather unexpected question, I am in no manner averse to immigrants, and I hope you will show the same attitude toward me, being that I am from the eastern United States.

Sincerely,

Genieva Bankmans

Nodding, Brevan returned the paper to his shirt pocket. "Hard-workin' woman with a sound brain in her head," he mumbled. Let Brenna nag him 'til her throat was bloody—he knew what he wanted and needed out of life. This Genieva Bankmans would do just fine.

Genieva Bankmans retrieved a small hand mirror from her purse and studied her reflection. Her hands shook unsteadily as she tucked a stray strand of hair back, fixing it with a loosened pin. Replacing her hat, she wrinkled her nose and stuck out her tongue—entirely disappointed at her appearance. Rubbing fiercely at the light freckles sprinkled across her nose and cheeks, she sighed, inwardly admitting no amount of prayer or wishing would make the unsightly pigments disappear. True, the natural rose-pink of youth colored her cheeks and lips perfectly. And her ever-changing hazel eyes—being green this day— were shaded by long lashes several hues darker than her rather plainly tinted brown hair. Returning the mirror to her purse, she inhaled deeply and straightened her shoulders and posture— attempting to appear a bit taller. Still, she knew her petite size provoked no menacing presence.

"He'll throw me right back on this train if I appear to be a weakling," she muttered to herself as the train slowed to a stop before the station. After disembarking, Genieva cleared her throat, stiffened her posture once more, and marched forward toward the station house. Apparently this Brevan McLean intended to meet her within—for not a soul was present on the station's outer porch.

• • •

Brevan McLean stood strong and intimidating in one corner of the train station. He watched as the train slowed to a halt and the passengers began to exit the coaches. One by one the passengers filed into the station. For a moment, his attention was captured by a small young woman stepping into the building. A spontaneous, amused grin spread across his handsome face. He was immediately impressed by what could only be dubbed *cuteness*. This girl—and she could hardly be more than a girl—was not an overwhelming beauty. This girl possessed a much more rare and appealing appearance in fact—that of being profoundly *cute*. The sparse freckles scattered across her nose broadened the smile on Brevan's face as he looked past her and out at the remaining disembarking passengers. He ignored the twinge of regret pricking at his heart—caused by the realization that he could never allow such a sweet-looking lass to turn his head again. In an hour's time he would be a married man.

"Excuse me," Genieva began, clearing her throat as she approached the ticket master's counter. "I'm . . . I'm looking for a man . . ." she began.

"There's a lot of women 'round these here parts a lookin' for men, my girl," the ticket master teased.

"I'm sure that's true, sir . . . far less than men

looking for women, however," she rallied. Genieva was determined not to let the stranger in the ticket window unsettle her any further than she had already managed to unsettle herself. The unnervingly attractive man standing in one corner to her left, however, looked over at her. He grinned a deliciously alluring grin, and Genieva inwardly thanked the heavens that this man was not Brevan McLean. She'd noticed the man the moment she'd entered the station, and the way he had knowingly glanced at her with those stunning blue eyes as she had passed him had nearly caused her to trip over her own feet because of his profoundly handsome stature and face. In truth, he was entirely too handsome. Men like him were no doubt an unendurable handful.

"I'm looking for a particular man," she continued. "His name is Brevan McLean. I'm to meet him here today and I'm not at all sure which . . ." Genieva was interrupted—gasped as she felt someone firmly take hold of her arm. Looking up, she saw she was held in the nearly painful grip of none other than the unnervingly attractive man who had been standing in the corner.

He glared down at her—though he spoke to the ticket master. "One ticket, Hubert. Back to Illinois, it is," the towering man growled.

"I beg your pardon, sir?" Genieva asserted in return, wrenching her arm free of his hold. "And just who are you to be telling me . . . ?" Her eyes

15

widened in comprehension. This man? This was the man who had found it necessary to advertise for a wife? This could not possibly be the man she was to meet.

"'Tis Brevan McLean, I am, lass. And ya're a liar," he accused.

"How dare you?" Genieva exclaimed. "How dare you accuse me of such a thing when it is completely unfounded?"

"Ya came here to marry me, did ya not?" the massive male growled.

"Yes. And you asked me to."

The ticket master's eyes widened as the conversation between the man and woman continued.

"I did not know ya were a wee runt of a thing! And ya look to have less than sixteen years upon ya! That was not part of the bargain," Brevan McLean grumbled.

"You're right, sir. Neither age nor appearance was part of the bargain. And I wasn't exactly expecting a great grouching bear either!" Genieva countered.

"And what exactly would ya be meanin' by that, lass?" Brevan McLean roared.

"The male ego," Genieva sighed. "Such a fragile thing. You may call me Miss Bankmans, Mr. McLean. Very well, ticket man . . . stamp the return ticket . . . but be sure to have the local newspaper print that the hotheaded Brevan McLean is not a desirable man to enter into business with. He turns tail at the first sign of unexpected circumstance."

Genieva looked up defiantly as she felt Brevan McLean take hold of her arm once more.

"There now, Hubert . . . ya wouldn't be havin' the time to witness a marriage, would ya now?" Brevan McLean asked the man.

Hubert chuckled and said, "Shore would, Mr. McLean. Shore would."

Moments after the local minister had pronounced them man and wife, Brevan McLean shook Genieva's hand firmly, fairly dragging her from the minister's home and most indecorously proceeding *not* to assist her up onto the seat of his wagon. He slapped the lines at the back of his team and began to talk. Not to converse—for there was a profound difference—Brevan McLean then talked to Genieva Bankmans McLean.

"I've got me a little brother, Brian. He married a bonny Mexican girl last spring named Lita. They be livin' on a cattle ranch 'bout a mile south of me own land. Me sister, Brenna, just married a nice lad named Travis. He's a good man. They live just west of me on another section." Genieva glanced away uncomfortably as Brevan turned his attention to her—caught her staring at him. "Ya won't see any red hair in the lot of us McLeans, ya won't. Me mother was a Creole girl from New Orleans. She married me father when her family went to Ireland durin' the war here. She had hair as black as obsidian and sky-blue eyes. Brenna is the image of her, she is. Me and Brian got the ugly mugs of the family."

Genieva nervously bit her lip. Brevan McLean was not at all what she had expected. On the one hand, this fact was a pleasant one—considering Genieva had been afraid she would wind up the wife of an ancient, wrinkled-up old prune of a man. All the same, Brevan McLean disturbed her. He was so handsome that a person could feel the very fact of it even without looking at him. She knew she would have to work hard to live up to his expectations. Yet that would serve—for no doubt it would serve her best to keep busy—both mind and body.

"There's no high adventure out here, Genieva. If that's what ya came lookin' for, it's disappointed ya'll be," he stated.

"I came to work. To make a life for myself," she reminded him, straightening her back in an effort to feel more certain of her decision. "And in this world a woman cannot do that without a man . . . no matter how unfair a fact it is." She could not help adding, "By the way . . . to dispel any misconceptions you may have . . . I'll be twenty years old in three months."

"It's only a wee miracle, that one," he mumbled.

The beguilingly attractive Brevan McLean didn't say one other word as they traveled toward his lands, and Genieva was soon lost in the beauty of her surroundings. There was no horrid, frigid wind from the lake here—only a soft, cooling breeze carrying the pleasing tune of a meadowlark's call on its breath. The scent of grasses and trees was heavenly, and all along the road there sprung wildflowers of every color and sort imaginable. A small chipmunk darted across the path in front of the team, and Genieva bit her smiling lip to keep from squealing out in delight. Chicago had been so noisy, smelly, and crowded. But here—here she felt as if her spirit were breathing for the first time since she was a child. The smooth rhythm of the horses—the fragrances of nature—the beauty of blue sky and mountains was perfect. Genieva relished it like nothing she'd ever experienced before. Time seemed unimportant—only the fact that her soul was free.

She was awestruck when her eyes, yet green in those moments, beheld one of the most beautiful sights imaginable. To her right, just beyond a neat-posted fence, stood an apple orchard—trees fully frocked in the most beautiful of white blossoms. The aroma of the blossoming flowers hung thick on the breeze, and even above the wagon's wheels rambling on the dirt road, Genieva could hear the soft hum of bees buzzing about through the tree limbs—performing the endless work for which they were created.

"That's the most beautiful thing I've ever seen,"

she muttered to herself, dreamily gazing at the orchard.

"That be me own orchard there. The house is just a ways now, and I've no doubt that me sister, Brenna, will be buzzin' 'round like the very bees in the blossoms," Brevan McLean grumbled. He suddenly smiled then—began to chuckle. Genieva looked at him, curious—puzzled by his change of manner. "That be the one good thing about yar appearance. Brenna will drop her teeth when she sees yar not a wrinkled-up old raisin of a thing, she will." Genieva could not hide the delighted grin spreading across her face at the sound of his chuckle. It was thoroughly engaging—and his accent was to her ears as the taste of sugar to her mouth.

The team turned the corner. A house came into view, and Genieva's hands clutched her stomach as it churned with anxious anticipation. She had never before considered there might be other family members to contend with. What if the rest of the McLean clan was as averse to her as Brevan had been?

As Brevan brought the team to a stop directly before the house, a beautiful young woman stepped out of it. The screen door bumped closed behind her, and she stopped—staring at Genieva in obvious wonder. Instantly Genieva felt like an alley cat keeping company with purebred Persians. She knew this woman to be Brevan's sister, Brenna—for she had the same dark hair and blue eyes that were Brevan's. She had not one freckle on her perfectly sculpted and small nose, nor was she irritatingly petite in her perfectly curved and balanced figure.

In the next moment, the young woman placed her delicate-looking fists firmly—one on each hip—and smiled with triumph. Clicking her tongue in scolding, she approached the wagon.

"Well, Brevan McLean. I'll say this for ya, I will . . . somebody's watchin' over ya from above," she said. She offered her hand to Genieva in greeting as the new bride climbed down. "I'm Brenna," she introduced herself. "Brevan's sister."

"I'm Genieva Bankmans," Genieva replied.

"Genieva McLean, it be . . . if brother Brevan has kept to his plannin'," Brenna said, winking at Genieva.

"He kept his word, yes," Genieva confirmed. "But he wanted to send me back when he first realized who I was."

Brenna laughed, then lowered her voice and divulged, "I don't doubt it one bit, I don't. He was hopin' for an aged, very plump, and very large woman that wouldn't distract him in any way, ya know."

"You'll be takin' Genieva into the house now while I unhitch the team, Brenna. And you, Genieva McLean," Brevan grumbled, glaring at his wife. "Ya don't be takin' to anythin' me brazen brat of a sister says."

"I'll make up my own mind about people and what they say, Mr. McLean," Genieva retorted.

"Listen here, lass . . ." he began with a growl.

"Strong things often come in smaller sizes, Mr. McLean. The same is true with people. So it may be in your best interest to cease in addressing me in such a condescending manner," Genieva interrupted.

"She's a wicked fairy, she is, Brenna," Brevan mumbled to his sister as he urged the team forward.

"Then ya got just what ya were deservin', brother Brevan," Brenna called after him. Turning to Genieva, she put a comforting arm about her shoulders and said, "I'm taken with ya already, Genieva McLean. The angels sent ya to care for me brother, they did."

"Don't expect too much from me, Brenna. I'll disappoint you. I've a way of doing that to people," Genieva warned as she entered the house that would now be her home.

"That's blarney if I ever heard it, it is," Brenna argued as the screen door closed behind them. "This is yar home now, Genieva. It's not a fancy place, for sure and for certain . . . but it's strong, clean, and cozy."

As Genieva looked around the room she had entered, pure delight began to sift through her being. It was a lovely home! This first room was large and open and obviously served as both kitchen and parlor. There was a large iron cookstove on one wall—a sink with a pump near to it wisely placed before a large window that looked out onto the orchards. A sturdy-looking table with four chairs sat in the middle of the room. All this was to Genieva's left. To her right was a smaller section of the room, complete with fireplace and large hearth, rocking chair, small table and lamp, and a short-length, worn-looking sofa.

"The bedrooms be at the back of the house this way." Brenna walked forward, passing through a door at the back of the front room. Genieva followed and was pleased to realize the heavenly scent of the orchards permeated the inside of the house as well as the air without. "There be three rooms at the back here. Mother and Father shared one before they passed on . . . that be Brevan's now. Brevan had me prepare this one for you," she said, entering the bright, welcoming room that was nearest the front rooms of the house. "It was mine before I married Travis. That's Irish lace at the windows, it is. Do ya like it?" Brenna asked.

Genieva bit her smiling lower lip as she looked around the comforting room. The brass head- and footboards were brightly polished, and the washbasin and pitcher sitting on a stand next to the bed were ivory, adorned with tiny pink flowers. There was a chest of drawers with an oval mirror above, and the walls looked freshly whitewashed.

"It's wonderful!" Genieva exclaimed.

Brenna giggled. "The window looks over the three sweet cherry trees at the side of the house. That's where the creek runs by," she explained. "Let me show ya the other rooms . . . though I'm certain Brevan's room is in its usual untidy condition."

Brenna explained the room next to Genieva's had been Brevan and Brian's when the family first moved to the West. It was unoccupied now— though clean and ready for use. The furthermost room was Brevan's, and Genieva's eyebrows arched in surprise as she entered it. The bed was unmade—the sheets and blankets lying in a twisted mass at the foot of it. The drawers to the bureau gaped open with the appearance of their contents having been rummaged through again and again. Miscellaneous pairs of trousers, soiled socks, and shirts lay draped over the bed, chest of drawers, and floor.

"Ya see, Genieva . . . he's nothin' more than a hog. It's a pig, he is, and that's the truth of it. Always worried about gettin' up early and finishin' chores. He falls into bed half-dead every night, tired and worn to the bone," Brenna sighed.

"Well, this is completely unacceptable," Genieva stated, gesturing to the cluttered room.

Brenna giggled—spontaneously hugged Genieva. "I knew ya'd be good for Brevan. The minute I set me eyes on ya."

"She's the livin' banshee, she is," Brevan McLean muttered to himself as he unhitched his team. "But if her work be as smart as her mouth . . . she might do in the end." He thought again of the expression that had crossed Genieva's face when she'd entered the station and seen him—he knew she had been unsettled by his appearance, and he smiled to himself—amused. No doubt he had the look of a great unkempt heathen from the Wild West to one such as her. He scolded himself inwardly for thinking she was attractive in those first moments before he knew her identity.

"And a good mornin' to ya, big brother Brevan," Brian greeted. Brevan looked up to see his brother approaching—sighed knowing he'd come to survey Brevan's would-be bride. "Would ya be a married man now then?" Brian asked.

"I would," Brevan answered plainly.

"And would the new Mrs. McLean be a tubby old wrinkled one? Or have the heavens been watchin' out for Brevan McLean again?" Brian's blue eyes sparkled with mischief as he winked at his elder brother.

"She's a scrawny brat of girl, with a tongue as sharp as a sickle and a nose as high in the air as the clouds above," Brevan grumbled.

"Ah. Then ya'd be tellin' me that she's the perfect lass for an old goat like you," Brian chuckled.

"As long as she's got the work of a horse in her . . . I do not care from whence she came or what she looks like."

Brian shook his head, smiling as he concluded, "That's a lie, it is. Ya're as much a man as me, brother Brevan. Dad didn't intend for ya to pass yar own life by to keep this land, he didn't. And well ya know it."

Brevan hung a harness on the barn wall. "It's me he left the land to, Brian. Dad worked himself into the grave to earn it, he did . . . and I'll not let it go because of me own weaknesses. I'm happy for you and Lita . . . and for Brenna and Travis, I am. But I've got me own duty . . . to our Dad." He paused for a moment, sighed, and chuckled as he looked at his brother—the near image of himself. "She's not gonna take much guff from the likes of me . . . I will tell ya that, Brian."

Brian smiled, "Then she'll be fittin' right into the family, won't she now?"

"I'll testify to that!" Travis Sinclair bellowed as he entered the barn. "Everyone knows what a feisty bunch the McLeans are. Good day to you, Brevan . . . and how would my new sister-in-law be faring?"

"She's merely me wife, Travis . . . no need to get soft on her," Brevan responded with indifference.

"I got me a look at her from the barn door just now, Travis," Brian explained. "She's a wee little bit of a thing . . . but bonny as they come. And I think she'll be keepin' brother Brevan in line, she will."

Travis Sinclair looked as nearly opposite of the two McLean brothers as was possible. He was short, tow-headed blond, and green eyed— yet handsome in a rather average way all the same.

"It will be good for Brenna. She worries about you so much, Brevan, that it's near to driving me insane," Travis said.

"Aye, don't I know it. Still, she means well . . . I know that," Brevan agreed, folding his strong arms across his chest. "Where's Lita, Brian? I've no doubt she'll be wantin' to come and gawk at Genieva as well."

"She'll be by any moment, she will. She's not been feelin' herself lately. I hope she's not comin' down with the chills or somethin' the like of it," Brian answered.

"So," Travis began, winking conspiratorially at Brian. "This . . . this Genieva you've gone and married so blindly . . . do you think she'll be capable of working like you expect her to?"

"She's small, 'tis true enough . . . but determined lookin' and sturdy," Brevan answered.

"And pretty?" Travis prodded.

"I'd say she's the very definition of cute and

adorable," Brevan answered. "Like a school girl the likes ya see in town."

"And . . ." Travis continued as Brian snickered, and a barely withheld chuckle began to manifest itself in his voice, "and . . . is she soft as velvet with a mouth that tastes of spring ripe berries?"

Brevan frowned as Brian and Travis both chuckled, knowing they had succeeded in irritating him. "I've no notion of how she feels or tastes, lads. I've not the time to waste that the two of you do on courtin' and flirtin' with me wife. It's hard work I'm lookin' for."

As Brenna and Genieva exited the house and walked toward the barn, all three men watched in momentary silence.

Travis patted Brevan's shoulder as if consoling him and said, "If you can keep your hands off that little morsel for more than two weeks, I'll give you that new heifer Brenna and I bought last month."

"Bring her on over now, Travis. For the lass is no temptation to me," Brevan grumbled.

Genieva's stomach began to twist itself into knots as she looked at the three men staring at her from the barn.

"There's me Travis!" Brenna whispered with excitement rising in her voice. She waved to her husband and pulled Genieva along with her. "Isn't he just the picture of a handsome lad, Genieva?"

"Oh, yes. Indeed he is," Genieva stammered. Her eyes locked with Brevan's as he glared at her.

"And brother Brian has arrived too. Ya'll meet the whole family this day . . . for Lita should be along soon. Come now, Genieva."

"So," Brian began, offering his hand to Genieva, "ya're the lass who's gonna to teach me big brother a thing or two, are ya?"

"I'm . . . I'm Genieva," she answered, accepting his hand. Brian had a knowing, mirthful glint in his eyes, and it unnerved her terribly.

"And I'm Brian. This is Travis, Brenna's . . . what is that me dear sister calls ya now, Travis? Ah, yes. This is Travis . . . Brenna's love muffin," Brian informed her, pointing to Travis.

"That's me, Genieva," Travis agreed, shaking her hand as well. "Love muffin."

Brevan sighed, obviously annoyed as Brenna giggled and linked her arm with her husband's.

Genieva smiled at their silly, flirtatious manner—yet bit her lip self-consciously as she looked again to Brevan standing so severe and frowning.

"Lita!" Brian suddenly exclaimed. Genieva was only somewhat aware of her mouth hanging open in astounded awe as she stared almost rudely at Brian's wife. There before her stood the most beautiful woman Genieva had ever seen—in her entire life she'd never seen such a beautiful woman!

"Hola," the dark beauty greeted in a melodious voice thick and rich with the sound of Mexico. She offered a soft and friendly hand to Genieva. Genieva could only nod in response, so the woman continued. "I'm Lita," she explained, her beautiful smile sparkling. "I'm so glad that Brevan has finally taken vows," Lita sighed. She placed one hand daintily over her heart and shook her head indicating concern. "We were all so afraid he would never settle down and start la familia."

Lita McLean's voice was as lovely as a songbird's, and the richness of her accent spilled from her lips like a dark, liquid confection. Her hair was thick and bluish-black—pulled into a braid hanging nearly to her knees. Her eyes were the deepest of brown, her cheeks rosy, and her lips the color of wine. Genieva sighed as she thought of her own pitifully common features in comparison.

All the same, Genieva was finally drawn from her wonderment and able to take Lita's extended hand. "It's so nice to meet you, Lita. I'm . . . I'm sorry to stare so, but you're so beautiful!" she said.

Lita giggled and placed a graceful hand on Genieva's shoulder. "Oh no, Genieva!" The scarlet of a lovely blush rose to her cheeks as she explained, "You flatter me, Genieva. I don't deserve such a compliment. I see myself every day in the . . . how you say? Espejo?" she asked, looking to Brian.

"Mirror," Brian answered.

"Yes, yes. The mirror. Every day I look into it and am sad to see myself looking back at me."

Everyone shook their heads in disagreement, and Genieva could only stand silent, unable to comprehend the reason for such a remark.

"Lita is forever and always goin' on and on about how ugly and fat she is," Brenna explained to Genieva. "She only does it to be makin' me feel a bit better, she does."

Brevan looked at Lita and spoke plainly, "Ya're lookin' as lovely as the summer skies today, Lita."

Lita's deepening blush did not go unnoticed by Genieva. Neither did the shy manner in which the dark-haired beauty momentarily cast her gaze to the ground.

"Muchas gracias, Brevan."

"So," Brevan began, turning to Genieva, "ya've met me brother and his lovely wife . . . and me wee brat of a sister and her love muffin ya have. I'll be takin' charge of yar time now, and we'll have a go 'round the place while I tell ya what needs to be done to keep things runnin' smooth." Hunkering down, he quite improperly took hold of Genieva's ankle, studying her shoe for a moment. Genieva thumped him squarely on the head with one fist—an entirely natural reflex to being so brazenly accosted. Brevan dropped her foot—looked up at her with profound irritation.

"Hey now, lassie. What would ya be beatin' me so for?" he asked.

Upon seeing the irate expression on his face, Genieva immediately began to wring her hands.

"Forgive me, Mr. McLean . . . but I am quite unaccustomed to being handled in a manner on which society frowns."

He seemed to completely ignore her explanation and simply reached down to take hold of her ankle once more—resuming his study of her shoe. "Are these the only sort of shoes ya would be ownin', lass?" he asked.

"Of course," Genieva answered, wrenching her ankle from his grasp again. She stepped backward several steps to ensure her ankle remained hidden—to ensure her modesty.

"Well, then day after tomorrow we'll be ridin' back to town to purchase ya somethin' more useful," Brevan informed her. He rose to his full, intimidating height—glaring down at her.

"Brevan McLean!" Brenna scolded. "She be your wife! Not some new horse ya've acquired. Next thing ya know ya'll be tryin' to nail her boots onto her feet ya will."

"Brevan wouldn't know what to do with a woman if she walked up and pinched him in the bum, for sure and for certain," Brian chuckled.

"Sí! Sí!" Lita added as she and Brenna broke into amused laughter.

Genieva looked up into Brevan's stern, frowning face—bit her lip to stifle her own need to giggle. It was obvious he was completely agitated. Yet his expression was somehow quite unexpectedly attractive.

"There's not a woman on this green earth ownin' the courage it would be takin' to pinch me square on the bum, Brian," he muttered, still glaring at Genieva.

"Oh, settle yar temper down now, Brev," Brian soothed, slapping his brother squarely on the back. "Genieva doesn't appear to be the bum-pinchin' type . . . now does she, Lita?"

Lita could only shake her head in agreement as she dabbed at the tears of laughter brimming in her eyes. Brenna began her giggles anew, and Brevan shook his head disgustedly.

"Ya be seein' now why I had to do most of the work on this farm me ownself all the bloomin' time, Genieva," Brevan grumbled. Taking hold of her arm, he led her away from the amused group of relatives. "Not a one of them can go through a single hour in the day without gettin' the sillies."

"Laughter is good for the soul, Mr. McLean," Genieva stated.

"There be a place and a time for everythin'," he growled. "But Brenna and Brian take too much time for foolish things." He looked ominously at Genieva and added, "If ya be the silly, lazy type, lass . . . let it be said now . . . and know that ya'll have to change."

Genieva clenched her teeth tightly—yanked her arm from his grasp. "I am not something you own, Mr. McLean. I am an individual, and I do enjoy laughter and fun. I also enjoy hard work and accomplishment. I consider myself to be well balanced, and you would do well to treat me as your equal rather than your slave." Smoothing the folds of her skirt, she added, "Furthermore, I would appreciate your adherence to a higher degree of propriety. My foot is my own as is my arm and . . ."

She was interrupted, however, as he once again firmly took hold of her arm and began leading her toward the house.

"We'll begin in the house, Genieva. It is to be yar main responsibility," he said.

"Don't let him bully ya around, Genieva," Brian called out. Genieva turned to glance back at the four onlookers. "Spank him hard on the bum if he tries it. That's what our mother used to do, she did," he added as Lita and Brenna broke into giggles once more.

"A word of warnin' to ya, Genieva," Brevan growled. "Ya lay yar hand across me bum but once, and I'll return the favor with spankin' ya over me knee, I will."

"I'm sure they're only teasing, Mr. McLean,"

Genieva assured him. "After all, this is such an unusual situation, and your family seems so . . ."

"When me mother died . . . and she slapped me on the seat of the pants when I did wrong 'til the day she did . . . Brenna took over spankin' me when I got out of hand. Teasin' it wasn't," he stated.

Spontaneously, Genieva's eyes dropped to the seat of Brevan's pants as he pulled her along. She bit her lip to suppress a giggle needing escape at the thought of a man this large being reprimanded with a good paddling.

The screen door to the house screeched open, and Genieva stood inside her new home once more.

"I raise meself from sleep at five in the mornin' sharp. I like bacon and eggs and fried potatoes for breakfast best. Biscuits, honey, or whatever else will do though. A man needs a good breakfast if he's expected to work through the day. I eat me lunch at noon and me supper at dusk," Brevan informed her—exactly as if he were instructing a new kitchen servant.

"I only know how to cook beans," Genieva responded with obvious sarcasm.

"Then you'll learn how to cook what I like," Brevan growled.

"Yes, I will. And you'll learn how to like beans." She watched as Brevan inhaled a slow, calming breath. Still, she was right, and he nodded— having accepted her countering.

He continued his instruction. "I like me house to be clean . . . well kept."

"Does that include your personal room?" Genieva asked, grinning.

"Me room is me room, Genieva. Ya can leave it to me."

"Don't you worry about things taking root in there and growing into wild, uncontrollable vines . . . creatures that will gobble you up in the middle of the . . ."

He quirked an eyebrow and looked at her inquisitively. He seemed puzzled by her exaggerated description of the possible consequences of bad housekeeping.

"Me room is mine, lass," he firmly repeated.

"Yes, sir," Genieva agreed, nodding. She was puzzled. For some reason she enjoyed teasing him. She liked the look of barely controlled irritation that crossed his face when she did. At the same time, however, she knew she would not want to be involved in a serious battle with him. She did not doubt the repercussions would be tempestuous—in the least.

"Brenna has shown ya the room that will be yars now, hasn't she?" he asked.

"Yes."

"Then I'll be bringin' yar trunk in for ya," he stated. He turned, leaving Genieva alone to consider the consequences of her rash decision making. Married to a complete stranger? What had she been thinking? Still, a more attractive, more interesting stranger there had never been. At least she was sure of that.

Brevan McLean had eventually ceased in giving instructions, and Genieva found her first quiet moments to reflect on the day. The sun was setting—sending waves of pink and lavender radiance across an endless ocean of sky. Travis, Brian, and Brevan sat on the front porch talking—their low, masculine voices lending a warm sense of safekeeping to the evening. Yet this sound did little to settle Genieva's uncertainty—for the deep, commanding intonation of Brevan's voice only served to remind her of the far-reaching consequences of her actions.

Brenna seemed to notice the look of uncertainty no doubt blatant on Genieva's face.

"It'll be fine, it will," Brenna whispered kindly as the three women sat at the table. She placed a comforting hand over Genieva's.

Genieva forced a smile and said, "Thank you, ladies . . . for the fine dinner. It was so kind of you to . . ."

"We're not ladies, amiga," Lita explained, placing her hand over Brenna's. "We're your sisters now—tus hermanas."

Brenna nodded—smiled at Genieva with reassurance. "He's brought up his battlements, he has, Genieva," Brenna whispered. Lita nodded and smiled in agreement. "He does it when he's tryin' to close himself away, ya see. He'll soften up, he will. Believe me—'tis well I know me brother."

Genieva shook her head—tried to smile. "He's fine. He's just fine. A little bossy, but . . . I'll learn to work around it."

"Brevan," Lita spoke softly. She dropped her gaze for a moment. "He would not have married with you if he had not liked you at once."

"Yes. He would've," Genieva argued. "He's not the kind to go back on his word."

"That is true," Lita confirmed. "Still, Brevan would not marry with someone he did not want to. Yes, Brenna?"

Brenna nodded. "He talks as if he's a heartless soul, Genieva . . . but he's not. You'll find it in time. He would not have brought ya home if he hadn't taken to ya right off."

An obsidian sky glistening with stars replaced the lavender of sunset, and Genieva Bankmans McLean lay in her new bed in her new home. Unable to sleep—for uncertainty gripped her in its cold, heartless fist—Genieva thought on the assurances of her new friends. Still, she felt so terribly alone—frightened. Days ago, when she'd left Chicago, it had all seemed so clear in her mind. This was her chance—her only chance at the life she wanted. In truth, it hadn't really been the life she had wanted—only better than the one previously placed before her. Yet now—now that she was here—married to the man who, through his letters, she'd secretly come to care for—she knew with all her heart—Genieva knew this *was* the life she wanted. More than that—this was the man she wanted.

Chapter Two

"The sun be nearly breakin' the horizon, Genieva." Brevan's heavy brogue drifted through Genieva's mind—through her dreams—and woke her. "The day begins early in this house, it does."

Genieva stretched with the contentment bestowed by a good night's sleep. She opened her eyes and slowly pulled herself to sitting. The sight of Brevan's serious, unsettlingly handsome face caused her to gasp. Her husband stood just there—in her room—just beside her bed— powerful arms folded across his broad chest.

"Oh!" Genieva exclaimed, realizing she had slept far later than Brevan had intended—and on her first night in his house. "I'm sorry. I'm not used to . . ." she began.

"Well, be gettin' used to it, lass," Brevan grumbled, his brow furrowing as he glared at her. "I've had me breakfast already this mornin', and I'm off to get the milkin' done. Brenna used to milk the cows, and I think that be somethin' you should do from now on. So, if ya'll be quick and put yar clothes on . . . ya can come to the barn with me and learn the task, ya can."

Genieva's temper flared to red-coal hot at his condescending manner. Still, she knew she was late getting up. She must give him some slack in the rope, or he might send her packing after all. Therefore, when he'd left the room, she quickly dressed, and pulled her hair back into a braid. Hurrying to the kitchen, she found him leaning against the sink—waiting for her with obvious impatience. Working the pump, she filled a glass with water and drank it as quickly as she could. Without a word, Brevan strode through the front door—and Genieva followed.

The first rays of sunlight were breaking across the orchard. Pink and orange, yellow and purple flittered across the bluest sky, and Genieva marveled at the beautiful sight.

Brevan began striding toward the barn. His stride was so long Genieva nearly had to run to keep up with him. "Now, there be three cows that need milkin' in the mornin'. Have ya milked before?" Genieva shook her head—feeling ashamed somehow as he frowned down at her. "Well . . . it be easy enough to learn."

Brevan showed Genieva where the milking buckets were kept and where to place the milking stool beside a cow. He sat down on the stool and began milking. Genieva felt her eyebrows arch—thinking the process looked easy enough—though somewhat uncomfortable for the cow. Brevan seemed to be pulling fairly hard on the nipples hanging from the cow's udder, and Genieva grimaced—compassion for the animal washing over her.

"There now," he said. "Ya see . . . 'tis an easy task, it is." Rising from the stool, he gestured she should take his place. Genieva drew a deep breath of determination and sat squarely on the stool. With not just a little trepidation rising in her, she reached out, taking hold of one of the cow's nipples with her thumb and index finger. Closing her eyes, she winced—turning her head as she tentatively pulled on the appendage. The cow remained still. Genieva opened her eyes and looked to the nipple. It did not spray milk into the bucket as it had under Brevan's efforts. Gritting her teeth, she looked at the nipple as she pulled again. Still nothing happened.

"There's a trick to it, I guess," she muttered, turning to look up at Brevan.

In that moment, Genieva was nearly awestruck as she witnessed a broad smile break across the Irishman's handsome face. His smile made him even more attractive—just the way the sunrise bathed the already bounteous and beautiful orchard in far deeper splendor. His smile was a brilliant sight, and Genieva was momentarily stunned silent.

Brevan chuckled—adding further charm to his already fascinating presence.

"Ya keep pullin' on the teat like that, lass, and she'll kick ya square in the stomach, she will." Still chuckling, he hunkered down directly behind her, reaching out and gripping the teat next to the one she'd tried. "Start up just under the udder . . . like this. Then squeeze as ya pull."

Genieva nodded and took hold of the teat once more—this time trying to imitate Brevan's actions. His hand cupped her own in an effort to assist her—sending her mind whirling—void of all rational thought. His very touch sent a wave of rapturous delight washing over her.

"No, no, no," he corrected. He must've felt her hand tighten—her body's reaction to his touch and proximity. "Relax yar hand, lass."

Reaching up with his other hand, he patted the cow reassuringly on the belly as he once again demonstrated the technique. Genieva closed her eyes for a moment—inhaling a deep, calming breath. She couldn't let this happen! She couldn't start thrilling every time he brushed her hand or smiled. Strengthening her will, she attempted to milk the cow again. This time she was successful in her effort. The quick stream of milk hitting the bottom of the bucket attested to it.

"I've got it now," she informed him—almost too curtly. "Thank you."

"This one . . . she's Matilda. Milk Macy and Mona, too. All right?" he asked, rising to his full height once more.

"Yes," Genieva answered, as she began milking.

"When ya're done with it, bring the milk in and put it in the three crocks ya'll find inside. Brenna and Lita will be over later for one each, and the other is ours," he instructed, turning to leave. Pausing he added, "When ya've finished that, I'll be in the east field. Come find me, and I'll show ya what to do next."

"Very well," Genieva responded without turning to look at him. She reasoned for a moment that her own father had been less parental in his tone than Brevan.

By the time she had finished extracting the milk from all three cows, her hands ached—throbbing from the efforts of unfamiliar work. After having poured the milk into the crocks, she rinsed the buckets thoroughly in the sink before slicing a wedge from the loaf of bread she found in the breadbox. Finding some bright red jam in a nearby cupboard, she spread it generously on the surface of the bread—her mouth watering excessively as she tasted the first bite of her breakfast. The bread and jam were delicious! She'd nearly finished her third helping when she heard the screen door screech open and turned to see Brevan enter the house.

"I'm sorry," she apologized after quickly chewing the morsel in her mouth and gulping it down. "I hadn't eaten anything."

"Breakfast is important . . . for sure and for certain," he commented, going to the sink and inspecting the buckets. "And Brenna's strawberry jam is the best I've ever had in me life, it is." Taking the three buckets by the handles in one hand, he resumed his instructional tone. "When ya've rinsed them in the mornin's, just hang these back where ya saw me get them from. Now . . . are you ready for a new task?"

Genieva quickly swallowed the last bite of bread and jam, nodding as she did so. "Then wipe the jam from your face, lass, and follow me," he said. A handsome grin softened the otherwise serious expression on his face.

Genieva quickly licked the corners of her mouth with her tongue. She was horrified—entirely embarrassed at having had jam on her face. Still, Brevan only chuckled. Reaching out, he wiped at her cheek with his thumb. To her utter astonishment, he licked the jam from his appendage. The gesture delighted Genieva—delighted her near to giddiness. Yet she forced her appearance to remain calm.

"Come along, then," he said, licking his thumb a second time. "There's much to be done today since I was gone for so long yesterday."

The day had been ever so long and fatiguing. Gratefully, Brenna had come over late in the afternoon and helped Genieva to get acquainted with the kitchen, stove, smokehouse, vegetable cellar, and cupboards. By dusk, the mouth-watering aroma of a beef stew permeated the house. Genieva wondered if she would be able to keep her eyes open long enough to enjoy it.

"Ya look so tired, ya do, Genieva," Brenna noted as they sat at the table together. "Ya've done too much for yar first day."

"No, I'm fine. Really," Genieva assured Brenna—though she covered her mouth as she yawned.

"Well, ya go to bed as soon as ya've eaten. And don't let him work ya so hard."

"I've got to earn my place here, Brenna," Genieva explained, yawning again.

"Brevan's got to earn the right to have ya, Genieva. He'll bully ya blue if ya let him. Ya make him not just a wee bit nervous, ya do."

Genieva smiled. Although she was tired nearly beyond clear thinking, she fancied that being worn out from hard physical labor was abundantly preferable to fatigue of the mind. "Clearing out that field was the hardest thing," she admitted.

"Oh!" Brenna agreed, rolling her eyes. "I hate that worse than spinach, I do." She shook her head, sighed, and continued, "Every year we have to clear the fields for the corn and gardens. But come summer when all the food starts comin' in . . . mmmmm! Brevan grows the best corn I've ever in me life tasted, he does."

"That I do, Brenna," Brevan affirmed as he entered the house. "It be worth the hard work. I think I can start the plowin' next week. Then when the corn is in, we'll start on . . ."

"Oh, preserve us, Brevan!" Brenna sighed. "The sun has gone down. Let her be for now."

"I've no doubt Travis is home waitin' on his own dinner, he is, Brenna. Off with ya now. Let me eat without yar eternal naggin' blisterin' me ears," Brevan grumbled.

Brenna stood and smiled at Genieva as she walked toward the door. She paused before leaving the house—looking at her brother.

"Ya let her rest, Brevan. It's not a mule ya've married," she said.

"I know that, Brenna. And remember, we won't be about in the mornin'. I've got to take Genieva into town for a new shoein'," he chuckled.

"Beast that ya are!" Brenna scolded, winking encouragingly at Genieva just before the screen door slammed shut behind her.

As Brevan dried his hands on a towel after washing them at the pump, Genieva raised her aching and tired body from the chair at the table and went to the stove.

"I've made stew for your dinner. I hope it meets with your approval," she announced. Her feet ached so thoroughly that she nearly limped back with the pot of stew, setting it down in the middle of the table.

As Brevan pulled a chair out, gesturing for her to sit in it, Genieva raised her eyebrows in surprise.

"I may be a beast in Brenna's eyes," he began. "But me manners can be polished when I want them to be." Genieva sat down and let him slide the chair in for her.

When they'd finished their meal, Brevan leaned back in his chair and sighed with the contentment of having enjoyed a good supper.

"A hard day's work feels good, doesn't it?" he asked.

Genieva nodded. "I suppose if you're used to it, it feels better than if you're not."

"Ya'll adjust to it, ya will. New boots will help. Yar feet won't wear out as fast then."

Genieva covered her mouth as she yawned. "Excuse me," she apologized. "I will adjust. I assure you of that."

"I know. Ya've worked hard today and proved yarself to be capable, ya have," he admitted as he pushed his chair back from the table. "Ya learn well and quick, ya do, lass."

Genieva sighed with relief. At least she had been able to prove herself for one day. But as her back and legs began to throb and ache with the unfamiliar strain of the work on a farm, she wondered if she would be able to keep up such a pace for an extended period of time.

"I've got a bit to do before I wear out, so ya go on to bed now. In the mornin' bright we'll go into town and find ya some suitable shoes. Good night then, Genieva," he said.

"Good night," she said. She yawned—watching him leave the house.

Every muscle in Genieva's body screamed with overexertion as she removed her day clothes and replaced them with nightwear. How different this life would be than the one at home. Hard work—work that would be almost unendurable at first would be what she would come to know. But far better it was than what she faced at home. Far better was a life married to a fantastically attractive man—a man who was ignorant to the fact—than life married to . . . Genieva laid her head on the fluffy down of the pillow and tried to think no more of it.

The next morning Genieva woke and rose as soon as she heard the front screen door slam, indicating that Brevan was about. The moon still shone in the dark morning skies, and Genieva shivered slightly as her feet touched the cold floor. If she were to have Brevan's breakfast before him when he returned, she did not have the time to dress properly. She simply tied her robe snugly at her waist and quickly braided her hair. She was pleased and relieved when she entered the kitchen to find that she indeed had beaten him to fixing his own breakfast. Working quickly, she lit the wood in the stove and put the cast-iron skillet on to heat. She beat four eggs and thinly sliced a large potato.

By the time Brevan had returned from his first chores of the morning, a fragrant and hearty breakfast greeted him.

"You see, I only needed to adjust to the earlier hour," Genieva informed him as his eyebrows rose in surprise.

"Well then join me for breakfast, lass," Brevan invited, sitting himself at the table.

At the first savory taste of the breakfast she had prepared for him, Brevan was impressed with Genieva's cooking. Although he hated to admit it, it was a finer-tasting breakfast than Brenna had ever cooked for him. He glanced up at Genieva— mesmerized for an instant when he noticed that the delicate color of her eyes had changed somehow. He could've sworn they'd been a hazel brown the night before. But in the bright morning light, as her eyes met his across the table, Genieva's eyes had somehow assumed a deep green hue.

The freckles sprinkled lightly across Genieva's nose gave Brevan's lips to forming an involuntary smile. Misunderstanding his grin, she nodded and asked, "It's good, isn't it?"

"That it is," he admitted. All the signs of fatigue she had worn to bed the night before had disappeared, and Brevan noted how radiant and cheerful her very countenance was. "Did ya sleep well, then?" he asked.

"Oh, yes," she assured him brightly as she spread jam on a slice of bread for herself. "It's so quiet at night here. One can completely relax . . . eventually."

"I guess the city was a bit loud," he commented.

"Yes. And stinky. I hated the odors of it. It's fresh out here, you know."

"I know," he agreed. Then, changing the subject, he said, "Lita and Brian were plannin' to go into town with us today. But I've just been over and Lita's feelin' a bit green, she is."

"Is it serious?" Genieva asked. Brevan watched, frowning in wonder, as the girl's green eyes slowly changed to an odd grayish blue.

"Uh . . ." he stammered, preoccupied by the transformation of her eyes. "No. In fact, though Brian's a fool at times and too blind to guess at it, I suspect that . . ."

"What?" Genieva prodded. But Brevan had already decided to keep his suspicions to himself.

"I suspect it's just adjustin' to this new life somehow," he finished.

"Oh, I see," Genieva muttered. Brevan knew by the expression on her face that she did not believe him.

"She's ripe from Mexico, ya see, lass. It's different here. Her English is good, but she's still havin' trouble once in a while," he babbled as he focused his attention on his breakfast.

"She's a rare beauty, isn't she?" Genieva asked.

51

"Yes. She's a bonny lass, that one." Brevan looked up to see Genieva's gaze was emerald colored—and intense on him. "How do ya do that anyway, lass?" he blurted out.

"What?" she asked—her eyes still emerald.

Brevan returned his attention to cleaning his plate. "Lita's father owns some land not far from here. Her brothers help him in the workin' of it. Maybe she's a bit homesick, is all."

"Well, I hope she feels better soon. When we've returned from town, you can show me how to get to Brian's place, and I'll check in on her," Genieva suggested. She rose from the table without finishing her breakfast and crossed the room to the sink.

Genieva scraped her plate of unfinished breakfast into the scrap bucket for the chickens. Her nerves were seething. "Yes. She's a bonny lass, that one," he had said of Lita. Genieva recognized the sharp burn of jealousy smoldering in her bosom. She silently scolded herself—but it did little to chase the emotion from her mind and body.

"I'll ready the wagon," Brevan said. "We'll leave in a few minutes, all right?"

Without turning to face him, Genieva nodded in acknowledgment. "Yes."

"'Tis a fine breakfast ya make, Genieva," he quite sincerely complimented as he let the screen door slam behind him.

● ● ●

"And what would be botherin' ya so early in the mornin'," Brevan asked, holding the lines loosely in his hands. The trip to town would take at least three quarters of an hour, he'd told Genieva as they had left the house.

"Not a thing. Why do you ask?" Genieva sighed—feigning ignorance. She was unnerved terribly by the fact Brevan could read her moods so well after less than forty-eight hours.

"Ah, it's lyin', ya are," he chuckled. "But, I suppose ya've got the right to keep to yarself when you feel like it."

"So," Genieva chirped happily—an attempt to change the direction of their discussion. "Why did your family leave Ireland?"

"That's a forthright question, it is . . . still, I'll be givin' ya an answer." Genieva watched as Brevan smiled the smile of a man reminiscing on pleasant things. "Me father wanted his own place, he did. He was tired of rentin' and payin' the landlord for land that he worked so hard. So, he asked me mother five or six years back what she thought of movin' all of us to America. Mother was more than a wee bit scared to come. We all were. All of us except me father. Dad knew what he wanted, and he usually got it. So . . . we came to America, and Dad sold every piece of silver and jewelry the family owned so he could buy the orchards. After he died two

53

years ago, our mother divided the land and orchards between Brenna, Brian, and me. Mother took ill and died only a few months later. Nothin' excitin' or adventurous about our story, lass. Plain and simple, it is," he finished. Genieva stiffened at the question he posed next. "And what brings ya out to this secluded land from Chicago, Genieva? I have to say straight out that ya're not what I expected to see gettin' off the train."

"I hated the city," Genieva answered honestly.

"Well, that I can understand. But have ya no family? Are ya orphaned then?"

Genieva swallowed hard and crossed her fingers where they lay in her lap—hoping he would let the issue go by as she answered, "I . . . I'd rather not speak of it, if you don't mind." She looked to him, her gaze boldly meeting his narrowed and curious eyes.

"Very well. I'll respect yar right to keep yar secrets," he grumbled.

"What . . . what . . ." she stammered, "what kind of person were you expecting to get off the train?" she asked.

Brevan shrugged—was quiet for a moment. "A woman of years beyond yars, for sure and for certain. Perhaps large and plump. Ya know, a woman who may have had a difficult time in findin' a husband for various reasons, ya see." Genieva nodded. "I know me reaction to ya wasn't with any manner becomin' a gentleman, lass. But don't think I'm disappointed. Ya're a hard worker. That's important in this kind of a life."

"I see," Genieva muttered.

"What were ya thinkin' when ya first set your eyes on me?" he asked, grinning with obvious amusement.

Genieva reflected on the moment she had first seen Brevan McLean—standing handsome and alluring in the corner of the room at the train station. Those moments before she had known he was Brevan were indeed moments worth thinking on. His astounding good looks had unnerved her to the point she had been thankful that the stranger was not the man she was meeting. He had appeared to be a man who would be controlled by no one—held back by nothing. And now, sitting next to him on the wagon, she realized her assessment of him had been correct.

"I . . . I was frightened of you," she forced out honestly.

"What?" he exclaimed. Genieva looked at him, finding he appeared sincerely surprised. "Frightened of me? Why would ya be frightened of me, lass? Ya didn't behave as if ya were."

"Well, it's just that . . . well, you can be very daunting. I think you're greatly aware of that fact too," she stated.

"I suppose I'm what ya might be callin' harsh

lookin', I am," he muttered almost to himself. "Brenna talks me brain loose a tellin' me that people think I'm mean . . . that I've no humor or kindness about me." He looked intently at Genieva and said, "Ya've no reason to be fearin' me, Genieva. I speak hard because I work hard, and I guess I expect too much from others at times. But I've the things in me for laughin' and dancin' and relaxin' just like any other man. I won't have ya fearin' me temperament, or me words."

It wasn't his temperament or his words that Genieva feared. Rather, it was his attractiveness and charisma—the kind of things that turned a woman's rational thought to oatmeal and her knees to water.

Still, she nodded and said, "I understand."

"Are ya in need of anythin' other than boots today, lass?" he asked unexpectedly.

"I . . . to what do you refer?" she countered, not understanding completely.

"I mean, do ya have clothes enough? Clothes that won't be gettin' too hot as the weather warms up? Gloves for workin' and the like?"

"I've clothing enough. Gloves, however . . ."

"We'll buy ya some boys' gloves. They should fit ya right and straight." He looked at her then, and she straightened where she sat when he added, "Cheer up there, lass. It will be a good life for ya, it will."

"I know that. I wouldn't have come otherwise," she assured him.

"Here then," he said, handing the lines over to her. "'Tis time ya learned to drive me team. Though they're a picky pair at times, they are."

When at last Genieva walked into the store in town, it was to face the storekeeper and his wife with windblown hair and a rosy face. The team had bolted when they neared town, and Brevan had insisted Genieva be the one to gain control of them. Thus, the moments just before entering the township were wild and windy as opposed to the rather slow pace of the ride previous.

"Hello," Genieva greeted, smoothing her wild-looking hair. She'd entered the store to find an older man and woman gawking at her.

"It's me new wife, Mrs. Fenton. This be Genieva McLean," Brevan decreed as he entered the store behind Genieva.

"Oh!" the woman exclaimed as a broad smile spread across her face. She came forward and offered a hand to Genieva. "It's so nice to meet ya, honey!"

"Thank you," Genieva answered, taking the woman's hand. "What a lovely store," she added, looking around.

"She's won me over, Gerard," the woman chimed, turning to wink at her husband. "I'm Lilly Fenton, darlin'. And this is my husband, Gerard."

"Hello," Genieva greeted, nodding in Gerard's direction.

"We're in the market for a pair of boys' workin' boots, Mrs. Fenton," Brevan announced. "She's got blisters already, she has."

"Oh my, yes, dear," the woman exclaimed as dramatic concern filled her features. "Shoes are so important. You come on over here, and we'll fix ya up."

Genieva followed the kind woman to the far corner of the store while Brevan remained behind with Mr. Fenton.

"So," Lilly Fenton began as she sat down and started rummaging through several boxes of boots. "You're the one who has finally cornered our Mr. McLean, eh?" Genieva looked at the woman—surprise readily apparent on her features. "I guess you know that every unmarried female in these parts has had her cap set for him since the McLeans moved out here . . . even a couple of married ones, if my memory serves me. But he's too smart to fall for any of them. You'll hear things now and again, I'm sure. People do gossip so terrible in these parts. But you don't pay them any mind, ya hear? It's all just gossip and nonsense . . . especially where that Amy Wilburn is concerned. Oh, how I wish her parents would send her away to have her . . . anyway," Lilly sighed, changing the direction of her babble, "I guess ya know we're all pretty concerned about the lack of rain hereabouts. No doubt you all will be lugging water from the crick for the crops if we don't see a change here soon. Here now," she said, holding out a pair of boots at last. "These look about your size."

"Thank you," Genieva agreed, nodding her head. "They look just right. May I . . . may I try them for certain, though?" Genieva studied the woman, amused at her exact resemblance to the elderly gossips she had always imagined small towns would harbor. Mrs. Fenton was short, round, and white-haired, with smiling eyes and chubby cheeks—a delightful-looking woman.

Lilly Fenton laughed. "Of course, honey! We have to make sure they fit right . . . else Brevan McLean would tan my hide, and don't I know it."

The boots did fit comfortably, and though they weren't in the least bit flattering to look upon, Genieva could see the sense in their practicality.

"We've got to have you a quilting bee, Mrs. McLean! It just won't do to have a young bride hereabout without a quilt for her new home! You have Brenna come in and talk to me about it," Lilly chimed. Her very voice held a tinkling quality that was soft on a person's ears. *Yes,* Genieva thought, *Lilly Fenton would make such a perfect gossip.*

"Oh, no. That's not necessary. I'm fine, really," Genieva assured her.

"Nonsense! It's bad luck to break with tradition, sweetie."

"I'll be waitin' in the wagon, Genieva," Brevan called to her as he left the store.

"Not one to sit on his backside too long, is he?" Lilly smiled.

Genieva returned her smile. Lilly Fenton was a kind woman even if she was a little generous in her conversation.

"How much do I owe you then, Mr. Fenton?" Genieva asked as she walked to the counter.

Mr. and Mrs. Fenton looked at each other with raised eyebrows—then back to Genieva.

"You're not serious, are ya, ma'am?" Mr. Fenton asked.

"Yes . . . actually," Genieva stammered.

"Your husband has paid for them already, dear," Lilly explained—her smile somehow sweetening even further.

"Oh. Of course." Genieva blushed at her own presumption.

As Genieva turned to leave, three young women entered the store. Each young woman appeared to be near her own age. They stared at Genieva—studying her from head to foot with obvious disapproval.

"Um . . . hello," Genieva offered. Each of the women forced a smile and nodded. "You'll excuse me," she mumbled as she moved past them and to the door. "Thank you again, Mrs.

Fenton . . . Mr. Fenton," she called over her shoulder.

"Is that's Brevan McLean's new wife? Well . . . *she'll* never be able to keep a man like him at home," one of the young women whispered as Genieva left the store. Genieva's ears burned at the assuming remark. Still, she kept her eyes forward and her head high as Brevan helped her into the wagon.

"I had no idea you were such a ladies' man, Mr. McLean," Genieva snapped as the wagon bolted forward. She found her anger was somehow directed at Brevan—not the young women in the store. She was angry with him for being so handsome—so entirely attractive to women—especially to herself!

"What?" Brevan asked.

"Who's Amy Wilburn?" Genieva inquired.

"Amy?" he mused. "Poor Amy. I suppose it was to be expected that Mrs. Fenton would mention the town scandal, it was. I feel sorry for the lass meself."

"Who is she?" Genieva repeated, irritated.

"She's a young lass in town who has unfortunately found herself . . . in the family way. It's unfortunate because there is no husband to her."

"Oh. I-I see," Genieva gulped. It was such a sensitive subject to be discussing with a man, and she suddenly felt very uncomfortable for having asked him about Amy Wilburn.

"And are the new boots tolerable then?" he asked.

"Oh, yes. They're very comfortable. Thank you for paying for them." Genieva swallowed hard and mounted her courage. She was not one who enjoyed being left ignorant of certain facts—especially when they concerned her. Therefore she abruptly blurted, "Those other women . . . the ones who came into the store just before we left . . . they don't think I'm capable of keeping you at home, as they put it. Are you a philanderer, Mr. McLean?"

Instantly Brevan pulled the team to a halt. He turned to Genieva—glaring down at her with a furious expression on his handsome face.

"I'm sorry to be so bold, sir . . . but I would like to know exactly where I stand and what to expect. If I'm to be the object of great ridicule and gossip, I would like to be as prepared as possible and . . ."

"I should turn ya over me knee and paddle yar bum, I should!" he shouted, and Genieva knew at once she'd been too blunt. "And I see now why ya're so interested in Amy Wilburn's story as well! I leave ya alone for two minutes in the store, and ya come out accusin' me of . . . of . . ." He was so angry that his face burned a fierce shade of red—his breathing labored. "The last man to accuse me of bein' father to Amy Wilburn's baby is still nursin' a broken nose!

Aye, I tell ya me mother's spinnin' in her grave over hearin' me own wife accusin' me of . . ."

"I merely asked a question, Mr. McLean. It was a perfectly legitimate one at that. After all, I've no experience with you other than through letters and just these past couple of days. I just wanted to be certain . . ."

Her words stopped as he reached out and firmly took hold of her chin. With his teeth tightly clenched, he growled down at her, "I'm no slimy snake, Genieva. Me parents raised me to be a good, moral man! I don't run around after women no matter what the storekeeper's wife says. Never have I done so, and never will I! And should me manly desires get the better of me, which they won't, then take comfort in the knowledge that I hold fully to the scripture tellin' a man to keep only to his wife!" He released her—pushing her chin ever so slightly as he did so.

Genieva cleared her throat and straightened her posture once more. "Very well," she said. "But in the future, I would ask that you please handle me with a bit less aggression."

She could feel the seething in him at such a reprimand and actually winced—for she thought his powerful grip would take hold of her once more. Instead, he inhaled deeply, and exhibiting great restraint, barked, "I will *handle* ya in whatever manner I feel is necessary, I will."

Unnerved slightly by a sudden odd thrill

springing up within her, Genieva corrected him again. "I am not your mule, Mr. McLean. I expect to be treated as your equal and without violence."

"Not me mule, ya say. Sounds to me like ya could put me mule's stubborn streak out like a candle's flicker," he grumbled as he snapped the lines, urging the team forward again.

" 'Tis a sad, sad story, it is," Brenna sighed as she helped Genieva to hang Brevan's freshly washed shirts on the line late that same afternoon. "Innocent she was . . . to the ways of the world, ya see. But she's a good girl, and things will be workin' out for Amy Wilburn eventually. As for the other three ya saw . . . vindictive as venom, they are. I've no doubt in me mind they're all plain furious at Brevan marryin' *you* and not choosin' one of them . . . as if he'd even waste his brain a thinkin' on any of those ugly sows."

"Mrs. Fenton seems nice, though," Genieva remarked. She grinned—unable to avoid being amused by Brenna's calling the young women in town "ugly sows."

"Oh, yes. No doubt she'll be makin' sure there's a bee held in yar honor. She's a kindly old lady. A bit too much on the gossip, though. She drowns in it like some men do in liquor."

Genieva smiled at Brenna's superb comparison. She knew she would have to take Mrs. Fenton's words very lightly.

Both women turned then as they heard the barn door slam shut. As Brevan walked from the barn toward the house, they watched in silence for a moment before Brenna whispered, "He's not as bad as he wants ya to think, Genieva. Just ya wait and see. He likes ya, he does. He would not have married ya otherwise."

"Well, I'm only here to . . ." Genieva began. But Brenna interrupted her.

"Me brother is so the handsome lad that it's frightenin', it is. And he's a lot of fun and kindness when he's not actin' up. Don't try tellin' me ya haven't already fallen for him, Genieva. For ya'd be lyin', and heaven's a watchin' ya."

"Oh, Brenna," Genieva scolded with a nonchalant toss of her head. She turned and continued to hang up the freshly washed garments from the basket at her feet. "This isn't like you and Travis." Pausing, she turned to Brenna. Only in that moment did she realize she had no knowledge of the circumstances under which Travis and Brenna had come together. "How did you and Travis meet and marry?"

"Oh, me Travis," Brenna sighed, staring toward the bright blue sky—a wistful smile spreading across her lovely face. "Travis was a cowboy. He was lookin' for a place to winter last fall, and he asked Brevan if we needed a hand. He'd been to the . . . to another place nearby . . . a rancher's land and been coldly turned away. The weather

65

was fairly fierce last winter, and before he knew it, he found himself on our doorstep the night of the first snow, askin' Brevan if he could winter out here. Brian had recently married Lita, and Brevan was wonderin' if he could keep up the place on his own, he was. So he told Travis he could stay the winter. I knew I loved him the moment I laid me eyes on him." She sighed heavily and smiled at Genieva. Genieva was delighted by the blush that suddenly rose to her sister-in-law's face. "Brevan came upon us sparkin' in the barn one day just before Christmas. Oh, he was angry! Shoutin' and callin' Travis a rounder and every such name." She laughed at the memory, and Genieva giggled, captivated by her story and fully able to imagine Brevan's reaction. "Travis shouted back and told Brevan he loved me and intended that I should be his wife! That was the first I had heard of it, and I thought I must be dreamin' it all. But we married in February, and here I am."

"And she spends far too much of her time tellin' her stories." Brenna and Genieva both startled and turned to find Brevan looming before them.

Brenna quickly punched him square in the stomach and scolded, "Ya scared the life out of me, ya did! Quit yar sneakin' about, Brevan McLean."

Unsettled completely by Brevan's sudden appearance, Genieva stepped back from him. In the process she caught the heel of her boot in the basket of laundry at her feet. Her arms began to flail as she struggled to keep her balance, and somehow her other foot became entangled as well. Brevan, reaching out and taking hold of the waistband of her skirt, steadied her for a moment. But Genieva watched in horror as Brenna gave Brevan's shoulder a hard shove from behind, sending the unstable duo tumbling to the ground to land in a heap. The force of Brevan's unbalanced weight drove the air from Genieva's lungs as she landed flat on her back in the dirt. As Brevan began to raise himself from his awkward position, Genieva gazed into his face. For a few lingering moments, his eyes captured hers in a curious stare.

"What kind of trick are ya pullin', lass?" he muttered. "It was brown yar eyes were a moment ago."

"Oh, get yarself off the girl, Brevan. Ya're crushin' the life out of her, ya are," Brenna giggled. "And I'll tell whatever story I want to tell, I will." Brevan raised himself. He reached out and took hold of Genieva's skirt band, pulling her to her feet to stand her before him.

"I'll turn ya over me knee and paddle yar bum good, Brenna," Brevan growled then, turning to his sister.

"Catch me first," she taunted as she lifted her skirts and ran off toward her own home.

Genieva swallowed the large lump in her throat as Brevan's irate stare turned toward her once again.

"I come out here to ask ya a question, I did," he growled.

"Yes?" Genieva prodded.

"I've forgotten it already. All this nonsense goin' on has taken it from me completely," he grumbled.

"Well . . . when you remember, just let me know," she assured him, bending down and righting the upset basket of laundry. Upon feeling Brevan's hand brushing at the seat of her skirt, however, Genieva straightened instantly. Whirling around, she slapped him soundly across one cheek.

He instantly took hold of her wrist and bent her arm behind her own back, holding it there firmly as he glared down at her. "I was only tryin' to help, lass," he growled through tightly clenched teeth. "Yar bum is covered with dirt."

"Well, I thank you to leave that as my concern," she retorted. "How dare you lay a hand on my . . . on my . . ."

"Bum," he finished for her. Brevan fought to stifle the grin begging to spread across his face as he held Genieva firmly in his grip. She was all too adorable—dangerously adorable. Especially when her temper was provoked as it was at that particular moment. He marveled again at the sudden change in the color of her eyes, now spitting deep brown in his direction. Only moments before, when he lay on her in a heap on the ground, he could've sworn he'd seen the same pretty eyes boast a strangely violet hue.

He loosened his grip on her as the grin threatening his lips won the battle of his self-control and spread across his handsome face. Genieva snatched her wrist from him and rubbed at it ceremoniously.

"Thank you," she spat. "Now, if you don't mind . . . I've got things to finish."

Brevan couldn't resist—though he tried to—and as Genieva turned from him and toward the clothesline once more, his hand impulsively sprang forth—slapping her firmly on the seat.

"A good day to ya then, Genieva," he chuckled as she stood inhaling long, deep breaths in an attempt to calm herself. He knew she would not give him the satisfaction of reacting to his gesture. Still, he was entirely amused as he returned to the barn in order to finish the evening feeding of the stock.

When Genieva could no longer hear Brevan's departing footsteps, she turned and looked in the direction in which he had gone. She watched as he entered the barn. She pressed a quivering hand to her bosom in a vain attempt to settle the frantic beating of her heart. Oh, how he upset her! She was horrified at the condition of every part of her body and mind at having been so close to him and having been the object of his singular attention once again. She would have to learn to be less unsettled in his presence—for it would be devastating should she slip somehow and give him any indication of the existence of the fast and furious attraction to him secreted deep inside herself.

Chapter Three

It was a brief matter of two days following Genieva's trip into town with Brevan that one of Mrs. Fenton's grandsons rode up to the farmhouse and handed a note to Brevan just after lunch.

"Help us all! Lilly's true to her word," Brevan moaned as he read the note. "Tomorrow. Tomorrow mornin', Genieva, lass . . . such torture I wouldn't wish on me worst enemy."

"What?" Genieva inquired, completely baffled. Brevan sighed and handed the note to Genieva.

"Read it then, lass. Read it, and weep the tears of a tortured woman," he mumbled with a manner of dramatics Genieva had not yet seen in him. He walked toward the orchard calling cheerily to the boy, "Tell yar dear granny 'thank ya' for me, William!" The boy nodded, waved, and rode off.

Genieva's curious eyes fell to the paper in her hand. There she read:

Dearest Mr. and Mrs. McLean,

I've only just arranged a quilting bee in honor of your recent nuptials and am writing to inform you that the ladies of the township, and outlying farms, will be descending upon your home tomorrow morning, bright and early, to create a lovely

quilt for you both . . . as a memento of your marriage. Not to worry, dear Mrs. McLean. We will provide everything that is necessary including a variety of delicious eatables.
Sincerely,
Lilly Fenton

Genieva's heart sank—depositing itself with a thud into the hollow of her stomach. She dashed after Brevan.

"Wait, Brevan," she called to him. He paused and turned to face her. "I don't want this!" she cried.

"When Lilly Fenton gets it into her mind that somethin' must be done, Genieva . . . there's no choice left to ya," Brevan assured her. "The best of it would be to just endure the thing, lass."

"But . . . who will attend? I don't know anyone. I . . ."

"I've no doubt that every female within fifteen miles of the town will be there, lass. They'll all want to burn their stares into yar face awhile. After all, ya've married the one man in town who never wanted to marry, ya have," Brevan explained.

"But . . . but I'm no good at these kinds of things, Brevan. I don't do well with people I don't know. How long will it take? Will it take long?" she asked.

Brevan only chuckled. He seemed to look at her with some sort of pity, and it deeply unsettled her. "It's one day, Genieva. Think of it that way. One day and ya'll have made it through another challenge." He smiled—a smile laced with sympathy—and walked toward the barn.

"How long does it take? What goes on?" Genieva asked Brenna as she helped her sister-in-law knead the bread dough on the table before them.

"Híjole! It takes eternity, Genieva!" Lita confirmed. She looked at Genieva with an expression of compassion. "But you'll have una hermosa manta . . . uh . . . a pretty blanket . . . a quilt to show when they are finished with you," she tried to encourage with a smile.

Genieva sighed, discouraged, as Brenna explained, "It takes the whole day long, it does, Genieva. The ladies, married and not, all come and quilt on the piece 'til it's finished. They gossip somethin' awful the long of it . . . and that can be a good thing, it can. For ya be learnin' all ya ever need to know about anybody." Brenna smiled with reassurance, "And besides, Lita and me . . . we'll be there with ya, we will. It won't all be strangers ya're sittin' with."

Still, sleep was elusive for Genieva that night. She thought back over the past few days. She still could not believe all that had happened. The great change in direction of her destiny was nearly incomprehensible. Almost overnight she had gone from the life she had known in aristocratic Chicago to the life she knew now—that of a woman married to a hard-working, ambitious, and stupendously handsome farmer, with instant relatives, responsibilities, and completely unfamiliar experiences. She was also beginning to understand why it would be greatly advantageous to work herself into a deep fatigue each day. It kept her mind from wandering to romantic daydreams of Brevan McLean. And he was ever so easy to daydream about. Simply watching him talk with Brian and Travis at the end of each day was mesmerizing—the way his jaw clenched tightly when he was irritated or the way his smile brightened his face when he was amused. Realizing that once again her thoughts had wandered to him, Genieva forced herself back into anxious contemplation of the quilting bee.

"There you are, dear!" Mrs. Fenton chimed as she entered the farmhouse the next morning. "Yes . . . yes . . . you are as charming as I remember!" the lady giggled, putting a friendly arm about Genieva's shoulders. "Now let's get this frame set up before the others get here," she mused, looking about. "We've got to make certain you've got some help in keeping that man warm at night, don't we?" Mrs. Fenton winked at her, and Genieva was eternally grateful for Lita's intervention at

74

that moment—for Mrs. Fenton's rather private remark had sent her blushing to fever.

"We were thinking it might be best to have the bee in the orchard, Mrs. Fenton. The trees will provide shade and it is un área más grande . . . a larger area," Lita suggested.

"Yes. What do ya think, Lilly?" Brenna added.

"I think that's a lovely notion, girls!" Mrs. Fenton chirped. "And won't our dear little bride think of the fragrance of blossoms each time she lays beneath the quilt with . . ."

"Yes, yes," Brenna interrupted. "Now, if you'll show us to the frame . . . we'll have Brian and Travis build it in the orchard, we will."

"You've lost all the colores from your face, Genieva," Lita whispered, softly pinching Genieva's cheeks as Brenna and Mrs. Fenton left the house. "It will be fine. It will be fine," she assured her, smiling with kindness.

Genieva looked into the beautiful brown of Lita's eyes and smiled. "She says such rather shocking things, Lita," she exclaimed in a whisper. "Doesn't she realize we only married for convenience?"

"No. She does not. And . . . it would go best if you let her believe that all is . . . that all is . . . normal between you and Brevan. She is the biggest gossip in the world. Smile your pretty smile, Genieva. The day will go quickly, and then you can share the quilt with Brevan."

Genieva's eyes widened with indignation, and Lita giggled, "I'm sorry, mí amiga. I could not resist it."

Genieva sighed and smiled herself. Lita and Brenna were wonderful women. She could not have wished for more perfect friends. It seemed pure miraculous luck that she should find two women as dear as they were so near to her now.

Half an hour later, Genieva found herself all too well settled next to Mrs. Fenton as nearly ten women worked simultaneously on the quilt. Most of the time there were several different conversations being held by small groups of individuals, but once in a while the entire group would involve each member in the same topic. As Genieva had feared, it wasn't long before the subject of the poor Amy Wilburn arose.

"I think it's just a pity . . ." one woman said. Genieva was nearly certain this woman's name was Mary Clawson. She was the blacksmith's wife—if she remembered correctly. "Poor Amy." Mrs. Clawson sighed. Nearly everyone else at the frame followed suit.

"Still . . . a woman has responsibilities to her own reputation. Her own well-being," Bertha Baumgardner reminded the group. Bertha was elderly, and impatient. She'd already sworn under her breath once at having to pick out two stitches. "I find it hard to be too sympathetic with her situation."

Genieva struggled to hold her tongue—to quiet her own opinion.

"Perhaps there be more to that story than most of us know," Brenna interjected. Every needle stopped mid-air as all eyes turned to stare at Brenna. Brenna shrugged and continued to stitch. "Has anyone here actually spoken with the lass since . . . since her condition was found out?"

"There's no need to speak with her, Brenna," one of the young, unmarried women corrected. "She's with child and not married. There's nothing more to be said."

Genieva drew in a deep breath—stabbed at the fabric beneath her fingers. This was Jenny Evans. Jenny had been the young woman to imply in the store, only days before, that Genieva was incapable as Brevan's wife. Jenny was an attractive young woman. Genieva could not deny that. Her hair was the color of morning sunshine, yet her eyelashes dark, long, and flattering to her blue eyes. "But then again," Jenny continued, "we all understand why you might feel inclined to defend her, Brenna."

Once again every needle halted—all eyes settling on Genieva.

Genieva could feel their burning, inquisitive stares but somehow managed to appear calm as she said, "I'm surprised a young lady, appearing to be so well-mannered, would imply such a thing at an event that is supposedly in my honor."

Genieva looked up, meeting Jenny's resentful glare. "Would anyone here like to tell me why it is that Brevan has been branded the miscreant in this situation?" All eyes dropped to the quilt as every hand began busily stitching. "Come now, ladies," Genieva coaxed, smiling. "Do you really suppose that were there any truth to this invented rumor . . . do you really think I would have married the man you all find so easy to slander?"

"He courted her just before . . . just before her condition became known," Jenny answered brazenly.

"He spurned her just before it! And well ya know it to be true, Jenny Evans!" Brenna growled.

"That's right. Brevan never courted Amy Wilburn," Mrs. Fenton agreed. "It's because she refuses to name the father that you all look to place the blame on him."

"And it's because all of you unmarried girls resent the young buck passing ya by that ya pin the deed on Brevan McLean," Mary Clawson added.

"So, am I to understand that Brevan never courted this Amy?" Genieva asked, staring at Jenny.

"Never," Mary confirmed.

"Still . . . it's the men like Brevan . . . the handsome and lustful ones who are, more often than not, responsible for the fatherless children in a town," Bertha grunted.

"Actually, that's not true. Isn't it more often the older, more established business-type men who begin to think themselves better than others, deserving of more, that leave a trail of poor desperate women with fatherless children in their wake?" Genieva suggested—pointedly looking to Bertha. She knew Bertha Baumgardner's husband had been mayor before his death.

Brenna stifled a giggle, and another elderly woman drew in her breath abruptly.

"A man's being handsome does not instantly mean he is lustful," Mrs. Fenton added. "More often it is the women of a town—the ones who blame him with lust—that are envious at not having him themselves. They're the ones who brand him as lustful."

Genieva looked up to Jenny, whose eyes smoldered like cinders at her. She sat between the other two girls that had been at the store, each of whom raised their eyebrows and looked expectantly at their friend.

"She's right," another woman whose name Genieva had forgotten added. "Brevan McLean is probably the most upstanding citizen in this community. And it does make a woman wonder at the other citizens in it who would suggest such a thing at his wife's bee."

Genieva smiled at the woman—noticing the guilt and glumness apparent on every face save Jenny's.

"Come now, ladies. Let's enjoy our time together. Actually, I'm very flattered that so many of you would find Brevan so attractive that you would assume any woman would be unable to resist him. And, I assure you, I realize now that we are wed you will cease to slander my husband's good name . . . knowing full well I would never slander any of yours. As for poor Amy . . . I believe there are almost always extenuating circumstances in these situations, and perhaps we should all be more forgiving and less judgmental." Genieva resumed her stitching. "Now, do tell me . . . is it always this dry here? Or is it just particularly so this year?"

"Humble pie! That's what they call it here, it is, Brevan!" Brenna laughed later that evening.

"Sí, Sí!" Lita exclaimed, laughing so heartily she doubled over with the weight of her mirth. "Humble pie. The most humble ever baked!"

"You women," Brian chuckled. "Just a bunch of cacklin' old crones, ya are."

"You've done us proud, Genieva. They'll not lock horns with you again for some time, I reckon," Travis added.

Brevan, however, sat solemn—appearing to be not in the least amused.

"Come now, brother Brev," Brian addressed him. "Don't ya find it amusin'? To see the look on Bertha Baumgardner's face alone would've been worth havin' yar toenails torn out for!"

"Amy Wilburn deserves far more sympathy than this town or the likes of all of you give her, for that matter. She's a poor soul led astray by some charmer among us, she is," Brevan growled.

"But we're not makin' light of poor Amy's situation, Brevan," Brenna assured him. "It's quite the opposite, it is. For that matter, Genieva nearly championed her."

Brevan shook his head and looked to Genieva, sitting solemn and without mirth herself.

"I'll say this for ya, I will," he began, "ya've got your wits about ya, and yar dealin' with those gossipin' hags today deserves more notin' than anythin' else ya've done thus far, lass." He shook his head as he stood and stretched his arms out at his sides. "I'd not spend an afternoon with them to save me own life."

"Ya look beat with a broom, Genieva," Brenna observed aloud. "It's best ya be gettin' to bed. 'Twas a long and tedious day of it. And before ya go . . . have ya shown that quilt we labored over so long to yar husband yet?"

"Oh," Genieva startled. "No. I haven't." Her bones and muscles ached as she went to her room and removed the quilt from the place she had laid it at the foot of her bed. It really was a beautiful piece of work. It held red and green squares and shapes of apples and leaves—a truly beautiful quilt.

"You see, Brevan," she said as she held it out for him to view, "it really is lovely, after all."

"It be a nice quilt," he bluntly responded. " 'Twill keep ya warm this cold winter."

"Now, brother Brevan," Brian chuckled as he walked quickly toward the door, "I thought that be yar own job!" And with a barrage of laughter, he jaunted out the door followed closely by his wife, sister, and brother-in-law, who all bid good night to Genieva.

Genieva smiled as she watched the couples disappear into the darkness—their playful conversation and laughter echoing on the breeze.

"He's a bleedin' idiot, that one," Brevan grumbled, a deep frown furrowing his brow.

"I think he's a breath of fresh air," Genieva sighed, turning toward her room.

"Well, he's been already inhaled, lass." The annoyance in Brevan's voice was so obvious that Genieva turned to look back at him. She found he stood angry before her. "Ya're strapped with the stale stench that's left in the family . . . namely Brevan McLean . . . the grouchy, philanderin', slave-drivin' Irishman!" he bellowed. He stormed past her and down the hall, slamming the door to his bedroom behind him.

Genieva tenderly folded the quilt—placing it in the linens trunk at the foot of her bed. She studied its crafted beauty one last time before closing the trunk's lid, noting how uniform all the stitches were, how tastily red were the apple pieces, and how the tiny cloth bees seemed to buzz—their soft noise humming in her mind. But as she closed the lid, her sweet thoughts vanished, replaced once more by uncertainty. Brevan had defended Amy Wilburn so vehemently. Was there truth, in fact, to the rumors? She shook her head, trying to dispel the disloyal thinking. Brevan was an honest, moral man. She was certain of it. She wouldn't have married him if her instincts had told her anything different.

But as she climbed into her squeaky yet comfortable bed, she wondered again how she had ever managed to find herself in such a position. She was not a farmer. She had no knowledge of farming. She was not a wife. And she had no knowledge of how to go about being married to a man, living with him day in and day out, and pretending everything was as normal as ever. She thought of her family, and a rush of guilt flooded her body. It had been a selfish act. Or had it merely been an act of independence?

Brevan nearly tore the shirt from his back as he removed it, angrily storming across his bedroom. *Why?* he wondered. Why was his name forever slandered, dragged through the dirt, whenever a scandal was about town? Why wasn't the finger pointed in the direction of the true and responsible culprit?

Amy Wilburn. He'd never given the girl the time of day—though he'd always been polite to her. Never had he given cause for gossip in her direction where he was concerned. Yet he pitied her—for he sensed the situation was not exactly what it appeared to be.

Exhaling a heavy sigh, he put a hand to his forehead.

And that poor lass in the other room. Poor Genieva, he thought. He was angry all over again for what the old and young biddies of the town had put her through. He knew she must doubt his honesty, his chastity. She hardly knew him from Santa Claus! And he'd snapped at her so. She was undeserving of it. After all, Brian was a jester—a freshness to any conversation. He'd been tired and taken offense at her complimenting his brother. Inhaling a breath of determination, he opened his door and marched out into the hall. Not pausing to knock, he pushed at the door to Genieva's room, barging in. He nearly laughed aloud when he saw her clutch the blankets to her throat—sitting prim and pristine in her bed.

"I'm apologizin' for snappin' yar head off, I am. I shouldn't have been so vexed," Brevan stated.

"It's fine. You're tired. I took no offense," she

responded. He knew she had taken offense. Still, he had apologized, so he nodded and turned to leave.

"Good night, lass," he mumbled over his shoulder.

Brevan McLean's conscience hit the pillow clear and guiltless.

Genieva raised her hands to her face. They were still trembling as she sat upright in her bed. Oh! How he'd startled her! She had not expected him to enter so abruptly and unexpectedly—not to mention so improperly attired! Still, she smiled as she recalled the expression donning his face upon entering. It reminded her of an expression a child might own had he been confessing to stealing a cookie from his mother's cookie jar.

What a different sort of man he is, Genieva thought, snuggling down into her bed once more. He was so serious, and so determined, that it nearly manifest itself as a flaw in him. But Genieva sensed a mischievousness or playfulness beneath the surface. He had, after all, apologized for snapping at her, therefore proving he had some conscience at least.

Chapter Four

Nearly two weeks had passed—two weeks since Genieva had married Brevan. With each day and night, Genieva began to enjoy the routine of her new life more and more. She had eventually adjusted well to rising before the sun and retiring long after it had set. She found she slept more soundly than she had ever before.

Lita and Brenna were frequent visitors. Genieva looked forward to each time they were near—for they shared wonderful conversation and laughter and confided in and encouraged each other.

On this particular night in mid-April, the couples met for dinner at Brenna and Travis's. Afterward, as Genieva stood at the kitchen sink drying the plates Lita handed to her from the rinse bucket, she noted how absolutely secure she felt—how thoroughly happy. Lita and Brenna giggled together at some humorous story of Brian's first attempt at fixing a loose shingle on the roof, resulting in his finding himself somehow flat on the seat of his pants in the dirt. Genieva smiled at the humorous story but also at the pure delight of her friends. Her attention was drawn to the conversation of the three men sitting on the front porch steps. She could hear the comforting lull of their low, masculine voices as they talked, and every now and again a wisp of their conversation was audible to her.

"I've got to get that field plowed this next week, I do," Brevan sighed. "Me corn is gonna be late gettin' in if I don't."

"Ya've had other things . . . distractin' ya, ya have," Brian chuckled. "Not that I blame ya now."

"Nothin' is distractin' me. Just the fact that Travis had to run off and marry Brenna, and Lita marry you, 'tis all. I've been havin' to break in the new help, I have. It's put me behind in me schedulin'." Brevan's explanation was followed by a yawn and another sigh.

"How do ya do it, Brevan?" Travis asked.

"How do I do what?" Brevan asked in return.

"How do you . . . how do you keep your hands off the woman?" Travis explained.

Genieva set the plate she had been drying on the counter, leaning forward in order to hear better. She briefly looked to Lita when the woman's elbow met with Genieva's ribs. Lita and Brenna were both listening intently as well— Lita arching interested eyebrows and nodding at Genieva—an indication she should keep her attention on the conversation going on outside.

But much to the ladies' frustration, a sudden breeze wafted through the open kitchen window— sending the wind chimes hanging just outside it dancing and tinkling with their piped tune.

"How irritatin'," Brenna grumbled when the next sound to sail on the breeze was the sound of all three men chuckling lowly and speaking in quiet voices now.

"I am sure he nearly ties himself to his bedpost to keep away from you, Genieva," Lita whispered, winking with delight.

Genieva shook her head and forced a smile. "I can assure you, Lita . . . I am no temptation to Brevan. And anyway, he is far too busy with his work to have time to even think of anything else."

"Oh, he's a good one at pretendin', he is," Brenna whispered. "But I'll tell ya this, Genieva McLean . . . Brevan is the most powerful man I've seen in me life when it comes to self-control. But even he'll break sooner or later and then . . ." Brenna shook her head and winked. "Well, ya'll have yar hands full, ya will. I hope ya're up to it."

"Sí!" Lita agreed. "It will throw you for a big fall the first time Brevan gives you his . . . beso . . ." Lita looked to Brenna inquisitively. "Beso?" she asked.

"Kiss," Brenna interpreted.

"Sí. The first time he kiss you, Genieva . . . you will fall hard," Lita finished, smiling with great certainty.

Genieva stared at Lita—suddenly very curious. She had not missed the reprimanding glare Brenna directed toward the beautiful Mexican woman.

"Of course . . . this is what happened the first time Brian kiss me, you see." Lita stammered. She cast her gaze down toward the sink and resumed rinsing the dishes.

"I see," Genieva muttered. Then, shaking her head to dispel the suspicions forming in her mind, she added, "But I don't fall easily, Lita. And I'm further assured I've nothing to fear where that circumstance is concerned anyway."

"Oh, mí hermana, it is nothing to fear. I promise you," Lita assured her sincerely, placing a hand on her shoulder.

Clearing her throat, Brenna rather abruptly changed the subject. "Um . . . I hope the two of ya are prayin' for rain, I do. I don't want to be carryin' bucket after bucket of water from the creek to water the gardens again this year."

"Híjole! That was terrible last spring," Lita agreed.

The men erupted into laughter once more, and Lita and Brenna continued to discuss the lack of rain. But Genieva's mind was elsewhere. Lita seemed far too sure of herself when it came to describing the effect of Brevan's kiss on a woman. Surely she was only judging from her experience with her own husband. After all, it was only natural to assume the brothers would share many common characteristics.

Still, as she and Brevan walked home at dusk later that evening, she found herself looking at him differently—pondering unthinkable possibilities. Had Lita been speaking from experience? She fought to drive the name of "poor Amy Wilburn" from her thoughts as well. To drive away the words *handsome rogue, dashing philanderer*.

"What?" Brevan asked as she continued to stare at him as they approached the house at last.

"Pardon me?" Genieva inquired.

"Ya're starin' at me like I've some creepin' crud about me," he grumbled. "Have I broken out in the pox?"

"No," Genieva admitted. "How ridiculous."

"What then, lass?"

"Nothing. I . . . I . . ." Genieva stammered. They stood at the front door to their house, and Brevan opened it, motioning for Genieva to enter. "Thank you," she mumbled.

Upon entering their home, Brevan reached over his head and took hold of the back of his shirt, pulling it off in one swift motion. The first few times Genieva had witnessed his now predictable habit of stripping off his shirt upon first entering the house each evening, her eyes had nearly bulged and exploded from their sockets. For the sight of his astounding physique had promptly caused Genieva further anxiety and discomfort. A man should not have the ability to inflict such nervous stress upon a woman, she told herself over and over. Yet he did unnerve her terribly, and the past weeks had only proved to Genieva that the fact would escalate with time.

"And what were ya three little witches cacklin' about over dish doin' this evenin'?" he asked as he went to the sink and worked the pump to draw water for his hands and face.

"Ever so much more interesting things than you three were," Genieva said.

"Really, now," he chuckled. "Well, the lads were askin' me tonight how it is that I manage to keep me hands from ya, Genieva," he stated. "Were ya answerin' the same question where I'm concerned?"

Genieva's mouth dropped open in astonishment. "No!" she gasped. "Of course not!"

"Ya don't find me temptin' then, lass?" he asked.

"I . . . I . . . I . . ." she stuttered. She was entirely astounded at his presumptuous remark.

"Hhmm. That's disturbin' news, it is." He turned toward her, glaring, and added, "But it makes us even, doesn't it?"

"It would seem so," Genieva mumbled. It was entirely too hurtful to hear it from his own lips—to hear he had no interest in her. Oh, she knew it well enough—but to hear him say it—it cut woundingly into her soul.

"Aye. It would," he agreed as he turned toward her. "I'm lackin' a hand towel to dry with, Genieva," he complained, walking to her with hands dripping wet.

"I'm sorry. I'll go get . . ." she said, turning from him—grateful for a reason to escape his further hurtful, verbal inflictions. But he reached out and took hold of her apron, spinning her back around to face him. Drawing it up from her skirt, he dried his hands thoroughly on it—all the while glaring down at her.

"Ya look tired, Genieva," he pronounced. "Ya should put yarself to bed, ya should."

Genieva brushed a loose strand of hair from her face and sighed. "I am tired. I work hard here, you know," she reminded him rather curtly.

"That ya do, lass." Then much to her disquiet, he reached out and rested his powerful hands at her waist. "Now, which bed are ya plannin' to put yarself in then?"

"Mine, of course. What do you mean?" she asked. Her eyes widened—her mouth gaping open as his insinuation struck her fully. As she felt him slowly begin to pull her body closer to his, she placed a tentative index finger against his chest in a gesture of stalling him.

"What a horrid thing to imply, Brevan. Especially when . . . when . . ."

"When?" he prodded.

"I'm going to bed now, Brevan. I'm tired," she finished. She felt entirely unstable.

Brevan released her waist. Yet one of his powerful hands cupped her chin firmly—drawing her face closer to his own. She could feel his breath on her lips as he spoke next.

"Ya see, Genieva," he began. " 'Tis harder for me than ya think."

"What?" she breathed, completely in awe of the effect his nearness had on her senses.

"Earnin' that heifer," he answered.

"What?" Genieva asked—breathless from his touch.

He released her and said, "Off with ya now, lass. Ya look done in."

Brevan watched Genieva slowly turn and disappear into her room, closing the door behind her. Running his fingers through his hair, he shook his head. Travis's heifer had absolutely nothing to do with Brevan's keeping his hands off Genieva thus far—it was pure common sense. He'd seen Brian and Travis both fall into that bottomless female trap. Blarney! There were even entire days that chores didn't get done on their lands because the two lovesick lads couldn't pull themselves away from those women long enough to concentrate on important things.

Brevan was smart enough to admit this adorable, sassy lass named Genieva had gotten to him. She'd distracted him enough that his corn was already late getting in. If he faltered—if he let a mere ounce of further distraction muddle his thoughts—the whole farm would eventually be lost.

Reassured, and with strength anew, Brevan retired to his bed. He'd get his corn in and have a new heifer too, he would.

Genieva didn't sleep well during the night. When she woke the next morning, her mind was still whirling—her nerves were agitated at the remembrance of being held by Brevan the night before. She could still sense his breath so close to her lips—so close that the taste of it was almost discernable. She busily worked all morning at her chores. Yet having finished the morning chores earlier than usual, she found she had merely created excess time to try to scatter the memory of Brevan's teasing from her thoughts. This was how she found herself mixing a cake when Brevan entered just before midday.

"Ya've certainly had the bee under yar saddle today, ya have," Brevan greeted Genieva as he entered the house. He paused at the pump to wash his hands.

"You mean a bee in my bonnet," Genieva corrected shortly.

"Same thing the way I see it. Whichever it is, ya've certainly worked fast this mornin'."

"Just wanted to get to some other things today. That's all," Genieva lied. She paused in beating the cake batter, setting the bowl on the counter as she turned to wipe the excess flour from the table.

"Get your fingers out of that cake batter!" she screeched when she turned back to her bowl in time to see Brevan plunge his index finger into the batter therein. Brevan turned to face her as he licked the batter from his finger. Raising his eyebrows with rebellion, he then dipped two fingers into the chocolate batter. He licked his fingers dramatically and with an air of superiority, causing Genieva's eyes to turn the color of the sweetness he was tasting. "I said, get your fingers out of that batter!"

As she stood before him, glaring daringly up at him, Brevan reminded her, " 'Tis my house too, it is. I'll eat what I want, lass." Triumphantly he placed the two fingers into the bowl of batter once more, swirling them in the mixture before drawing them out and smacking his lips after he had licked them clean.

The anxiety she'd endured throughout her morning, coupled with fatigue from her sleepless night, found Genieva's temper indeed provoked. Taking the wooden spoon from the bowl, she tapped it ceremoniously on the side of the dish to lessen the amount of batter clinging to it. Then, inhaling deeply, she soundly spanked Brevan across the seat of the pants with the spoon.

"I think Brenna was right to spank you once in a while . . . especially when you involve yourself in such a childish act!"

At once, Brevan's eyes narrowed—his chest rapidly rising and falling with indignation. Taking hold of Genieva's wrist, he turned her abruptly away from him, slapping her smartly on her own behind.

Genieva wrenched her hand free of his grasp, shouting, "How dare you? How dare you lay a hand on my . . . on my . . ."

"Bum," Brevan finished for her. "We had this same conversation a few days back, I think. The word is *bum,* Genieva."

Throwing the wooden spoon to the floor, Genieva reached around and spanked the seat of his pants as hard as she could with her own hand.

"Genieva," Brevan warned. "I'll turn ya over me knee, I will, lass."

"Don't threaten me," she ordered. Reaching for the bowl of batter, she lifted it high above her head.

"Ya wouldn't dare, lass . . . for the consequences would be beyond yar toleration," he growled. "Ya won't be able to sit yarself down for a week!"

But Genieva's temper was provoked, and, tipping the bowl, she poured the batter over Brevan's head. He made no effort to escape— only stood glaring at her as the brown confection dripped from his chin, nose, and hair. As he wiped a dab of batter from his left eye, Genieva's hand flew to her mouth, and she gasped. She was suddenly horrified at her own action—for she knew there would indeed be a price to pay.

"I-I'm sorry, Brevan. But . . . but you provoked me so," she stammered.

"Maybe. But ya better run all the same, lass. For I'll not be gotten the better of, I won't," he threatened.

Genieva knew by the flame smoldering in his eyes he meant his remark literally. Lifting her skirts and petticoats, she turned—fleeing from the house as quickly as her rather cumbersome work boots would allow. When she felt she had reached a safe distance, she stopped to catch her breath. Looking back at the house, she gasped as she saw Brevan step onto the porch, run his hands through his batter-saturated hair, and wipe the stuff on his trousers before catching sight of her.

"You!" he shouted, shaking an index finger angrily in her direction. "Ya better make for the hills, lass!"

"Oh, no, no, no!" Genieva whined as she saw him quicken his stride toward her. Turning, she began running again. There was no guessing what he would do to her were he to catch her. Genieva had visions of herself bent over his knee—her backside being abused with a switch. She knew he would overtake her in a moment. Stopping short, she turned to face his wrath, raising her hand to halt him.

"Brevan," she panted breathlessly. An odd flutter permeated her bosom at the sight of Brevan advancing on her. "Only wait." Brevan paused for a moment in his pursuit of her. "Forgive me. I don't know why I lost my composure. I . . . I . . ."

As he lunged forward, taking hold of her shoulders with his cake-battered hands, she could only stare apprehensively at him. Genieva could see his jaw was tightly clenched. As he began frantically looking about, she knew her vision had been correct and that he was, indeed, searching for some utensil to use for her paddling. Instinc-tively, Genieva's desire to preserve her dignity triumphed, and she shoved him as hard as she could—causing him to stumble backward and land squarely on his behind in the dirt. Her original intent had been to run. To flee for safety until her husband's temper was squelched. But as she studied the mighty man sitting in the dirt—hair, face, arms, and shirt covered in brown batter—amusement swelled within her. Even mercilessly biting her lip couldn't stop the giggles from erupting.

"You look like you've been in a fight with . . . with . . ." she struggled as her laughter increased.

"Don't say it, Genieva! Don't ya dare to say it!" Brevan growled, shaking his finger at her again.

"With a cow sufferin' from a bad case of the runny dung," Brian's voice interrupted from one side of them. Genieva looked to see her brother-in-law approaching from the orchard.

"Ya keep yar mouth to yarself, brother Brian," Brevan warned as he stood. "She's poured a bowl of batter over me head, she has!"

"And well ya deserve it, Brevan. I've no doubt in me of that," Brian chuckled, wiping the moisture of laughter from his eyes. "But I'm not goin' to find meself in the middle of this. I'm afraid ya're on yar own, ya are, Genieva."

"Brian, please," Genieva pleaded as Brevan lunged forward, taking hold of her arm tightly.

"Leave me out of it, lass. I've learned me lesson when it comes to battle with me brother." Turning his attention to Brevan, Brian added, "Why don't ya just kiss the lass, Brevan, and get it done with? Travis's heifer isn't worth the torture to yarself, it's not."

"What?" Genieva exclaimed. "What are you talking about?"

"I'll thank ya to keep yar nosy snout out of me business, Brian," Brevan growled. "Now, off with ya. 'Tis a private matter between the lass and me."

Genieva watched Brian saunter off, chuckling to himself, and her anxiety heightened. When she looked back to Brevan, she watched, aghast, as he ran his fingers through his matted hair once more before taking hold of her shoulders.

"My dress," Genieva whispered as she looked

at the brown handprints staining the sleeves of her clothing. A conquering grin spread across Brevan's handsome, batter-caked face. He tore open the front of his shirt. "What are you doing?" Genieva asked. He did not answer, simply wiped at his chest with one hand, coating it thoroughly with the cake batter that had found its way there. Ceremoniously, he held the sticky hand before Genieva's face, ensuring her vision of it. "Don't," she begged an instant before his hand lost itself in the softness of her hair. As she began to struggle in an attempt to escape any further harassment, she found herself suddenly and unexpectedly bound tightly in Brevan's arms—her soft, feminine form held improperly against his strong, masculine one.

"What's the old sayin' there, Genieva?" he asked. "Ya seem to be the expert here on them. 'If ya make yar cake batter . . . be prepared to eat it too?' Would that be close enough?" With a victorious chuckle, he ran his unshaven, cake-batter–covered cheek against her own—repeating the process on the other side of her face.

"Oh, let me go!" she cried. "You're a mess!"

Brevan laughed, and Genieva sensed his anger was gone—lost as hers was in the complete and utterly ridiculous situation.

"Let me be warnin' ya, lass," he began—wiping his chest again and spreading the mess across her forehead and chin, "I like to be tastin' batters and doughs when a woman is bakin', I do. It would go much better for ya if ya'd learn to give me a little taste here and there of yar own free will."

"Very well. Whatever you want. Now just let me go," she pleaded.

"Ah, but there's one thing more first," he muttered. "Ya see, Genieva . . . me brother is right, in his own shallow way."

"What do you mean?" Genieva asked, preoccupied with the uncomfortable, sticky sensation the batter caused on her face.

"I think ya've been curious about the quality of me kissin' abilities, ya have."

"What?" Genieva breathed. She couldn't believe what he was suggesting. "I couldn't care less about what it feels like to be kissed by you, Brevan McLean. That is most assuredly the very last thing on my mind!" she lied.

Lowering his voice, he said, "Come now, lass. Let's be havin' us a kiss. Then we'll both know that it's not somethin' we want to be wastin' any more time considerin'. We'll get more done that way, and ya won't find yarself trippin' over the laundry anymore." Genieva shook her head, unbelieving, but he continued, " 'Tis the heat and lack of rain that's got us on edge, ya know. Now let's get this out of the way, so we'll have one less thing pickin' at our brains."

"It's not picking at my brain," Genieva lied

again. And it was, indeed, a lie, for she had spent many an hour during many a day daydreaming on the idea. Yet as his charming smile brightened his face, Genieva was so entranced by his attractiveness, that when his head descended, his lips placing a light but lingering kiss on her cheek, she did not move to escape him. Putting one hand lightly at her chin, Brevan tipped her head slightly, and for the first time, Genieva experi-enced the fascinating touch of his lips to her own. He kissed her lips softly and quickly several times in succession before gradually coaxing the intimate ritual into a deeply stirring and passionate exchange.

Genieva's mind and body fought the complete elation threatening to overtake her common sense. Brevan's kiss was dangerous to her mental stability. She had known that it would be. Yet, she had dreamt of it at night, thought of it in daylight, and wanted to experience it since the moment she had first seen him almost two weeks before. His body was warm and solid—his mouth hot and convincing in its endeavor to prove to her that her dreams could not compare to the reality of him.

"How convenient," he mumbled when he at last released her from his merciless and irresistible embrace.

"What?" Genieva breathed, still overcome with the tingling sensation numbing her limbs.

"I said, how convenient . . . that the pond be so close," he explained.

"The pond?" Genieva asked, puzzled and breathless.

Brevan swiftly gathered her into his arms—picking her up and slinging her over one shoulder as if she were no more than a sack of flour.

"We both need bathin', we do. 'Tis easier by far to jump into the pond with ya than to tote the water into the house and pour it into the tub," he chuckled as he strode toward the pond.

"Don't you dare! Brevan! Stop at once!" Genieva screeched. Yet, mere seconds later, she felt the rather refreshing coolness of the pond's waters engulf her. Standing up and gasping for breath, she pushed her sticky and now wet hair back from her face. Brevan laughed and swam past her to the middle of the pond, where he disappeared several times beneath the water's surface in an effort to cleanse himself of the cake batter.

"Here, lass," he called to her, stripping off his shirt. "A washcloth for ya." He threw the wet article of clothing at her, hitting her squarely in the face.

"I can't believe you did this to me! You are an utter pest!" she cried as she began to wipe at her face and hair with the wet cloth. "I am completely soaked to the skin, Brevan." She ducked as one of Brevan's boots barely missed her as it flew through the air over her head, landing soundly on the bank of the pond. The other boot followed, and he only chuckled.

"Ya look like a drowned kitten, lass," he remarked. Swimming back to her, he stood and walked to her. Reaching down, he took hold of her ankle, and she toppled back into the water sitting down solidly in the mud beneath. "Get your boots off and come swimmin'," he demanded.

"I don't like water," Genieva argued. It was true. Even as a small child, she had harbored an intense fear of bodies of water. She watched as her own boots landed with a thud next to Brevan's on the bank.

"Ya don't swim then?" he asked.

"No," she confessed.

"Then it's time ya learned, it is." He took her hands and pulled her to her feet. "But not in that mess," he muttered, tugging at her skirt. "Take this bolt of fabric off yarself now."

Genieva's eyes widened. "I will not!" she avowed.

"You'll sink and drown otherwise, lass," Brevan informed her as he turned her away from him and fumbled with the fastening hooks at her skirt waist. In a quick moment Genieva felt her skirts and petticoats slip into the water about her ankles and she squealed in horror as Brevan turned her to face him again, took her waist between his powerful hands and began to pull her further into the deepening water. Soon the surface of the water was lapping at her chin, and only the tips of her toes could feel the squishy mud beneath her feet.

How had she gotten from a morning filled with hard labor at chores to splashing in the pond while covered in cake batter? Genieva looked about her as Brevan pulled her deeper.

"Brevan, please!" she pleaded. "I don't like the water!"

"Ya have to trust me, Genieva," Brevan told her calmly. "I'll not let ya drown."

"I know. Who would work for you then?" she snapped at him.

"I don't know. Maybe somebody who would let me stick me fingers in the cake batter once in a while and not spank me on the bum for it," he suggested, obviously amused at Genieva's disadvantage.

She could no longer feel the bottom of the pond with her toes. She realized the only things keeping her head above the water were Brevan's strong hands at her waist and instinctively threw her arms about his neck for support. She was frightened and drew her body next to his for safety. As his arms slid around her—held her tightly to him—she knew he would not let her slip beneath the water's surface.

"Ya have nothin' to fear, lass," Brevan assured

her then. "I taught Brenna and Lita both to swim last summer, I did."

Immediately Genieva's renewed fear caused her to stiffen, and she tried to push herself out of his embrace. "I don't want to learn to swim," she argued.

"Well, I lost me chances at a new heifer today, I did. And it's yar fault. So, I think it's time ya sacrificed somethin' yarself," he told her.

"Whatever are you talking about, Brevan?" she asked. She didn't understand why Brevan, Travis, and Brian were forever referring to Travis's new heifer.

"I'll just get ya used to the water today, lass. We'll swim some other afternoon. I've wasted enough time on silliness just now." He positioned one of her arms to crook the back of his neck. "It's not so bad, is it?"

Genieva was conscious of Brevan's powerful chest against her own—of the muscles in his arms as he held her in the water.

"No. It isn't," she admitted. She still hated the water, but the closeness and feeling of privacy at having Brevan's complete attention was worth enduring her fears.

"Ya have to relax once in a while, ya do. Swimmin' is fun. It's coolin' on hot days, as well." Brevan lifted a hand out of the water and brushed a strand of hair from Genieva's forehead. "Now, I'll take ya back in and go back to the house.

Don't look so disturbed, Genieva, lass. I'll give ya a minute to put that cumbersome clothin' of yars back on." As he started to push her backward toward the shore, he muttered, "Might as well make the loss complete." And he forced one last exhilarating kiss to her mouth.

Genieva was overcome by the floating feeling of being in the water—of being held by Brevan and kissed by him.

Moments later, as she stood waist deep in the pond watching him retrieve his boots from the shore, he said, "Ya see, lass . . . it's not worth wastin' time wonderin' about, is it?"

"No," she answered flatly. Yet, as she watched him saunter away toward the house, she could only long, in vain, to feel his lips meet hers again.

As she stood at the pond's shore fastening the waist of her skirt, Genieva glanced toward the orchard—and saw him. There among the trees, sitting on a tall bay horse, was a dark-haired man with a heavy mustache—a sombrero hanging at his back. His manner of dress indicated he was obviously a native of Mexico. His physical features were striking—Genieva noted he could be considered mildly attractive. The man smiled broadly, nodding his head in Genieva's direction as he rested his arms on the horn of his saddle. He stared at her—brazenly.

Genieva, instantly aware of her previous state

of indecency, picked up her boots and turned, walking briskly toward the house. It wasn't until she felt she was a safe distance from him that she turned to look for the man again. He was gone. The orchard was empty once more.

Entering the house, she gasped as Brevan unexpectedly stepped in front of her, fastening a pair of dry trousers.

He chuckled as he looked down at her and muttered, "Yar smaller even yet when yar drippin' wet."

"Well, I do wish you would forewarn me of your lecherous friends lurking about in the orchard before you dunk me in the water. He just sat there on his horse watching me like there was nothing at all wrong with it!" Genieva scolded—embarrassed by the way Brevan himself so thoroughly studied her.

"What? Who was watchin' ya?" he demanded, taking her shoulders roughly between his hands.

Genieva was terribly unnerved by the expression of rising concern on his handsome face.

"A . . . a man," she stammered. "He rode a bay horse and . . . and had black hair . . . a mustache." She paused, speaking her thoughts aloud. "Oh. Is he a friend of Lita's then?"

"Where in the orchard?" Brevan growled.

"Near the pond. But he's long gone now, Brevan. Why are you . . . ?" she began.

Brevan bolted past her and out the door. She turned to see him in a dead run toward the orchard.

Genieva was sitting in her bedroom brushing out her wet and matted hair when he returned some time later.

Bursting in upon her, he asked, "Ya've never before seen that man, have ya, lass?"

"No," Genieva answered. As she looked up to him, she had the overwhelming desire to cup his face in her hands—to soothe the frown on his brow. "Why?"

"If ya ever be seein' him again, ya tell me the minute ya're away from him."

"Is . . . is he an undesirable? A criminal?"

Brevan threw his head back in a sudden, rather boisterous laugh. "Yes and no. Not literally a criminal . . . yet."

"Who is he?" Genieva ventured.

"Never ya mind who he is. It doesn't matter. Just keep out of his way, and let me know if ya ever see him again," Brevan commanded. Looking around at the floor, he ran his fingers through his hair with obvious frustration. "I've wasted the whole afternoon, I have. Bein' silly and chasin' idiots," he grumbled as he turned and left.

Genieva's mind was taxed for the remainder of the afternoon and long after dusk. When Brevan finally returned from choring, he appeared to be even more tired than usual and hardly touched his supper. He said very little and went directly to bed when he'd finished eating.

Once Genieva had finished cleaning up after the meal, she stood at his door for a moment and listened. She heard not a sound and assumed he was already asleep. Going to the hook behind her bedroom door and retrieving her shawl, she looked at the clock on the fireplace mantel. It was only 7:30, she noted. Surely Brenna would still be awake. She quietly left the house, intent on discussing the day with her friend.

Brenna's face went ashen as Genieva told her about the man in the orchard. Genieva knew that, when Brenna finally had regained her composure and commented on the incident, she was hiding something. Brenna held knowledge she was plainly afraid to reveal.

"I . . . I'm not sure who it was, Genieva," Brenna stammered. "There are many, many families from Mexico in the area. It could've been one of any number of vaqueros workin' or livin' nearby."

"Brevan seemed to know who it was . . . specifically," Genieva urged.

Brenna tossed her head and sighed with feigned indifference. "Well, it's hard to say. Brian said he came upon the two of ya wrestlin' about somethin' fierce today." It was apparent

Brenna did not want to be hounded about the matter. Genieva would respect her friend's desires for privacy.

"He kept digging his fingers into my batter," Genieva explained. "Not once . . . but again and again."

Brenna laughed. "He's terrible with batters and doughs, he is. Can't keep from them. Don't be too hard on him though, Genieva. It's one of the few weaknesses he has that he lets us see plainly."

Brenna and Genieva both turned then to see Brevan storming into the room—his fierce stare affixed solidly to Genieva's bluish-tinged eyes.

"I'll put you to sleepin' with me if I can't trust ya to stay in at the late hours, I will!"

"What?" Genieva mumbled. "I only came to visit with . . ."

"Ya didn't have the consideration to let me know ya were goin'! Ya've scared the life out of me, ya have!" he bellowed.

"She's only come for a visit, Brevan," Brenna explained.

"And I was supposed to know that by readin' her mind, I guess. 'Tis not a night that ya should be wanderin' about alone, lass." His voice had calmed—but Genieva sensed the residue of some form of fear in him.

Genieva looked from Brevan to Brenna—who dropped her gaze to the floor.

"Why not?" she asked. "I've come alone other times."

"I'm . . . I'm uncertain who it was that ya were seein' in the orchard today. But I'm fairly certain of what ranch he's from, and I'm not sure it's wise for ya to be out alone after dark," Brevan explained. Genieva knew he held information in secret still. He wasn't trying to frighten her, she knew. Yet she was frightened.

"All right," she agreed simply. "I'll be more thoughtful before I go out alone at night if you think it's necessary."

Brevan sighed and smiled slightly. "Good. Then let's be gettin' back. I'm tired this night."

Brevan was unusually talkative on the walk home. His babble was almost constant and bounced erratically from one subject to the next without ever touching once on the man in the orchard.

That night, as she lay in bed, Genieva's sense of security was breached by the realization of Brevan's uneasiness—never to be entirely intact again.

Chapter Five

The next afternoon was pleasant in its comfortable warmth. Genieva buried her face in the freshly sun-dried sheet before tossing it into the bushel basket at her side. She loved the smell of clean laundry fresh off the line. Caring for the laundry was somewhat relaxing—for it was practically the easiest responsibility she had on Brevan's farm. The warm sun and slight breezes had dried the bedding quickly, and Genieva intended to hang some other clothes out before the sun began to set. As she reached to remove another sheet from the line, she couldn't keep her gaze from wandering to where Brevan was working in the field—he'd been plowing all day.

Brevan and the team of black mules had created quite an impressive number of straight, even furrows. The field, intended for corn, was nearly ready for planting. Brevan had told Genieva he planned to start the planting the very next day. Genieva watched him for a few moments, marveling at the strength it would take to work so physically hard for such long hours. He was a determined man, and the profound determination in him was admirable. As Genieva continued to watch him plow, it appeared as if the mules were having some difficulty, for the animals halted abruptly. After snapping the leather at their backs several times and finding the command a vain attempt, Brevan slipped the lines from around his shoulder and released the plow as he walked forward to investigate. Hunkering down, he studied the ground in front of the plow for a moment. Genieva saw him reach down and unearth a large clump of roots. She smiled to herself as she watched the magnificent man—he was truly unlike any other man she'd ever known.

As Brevan reached down to pull at another clump of undesirable substance, the unexpected repeat of a shotgun somewhere near spooked the animals, and the team bolted forward. In their startled state, the mule team took no notice of their master. Genieva watched, horrified, as the plow, still connected to the animals by the whippletree, tipped forward, knocking Brevan to the ground. From where she stood, Genieva could see the sharp blade of the plow being pulled behind the team slide over Brevan's body as he lay in its path. He shouted—an indication of extreme pain. Genieva dropped the sheet she had been holding and ran to him.

The sight meeting Genieva's eyes upon reaching Brevan was terrifying! There he lay—facedown in the soil. The back of his shirt was already saturated with bright red blood—spilling from a wound some six inches long, running vertically down the right side of his back.

Dropping to her knees beside him, Genieva cried, "Brevan!" as her hands flew to her mouth in panic.

A painful grimace constricted his face, and he panted as he said, "Quickly, lass. Get me to the house, now." As his powerful arms raised his hulking body, he added, "Hold the mess together with your hand, Genieva. I can feel that it's deep."

"I-I-I don't know what you mean?" she stammered. Her own body was shaking with anxiety and horror.

"Pinch the wound closed with yar fingers, lass!" he shouted, as he staggered to his feet. "I've no hands growin' out of me back, now have I?"

Before that moment, Genieva had always thought herself far from squeamish. The sight of blood had never weakened her stomach or knees before. But this was Brevan's blood running in crimson streams down his back—Brevan's flesh mangled before her!

"I-I don't think I . . ." she began.

Brevan took hold of her wrist, demanding, "Pinch it closed now, Genieva McLean, and help me into the house."

When he'd released his hold on her, she watched as her own hand took the wounded flesh of his back in a firm fisted hold. Blood immediately seeped through her fingers and began running down her forearm. As Brevan stumbled toward the house, the warm blood tracked red rivulets down Genieva's own arm. It quickly began dripping from her elbow to the ground, leaving a trail in the soil as they went.

"I'll get you into the house—then I'll get Brenna. She'll know what to do," Genieva said.

"I know what to do, Genieva. You can dress the wound yarself, ya can," he groaned as he stumbled momentarily.

"Me?" Genieva choked. "I've never had to . . ."

"Well then, lass . . . there be a first time for everythin', they say."

When they had entered the house, Brevan immediately began ordering Genieva about. This time, however, she did as he directed—for she knew she needed his strong, commanding manner in those moments.

"Quickly, lass. Light the stove aflame, and get some water to boilin'. Needle and thread are in me mother's old sewin' basket in the spare room. Boil the needle and thread in the water while ya be cleanin' this mess up," he ordered, as he groaned between breaths.

"Needle. Thread," Genieva muttered anxiously as she sought the items after setting a pot of water on the stove. "Boil them in the water," she continued to mutter to herself, returning to the kitchen and dropping the items into the pot of water. But as she realized why Brevan had ordered her to boil the needle and thread, what little pretty pink coloring remained in her lovely

116

face left it completely, and she stared at him in horror. "You want me to . . . to sew it up?" she squeaked.

"How else would ya be thinkin' it's meant to heal, Genieva?" he growled. "Now, wipe this mess from the cut, and make certain it's stopped runnin' blood." He closed his eyes tightly and ground his teeth. Genieva knew he must be enduring excruciating pain.

"I'll fetch Brenna, Brevan. She will be able to deal with this much better than I can. I'll be back as soon as possible," Genieva said as she lunged toward the door. Brevan caught hold of her wrist, however.

"Ya're me wife, Genieva. Ya're responsible for carin' for me as I am for you. Ya let that water boil for five minutes, and then ya stitch this cut closed and put me to me bed. Better get used to the harsh life we're livin' out here. Else ya'll not make it to yar twenty-first birthday," he growled. The pain inflicted on his wounded body was dreadfully evident on his face as he scowled. Taking a deep breath, and swallowing the thick lump of fear in her throat, Genieva pushed his hand from her wrist. Hurrying to the cabinet, she fetched a clean cloth with which to wash the wound.

Her hands trembled, near to uncontrollably, five minutes later as she endeavored to thread the needle with the wet, sterilized thread.

"All right, all right," she soothed herself as she knotted the thread and turned to face Brevan.

"Just pinch it together and sew it closed," Brevan instructed as he turned away from her. "Neat and tidy is not what ya're strivin' for, Genieva."

"Brevan," she began. "I-I don't think I can do this. It's going to hurt you so."

"Genieva . . . I need to get to restin' up. The plantin' won't wait, and I've got to finish that field. Sew the vile thing shut so I can get to me bed!" he growled.

Genieva knew the wound pained him unmercifully. Thus, as tears flooded her cheeks, she pinched the large laceration together and began to stitch it. Brevan only flinched once—the first time she pricked his tender flesh with the needle. It was a horrible task to perform, and she wondered how physicians tolerated such things.

It was not a pretty sight she studied when she'd finished the stitching of Brevan's flesh. She could only bring herself to initiate twelve large stitches—stitches that were too far apart—but it was all she could do. The bleeding had slowed, and she washed the area once more.

As she helped Brevan stand, she was immediately frightened at the pallid tinge and weariness of his face.

"Put me to bed, and leave me be. I'll be fine in the mornin', I will," he assured her. "Ya cleaned it good didn't ya, lass?"

"Yes," she answered as she helped him down the hallway to his room.

"Me arms are weak, Genieva. Help me now," he instructed. "I don't think I can be takin' me boots off me own self."

"Sit down, Brevan. I'll do it," she affirmed. He sat down on his bed, wincing as he did so. Genieva struggled with his boots but was able to remove them.

"Thank ya, Genieva," he muttered. His eyes were already closing, worn with fatigue.

"You'll sleep better without your socks and . . . and trousers, Brevan," Genieva reminded him.

"Fine then, lass. Take them off as well. Strip me naked if ya must—just let me rest." His voice was filled with frustration and fatigue.

Genieva removed his socks and settled for loosening the buttons of his trousers. She helped him to lie as comfortably as he could on his stomach. He was sleeping before she even left the room.

"What frightened the mules?" she asked herself aloud as she sat at the table in the kitchen with a glass of refreshing water after having sponged Brevan's blood from nearly every surface in the room. She was sure she had heard a gunshot. It had been close too. But Brian and Travis never hunted close to the houses.

"What's goin' on, Brevan?" Brian shouted as he stormed into the house.

"Shhh!" Genieva shushed him. "He's resting." How relieved she was for dear Brian. He would know what to do—she was certain.

"Resting? His idiot mules just came tearin' through me strawberry patch, Genieva! The plow they were draggin' behind them destroyed half of it, it did! And he's restin'?" Brian started for the hallway, but Genieva stood, stalling him.

"There's been an accident, Brian. Brevan bent down to clear the path for the plow, and a gunshot frightened the team, and they bolted. They pulled the plow with them as they went, and it cut Brevan's back so badly that I can hardly imagine a man living through such an injury! I was afraid to leave him here alone to go for help. I didn't even think about the team being loose."

"Well take me to him, Genieva! Is he well? Did you tend to the wound?" Brian asked, his anger turning to deep concern as they made their way to where Brevan lay.

"I did the best I could, Brian," Genieva said, as she removed the light sheet she had placed over Brevan. Immediately the tears streamed down her cheeks once more at the sight of the blood-saturated cloth she had laid over the wound to protect it.

"St. Patrick's snakes a slitherin'!" Brian exclaimed, astonished at the severity of the wound as he gazed down at it. "Is he breathin' still, Genieva?"

"He's sleeping. He seems to be . . ." she began.

"Such a wound, lass! Such a deep and painful wound." Reaching down, Brian affectionately squeezed one of Brevan's hands lying on his pillow near his head. "Ya watch him close, Genieva. Infection could kill him."

"I-I cleaned it as good as I possibly could. I used the iodine . . . I . . . oh, Brian!" she cried, burying her face in her hands.

"Now, now, lass," Brian soothed, gathering her into his arms. "He's the strongest man I've ever seen in me life, he is. No doubt he'll be up in the mornin' and referrin' to that horrible sight as his wee scratch." As he smoothed her hair, Genieva let her tears soak his shirt at his shoulder. "Ya're tired, ya are. I'll send Brenna and Lita over to keep ya company, and the three of ya can take yar turn sittin' up with him tonight. It'll make ya feel better."

Removing herself from his arms, Genieva dried her tears with her apron and nodded. "It will help me to have them here, Brian. Thank you. Oh, and I'm so sorry about your berry patch."

Brian smiled with understanding and shook his head. " 'Tis nothin' to speak of, Genieva. Nothin' at all." He frowned then, inspecting once more the massive wound on his brother's back. "I'll send Brenna and Lita over right away, lass. Ya're not to worry. I tell ya, he's stronger than a bull, that one."

• • •

Brenna and Lita gasped in perfect unison when Genieva pulled back the sheet and revealed to them Brevan's terrible laceration.

"Genieva!" Brenna exclaimed in a whisper. "'Tis a foot long if it's an inch!"

"Oh, no!" Lita disagreed. "A foot deep! Oh, Genieva! How did you manage it?"

"Brevan's a very authoritative man, you know," Genieva whispered her answer, motioning for the two women to leave the room with her.

As the three women walked quietly down the hallway, Lita took Genieva by the shoulders and turned her toward her own room. "Aquí, mí amiga," she directed as she pointed to Genieva's bed. "You need to rest. You look so tired and worried. Brenna and I will sit up with your husband."

"Oh, no, I can't!" Genieva argued.

"You must, Genieva," Brenna insisted. "I know me brother, and he'll be hard to handle tomorrow, he will. He'll be steamin' angry that the field won't be gettin' plowed, if the pain itself doesn't make him a rabid animal."

"But I-I can't just . . ." Genieva stammered.

"To bed with ya now, Genieva," Brenna ordered as she closed the door behind her.

With pangs of guilt and trepidation, Genieva did retire to her own bed—and she cried pitiful tears as she thought of how horrid it had all been.

What would she do without Brevan if he were stricken ill and taken from her? It frightened her to realize that she already knew she would never recover from losing him. Never recover from losing the great stranger of a man she was so thoroughly in love with.

It was hours and hours later when Genieva woke. She was certain she had heard the deep intonation of Brevan's voice. Quickly she threw back her blanket and walked down the hallway to his room. She stopped before his doorway, however, when she heard another voice—Lita's.

"Brevan, mí amor," the woman sobbed. "Perdóname. Forgive me. I should've . . . I should've . . . this is all my fault!" she cried softly.

"Ah, hush, Lita," Brevan assured her. Genieva peeked carefully around the doorway. Brevan was still lying in his bed—on his stomach. Lita sat on the floor next to him holding one of his large hands against her cheek as she wept. Instantly, an overwhelming anxiety and jealousy washed over Genieva. Yet she stood still and hidden as she continued to eavesdrop.

"This . . . none of this has ever been yar fault, and well ya know it," Brevan continued in a scolding manner.

"But Genieva said she heard . . ."

"Genieva imagined it, Lita. The animals startled 'tis all. 'Twas me own fault, I'm certain of it."

Now anger and indignation compounded Genieva's plaguing emotions as she listened. She knew she had heard a gunshot. She knew it!

"But, oh, Brevan . . . what if Genieva should get in the way somehow?" Lita asked.

"She won't, Lita. I'll see to it. I'll make sure of that. Ya just worry about yarself, lass. Ya'll be needin' to be more careful now, and ya shouldn't be losin' sleep like this either. It's not good for you or . . ." As Genieva watched Lita lean over and kiss Brevan affectionately on the forehead, her temper flared, and she stepped into the room.

"Oh, you're awake," Genieva stated flatly.

"Oh, yes! He is quite well, Genieva!" Lita beamed.

"So I see," Genieva agreed. "Well, off with you now, Lita. I'll sit with him awhile. You need your rest after all."

"I am tired," Lita admitted as she rose. Reaching out, she took Genieva's hand and squeezed it with reassurance. As Genieva looked into Lita's beautiful brown eyes, her anger began to dissipate. Surely she had misunderstood the implications in the conversation she had overheard. Lita appeared so unruffled and sincere.

"Brenna is resting in the spare room. Would you mind if I take your bed?" Lita asked.

"Of course not, Lita," Genieva assured her. She smiled at the woman, and when Lita had left, Genieva turned her attention to Brevan.

"Feeling better?" she asked shortly.

"Ya shouldn't have let her stay up so late, Genieva," Brevan barked at her.

"Brenna insisted that we take turns, Brevan. It wasn't my idea," she defended. "And anyway, you seemed rather smitten with her company."

"She needs her rest, lass," he continued to bark, lowering his voice.

"We all need our rest, Brevan," she reminded him rather too curtly.

"'Tis true enough. But Lita . . ." he paused, seeming uncertain about whether he should continue. "Lita must think of her baby now."

Genieva sat down on the chair near his bed. She was so stunned—as if someone had simply hit her over the head with a board.

"You mean she's . . . Lita is . . ." she mused.

"The word is *pregnant,* Genieva. 'Tis a proper word, ya know," he snapped at her.

"Why hasn't she told any of us? Why hasn't Brian said anything? He's the one that suggested she come over here!"

"Brian doesn't know of it yet."

"You mean to tell me . . . she's confided this profoundly intimate secret to you, and not to her own husband?" Genieva's heart began to pound—furious with anxiety again.

"I guessed at it. Brian, good and true man that he is, doesn't see things on the end of his nose sometimes," he groaned. It was obvious the wound was paining him once more, for he clenched his eyes tightly shut and held his breath for a moment.

"By the way, Brevan," Genieva charged forth, "I did hear a gunshot that spooked the mules today."

"I know," he admitted. "I heard it too, I did."

"You heard it?" Genieva asked. "Then why did you tell Lita that you didn't? You made me look like a fool in her eyes."

"There's no sense in worryin' her, there isn't. She's blamin' herself as it is."

"Why should she blame herself?"

"I'm tired, Genieva. Me back hurts . . . me head is poundin', and me field is waitin' to be planted. Just let me rest now. And it's not necessary for ya to stay here with me," he grumbled.

"Well, I can't very well return to my bed to sleep, so I might as well . . ."

"Me own bed is big enough for the both of us, Genieva. Just stop yar endless chatter, and let me rest," he moaned. He was hurting, and Genieva forgave him instantly for being so curt with her—and for suggesting such an inappropriate resting place for herself.

"I'll leave you then. Don't worry about your field, Brevan. It will still be here when you feel better." But as she rose to leave, he caught hold of her hand. She turned to find him glaring up at her, an expression of warning blatant on his face.

"Don't argue the gunshot with Lita, Genieva. It

126

will worry her more than ya know. Let it die," he whispered.

Wrenching her hand from his grasp—for his touch unnerved her—she said, "As you wish, Brevan. Sleep well."

"Brian was over early this mornin', Genieva, and finished the plowin'. I'll help ya plant the corn, I will. Then Brevan won't be forcin' himself to work before 'tis safe for him," Brenna informed Genieva at the breakfast table. Lita had left early—before Genieva had awakened—but Brenna had waited and fixed a fine breakfast.

"Did you know that Lita is . . . ?" Genieva stammered.

"That she has a wee bun in the oven?" Brenna finished joyously. "Oh, yes! She told me just this mornin' on her way to tell Brian. I've no doubt he'll be walkin' on the air all day now. When did she tell you?"

"She didn't," Genieva answered flatly before shoveling a pile of scrambled eggs into her mouth with her fork.

"How did ya know it then?"

"Brevan told me."

"Brevan? Ya mean Brevan knew before the rest of us? Before Brian?"

"Yes."

Genieva looked up, startled when Brenna giggled merrily. "Oh, Brevan. He can read a person through and through, ya know. He guessed at it. He must've."

"He said as much," Genieva confirmed.

"Oh, how I wish it were me," Brenna sighed. "A baby! Just think, Genieva. How wonderful!"

"Yes. And I'm sure it will be a beautiful one as well," Genieva agreed.

"For sure and for certain!" Brenna giggled. "With me brother's handsome looks and Lita's heritage combined."

"Yes. Lita is beautiful. And as for your brother . . ." Genieva could not finish her thought—for a horrid idea had been forming in her mind since she'd overheard the conversation between Brevan and Lita—and now it was threatening to further pollute her thoughts. It just seemed too unnatural for Brevan to guess at Lita's condition while Brian remained ignorant of it. Shaking her head, Genieva tried to dispel the unthinkable vision from her mind. She tried to dispel the name of Amy Wilburn echoing throughout it as well.

"You and Brevan will have beautiful babies as well, ya will," Brenna said softly, smiling and winking at Genieva.

"Children are not on his list of important chores, Brenna," Genieva corrected her, blushing vermillion, however, at the thought.

"But gettin' me corn in is," Brevan growled as he entered the kitchen.

Genieva and Brenna both turned to face him, and Genieva was on her feet instantly at seeing his state. He was pale and obviously weak—for he put his hand out to steady himself against the wall. His trousers threatened to slip from his hips—for they remained unfastened.

"Get yar scrawny body back into bed, Brevan McLean!" Brenna ordered as Genieva rushed forward, tugging at the waistband of his pants to secure them.

"I've got to get that corn in, Brenna," he mumbled. As he stumbled forward, Genieva's smaller form struggled to support his incredible bulk.

"You've got fever," Genieva mumbled. "He's too warm, Brenna," she called over her shoulder. She felt warm moisture on her hand as she fought to help support him as he teetered backward. Drawing her hand away to examine it, she gasped as she saw the bright crimson blood there—fresh and wet. "And you're bleeding again."

"That field has to be planted, Genieva," he breathed, taking her face tightly between his two powerful hands and glaring down at her.

"I'll plant the field for you, Brevan. I promise. But you must rest," she told him. His condition frightened her! It frightened her more than anything she had ever in her life encountered.

"I-I . . ." he stammered before his full weight descended on Genieva, knocking her to the floor. The crushing mass of his unconscious body descending onto her own, forced the breath from her lungs, and Genieva was momentarily paralyzed for lack of it.

"He's as stubborn as anythin' I've ever seen, he is," Brenna complained as she worked to help Genieva push the great man off her own body. "Leave it to Brevan to pass out on the kitchen floor with only the two of us to be draggin' him back into bed."

Yet Brevan's unconscious state was very brief. He woke almost immediately.

"Ya ask Brian to plant me corn for me, Brenna. It has to be done in the next couple of days. I'm late with it this year, I am," Brevan mumbled as Genieva and Brenna helped him to his feet.

"Let's get ya to bed, Brevan. Quit worryin' about that corn! It's yar healin' that's important," Brenna scolded him.

"'Tis but a scratch, Brenna," Brevan barked. "Let me be!" He pushed Brenna away from him, putting one arm about Genieva's slight shoulders for support. "Get to askin' Brian about that corn, lass!"

Brenna sighed heavily. She shook her head as she said, "Crack him over the head with a hammer if ya must, Genieva. But get him to bed and to sleep so we won't have to put up with his bellowin' for another minute! I'm off to speak to Brian, I am." Irritated, she slammed the front door as she left.

"You shouldn't be so short and demanding with your sister, Brevan. She's been a great help and . . ." Genieva began.

"I know, I know," Brevan interrupted. "Now, I'm feelin' a bit dizzy again, I am. Get me to me bed, lass."

As they approached his bed, however, Genieva stood before him, taking his arms in order to guide him into lying down on his stomach.

"Your wound is bleeding again. I'm afraid I didn't get it stitched very thoroughly," Genieva mumbled.

At that moment, however, Brevan's weakened state caused him to stumble and his great hulking form was once again too awkward and heavy for Genieva to support. Before she could react and move out of the way, she felt herself fall back on his bed, his massive weight crushing her an instant later as he fell on top of her.

"Brevan," she gasped, pushing on his shoulders in a pointless effort to remove him. "Brevan, wake up and move!" When she found it impossible to move him, she took his face in her hands and lifted his head to look directly into it. "You are smashing me flat! Wake up!" She slapped him all too gently on the cheek, but his head only fell against her neck when she released him.

Struggling for breath—for he was astonishingly heavy—Genieva tried to squirm her way out from under him. She soon realized she was trapped, however. Perhaps if she could maneuver her legs to one side a little, she could free herself. Yet it was to no avail. They hung off the bed from the knees down, rendering themselves in too difficult a position to be used to pry Genieva loose.

"What goes on here?" Brevan's slurred words came as he tried to raise his head. "What are ya doin', Genieva?" he asked looking at her.

"You are smashing me! Get off, you big oaf!" Genieva groaned. She could tell then that he was still close to being unconscious, for his glassy eyes narrowed.

"Make sure Brian gets that corn in, Genieva," he mumbled as he stared down into her eyes.

"Hang the corn, Brevan!" she shouted then, pushing at his shoulders. "Get off me before I'm crushed to death!"

With a profound effort, Brevan placed his hands on either side of Genieva's body and tried to raise himself, only to collapse on top of her once again. "I'm as weak as a bloomin' calf, I am," he panted.

"Just help me to roll you off," she groaned as she pushed at his right shoulder to guide him to roll left.

With a pain-stricken moan, Brevan mustered what little strength was left to him and rolled to his side. Genieva drew a deep breath before sitting up.

"You weigh more than . . ." she began. But when she looked at him lying pale and silent on his side, she knew he was unconscious again. Anxiety gripped her once more, and she laid her hand gently on his chest to make certain that it did indeed rise and fall with life-sustaining breath. His flesh was hot to the touch, and the fever of it caused her hand to tremble. Tenderly she caressed his rugged and unshaven face, praying silently for his well-being.

As Genieva studied Brevan's face—a face that even in sleep donned a pain-stricken frown—her heart swelled with what she had already come to know as her astounding love for him. What manner of marvelous man was this that she was blessed to be married to? Hard-working, handsome, and capable of anything. Gently she smoothed the frown from his tired brow. Caressing his desirable lips with her fingers, she remembered the taste of them the previous day in the orchard when he had kissed her.

Suddenly, as if his subconscious had read her mind, Brevan's eyes burst open—their deep blue mesmerizing Genieva. In a moment, she gasped, realizing that he was conscious. Even if she had wished to she could not have avoided him as he reached out unexpectedly, slid his hand around her neck, and quickly pulled her face to meet his own. His magnificent kiss was feverish in its heated thirst—exhilarating—as he seemed unable to quench some deep craving hunger! And when he pulled her down onto the bed next to him, covering her chest and shoulders with his own—delivering an intensely unbridled continuance of it—Genieva's breath was once again wondrously seized from her body. Truly, it could only be dubbed a bewitching skill that he owned—for his kiss rendered her powerless to resist relishing in it. His mouth was warm and demanding, even for his weakened state, and each time she drew breath, Genieva basked in the pure pleasure and taste of Brevan's affectionate wizardry.

Still, a horrible feeling of uncertainty nagged at Genieva's mind, and she reached up, pushing his face away. "Brevan," she asked, breathless from his kisses. "Y-you do know it's me, don't you?"

His glassy stare seemed unable to take note of what she had asked. He only grabbed the wrist of her hand pushing at him, pinning it to the bed as his mouth sought to enslave hers once more. After one final fervid and fevered kiss, he fell unconscious again, and Genieva pulled herself from beneath him. Though the kiss of the day before had been the stuff of dreams, this kiss was different—issued with a powerful something she could only define as wanton passion.

He slept quietly—the frown gone from his face at last. As she watched him for some time, Genieva wondered if he had known it was she he had ravished with affection. Or had his mind, in its fevered state, envisioned someone else in his arms and bed? Her mind fought back the name echoing throughout it—*Lita*.

The April sun was warm and the lilacs fragrant as Genieva drove the stick into the soil. She dropped a few corn kernels into the hole, using her foot to cover it with dirt. Having never planted before, planting the corn was a tedious chore for her. Still, she knew how important it was to Brevan—how important it was to have it done immediately. Brevan had married Genieva to help him with the farm. She knew it was her responsibility to get the planting done, especially since Brian and Travis had left for two days on important business. Though Brenna had offered to help with the planting, Genieva knew Lita was not well and needed Brenna with her while Brian was away. Brenna had shown her how to plant, and, being assured she now had a proper knowledge of it, Genieva had begun the planting herself. As she continued the monotonous process of planting, she began to dread having to haul water from the creek to the field. Hauling water would indeed be necessary—for there was no sign of impending rain.

Brevan had not stirred since the previous morning. Genieva worried over him with every step she took—with every kernel that she buried in the soil. From time to time, she would leave the field to return to the house and check on him—for she feared that, even though his fever had gone, something might cause him to take a turn for the worse once more.

Genieva's legs, arms, back, and every other part of her body ached as she carried bucket after bucket full of water to the field. Each seed must be watered. It had taken her a full day to plant the corn, and she knew it would, no doubt, take this entire new day to water it sufficiently.

As the sun set that evening, Genieva sat at the kitchen table. Her body was racked with aching and soreness. Even for having worn gloves, blisters had formed on her tender palms. Her hands throbbed and stung, ached with the soreness of unfamiliar hard labor and the sting of swollen blisters. She placed cool, damp cloths on them, but it did little to soothe her pain. Still, it was done—after two days of hard labor the like Genieva had never known—Brevan's corn was planted and watered in the field.

"Get yarself to bed, Genieva." Brevan's voice echoed through her mind. She found it hard to raise herself from the great fatigue forcing her to sleep as she sat—head resting on the kitchen table. "Genieva," his voice echoed. This time she opened her eyes. She looked to Brevan standing near the table, glaring down at her.

"What are you doing up? You need your rest. And

just give me a moment, Brevan," she mumbled. "I'll just sit here a moment." Genieva was so exhausted! Her mind hardly registered that this was the first time Brevan had been about since being injured. Even when she felt herself hoisted from the chair and into strong arms, she was so worn and weary that she did not rouse more than a moment— just long enough to enjoy the pleasant smell of Brevan's skin as her head lay against his shoulder.

Brevan laid his wife gently on her bed. She flinched as her hand hit the pillow, and he took her small hand in his own, studying her palm. A deep frown furrowed his handsome brow as he gazed at the horrid blisters there.

"What have ya been doin', lass?" he muttered to himself. The other hand was just as blistered. Laying her hands gently on the bed and taking the lantern hanging in the kitchen with him, he hurried out of the house and to the field. He stood, astonished at what he saw.

"Surely Brian has done this," he whispered. But when he drew near to the field and saw the small size of the boot prints in the soil, he knew. Placing his own boot next to one of the impressions in the dirt, he knew at once that the tiny boot print belonged to Genieva. Her boot prints led from the creek to the field as well. Her boot prints were near the empty buckets and seed sack sitting against the outer wall of the barn.

Guilt enveloped his conscience as he quickly made his way back to the house. He entered her room to find Genieva still slept—the deep sleep of one worn to the bone. Gently, he removed her boots and stockings to find her feet blistered and red as well. He removed her skirt and petticoats—all the time pitying women for having to wear such cumbersome gear. He rolled her onto her stomach and unbuttoned her shirtwaist, gently turning her to her back once more in order to remove it. Not once did she stir from her fatigue-induced slumber. Brevan frowned—shook his head as he fumbled with the fastenings of her corset.

"What devil invented such a device of torture?" he muttered as he removed it—leaving her looking more comfortable in just her camisole and panta-loons.

Going to the kitchen, he poured the hot water from the kettle on the stove into a basin of cool water from the pump until the mix produced a warm and comfortable temperature. He shook his head in disbelief as he carefully bathed Genieva's dusty arms and face. As his hands worked to freshen her neck and shoulders, he was still amazed at what he assumed had occurred while his own body nursed his wound. From all appearances, this small, freckled woman had planted his cornfield and hauled buckets of water from the creek to ensure its need of moisture was met. He was angry with Brian for letting her do the work. And where had Travis been all the time?

Brevan pushed Genieva's pantaloons up over her knees and washed her feet and legs as well before covering her with a light sheet. As he sat studying her peaceful face, he wondered at how one such as he could find such a woman with such little effort. It was as Brenna had told him—someone was indeed watching over him.

"I fear that ya deserve far better than Brevan McLean, lass," he whispered, closing the door to her room behind him.

"Brevan, ya know Travis and me had to check with the land office," Brian explained the next morning as he and Brevan carried water from the creek to the fields and garden. "He's gettin' desperate, he is, and we, neither one of us, wanted to travel alone, we didn't. I've got to think of me own wife and child now too. But I swear it to ya now that I did not know Genieva was plannin' on plantin' the crop herself, brother . . . or I would've waited all the same."

"I know, Brian. I know. I've not the right to be angry with ya. And I thank ya for finishin' the plowin', I do," Brevan said. Both men turned as Genieva approached.

"And good mornin' to ya, Genieva," Brian called merrily.

"Good morning, Brian. Should you be exerting

yourself so soon, Brevan?" Genieva asked—her expression that of concern as she studied Brevan intently.

"I should," he answered. " 'Tis an admirable job ya've done in the field, Genieva," he added.

"You said it had to be done," she responded.

"I didn't mean that *you* had to do it, lass."

"It was my responsibility. Not Brian's," she reminded him. Genieva smiled, overjoyed at seeing Brevan's strength renewed. He was whole once again, and she felt relief at the knowledge. "I'll get some more buckets and help," she offered.

"No," Brevan growled. But his frown softened, and he added, "When yar hands have healed, ya can water, Genieva."

Looking at her sadly blistered and terribly sore palms, she muttered, "But the gardens and fields must be watered, Brevan. There hasn't been any rain."

"Brian will help me for now, he will," Brevan informed her. "Lita has been ill. Ya run over and keep her company while her husband is here."

"Yes. Do that for me, will ya, lass?" Brian asked. "She's been feelin' so badly these past couple of days. She could use a friendly visit from ya, she could."

"But the watering," Genieva argued. "It has to be done, and I'm not sure Brevan should be . . ."

" 'Tis well and strong I am, Genieva," Brevan

interrupted. "Me back is sore, but the rest of me is ready enough."

"All right," she agreed a little unwillingly. But should she take to admitting the truth to herself, she was uncertain as to whether or not she would enjoy the visit with Lita. Something wasn't right. Genieva knew some substantial and unspoken secret was being kept from her concerning Brevan and Lita. Certain obvious events, such as the conversation she had overheard between them the first night Brevan was injured, testified to this—as well as other subtle, less noticeable things. She also still found it perturbing and odd that Brevan would know of Lita's condition before her own husband was aware of it.

Still, as she meandered toward Lita and Brian's house, she tried to put her anxieties to rest. Surely she just imagined there to be more between them than there truly was.

"Mí amiga! Genieva!" Lita called from her chair on the front porch as Genieva approached. "You have come to keep me company, no?"

Immediately, guilt began to gnaw at Genieva. Lita was a beauty in both body and spirit, and Genieva was reassured in her sense that this woman would not be capable of such things as Genieva's insecure mind had been imagining.

"Brian has told you, no? He has told you that we are to have a bebé?" Lita asked, gesturing toward a nearby chair.

"Actually, Brevan told me," Genieva answered, smiling pleasantly as she accepted the chair.

"He is well then? I was so worried for him, Genieva," Lita sighed, placing one of her dainty hands at her bosom. "That was the worst cutting on a person I have ever seen! I don't know how you managed to sew it yourself. I would have died! Muerta! On the floor next to him!"

Genieva shook her head, agreeing with Lita. "I don't know how I did it either. When you have to . . . well, you have to, I suppose."

"Híjole! I don't know," Lita sighed. "You will have to help me have the bebé, Genieva. You are so brave, and I will need you there."

"I'm not brave, Lita," Genieva corrected her.

"Sí! Yes, you are. Not only did you sew up Brevan's back, but you came here to marry him when you did not even know him!" Lita clicked her tongue and nodded with reassurance. "You are brave, Genieva."

Again, guilt began eating at Genieva's heart— but for different reasons. Brave? No. A coward, yes! To leave as she did—it was pure cowardice. Genieva wondered if she would ever be able to confide in Lita. Would she ever be able to tell any of them the story of why she had found the courage to marry someone she had never met? Most likely not. She would remain a coward.

"Brenna is wanting a bebé badly, too. Especially now that Brian and I are having one," Lita announced. The Mexican beauty placed her hands low on her stomach and smiled as if she held some secret and joyous knowledge no one else could understand. She looked to Genieva and said, "You need to have Brevan give you a bebé soon and then todos los niños . . . all the childrens can be perfect friends . . . playmates!"

Genieva shook her head and laughed. "I'm here to help him with the farm, Lita. Nothing else," she explained.

Lita's brows puckered in a disapproving frown. "Babies come from God, Genieva. They are a blessing to men and women. You do not want babies?" she inquired shortly.

"Of course I do! You don't understand, Lita," Genieva defended. "I want them ever so badly! But . . . but it's not what Brevan wants of me. It's not why he had me come here."

"Brevan is a good man, Genieva. He would not marry with you just to have your hands to work his farm," Lita stated. The expression on her face was stern and, Genieva fancied, rather reprimanding. "He would not have married with you if a worker is all he had wanted. He could have married with any woman then. No. He married you because you are *you*."

Genieva smiled kindly at Lita and went on to talk of other things. "Were the rains this sparse last spring?" she asked.

"Not this bad," Lita answered, looking up to the

sky as if expecting to see it filled with thunder-clouds. "This is dry. And the crops must have water. The apple trees have deep enough roots that they can do fine for a short time. But soon they must have rain too."

"My hands were bleeding by the time I finished bringing the buckets from the creek yesterday," Genieva mentioned, looking at her sore, cracking palms.

"You must wrap them in rags, Genieva. Just gloves do not protect enough. And I have something inside—some salve that will help them to feel better."

As the audible sound of an approaching wagon suddenly caught their attention, both women turned to stare in the direction from which it came. Two women were in the wagon—one obviously older than the other. The younger looked to be about Genieva's and Lita's age.

Lita smiled and stood, waving one hand happily. "Hola! Amy . . . Mrs. Wilburn! Hello!"

Upon hearing the names, Genieva immediately jumped to her feet beside Lita. She was far more interested now in the approaching wagon.

"It's Mrs. Wilburn and Amy. Mí casa is one of the few where they are welcome now," Lita explained sympathetically.

Genieva watched with avid curiosity as the women climbed down from the wagon and came to stand before them on the porch.

"Mrs. Wilburn!" Lita exclaimed, hugging the woman. "And Amy. You look so pretty."

The lovely, brown-haired girl dropped her gaze to the floor of the porch, and Genieva could not help but notice the time of her baby's coming was near. The girlish curves Amy Wilburn had no doubt once boasted were replaced with the new figure of an expectant woman.

"This is Genieva," Lita said, turning to Genieva. "She is the lucky one to have married Brevan!"

Genieva smiled as Amy's eyes immediately met hers—searchingly. There was a sweet and repentant soul showing brightly in them, and Genieva could not help but pity her.

"It's so nice to meet you both," she greeted, extending a hand to Mrs. Wilburn.

"We've heard so much about you," Mrs. Wilburn offered, smiling. The elder woman did indeed wear a smile—yet her overall expression was that of worry and fatigue.

"Is that good or bad?" Genieva teased. She would be friendly to both women—no matter what the circumstances behind Amy's condition. She was determined to show them kindness.

"Good, of course," Mrs. Wilburn assured her.

"How is the bebé, Amy?" Lita asked. Genieva quickly glanced to Lita. It seemed a very bold question.

Amy continued to study Genieva but answered, "I think fine." Then, still looking to Genieva, she added, "It's no great secret, Mrs. McLean. I'm the talk of the county, and I know it."

Genieva blushed—embarrassed at having let her thoughts show so obvious on her face. Insecure thoughts began growing in Genieva's mind again as she looked back to the attractive girl.

Amy was taller than Genieva—her skin was porcelain—her eyes a bright blue, not unlike Brevan's. She was lovely—would no doubt easily catch any man's eye.

Genieva looked to Lita as her friend suddenly announced, "Brian and I . . . we are going to have a bebé too, Amy!"

Mrs. Wilburn squealed with delight, throwing her arms about Lita's shoulders with true affection.

"That's wonderful, Mrs. McLean!" Amy agreed.

"You and I, Amy . . . we share even more now, no?" Lita giggled. Genieva did not miss the twinkle in Amy's eyes, or the one in Lita's. She wondered what else they held in common. Lita's answer to her own question sent a shudder throughout Genieva's body. "Blood is a thick bond, Amy." Lita's face was serious and encouraging to Amy. "You'll always have me here . . . as a friend."

Amy nodded and brushed a tender tear from her cheek. Genieva, however, was beginning to feel ill.

"I think I had better get home, Lita," she announced abruptly. "I'll let you all visit. It was nice to meet you both. Please stop in on me if you're ever over our way," she offered a bit insincerely.

Walking home that afternoon, Genieva was lost in her frightening thoughts—thoughts of Lita and her baby—of Amy and her baby. How could Lita and Amy share a blood bond unless Brevan was the father of Amy's baby? There was no other way about it. And what if . . . she shook her head. The thought was too lewd—too disloyal. Yet what if the paternity of Lita's baby were in question as well? Turning away from these devious thoughts, she concentrated on her own wounded hands—on the fear she had felt when Brevan lay hurt in his bed. Most of all she thought of Brevan. Thinking of Brevan took the other terrible contemplations from her mind. The mere thought of Brevan was like having her spirit take flight over the fragrant apple blossoms hanging so heavy on the trees. The vision of his handsome features of face and body—of his wit and commitment to his land—it was uplifting. And the memory of his succulent kiss? The memory of his kiss was exhilarating!

"Hola," the rider called.

Genieva had been so immersed in her own thoughts she hadn't heard the soft trot of the approaching horse and rider at first. Now, however, she turned around, shading her eyes from the sun hanging intense and bright in the sky.

"Hola!" the rider repeated. "Eres tú la esposa de Brevan McLean?" he asked.

"I'm sorry," Genieva apologized. "I don't speak Spanish."

"Forgive me then, señora. I ask only if you are the wife of Brevan McLean?" The large man reining in his horse just before her smiled down at Genieva. He donned a heavy black mustache and a well-worn sombrero—similar to the one that Genieva had seen hanging from Lita's bedpost—and the one donned by the stranger in the orchard. The man was somewhat handsome—perhaps in his late fifties.

"Yes. I'm Genieva Bankma . . . McLean," she affirmed.

"I am Juan Miguel Archuleta, señora," the man greeted, offering his hand to Genieva. "I am Carmalita's papá."

Genieva reached up and took the man's offered hand, shaking it firmly. "Carmalita?" she asked. Then, as she realized to whom the man referred, she added, "Lita! Oh, how wonderful to meet you!"

"You are not what I expected to find," he commented.

"I believe Brevan finds more value in a person who can work hard than in one with beauty," Genieva explained.

"Then, you are not a hard worker?" he flattered.

"I see where Lita gets her charm, Mr. Archuleta," Genieva giggled. "Have you come to visit her?" she asked. "I believe she has some exciting information to share with you."

"Sí. I was passing by. I am glad to have seen you, Mrs. McLean," the man said as he touched the brim of his sombrero and rode away.

He seems a charming man, Genieva thought as she watched him ride toward Brian's and Lita's home.

"Have you finished the watering?" Genieva asked Brian as she entered the house to find him sitting at the table with a tall glass of water before him. He looked tired—his face covered with dust and streaked from perspiration.

"For today. At least, here," he answered. "Now I'm to drag Travis off to help me with me own crop waterin', I am."

"I just met Lita's father on the way home. He seems quite charming. I can see where she gets . . ." Genieva gasped as Brevan stormed through the front door, firmly took hold of her arm, turning her to face him.

"Juan Miguel?" he nearly shouted. "Juan Miguel was on me very land this day?"

"Well, actually, it was near Brian's and Lita's. Why are you so . . . ?"

"Ya spoke with him? What did he say to ya?" Brevan growled.

"I'll get home this instant, I will," Brian muttered. Genieva marveled as he fairly leaped from his seat, dashing out the front door.

"Brevan, what are you so upset about?" Genieva asked, wrenching her arm free of his grasp.

"I . . . I . . . ya should be careful of strangers, Genieva," he stammered, still violently agitated.

"But . . . he's Lita's father, isn't he?" she inquired.

"Ya stay away from him, Genieva. He's not to be trusted," Brevan told her, his voice booming with angry emotion.

"Don't raise your voice to me that way, Brevan! If there is something amiss with him, then tell me of it, and I'll stand clear. But don't shout at me so," she scolded.

"Stand clear of Juan Miguel, Genieva," he growled, wagging a warning index finger toward her. "Do ya understand me?"

"I suppose so," she conceded, miffed.

"I'm going over there to check on things," Brevan announced as he started for the door.

"Brian's capable of protecting Lita, Brevan. She's his wife," Genieva spat.

"I've no doubt of it. But a man can always use assistance when trouble comes, Genieva. And by the way," he added, taking hold of her chin firmly so she was forced to meet his glare. "Ya're my wife, lass. So you'll do as I say. Ya stay far away from Juan Miguel," he ordered. He turned—the front door slamming behind him as he left.

Chapter Six

Genieva thought often of the anger provoked in Brevan when she had told him of her meeting with Lita's father. She had sensed it was a matter no member of the family wished to discuss. So, naturally her mind began to concoct many different reasons for Brevan's hatred toward the man. Perhaps Juan Miguel had treated Lita badly as a child, Genieva mused one day sometime later as she carried bucket after heavy bucket from the creek to the cornfield. Yet Juan Miguel had seemed quite charming. Then again, people who treated others badly often did appear pleasant outwardly. Perhaps Juan Miguel harbored some immoral vice, such as gambling—or maybe he was too friendly with liquid spirits. These same thoughts had presented themselves time and again to Genieva's mind over the past few days. It frustrated her, but as always she sighed, shrugged her shoulders, and tried to put it from her mind.

Genieva poured the bucket of water on a thirsty yet thriving corn sprout. She and Brevan had worked diligently each day, and often late into the night, watering the corn and gardens. Wiping the perspiration from her forehead, she stood straight and arched her back—aching mercilessly from carrying the heavy buckets.

"Get a move on, lass," Brevan ordered as he approached from behind her—a bucket in each hand. "The sun will be settin' soon, and we'll be doin' this in the dark again, we will."

"I have to have a moment to replenish my strength, Brevan," Genieva said. "I won't be worth my weight if I collapse here in the field, now will I?"

"Ya don't weigh all that much to begin with, Genieva," he grumbled, dumping his buckets and turning toward the creek once again.

Genieva was not in a mood to nurture his sarcasm. She turned, intending to meet him headlong in a verbal battle—knowing she was worth far more than any other woman he could have been saddled with. Yet as she turned, she found herself staring at three approaching horsemen—her argumentative words stuck in her throat.

All of the men on horseback wore sombreros—similar to that Juan Miguel wore when she had met him. The three men reined in before Brevan. Genieva noticed Brevan's broad shoulders already rose and fell with angered breathing. Upon having a closer look at the men, Genieva instantly recog-nized the one in the middle—the one mounted on a tall bay. He was the stranger from the orchard.

"Get off me land, Cruz!" Brevan shouted.

"Mí amigo," the man from the orchard greeted.

He smiled, flashing a dazzlingly white set of teeth. "Mí hermanos and me have only just come back from to see our querida hermana."

"Then what are ya doin' here? Ya know ya're not welcome on me lands," Brevan growled.

"Joaquin, Mateo, and me . . . we wanted to see your esposa," the man explained—his eyes lingering on Genieva. His gaze was not that of proper admiration, and it sent a chill rippling down her spine.

"Ya've seen her already, Cruz . . . and once is too many a time," Brevan growled.

The man named Cruz chuckled slyly and continued to speak to Brevan. "And you," he said, nodding in Brevan's direction. "We hear you had a little accident in your field, hombre." The man chuckled again and added, "But you . . . you're a big man. You're tough, no?"

"I'm bigger and tougher than you'll ever be, Archuleta," Brevan mumbled. The threatening intonation in both men's voices frightened Genieva. These were polite words being spoken by men who hated each other. Archuleta, Brevan had called him. Was this man akin to Lita as well?

Cruz laughed again and warned, "Be more careful, hombre. You'll get hurt."

Brevan lunged forward, but Genieva reached out and took hold of his arm, staying him.

"Let it pass you by, Brevan," she whispered.

"Come, Cruz," one of the other men urged.

Genieva noted this man didn't smile as the other two did. His expression was one of concern and doubt. "It's time we went for home." Though this man looked the image of Cruz in every physical respect, there was a definite difference about him. Genieva noted this man lacked the wicked glint to the eye that his brother's held.

"Joaquin is a wise man," Brevan agreed. "I want no trouble from you this day."

The one named Joaquin tipped his sombrero to Genieva, and she nodded. This man meant them no harm. She was certain of it.

"We go, McLean," he said, and he turned his horse. The third man did the same—obviously intending to leave. Cruz paused, however. He leaned forward, staring lecherously at Genieva as his grin broadened.

"Cruz!" Joaquin shouted. "Apúrate! Ándele!"

Cruz Archuleta turned his mount at last, glancing at Brevan once more with an air of superiority, causing Genieva's own anger to heighten.

When they had gone, she shouted, "Enough!" Brevan turned to face her, and she lunged at him, taking hold of his shirt in her tiny fists. "What is going on here, Brevan? I have a right to know!"

"Nothin'," he answered.

"Don't lie to me anymore," she demanded. "What is going on? The man named Cruz . . . he's the one from the orchard. And he implied . . . did he have something to do with spooking the mules the day you were hurt? Are these men Lita's family as well? Answer me, Brevan! I have a right to know what's going on here!"

"Lita is a fine woman," Brevan responded through clenched teeth. "But her family, her father and her brothers . . . they are not the kind of men I want on my lands."

"Why?"

"It's all ya need to know, Genieva. They cause trouble, and I've no time for trouble," he answered.

"I know, I know, I know!" Genieva whined. Fatigue had gotten the best of her patience. "I know! You don't have time for anything other than your work and this land and your apple trees and your corn. I know. You drive me mad with saying it all the time! I don't need incessant reminding of how you have no time for anything else but this farm." She watched as Brevan's eyebrows arched in surprise at her outburst. Turning over one of the empty buckets she had just dropped to the ground, she sat down solidly on it. Folding her arms across her knees, she rested her weary head on them.

"I'll forgive ya for yar snappin' ways 'cause I know ya're tired, but . . ." he began.

"Oh, don't be so benevolent on my account, Brevan," she snapped again. "I agreed before I married you to work like a mule, so I know I don't have any right to complain. Still . . . I'm sick to death of hearing about how you have no time for trouble, no time for silliness, no time for supper, no time for sitting still, no time for . . .”

“No time for you, ya mean to be sayin’,” he interrupted. Genieva looked up at him, her mouth gaping open indignantly, as he continued, “Ya’re miffed because I don’t spend me time courtin’ after ya the way Brian and Travis do Lita and Brenna. And now that Lita’s got her wee bun, yar female side is thinkin’ of children and . . .”

“What do you mean, my ‘female side,’ ” Genieva shouted, standing and glaring daringly up at him. “And don’t flatter yourself by thinking every woman on the earth dreams of having your children, Brevan. I believe there will soon enough be plenty of your . . . your lineage toddling around town! Don’t lump me in with the women who found you literally irresistible!”

Instantly, both by her own conscience and the look of disgust and betrayal apparent on Brevan’s face, Genieva was awash with guilt. Why had she been so hateful to him? Yet she knew why. It was because he had been too close to the truth, to hitting the proverbial nail on the head. He’d stumbled on the truth of it all, and she’d snapped back hatefully because of her own pride. Of course she wanted his attention! Of course she wanted his affection! It was only natural when you loved someone to covet these things from them.

“That was cruel and slanderous, Genieva,” he

mumbled. The set of his mouth, the lack of spark to his eyes told her she had committed a grievous error in battling him with such hurting words.

"I'm sorry, Brevan. I'm just so tired. I'm sorry. Please don't . . ." she began. But he looked away to some point above her head as his jaw clenched and unclenched angrily. Panic began to engulf her, and she took hold of his shirt in her fists once more. "Please, Brevan. I'm just so . . . so tired all the time, and I say things I don't mean. Please, don't stay angry. Forget that I said it. You know I don't mean it." Reaching up, desperate for his forgiveness, she boldly took his face between her hands, forcing his gaze to meet her own.

Brevan resisted her tugging at his face only for a moment, and when he did meet the pleading of her eyes, he was instantly astonished. Her eyes, deep green only moments before, were a pale blue. A grayish, steel blue he had learned indicated a torment of some sort within her.

"I'm only tired, body and mind, Brevan," she continued to plead. A deep guilt struck his heart—guilt at working her so hard—for he knew he did it so she was ever out of his way. It was the only way to keep his thoughts from straying to her constantly. She was so adorable, so beautiful—so desirable. He knew he must keep his head about him where she was concerned, and hard labor was the only thing he knew to do it.

Brevan grinned sympathetically at Genieva, and she felt suddenly self-conscious and uncomfortable at having talked to him so revealingly—at having touched him. Quickly she dropped her hands and her gaze from him.

"Do yar feet hurt then, lass?" he asked. Genieva frowned, puzzled by his question. "Yar feet. Do they pain ya now?" he repeated.

"No more than every other inch of my body," she muttered, as she began to sit down on the bucket once more. She gasped, surprised when he reached down and lifted her into his arms, striding determinedly toward the orchards. "What are you doing? Put me down," she whined, struggling—but only slightly—for it was ever so heavenly being held in his arms.

"Sore feet are bad, they are. They make the rest of yar body ache. If ya can relieve the ache in yar feet, ya can relieve the rest of it," he informed her. Abruptly he stopped at the edge of the pond and sat her on the ground. Quickly, before she could begin to argue, he pulled off her boots, then sat down next to her and removed his own. He swiftly pulled his shirt off over his head and tossed it aside.

"Brevan . . . I told you . . . I hate water. It frightens me. I'll feel worse than I do now if you force me to . . ." she argued. But Brevan was obviously feigning ignorance because he pulled her to her feet and began struggling with the button at the waist of her skirt. "Brevan!" she reprimanded, slapping him smartly on the hand.

"This cumbersome cloth will drag you to the bottom, it will," he argued, slapping her hand in return. "It's gettin' dark enough that I can't see me way well anyway. And besides, I've seen ya in yar unmentionables before."

Before Genieva could argue further, she felt her skirt drop to the ground. She barely managed to retain one of her petticoats with one hand as Brevan lead her into the water with the other. The water was still warm from the hot rays of the day's sun, and it did feel soothing on her tired feet. As the water lapped up against Genieva's chin, she gasped and reached out, taking hold of Brevan's broad shoulders. She shivered with delight as his hands encircled her small waist, pulling her against the protection of his capable body. She could not help but gaze in wonder into his face—for she usually only saw it from a position below him. But as she looked directly into his eyes—their faces on an even level because of his supporting her in the water—she marveled at the beauty of his physical combination.

"I'm sorry I said those things, Brevan. I really am sorry. I have to know that you're not going to hold my behavior against me. I won't be able to sleep otherwise," she confessed to him.

• • •

Brevan was again captured by the color of her eyes. The moon, showing itself fully over the horizon in that moment, cast its bright white light across the pond's surface. That light reflected in Genieva's beautiful, now violet eyes. *Why this color now?* he wondered.

It had been nearly two weeks since Brevan had kissed Genieva first in the orchard and pond and then in his room when he had been incoherent. As she studied his face now, so close, so tantalizing, the moisture in her mouth increased tenfold. She let her eyes linger for a moment on his mouth as it dipped below the surface of the water—as he spit a drizzle of water out when he bobbed up. So badly did she want him to kiss her that she feared she might just reach out and take the kiss—no longer able to resist doing so.

"Did you hear me?" she asked, realizing the day must end and that she must escape him or make a fool of herself.

"I heard ya. I just think ya need to stew in yar own juice a minute, lass. For it was a cruel thing to say to me," he reminded her. Genieva felt his hands leave her waist as they slid to her back, holding her even more firmly against the strength of his body. "I work ya too hard," he muttered as his eyes seemed to intently study her every feature. "I do. I admit that to ya. And I'll try to be more thoughtful of it from now on. But," he paused, and Genieva felt an anxiety rise in her chest. "But why do ya think I fathered Amy Wilburn's baby, lass? And don't deny it . . . for it's all too obvious that ya do."

Genieva cast her gaze to the water's surface for a moment. Yet when he cleared his throat with impatience, she looked back to him.

"I don't believe it's because of the gossip," he said. "Ya're not the type of woman who takes gossip to heart. Why then, lass? Why do you think it was me?"

"I-I . . ." Genieva stammered. "It is the gossip," she finished, not wanting to reveal the suspicious side of her nature any further. "And she is a very pretty girl. Men like you . . ."

"Men like me? What are ya meanin' by that?" he asked. Genieva began to breathe more rapidly. He was calm, he wasn't angry with her, but he was too close to her. He held her now tightly— his strong arms wrapped completely about her.

"Men who . . . men who . . . men who catch the ladies' eyes. You know. The charming ones who woo them into . . . into faltering," she stuttered.

"Charmin'?" he chuckled. "Oh, Genieva. Surely ya'll not be accusin' me of bein' charmin', now?" He spit a tiny stream of water from between his teeth, hitting her square on the chin so that she looked up at him. "And to be sure and certain . . . can ya really see me, Brevan McLean, the lad with no time for anythin' but the farm . . . wooin' a woman into 'falterin',' as you put it? Come now, Genieva. Tell me how realistic be that?"

Genieva gazed into the sapphires that were his eyes—knowing he would have to do far less wooing than most men. She watched as he once again let his tantalizing mouth dip beneath the surface of the water to moisten his lips and chin.

"I-I . . . I'm not familiar with that side of your nature. But it doesn't mean that it doesn't exist," she answered finally.

His eyes narrowed, and he whispered, "Then I'll tell ya, lass . . ." His face was straight, and she knew he was sincere in what he was telling her. "It's the sound of vanity, it is . . . and I don't be meanin' it that way. But if I had a mind to do it, I've not the one doubt that I could indeed seduce any woman I put me mind to corruptin'. But I'm *not* the like of a beast that causes ruination of lives and leaves fatherless children aboundin'."

Genieva began to shiver in spite of the warmth of the water. Brevan dipped his mouth below the surface once again, and when he then tipped his head back to submerge his hair and the top of his head in the water, Genieva thought she might fly apart so desirous was she to place a kiss on his neck stretched out before her. He looked to her then and must have sensed her discomfort. Chuckling he added, "And besides, lass . . . I've not the time for it."

Genieva smiled then and sighed—relieved he was no longer angry with her and could make light of her unkind remarks.

"Now," he said, taking one of her hands from his shoulder and placing it at her nose. "Pinch it shut and hold your breath."

"Oh, no, no, no! Please, Brevan! I don't like the water!" she pleaded.

"Ya will, lass. I promise ya that, someday, ya will like it," he said, and when she was ready, he pulled her beneath the surface for a few brief moments.

When they surfaced again, Genieva drew in a deep breath, brushed the water and wet hair from her eyes, and looked at him. He bobbed up and down before her, grinning triumphantly.

"The achin' is goin' away, isn't it?" he asked.

Genieva nodded. "The ache in my feet feels better," she admitted—though the aching in her heart had worsened. Oh, how she loved him—after such a short time, such a strange acquaintance! Yet she loved him completely—to the very depth of her very soul!

"Kick that last petticoat off then, lass. It's time ya were learnin' to swim," Brevan said, giving a tug on the cumbersome fabric. Hesitantly, Genieva did as instructed and watched as the white petticoat floated to the water's surface—looking ghostly in the moonlight.

Brevan began Genieva's instruction by laying

her on her back in the water while supporting her. She was amazed at how easily her body floated in the water, and some of her fear of it was lost that night in the pond.

He pulled her vertically against himself once more after some time and said, "Ya see, it's refreshin', relaxin', it is."

She smiled, nodding in agreement. "You're right. And I do feel better."

"Yar temper won't be spittin' at me any time soon then?" he chuckled.

"No," she assured him. One last time she watched as his mouth disappeared beneath the surface of the water for a few moments, only to resurface and flash an alluring smile.

"Well, I suppose you'll be wantin' yar privacy to get out now," he teased.

"It would be proper," she assured him. Slowly he pushed her gently backward as he began toward the shore. He stopped abruptly, however, and dipped his mouth beneath the water's surface again.

"Why do you do that?" she asked, curious.

"It helps . . . satisfy me thirst," he mumbled pointedly.

"You're thirsty?" she asked innocently. "We're out in the middle of a pond, Brevan." It did seem an oddity.

"*Liquid* refreshment has nothin' to do with it, Genieva," he muttered, grinning.

Genieva was tired and simply shook her head. She was too tired for him to talk in riddles. She turned toward the shore, but his arms tightened about her waist, and he backed into the deeper water once more.

"What are you doing?" she squealed, turning in his arms to face him and clinging to his body for support.

"I have to keep me feet on the ground, lass," he mumbled. As his eyes locked with her own, her heart began to pound furiously. "I've got this farm to run, to make profit, I do. It's our life, and I've got to keep me feet on the ground when I'm on it. But me feet aren't back on that ground yet, and I'm havin' a moment of weakness, Genieva. And heaven help me . . . for I'm givin' into it."

Then it did seem as if the very heavens themselves opened, pouring down warm, life-giving sunlight. For a moment after Genieva watched Brevan's mouth dip below the water's surface one last time, he embraced her tightly and favored her lips with a fierce and driven kiss.

It was apparent to her he had meant to kiss her once, firmly and quickly—for when his lips left hers, he looked at her, shaking his head, and mumbling, "I'm too tired, and me strength of resistance slumbers without me," an instant before the passionate heat of his mouth commanded her own in a kiss so perfectly superb it nearly induced Genieva unconscious. Her skin burned

165

where her body pressed securely against his, and her mind whirled with visions of the magnificence of his face and form. She had to gasp for her breath once when his mouth left hers and kissed her fiercely on her neck just beneath her ear. He'd taken her breath from her again, and it frightened her. One last time Brevan kissed her demandingly—thoroughly—before breaking from her and walking with her in his arms toward the shore. She could only stare at his mouth in silence—awed that she had actually been the object of its attention. Finally, she looked up into his eyes—narrowed and serious—and thought it was truly miraculous that such a man as he had just blessed her with attentions—attentions she had no right to even dream of receiving from him.

When they stood only waist-deep in the water, he released her. The cool evening breeze was cold on Genieva's moist skin, and she hugged herself tightly. She watched as he left her standing in the water while he reached down and retrieved his boots from the shore.

He began walking away, but paused and said over his shoulder, "We're even now, we are. An eye for an eye. Yar accusation is forgiven by me . . . and I hope now that—that me behavior just this last minute is forgiven by *you*." Then he left. Genieva, still warmed by his kiss, stood watching him walk toward the house.

Chapter Seven

There was no more of it. No more unexpected visits from Lita's family and no more kisses the fabric of dreams from Brevan. For the following weeks and weeks, Brevan and Genieva labored each day from before the sun rose until it was long gone from the skies. The rain had not come, and every small stalk of corn, every garden plant, every tree had to be watered by hand.

Genieva awoke each morning already greatly fatigued from the previous day's endeavors. And she was asleep each night before she was settled in her bed. The strain on Brevan was even worse, for he did the other chores on the farm before Genieva rose each morning.

Through it all, the few moments of respite allotted Genieva at the end of the day were spent learning to swim. At first she had taken to wading in the pond each evening while she waited for Brevan to finish seeing to the stock. He never came into the water with her again, and she could only assume it was because he viewed himself as having even less time for frivolities than he usually did. Yet she began to enjoy her private swims. It helped relieve her aching body and mind each evening.

All at once, it seemed, it was mid-June. Still the

rains were lost to the farmers, and Genieva worried for everyone. She had come to know how important the crops would be to them. It was their very livelihood. Travis and Brenna were rarely visiting—for their crops needed tending too. And poor Brian! Genieva felt especially for Brian—for Lita could not assist him with lifting and carrying water. As for the Mexican beauty, Lita was pleasantly rounded in front and looking more beautiful every day. Genieva envied her for having her husband's complete devotion and love—and for carrying her husband's child.

Even though the Archuletas had not attempted to aggravate Brevan again, Genieva often wondered at the secrets. What was the cause of the friction between Lita's family and Brevan? It nagged at her. Yet since she knew better than to attempt to ask anyone about it, she simply tried not to think of it.

And then, one warm summer morning, Genieva found herself with a very rare free moment to spend with Lita, who had come for a brief visit and a walk. As they spoke, they strolled leisurely through the orchard, meandering beneath the trees.

"The apples are heavy on this year," Lita remarked. "Even without the rains."

Genieva looked up to see that, indeed, the tree branches were already heavy with small, green fruit. She felt an odd excitement rise within her—

for it was inspiring to see the literal fruits of Brevan's labor—and of her own.

"How will I do it?" Lita asked with an unexpected sigh of discouragement. Genieva looked to her friend and her frown of concern.

"What do you mean?" Genieva asked.

"You've never seen the harvest of the apples, have you, Genieva?" Lita asked. When Genieva shook her head, Lita continued, "It is work. Work as hard as watering these plants by hand. Apples, apples, apples! Apples that must be picked, then washed, and dried in the ovens or sun. Apples that must be delivered to people who buy them. Applesauce, apple pie, apple jelly, apple preserves. Apples, apples, apples. And me with a new bebé coming just at that time. How will I do it? Already my Brian is so tired at the end of the day. I am no use to him. Useless."

"We'll all help him, Lita," Genieva assured her. "What you can't do, we will make up the difference. You and Brian would do the same for all of us. You've done it before. It's nothing you should be worrying about. You have to think of the baby." Genieva smiled as Lita sighed and nodded.

Embracing Genieva affectionately, Lita giggled, "My turn will come to help you, no?"

"Esto es tan dulce! Yes . . . this is very sweet."

Genieva spun around to find Cruz astride his tall bay, watching them with an amused grin on his face.

"Vete de aquí, Cruz!" Lita ordered him.

"Lita . . ." the man whined, putting a hand over his heart as if his feelings were hurt. "I've come to check on you and the bebé. How come you're so mean to your favorite hermanito?"

"Ándale, Cruz. Brevan will kill you if he finds you here in his orchards," Lita threatened.

"No! Really?" Cruz mocked. "Is this so, señora?" he addressed Genieva. "Will your apuesto esposo kill me if he finds me here with you?"

"I wouldn't risk it if I were in your boots, Mr. Archuleta," Genieva answered. She took a step back, linking her arm through Lita's as Cruz dismounted and walked toward them.

Cruz stood directly in front of Genieva now. His manner toward her was more than threatening—it was lustful. Still she raised her face to meet his stare defiantly as he spoke.

"Your husband . . . él es un hombre violento . . . a violent man. But me . . ." he whispered as he studied Genieva from head to toe. "I can be nice—especially to una mujer bella . . . a beautiful woman like you, señora."

"Don't you talk to her like that you . . . you . . . usted es el diablo, Cruz!" Lita defended.

"Cállate!" Cruz shouted at his sister. Returning his undesirable attentions to Genieva once more, he whispered, "What you think, señora? You find me handsome, no?"

"No," Genieva stated. Cruz took Genieva's

chin tightly in his grasp, glaring daringly at her.

"Do not lie to me, mí amor. You should enjoy my attentions," he growled.

"Run, Genieva!" Lita cried, suddenly pushing her friend aside. "Bring Brevan, apúrate!"

Genieva stood stunned for a moment as Lita lunged forward and began beating on her brother's chest. Cruz caught Lita's wrists in his hands and threw her brutally to the ground.

"No!" Genieva cried, dropping to her knees beside her friend. Lita nodded, indicating she was unharmed. Genieva looked up to find Cruz looming over them—a wicked smile spreading across his face.

"Whose bebé is that in your estómago, Carmalita?" he asked. "Does it belong to the man you married? Or to the one you love?" Cruz chuckled as Genieva frowned at him.

"What would you know about love, Cruz? Monstruo!" Lita cried out at him.

"I know plenty, hermanita," he growled. Then, reaching down, he took hold of Genieva's arm and pulled her to her feet. Genieva glared at him in defiance as he mumbled, "I see why the hombre wanted you, niña. You smell very delicious to me." He pulled her against him, and Genieva struggled to escape before his mouth could find her own. Grabbing her long braid, however, Cruz pulled her head back painfully and glared at her. "The way to anger a man, to provoke him into doing what you want, is with his esposa."

"Release her, Cruz!" Lita screamed as tears of anger and frustration flooded her cheeks. "Let her go!"

"Cállate, Lita!" he growled at his sister. Licking his lips, he moved to kiss Genieva. She spit in his face, causing him to release her in order to wipe the saliva from his eyes.

Helping Lita to stand, Genieva told her, "Go quickly, Lita. I'll not let him harm you or the . . ." Her words were lost in her cry of anguish as the back of Cruz's hand struck her hard across her left cheek, sending her plunging to the ground. She felt the warmth of the blood at the corner of her mouth an instant before she tasted it. Lita was at her side in a moment.

"I'll kill you, Cruz. If you ever touch her again, I will kill you, diablo!" she cried.

Cruz only stood chuckling and looking down at them amusedly. "Many men have threatened that to me where women are concerned, Carmalita. Why you think I will be afraid of you doing it?" He laughed, triumphant and completely amused with himself. "Look at Joaquin. Coward! He thinks only of that Amy Wilburn. That girl in town with a bebé coming and no esposo. He's a fool, for he knows who its papá is. He knows it is me, his own brother, who caused her to be that way, and still he thinks of her, and I stand here healthy and alive."

"Que está mal! Evil!" Lita shouted. "El diablo! Mama would drop dead of your actions if she were alive still. She would hate you for it!"

The triumphant smile left Cruz's face as he glared at his sister. "Mama loved me, Lita! I, Cruz Mondragon Archuleta . . . I was her favorite niño. You would be the one she would find shame in . . . for you did not do what Papá sent you to do. You turned from him when he needed you."

"It was wrong! All of it!" Lita cried. Cruz slapped her mercilessly, and she buried her face in her hands.

"Cállate, Lita! I hate your voice." He looked again to Genieva, and she began to scoot back, trying in vain to escape his grasp. Pulling her to her feet, he growled, "Por favor, mí amor. Do not fight with me." And he forced a wet, detestable kiss to Genieva's neck, causing her to cry out in anguish.

"Leave them, Cruz!" another voice shouted from somewhere near. A moment later Joaquin rode up, his face angry. "Leave the women, que cobarde! Coward!" Joaquin growled at his brother.

"You? You call me coward? You, sitting there on Papá's horse, judging me like you're San Martín de Caballero? Where's your woman, Joaquin? I tell you where she is . . ."

Genieva gasped as Joaquin pulled a pistol from his belt and leveled it at his brother. "You will not speak of her, Cruz. I will shoot you here in this orchard if you do. Ride home."

Cruz glared defiantly at Joaquin for only a minute before mounting his horse and spitting on the ground in front of Genieva.

"Your husband . . . he may be a strong hombre. But Cruz Archuleta is stronger!" Cruz shouted. He spurred his horse and rode away.

"He . . . he is loco, Joaquin! Loco!" Lita cried as she fell into her brother's embrace once he had dismounted.

"Are you well?" the man asked, placing one hand on Lita's protruding belly.

Lita nodded and wiped the tears from her cheeks. Then, turning to Genieva, she gasped and began dabbing at the corner of Genieva's mouth with her apron.

"Brevan will kill Cruz for doing this to us!" she mumbled.

"Do not tell him, Lita," Joaquin stated. Genieva looked to him in disbelief. Understanding her puzzlement, he explained, "It is what Cruz wants you to do. He knows Brevan would come for him, and then Cruz would kill him easily."

"No one can kill Brevan easily," Lita argued, straightening her shoulders defiantly. "He is a great man . . . a strong man . . . stronger than any of the Archuleta men."

Joaquin glanced away for a moment before looking to Genieva again.

"Cruz would not meet Brevan alone, señora," he said. "It would be . . . how do you say, Lita? Tricked? Catched?"

"Ambushed?" Lita suggested.

"Sí, ambushed. Cruz would kill him."

Genieva put a trembling hand to her cheek. "We'll say . . . we'll say I fell, Lita. If he notices, we'll tell him I fell. Say nothing to Brian, Lita."

Joaquin nodded. "I am sorry, Lita. I try to watch him closely . . . but there are times when I cannot."

Lita cupped her brother's chin in her small hand. "You give the Archuleta name some hope, Joaquin. You are the good niño." Then, dropping her gaze to the ground, she added, "I am sorry for your Amy, Joaquin."

Joaquin's jaw clenched tightly shut. He looked to the sky for a moment. "I have failed her, Lita. For I have not talked to her since she . . ."

"It is natural, mí hermanito. But where Cruz is concerned . . . it may be that she . . . that she was forced to . . ."

Joaquin nodded. "Still, it is hard." He paused a moment, then nodded to Genieva. Mounting his horse, he looked to Lita and said, "Good-bye, mí hermanita," before riding away.

"He is a good man, Genieva," Lita said as she watched him go. "Joaquin and Cruz, they are opposite . . . good and evil."

"Cane and Abel," Genieva mumbled.

Lita looked to her and smiled. "Sí. Cane and Abel. You must not tell Brevan of this, Genieva." There was an expression of utter panic in Lita's eyes, and Genieva understood it all too well.

"I know. He doesn't want your brothers on his land."

"That is true. But that is not why you must keep silent. If he knows Cruz touched you . . ."

"I know. He doesn't want your brothers touching any of his property," Genieva sighed as she turned toward the house. "Why didn't you tell me, Lita," she asked then, "that you knew who fathered Amy's baby?"

Lita shook her head and smiled nervously. "Would you want to tell the wife of your brother-in-law that your own hermano was . . . I didn't want you to think less of me, and anyway . . ." Lita looked away, obviously ashamed of Cruz's actions. "No one else knows of it."

"Brian?" Genieva asked.

Lita shook her head. "Not even Brian, and I feel bad keeping it from him. Yet I do not want to see my husband killed . . . or yours. It would make great anger in Brian or Brevan. I think you know that."

Genieva nodded. Whatever it was that kept the two families fighting, knowing that Cruz Archuleta had been the cause of a girl's ruination would indeed provoke Brevan and Brian further.

"We'll tell him I fell," Genieva reminded Lita once more before they parted at the pond.

"What's the matter, lass?" Brevan asked Genieva later that night as they sat at the table eating dinner. "Ya're pickin' at yar food, and it tells me somethin' is taxin' yar mind, it does. Does yar face pain ya? It looks like it must. Ya must not be so clumsy near the woodpile, Genieva."

Genieva had lied to Brevan—just as she had told Lita that she would. She had told him nothing of Cruz and Joaquin in the orchard but rather had told him she had stumbled and fallen into the woodpile. He had accepted the excuse easily enough, but now her conscience bothered her. She shook her head and smiled nonchalantly.

"Nothing is bothering me, Brevan. I suppose I'm only just tired this evening."

"We're both tired every evening, Genieva. Ya're hidin' somethin' from me. I can see it in yar eyes." Brevan's eyes narrowed. He rose from the table and went to stand over Genieva. "Tell me what it is. It's plain as if ya wore a sailor's tattoo across yar face, it is."

Genieva rose from her own chair and walked away from him. She couldn't stop her hands from wringing her apron, and she knew her face was turning crimson with guilt. "It's nothing, Brevan. And anyway, I told Lita that I wouldn't . . ."

She felt herself whirl around as Brevan took

hold of her arm and turned her to face him. "Ya tell me, Genieva. Is somethin' wrong with Lita? Has she fallen ill?"

The concern on his face was astonishing. Genieva knew he was truly and deeply concerned for the woman. "No, no. She's fine. It's just that . . . in the orchard today . . . I was . . ." she paused, afraid to tell him anything. To tell him the entire truth was unthinkable.

"Go on," he commanded. Still she paused until he said, "I saw the shoe prints in the orchard today, Genieva. Has Lita been meetin' with her brother Joaquin there?"

"Yes," Genieva sighed with relief. He had given her the opportunity to squirm out of her lie—at least a little.

"Joaquin." Brevan's chest began to rise and fall with fury. His jaw clenched tightly shut—his fists opened and closed violently.

Genieva panicked and knew she must keep him from finding out about Cruz's being there as well—and about what else had happened. She didn't know why her husband should be so furious at his sister-in-law's meeting with a member of her own family, but she sensed he was preparing to confront the woman about it.

"Brevan," she pleaded. "Please. I told her I wouldn't tell you. She knew how angry you would be. But he's her brother! I don't understand . . ."
Brevan turned and stomped across the room

178

toward the door. "No!" Genieva called out, following him and taking hold of his arm to stall him. "No, Brevan! Leave her alone. It only makes sense that she should want to see him."

"It only makes sense?" Brevan shouted. "There is not one good quality in any of her brothers, Genieva! I will talk to her about this. She knows the conditions. She'll hear me out, she will!"

"No! Brevan, please," Genieva cried, taking his face in her own small hands. She feared for him. She feared that if he approached Lita about it and Lita's conscience was as guilt-stricken as her own, she might falter and tell Brevan the whole truth of it. "Please, stop and think before you charge off to reprimand her." Brevan paused, glaring down at her. "Relax that ever-present pucker on your brow and think." Genieva smoothed the frown on his forehead with her thumbs and spoke quickly and plainly. "He is her brother, Brevan. It is obvious they care deeply for each other. It is natural she would want to visit with him."

"It's not their visitin' that worries me, Genieva. It's the reason for which they visit," he grumbled. Removing Genieva's hands from his face, he squeezed them slightly and held them at her sides as he continued, "Ya're ignorant in this situation, Genieva. Don't make to involve yarself in it while that ignorance persists."

Yanking her hands free of his grasp, Genieva

glared at him resentfully. "The only reason I remain ignorant is because no one will educate me in the matter. Furthermore . . . I'm not so ignorant that I don't see the true reason you are either forever protecting Lita or scolding her."

"And what might that reason be, Genieva? Do you fancy I have some sort of strange attachment to me sister-in-law? That's it, isn't it? Yar wee brain has concocted some perverse idea that I favor Lita somehow, it has."

"I-I . . ." Genieva stammered, looking away unsettled. She had done it once more. Fear and desperation this time were what caused her mouth to utter what her unconscious mind suspected.

"Let me clear things up for ya, lass. Lita is me sister-in-law—Brian's wife—and he loves her completely. I've no feelin' for her other than that of a brother-in-law who worries about his own brother's happiness. If I had felt anythin' else I would've . . ." Brevan interrupted himself. He straightened his shoulders and continued to glare angrily at Genieva. "There're things here that ya don't know, Genieva. Things ya don't need to know. But I'll tell ya this—if I ever catch Joaquin Archuleta on me property again . . ." He was silenced instantly as Genieva's hand covered his mouth tightly.

"Don't even speak such threats, Brevan. Don't even speak it," she repeated.

Taking her wrist in his hand, Brevan removed her palm from his lips. "Don't push me too far, lass. I admire yar ability to work hard. And I admire that ya have wisdom and wit in yar mind. But I warn ya, don't push me too far. I'm responsible for this family. I'm the head of it still. And I'll do what has to be done to protect and further it. 'Tis Brian's baby that Lita carries. The McLean bloodline. 'Tis also the McLean blood helpin' to give life to Brenna's baby, and I'll not see either harmed."

Genieva's mouth dropped open in surprise. "Brenna's baby?" she asked.

"She hasn't told ya? Yes, Brenna's baby . . . and Travis's. Due to arrive in the late winter, it is."

Genieva looked away from Brevan—an odd and uncomfortable ache throbbing in her chest at learning the news of Brenna.

"If you're so worried about the babies, Brevan . . . then you'll not upset Lita any more than necessary," she said.

"I admit . . . ya are wise to remind me of that," Brevan mumbled, his voice softening. "Perhaps ya should retire for the day, Genieva. Ya look a bit green, ya do."

Later that night, Genieva was still unable to sleep. She'd decided a walk near the pond might help her to relax. As she stepped from the porch and into the night air, however, her attention was caught by a flicker of light in the barn. Carefully she approached. What she saw within caused her physical illness. There in the barn stood Brevan. He was dressed only in his trousers and boots. Before him—sobbing quietly—stood Lita. He seemed to say something soothing to her and reached out, tenderly stroking her hair. His powerful hands took her shoulders, pulling her toward him, and he kissed her soundly on the forehead. He smiled and put a finger under her chin to tilt her face upward. She smiled back and embraced him quickly.

Turning from the sight, Genieva fled back into the house. She sat trembling on her bed—until she heard Brevan's heavy footsteps in the kitchen some time later. Why were they meeting—her husband and her sister-in-law? What matters could they be discussing so intimately at such an odd hour? Genieva's mind was plagued all through the night with possibilities. So plagued that by morning she was terribly ill. Sick enough that her stomach was wrenching and she was unable to rise from bed until near the supper hour when Brenna arrived for a visit, having heard she was feeling badly.

"Brenna," Genieva began timidly. "Brenna, it is Brian's baby that Lita carries, isn't it?"

Brenna's mouth gaped open in astonishment. She dropped the potato she'd been peeling.

"Genieva McLean! What a thing to say! How

could ya even . . ." But Brenna stopped her scolding when Genieva turned toward her, tears streaming down her freckled cheeks. "Why would ya even think to ask a question like that, Genieva?"

"There's some sort of . . . some sort of unspoken agreement between Brevan and Lita, Brenna. And don't tell me you don't sense it! I'll know you're lying. They harbor a secret that I'm ignorant of. I saw them last night . . ." she whispered, heartbroken at the remembrance, "in the barn . . . together. It was not the usual conversation or affections exchanged between in-laws, Brenna. I think . . . I suspect . . ."

"Don't speak it, Genieva. It's not true, and ya know it!" Brenna interrupted.

"But they were there . . . in the barn, Brenna. He held her to him so tenderly and kissed her fore-head . . . the actions of two people who are . . . who are . . ." She couldn't finish her thought, and the tears flooded her cheeks more heavily.

"Of two people who are tortured by a secret, Genieva," Brenna finished guiltily. "And ya're right. There is somethin' they hide from ya . . . but only you. Brian and I know of it already."

"It's a bit clearer now, you know," Genieva sobbed. "The reason he hasn't a shred of interest in me . . . other than as his farmhand. And she is very beautiful."

"Oh, no, no, no! Ya're thinkin' completely

183

wrong, Genieva," Brenna exclaimed, gathering her sobbing friend into her embrace. "Lita and Brian love only each other, Genieva . . . completely and only each other. But Brevan and Lita do share a bond, a knowledge that the rest of us cannot pretend to understand. For ya see, it was Brevan Lita came here to marry."

Chapter Eight

Genieva could only stare at Brenna. Lita had wanted to marry Brevan? Is that what Brenna meant? If so, then Genieva's worst fears had been amply realized. Had it been arranged—had Lita been the first woman who was supposed to have been his bride?

"Genieva, the pink is completely lost from yar face, it is!" Brenna noted aloud. Carefully she put a consoling hand over Genieva's. "It's not at all what ya must be thinkin'," she assured her. "Not at all. Lita only came last night to confess to Brevan about meeting Joaquin in the orchard yesterday. I guess you had already told him of it, and he pitied her, for it is sad that her family . . ." Sighing heavily, she began again, "I must tell ya the whole of it, Genieva . . . if ya're to understand everythin'. Ya see . . . Lita's family owned part of the orchards Brian and Lita own now. In fact, the Archuletas owned nearly all of that land. Her father raises cattle as well to sell for beef. Lita's mother was a dear soul . . . simply an angel. But her father . . . well, let me begin with our own father's death two years back."

Brenna led Genieva to the table where they sat down, and Genieva listened as Brenna began her tale.

"Dad was out in one of the fields plowin' one evenin'. I remember a storm was rollin' in from the mountains, but he wanted to finish the field. He was such a hard worker. Just like Brevan, he was. Anyway, mother went out toward the field as Brevan, Brian, and I watched her from the porch. Halfway between the house and the field where Dad was, she stopped and turned. We had all heard it, but it was unfamiliar to us, ya see. We thought it was just the thunder from the storm that was comin' our way. But then we saw them . . . an enormous, angry herd of cattle runnin' right toward our place. Somethin' about the storm had scared them when Mr. Archuleta and his sons were bringin' them in, and the stampede was fearful and headed right for us. Dad must've seen it from the field, for before Brevan was even close to mother, Dad reached her and pushed her out of the way, he did. The cattle were headed for the new orchards where Dad had just planted some young trees. He thought he could beat the herd to the orchards and close the gates so that the cattle would turn. But the cattle were fast, and the ground shook with the mad poundin' of their hooves. And Dad . . . Dad was in the way. They trampled him to death while Brian and I held Brevan from jumping into their midst as well."

Brenna paused and brushed the tears from her cheeks with her apron. Genieva shook her head, astonished and horrified. "How terrible! How absolutely unbearable," she whispered.

Brenna sniffled and continued, "Mother fainted and was feverish for several days. Even when we buried our Dad, I'm not sure her mind was with us entirely. Mr. Archuleta and his family, includin' Lita, attended the small service we held, and Mr. Archuleta apologized. Lita's mother was a sympathetic and very proud woman, and she insisted that Mr. Archuleta give our family his best orchards as compensation for the new trees the cattle trampled and as an offering of their sorrow for Dad's death. Mother was too ill to deny the gift, and Brevan—ya see, he was the head of the family now—Brevan was too angry and hurt to refuse it. He accepted the offer, though it was so obvious to all of us that Mr. Archuleta did not want to give us the land and orchards. The look on his face frightened me. I remember it, I do. But Lita's mother insisted on it, and the land became part of our property.

"Mother never did get well, Genieva. She blamed herself for Dad's death, and she fell very ill with a terrible cough and fever. She died only four months after Dad. Some time passed, and we learned from the people in town that Mrs. Archuleta had died as well. Consumption, it was. Mr. Archuleta knew he couldn't demand his lands back. Legally they were ours. Brian and Travis even went to the land offices awhile back to make sure. And they are ours still. But Juan Miguel wanted them back, he did. He coveted them. And he sent his only daughter to get them back for him."

"Brenna," Genieva began, "I'm so sorry."

Brenna nodded. "It's all right." She swallowed and seemed to force the tears in her eyes to keep from escaping as she continued, "I'll explain the rest now. Juan Miguel rode over to the house one day, and he brought Lita with him. She's very beautiful, I'm sure ya've noticed, and he intended to use her beauty to his own advantage. We all went out onto the porch to meet them, and Brevan greeted him pleasantly enough. 'I'm here to give you mí hija, McLean . . . my daughter. She will be your esposa,' he told Brevan. I remember Brevan laughed out loud and asked Lita's father what he meant. Mr. Archuleta explained that he felt responsible for the loss of our parents. He was lyin', he was, and well Brevan knew it. Brevan told him he could have his lands and orchards back, but Mr. Archuleta had gotten greedy. He wanted Lita to marry Brevan, the head of our family, so that he could gain power over all our lands. Brevan knew what he meant to do, he did, and he refused. Mr. Archuleta made Lita get down from her horse, and he told Brevan that he must accept his gesture of friendship or there would be dangerous consequences. Then he simply rode away, leavin' his daughter like an abandoned pup on the doorstep. And poor ita . . . I felt so sorry for her. I remember she walked up to Brevan and said, 'Mí papá has given me to you, señor. I am yours.' She reached up and kissed him right on the mouth, she did. Such a kiss I had never seen meself. 'Twas long and very intimate in nature."

Genieva was suddenly uncomfortably hot and irritable. She squirmed uneasily in her chair as Brenna continued. "Brevan was kind to her, of course. He did not scold her or push her away, but when she had finished . . . when she had finished . . ."

"Offering herself to him," Genieva spat out, completing Brenna's sentence.

"Yes, that's it. When she had finished offerin' herself to him, he simply said, 'Yar father is wantin' me lands, he is. And he'll not have them. I've offered to give him his own back, but he's a greedy man, Miss Archuleta. I'll not marry ya and fall into a trap that will take everythin' me father worked for away from his children.' "

"So Brevan didn't marry her simply because he didn't want her father to order him around and gain control over the farm and the rest of you," Genieva surmised.

"Brevan didn't marry her because he had not the desire to do so, Genieva," Brenna corrected. "Lita told us, then, that her father had threatened to beat her if she returned to his home without securin' Brevan as her husband. We all felt sorry for her. Brevan told her she was welcome to stay with us until somethin' could be worked out." Brenna dropped her gaze to the floor and lowered her voice as she spoke next. "I won't be lyin' to ya, Genieva. Lita did not give up on Brevan. After all, it was her father's wish that she marry him, and she is a loyal sort. But all the time, Brevan and I could see the spark in Brian's eyes when he looked at her, and the twinkle in hers when she looked at him. And one day, Lita went into the barn where Brevan was milkin' the cows. I walked in the moment she bent over him, her arms wrapped snugly about his chest as he sat milkin'. She began kissin' his cheeks and neck, but he stood and pushed her away. 'If ya be wishin' to marry me brother, Lita,' he told her, 'then ya best be forgettin' what yar father wants and start workin' on what you want of it, lass!' "

Genieva closed her eyes tightly against the vision forming before her—the vision of Lita and Brevan involved in an intimate moment. But the darkness only helped make the picture more vivid and hurtful.

"I think it was Brevan's strength that finally helped Lita to find her own, and she went directly to Brian and confessed her feelin's for him. They were married soon after, and I will tell ya now, Genieva, that Juan Miguel Archuleta, Lita's father, was as angry as the devil. He carries a bull whip with him, he does . . . and just after the weddin' he rode into the church yard like the screamin' banshee and cracked his whip on the ground like a madman as he began shoutin' at Lita. He called her a traitor to her family. Lita's brothers rode up behind him and began ridin' in a great circle around Lita, Brian, and Brevan, shoutin' at the top of their lungs. All of her brothers except one. Joaquin is Lita's twin brother, he is, and he's loyal to her. But he's loyal to his father as well, so he does nothin'. He is a friend to Lita but works his father's land too. Now her brother, Cruz . . . he is his father's image in face and spirit, he is. To tell the truth of it, he's far worse than even his father. For he has a deep streak of cruelty that I think even Juan Miguel lacks. He frightens me. Anyway, after they finished shoutin', Lita's brothers left, but before he followed them, Mr. Archuleta told Brevan that all the McLean lands would be his . . . that he would have them anyway."

Brenna was silent for a moment, and Genieva was thoughtful. When Brenna did speak again, it was with a smile and a comforting arm about Genieva's shoulders. "So ya see, Genieva . . . Lita loves Brian. And Brevan . . . well, I think Lita still fears for him. Brevan becomes furious when Joaquin visits because he doesn't trust him. Do ya understand it all now? Do ya see now why he was angry with her for meetin' Joaquin? And, Genieva, do ya see that Lita and Brian love only each other? Brevan is not in love with Lita, Genieva."

"So," Brevan began, as he sat down to supper that evening, "Brenna's told ya about the Archuletas, she has."

"Yes," Genieva affirmed. She had known Brenna would confide in Brevan about the conversation the two women had held earlier in the day. Brenna and Brevan were too close to hide things from each other. "And I don't know why you felt you had to keep such a thing from me."

"Lita doesn't want the world to know about it, lass. I'm sure you can understand that."

"I'm not the world!" Genieva cried. "I'm her sister-in-law and your wife! I should be told such things! I thought you and she . . . I thought you were . . ."

"Her lover?" Brevan finished.

"How dare you use such vulgar terms! But . . . but yes," she stammered. "Then I walk out to the barn last night and see you and her . . . the two of you . . . I see . . ."

"Ya saw nothin', lass," Brevan confirmed casually.

"Nothing?" Genieva exclaimed. "Put yourself in my shoes for a moment, Brevan. I did not know you and she shared all these little secrets! My natural assumption was . . ."

"I know what yar assumption was, Genieva," he growled, rising from the table and leaning forward to glare at her. "Ya've a filthy mind, ya have . . . interrogatin' Brenna all evenin' and askin' her whose baby it is that Lita's carryin'! I ought to turn ya over me knee and paddle yar bum, I should! What a thing to even think of, Genieva!"

"Well, I-I . . ."

"She came last night to confess to me that she'd been meetin' with Joaquin in the orchards. 'Twas her conscience that brought her here, and if ya had any conscience yarself, ya wouldn't be so suspicious of yar family." He sighed heavily and continued, "Ya spent too much time in the city, ya did. He's me brother, and she's his wife, and I'm happy for them, I am. And even if I was the scum it takes to do such a thing as ya're implyin', I wouldn't do it to me own brother!" He slammed his fist on the table, walked to where Genieva sat, and, taking her arm, pulled her to her feet. "Brenna says yar problem is jealousy, it is."

"What?" Genieva gasped as he glared down at her.

"Brenna says ya wouldn't even conjure up such ideas if I did me duty as a husband and made ya certain I'm faithful to ya."

"Brevan, I'm sorry," Genieva said as she tried to pull her arm from his grip. "I didn't know the situation. Naturally I assumed . . . I'm sorry. I understand now. If you had just told me, I wouldn't have . . ."

Her words were choked into silence as his free hand took hold of her chin firmly, forcing her to look up at him.

"It bothers ya, doesn't it?" he asked. "It eats at ya that before Brian and Lita were married I had me fill of her kisses. Well, I'll have ya know, Genieva, I never once asked for her attentions. I never once kissed her first."

"But you let her kiss you. You didn't . . ."

"Would ya rather that I humiliated her all the more? More than her own family had already done?"

"No. No of course not," Genieva sighed as tears fell from her eyes, streaking her cheeks in salty streams. She pushed at his hand holding her chin, and he released her.

"Ya need a part of me, don't ya, Genieva?" he asked unexpectedly.

Puzzled by his remark and tired from the long day, Genieva shook her head. "What are you talking about?"

"Ya need to own a part of me. Ya need somethin' of me that's yars alone. Somethin' that will confirm to ya that I'm nothin' if not loyal to only you." Brevan took hold of her waist

194

and pushed her backward until she was pressed firmly against the kitchen wall. "I've kissed ya enough to know that ya fancy it when I do, I have, Genieva." Genieva looked up at him with defiance—but he only continued. "Don't try to look so stern as stone, lass. I know it's true, and I'll tell ya this . . . that's the part of me . . . the part of Brevan McLean that I give to ya now. I've had the taste of Lita Archuleta's mouth, Genieva, but never the mouth of Lita McLean. And I've kissed a few other lasses in me life . . . but ya're me wife now, Genieva. Like it or not, ya are that. And ya need to know ya're the only woman I'll ever be kissin' now. And ya need to know that it's me own choice, and I'm not at all disappointed in the choice." Pressing his massive form firmly against hers and pinning her arms at her sides with his powerful hands, he whispered, "Now, look at me, lass. Do ya see me lips? Me very mouth? Well, it's yars, it is. All ya have to do is ask for it."

Genieva's eyes were instantly drawn to his lips. She watched, drenched in delirium, as he moistened them slowly with his tongue. She tried in vain to steady the nervous breathing causing her bosom to rise and fall more heavily than usual. He bent and kissed her chin lightly—next letting his lips brush against her cheek.

"One word from ya, Genieva . . . anywhere . . . any time of the day or night. I give ya me promise that me kiss is yar own. Me mind may be taxed with worry, me body may be tired from the work of the day . . . but me kiss is yars, lass." Brevan raised one of her fisted hands to his lips and kissed it softly. "And I tell ya this as well," he whispered, "I'll take pleasure in it, I will. More than I care to confess."

Genieva was bewitched by his eyes as they narrowed—his gaze capturing her own. Breathless from his taunting, she whispered, "I could never ask such a thing, Brevan. You know I would never ask you to . . ." Her quiet words were lost as a knowing grin spread across his face.

"Aye, then let yar eyes do the askin', Genieva," he offered.

"What?" she breathed as his hand slowly slid up her arm, coming to rest at the back of her neck.

"Yar eyes will speak to me, Genieva. I can read their colors, I can. And they're invitin' me now. Their askin' for a kiss, they are," he whispered. He stepped back, pulling her away from the wall and against his body as he wrapped her tightly in his mighty embrace. He pressed his lips to her neck and whispered, "They're askin' me now, Genieva. For it's the color of amethyst they are." He took her chin in his hand and looked directly into her eyes once more. "Of violets in the bright mornin' sun."

"You're a horrid tease!" she cried out in a whisper. Pushing herself from his arms, she turned away, flustered—her cheeks bright scarlet.

"Sometimes," he agreed. Forcefully taking her in his arms again, he added, "But not now."

His kiss was miraculous as he gave it to her. Genieva struggled to catch her breath as his mouth worked to prove to her he was sincere about his kiss being her own. Her mind was whirling—unable to think of anything save the pure and complete enchantment he was able to work throughout her! She feared her lungs might burst—that her heart might pound so fiercely as to work itself to quitting! As she found herself returning his kiss, she realized he was far too superb—too skilled. Certainly a man able to kiss a woman so thoroughly as to cause her body to threaten her mind with unconsciousness was all too familiar with kissing a woman.

"Stop it," she mumbled, tearing her mouth from his. She began pushing against his chest. "You're only mocking me." Backing away from him as she fought to catch her breath, she bumped into the wall, causing her knees to buckle. At last she crumpled to the floor.

Hunkering down before her, Brevan brushed at the lone tear traveling down her face with the back of his hand.

"No, Genieva," he assured her softly. "No," he repeated as he took her face in his hands and kissed her lips lightly—tracing their petal softness with his thumb before dropping to his knees and pulling her into his arms once again.

The raging flame inside Genieva ignited instantly. Brevan's kiss coaxed her into a state of being completely and blissfully unaware of anything but the glory of receiving his affections—of his lavishing his absolute and thorough attention upon her alone.

The knock on the front door, coupled with Brenna's calling to anyone inside, broke the spell for Genieva, and she tried to pull away from Brevan.

"Ignore her," he whispered, trying to reinstitute their union.

Putting her fingers to his lips to stop his advance on her own, she shook her head. "She had wanted to borrow a pie plate, and she forgot to take it with her before. And . . . I-I think you've proven your point, Brevan."

Sitting back on his heels, Brevan grinned with triumph "I hope so, I do. Now run answer the bloomin' door, lass. Before me sister starts to suspect that ya've gotten to me at last." With a wink, he stood and walked down the hall and into his room.

In the morning, Genieva awoke revitalized. She knew the story, at last. Finally she had an understanding of all that was going on between

Lita and Brevan—and their families. It was an immense relief. Coupled with the pure elation still filling her over having finally been the recipient once again of Brevan's marvelous kiss, her day was brightened, and her chores seemed less severe.

The plants were dry. Their thirst was profound, and Genieva wondered if she and Brevan could provide what they needed for much longer. The creek from which they drew water to give to the gardens, fields, and orchards was becoming dangerously shallow. Even the pond had lost a good foot of its depth. And now, with Brenna expecting a baby as well, Brevan and Genieva spent every other evening helping either Brian or Travis to water their fields.

The second week in July began, and Brevan told Genieva that unless rain came in the next few days, the crops would be lost. They would save most of the apples, but the corn and gardens would be lost. She went to bed that evening worried and anxious. Even the soothing, cool breeze did nothing to lull her to sleep.

Hours into the night, Genieva awoke from a fitful slumber. What did she hear? Was it what she hoped? She fairly leapt from her bed, dashing out of the house—not even pausing to snatch up a robe or shawl to cover her nightdress. Running down the front steps in her bare feet, she felt tremendous joy as the first drops of refreshing rain fell on her cheeks. Looking down, she watched as the dust blew about on the ground—quickly settling as the light shower turned into heavy rains almost immediately.

Her quiet thoughts of thankfulness were interrupted as Brevan came bounding toward her from the barn.

"It's rainin', lass!" he shouted as he reached her. Genieva was delighted by the sheer magnificence of his smile. She saw it so rarely, and at that moment it seemed to her as if there were no more beautiful a sight on earth. "It be goin' to rain like I've never seen it rain here before! Do ya know what this means, lass?" he asked.

"It means I won't have to carry water in buckets tomorrow to water the plants," Genieva sighed with relief.

Brevan laughed and agreed, "That it does, Genieva! That it does. But it means our crops are saved as well as our strength!" Stripping off his shirt, he flung it to the ground, spread his arms wide, and tilted his head back, letting the rain fall freely on his face and body. "Oh, blessed night be this, lass!" Looking at her—an expression of resplendent joy on his handsome face—he placed his fists firmly at his hips and began dancing about. Genieva smiled as Brevan danced a literal Irish jig—a jig one might expect to be more aptly performed by a leprechaun. It looked rather odd to see such a large man dancing about in the mud in such a manner, and Genieva couldn't stop a giggle from escaping her throat.

"Come then, lass," he chuckled, extending a hand to her. "Genieva and Brevan McLean will have their harvest this year, they will." Taking her hand, he began to lead her in any number of folk-dancing maneuvers.

Genieva giggled delightedly as they danced about, splashing the puddles beneath their feet. When she began to feel dizzy from their spinning about, she pleaded breathlessly, "Oh stop, Brevan. I'm going to be sick!" The rain was falling harder now, and the air had turned colder. "Let's go in. We'll catch our deaths out here," she suggested, hugging herself as her teeth began to chatter.

Unexpectedly, however, Genieva found herself wrapped tightly in Brevan's arms. "Ya'll be waitin' a wee minute more before ya leave me, ya will," he said as his disturbing gaze never wavered from her. "I'm as dry through and through as the plants ya've been a strivin' so hard to save, Genieva. I think it be time ya were workin' to be quenchin' my thirst now."

Though her mind immediately registered his inference, Genieva was powerless to resist him as he took her face firmly between his warm, wet hands, tilting her head backward. The unexpected touch of his mouth to her throat caused her knees to buckle, and his arms wrapped around her waist to support her as he continued to let his mouth ravenously savor the tender, sensitive flesh of her neck. Reaching up, she placed her hands on his shoulders and tried to muster the strength to push him away. It unnerved her that she should feel so completely powerless to resist him—that she felt the necessity to try. Every muscle and bone in her body seemed to have turned to liquid, and she could only find the strength to keep her heart from bursting within her bosom. Thus, she ceased in her pitiful attempt to deter him, surrendering to his attentions.

Genieva had heard stories of women who had been unable to resist men, and to be honest with herself, she had always been fairly judgmental of them—until the next moment. As Brevan McLean turned his attentions from her neck, gazing into her eyes momentarily before hi head descended to hers, his mouth capturing her own in a heated, demanding kiss—Genieva under-stood—understood how a man such as Brevan McLean could vanquish the resistance of any woman! It frightened her—for she feared that, though she had endured much and been always strong, Brevan McLean's kiss would somehow be her undoing. It had been weeks since she'd tasted of it—been rejuvenated by it while at the same time being rendered weak in his arms. She thought it was good he hadn't kissed her for so long—for she estimated it would take her another two weeks to gain control of her senses after this.

The rain was cool and refreshing on her face, and Brevan's kiss was hot and sweet to her mouth. Yet suddenly he moaned—broke from her and arched his back as if in great pain.

"Brevan?" Genieva cried out as she saw the look of agony on his face.

"Me back, lass," he breathed before dropping to his knees in the mud. Genieva saw it then— the small knife—the blade buried in Brevan's back—the handle protruding from his back. Frantically she looked around, huddling over him protectively, as she heard the approach of a horse. Horror struck her as, looking up, she found herself staring into the cruel and triumphant expression on the face of Cruz Archuleta.

"What's the matter, McLean?" the man chuckled. "Have ya got a knife in your back, hombre?"

"Not at all, Cruz. 'Tis but a wee splinter," Brevan growled. Reaching around, Brevan pulled the knife from his body. "Get off me land, Cruz," he ordered, groaning slightly from the pain of the wound.

"This . . . all this will be my father's soon enough," Cruz threatened. Chuckling, he added, "And your wife will be mine."

"I said, get off me land!" Genieva watched as

Brevan, taking the knife firmly in hand, reached up and drove the weapon into the neck of Cruz's bay. The horse reared, neighing with pain, and only just missed trampling Brevan—for Genieva pushed him out of the way before it bolted off in the direction from which it had come.

"Baboso! You will pay for that, hombre," Cruz shouted over his shoulder. He managed to gain control of the horse finally—glaring hatefully in Brevan's direction as he rode away at last.

"Boil up that needle and thread, lass," Brevan muttered as Genieva helped him into the house.

Chapter Nine

The next morning Genieva set out to tell Brian what had happened. The threat from the Archuletas, especially Cruz, was too dangerous for Brevan now. Brian must be told about the intensity of the danger. Cruz had openly attacked Brevan—and Genieva knew it would not be the last time.

"Juan Miguel . . . he's bidin' his time, he is," Brian said, after he'd listened to Genieva's telling of Cruz's attack on Brevan. "What's he waitin' for then? Why does he send Cruz? He's a proud man. If he wants Brevan dead, it seems he would've done it by now."

Lita swallowed hard and timidly spoke. "H-he . . . he thinks that Brevan is . . . the father of our bebé, Brian," she whispered.

"What?" Brian exclaimed, looking at her in astonishment.

Lita looked to Genieva, who nodded in understanding and spoke for her, "He thinks you love Brevan, but he knows Brian is your husband. He cares enough for you that it muddles his thinking, and it keeps both Brevan and Brian safe for a time."

Lita nodded and looked to Brian with tears in her eyes. "He wants Brevan dead, Brian. He wants this land. He'd have taken it by now if it weren't for the fact that Cruz, idioto, told him that he thinks it is Brevan's bebé I carry."

"Ya mean to tell me, Lita," Brian began, "that yar father thinks no more of ya than that? He thinks ya are capable of . . ."

"Cruz *is*. Cruz is the father of Amy Wilburn's bebé, Brian. Why should mí padre think any less of his other children?" Lita buried her face in her hands and began to sob bitterly. "I'm sorry, Brian! I'm so sorry. I thought I could help your familia somehow. I never knew I would cause it to be worse on you."

Genieva watched as Brian dropped to his knees on the floor before Lita. Taking her face in his hands, he wiped at her tears, placing his own cheek against hers as he soothed her.

"Oh, Lita. Ya should've told me, lass. It does not fall on yar shoulders to protect me brother and me."

"You mean to be saying," she sniffed, "that you are not angry with me for . . ."

Brian shook his head. "No, lass. I love ya all the more for it."

Genieva dabbed at her own tears. It was a personal moment for them both, so she excused herself with, "I need to get back to Brevan."

Yet Genieva knew Brevan would not need her at home. No. Ever diligent, ever hardworking, Brevan would be out tending to his crops or his stock or fixing something in need of fixing. As Genieva truly had no rapturous desire to tend to her own chores, she rather ambled along the dirt path leading her home from Brian and Lita's house. The rain had breathed freshness and color to every flower and tree along the path. Thus Genieva felt a smile on her face as she watched a small striped chipmunk scamper through the wildflowers.

As she strolled somewhat lingeringly, she thought of the depth of the love Brian and Lita shared. She had seen it in their eyes many times since coming to live with Brevan—but never so obvious, nor as earnest, as it was that morning. She understood Lita's frantic desire to protect her husband and his brother. She would've done no less to protect them both. It touched her immensely to think of Brian's instant understanding. He had not scolded or tormented Lita for what she had allowed her father and brothers to think of her. He had recognized her sacrifice for his sake.

Genieva reached down and plucked a wild daisy, studying it intently as she thought of Brevan and how wonderful it would be should he ever look at her the way Brian looked on Lita. She closed her eyes and tried to imagine the expression that might be apparent on Brevan's face were he to know she had made such a sacrifice of her moral reputation on his behalf.

Still, a vision of what his expression would be should she confess to him having withheld the truth about what had happened with Cruz in the orchard played itself more vividly before her eyes instead.

"Do you dream of me, niña?"

Genieva gasped—opened her eyes to see Cruz approaching. He walked toward her, leading a black horse by the reins.

"Don't come near me," she warned him, her heart hammering brutally within her chest. How would she avoid him? She knew he meant her harm.

"Oh. You are hurting my feelings, señora," he whined, putting his hand to his chest and scowling. "I do not mean to harm you."

"Then walk on. Leave me alone."

"I do not mean to harm you at all. What I mean for you is much more pleasant, niña," he explained, lunging at her suddenly and taking hold of her wrist. Genieva cried out as he twisted her arm, holding it firmly against her back as he whispered, "I mean to pay your esposo. I mean to return the favor he did my sister. She carries his bebé, no? Sí. You know it is true." Genieva tried to struggle, but he twisted her arm more violently, causing tears to swell in her eyes. "So, I think your husband, mí amigo Brevan McLean . . . I think his wife's estomago should grow with a bebé, too. You agree, no? I think it should be my bebé, señora."

Genieva's stomach threatened retching, and she turned her face toward Cruz's then, spitting at him. He shoved her forward violently as a result, and she stumbled to the ground.

"Idiota!" he shouted as he wiped her saliva from his cheek. "I meant to be nice to you, señora. But I see you are proud. I do not like too much pride in a woman."

"He'll kill you if you touch me," Genieva sobbed as Cruz Archuleta took hold of her arm once more, pulling her to her feet.

"Are you so sure, niña? Perhaps he is like my brother, Joaquin. Joaquin cares nothing for his woman now. Maybe your hombre will be the same to you."

The thought put into Genieva's head by the evil creature before her imprinted itself on her already insecure mind. Perhaps Brevan would simply turn her out. Yet her reason and knowledge of her husband's character instantly reaffirmed itself to her.

"He'll kill you," she assured him.

"I should do no less," Joaquin Archuleta said, stepping from behind a nearby piñon tree. "Let the woman go, Cruz. Papá would not send you to do this."

"Mí papá does not tell me everything to do as he does you and Mateo, hermano. I am my own man," Cruz growled.

"Then act like one, hombre. Quit hurting

innocent women. Are you afraid to fight men, Cruz?" Joaquin mocked.

Immediately Cruz released Genieva, turning to face Joaquin with one hand poised above the pistol at his hip.

"I dare you, hermano. I dare you to speak those words to me again," he threatened.

"Go home, Cruz. I have more reason to kill you than you do me. And I'm faster at the draw. Go home," Joaquin growled.

Cruz's jaw was firmly set, but he paused, seeming to consider for a moment.

Turning to Genieva, he mumbled, "You and me . . . we are not through, niña. And I tell my brother that he should watch behind him from now on . . . for he is no safer than you or your husband." Angrily mounting his horse, Cruz Archuleta rode off at a full gallop.

Genieva immediately turned to face Joaquin. He stood pale and somber as he watched his brother ride away.

"He's intimidated by you. Thankfully," she said.

"He is growing confident in himself. It will not be long before he grows impatient with mí padre and does more things that he does not order," the man told her. "Papá does not wish to kill Brevan or Brian, señora. Only to . . . to harass Brevan so that he will give him all his lands. I have just been to tell this to Lita."

"I can't believe you," Genieva admitted to him,

however. "Cruz attacked Brevan only last night. He . . ."

"Mí padre knows not of it. Cruz has a bad part in him. I will tell papá what has happened. But your man . . . Brevan is in danger still. Cruz is having his own reasons now for hating your husband. And he wants to win the lands for my father." Reaching out and taking Genieva by the shoulders, he frowned, adding, "You must not tell Brevan of this. It is what Cruz wants you to do. It would make Brevan loco with anger, and he would come for Cruz. But Cruz is a coward, and he would wait with other men for your Brevan. Brevan McLean . . . he is a strong, powerful hombre. But Cruz would have others to help him. You must not tell Brevan of this. Cruz is purposely trying to provoke him."

"But I can't keep this from him. I can't lie to him," Genieva explained, her eyes pleading with the man for understanding.

"Then you must keep him from coming after Cruz. It is what Cruz wants, señora. He will be too ready for Brevan." When she had finally nodded in agreement, Joaquin released Genieva. "I must follow Cruz and see him go home. You need to be more careful being out alone. I cannot always be near to help you." He whistled sharply, and a paint horse appeared from behind another tree some distance from where they stood. Genieva watched as Joaquin mounted the animal, but as he turned it in the direction in which Cruz had ridden, he paused. Looking down at her, he said, "I will tell papá that Lita carries the bebé of her esposo. He will be happy to know the truth," and he rode away, leaving Genieva alone once more on the path toward home.

Genieva's anxiety was lessened a little when she saw Travis's wagon waiting in front of the house. Brenna would give her comfort, and she would find the strength to hide the knowledge from Brevan of her encounter with Cruz. The other wagon waiting in front of the house, however, was unfamiliar to Genieva. As she ascended the front steps, she wondered who had come from town for a visit.

Upon entering the house, Genieva's hands flew to silence her gasp as she recognized the gathering of visitors sitting here and there about the room. Brenna and Travis sat among the group, looking pale and uncertain. Her eyes fell to Brevan, who stood leaning in the hallway doorframe, and she let them plead with him for support. How would she endure this? Had the truth already been told in her absence? Was she now the object of so many inquisitive eyes because the entire story—the reason she had come to Brevan—had been revealed to him already?

"Well, hello, Genieva," her father greeted—his voice thick with sarcasm.

"Father," Genieva muttered.

"My darling!" her mother chimed, standing and rushing toward Genieva. Her mother gathered her into her arms as if she were a lost kitten. "Oh, my darling! We've been so worried!" her mother exclaimed. "How could you, Genieva? How could you do this to us? To worry us so? And to disappoint us in not following through with your duty?"

"Andre was devastated, Nieva!" Genieva's younger sister, Maureen, scolded. "You've simply broken his heart! Not to mention the humiliation that . . ."

"Enough, Maureen," Genieva's father grumbled.

Genieva looked at each member of her family standing before her. Her father, Evert Bankmans—strong, stern, ever frowning. His hair was near to white with his aging, but still he was a handsome man. Her mother, Abigail Jefferson Bankmans, wore the eternal expression of concern she always did. She was still short and plump—her hair as lacking in gray as the day Evert Bankmans had wed her. Maureen was still beautiful and obviously quite aware of the fact. She bore the same hair color as Genieva but had been blessed with a purely perfect complexion, void of freckles. Her eyes, though a lovely shade of brown, were not as intriguing as were Genieva's. Brevan remained still and composed in the doorframe, but Brenna's eyes were wide with astonishment, and Travis's brows arched with the same emotion.

"I can't believe it," Genieva's father muttered, glaring at her—disappointment blatant on his face. "To shame the family so. To promptly run off the day before your engagement was to be announced. The Stewarts are infuriated, Genieva Bankmans."

"McLean," Brevan corrected, remaining unmoved—his arms folded determinedly across his broad chest. "Genieva McLean it be now, sir."

Genieva could see the irritation boldly engraved across her father's face. No one had ever dared to correct Evert Bankmans! He tried to appear as if he hadn't heard Brevan's comment, however. "This is outrageous, Genieva," her father continued.

Maureen approached her sister then and, dropping her voice, said, "This one is unearthly handsome, Nieva . . . but to simply brush aside Andre . . . it just isn't done. You should hear what people are saying."

"I don't care what people are saying, Maureen!" Genieva exclaimed. Turning her attention to her father, she took a deep breath and charged forward verbally, "I'm not something you own as you do a horse or a dog, Father. I'm a human being. An individual, and this is my life. I thank you and mother for giving me my life . . . but you can't expect to direct it for your own purposes. I left to find my own way . . . my own life. And I've found it." She glanced at Brevan briefly and was encouraged when she saw a supportive nod in return. Brenna smiled triumphantly, and Travis gave a heartening wink.

"How dare you talk back to me so, child!" her father bellowed. Taking hold of her arm firmly, he ordered, "Pack your bags at once, Genieva! We'll straighten this mess out at home!"

"Oh dear, oh dear," Genieva's mother whined as Brevan took her gently by the shoulders and moved her aside, advancing on Genieva and her father. Travis too stood firm—defiance apparent in his stance. Brenna looked to Genieva then expectantly to Brevan and back.

As Brevan approached, Genieva's heart began to pound with a wild force. Would he help her father pack her off to Chicago? He had never wanted her in the first place. It was surely a way out for him.

Yet as Brevan laid one powerful hand on her father's shoulder, saying, "You'll be excusin' me now, Mr. Bankmans," his eyes told her he would champion her instead. Taking the wrist that her father had held in his grasp, Brevan pulled Genieva to him as he spoke to her father. "You'll not be takin' Genieva anywhere, ya won't. She's me wife, Mr. Bankmans, legal and otherwise."

"Brevan," Genieva pleaded in a whisper as she let herself be bound in his embrace. Her arms slid about his waist—she laid her head against the firm strength of his chest.

"An annulment will not be hard to come by in light of this situation, man," her father threatened.

"You'll not have her so long as there's breath left in me," Brevan growled. "Besides . . . to me own knowledge . . . annulment requires that the marriage is yet unconsummated."

Genieva tightened her embrace around Brevan as every shred of her soul hoped his attempt to deter her father would not fail. When he groaned slightly, she remembered the wound at his lower back and loosened her embrace.

"Oh, my!" Genieva's mother gasped. "Cover your ears, Maureen," she ordered as the youngest daughter's eyes widened with understanding.

"I'm a powerful man, Irishman. I've friends in important positions. I assure you . . . it can be done," Evert Bankmans growled.

"You'll not have her. You'll have to kill me first, Bankmans," Brevan stated calmly.

"I'm not averse to it, Irishman."

"Then you'll commit more than one murder to do it, sir," Travis growled, stepping forward.

"Evert!" Genieva's mother exclaimed.

"I'm not doubtin' that a man who would force his own daughter into a marriage she did not want would be able to kill his own son-in-law," Brevan said through clenched teeth. Genieva could feel the muscles in his body tightening, and

216

she released him, turning in his arms to face her father. She had meant to meet her father in complete defiance—telling him he would have to kill her as well before she would return with him.

Yet in that same moment one of Brevan's powerful hands pressed firmly on her stomach, sliding downward and coming to rest directly on her abdomen as he said, "But it be my child she may be a carryin'. What then, Bankmans? Ya would strip a wife and her child of the man they both belong to? Strip yar own daughter of her lover and husband? Yar own grandchild of its father and protector? What kind of a man are ya? Or are ya a man at all now?"

Genieva saw the look of wonderment passing between Travis and Brenna before her mother gasped, exclaiming, "Cover your eyes, Maureen!" as she put a hand dramatically to her throat. Maureen only continued to stare in dazzled amazement, and Genieva closed her own eyes, letting her head fall back against Brevan's powerful shoulder—her hand lacing fingers with his that lay on her abdomen. For all that he viewed her as a burden, he would protect her. He would not let her be taken back to Chicago.

Genieva opened her eyes to find her father still standing before her, a look of defeat and guilt mellowing his features.

"I'm happy here, Father. For the first time in my grown-up life, I'm happy. Doesn't that mean

217

anything to you? Don't you care about me and what I need?" Reaching out, she took Maureen's hand in her own as she stepped out of Brevan's protective embrace. Smiling at her sister, she said, "Don't do it to Maureen either, Father. I beg you. Don't give her the need to run from you like I did."

Maureen smiled at her elder sister and returned the comforting squeeze of her hand. Drawing in a breath, she turned Genieva's hand over in her own and studied it carefully. "Nieva! Your hands! They're so roughened and dry!"

"They're working hands now, Maureen. It's fine," Genieva assured her, studying her own hands with a measure of disappointment.

"They work to make a home and a man happy in it, lass," Brevan said to Maureen. He took Genieva's hands in his own. "They're skillful, hard workin'," he whispered. He slipped Genieva's hand beneath his shirt then—moving it slowly over his warm skin and chest. "And they feel good here." Genieva smiled at the two sets of eyebrows arching once more on the faces of Brenna and Travis.

"Oh, my! Oh, my!" Genieva's mother whimpered, fanning herself fiercely with one hand as she witnessed the brazen caress. Genieva nearly giggled out loud as her mother began to sway back and forth slightly—her other hand going to her forehead.

Genieva's own hand prickled with excitement at the feel of Brevan's skin and muscle beneath her palm. She silently scolded herself for letting the simple touch affect her so completely.

"Now," Brevan began, addressing her father as he dropped Genieva's hand, "ya're more than welcome to stay here with us . . . for a visit, if ya like. All of ya . . . Mr. Bankmans, Mrs. Bankmans, and wee little sister too." His voice was stern as he continued, "That is . . . assumin' ya've accepted the situation and settled yar mind where Genieva's concerned."

Genieva watched with great trepidation as her father's chest rose and fell heavily with withheld anger. Her mother frowned—silently pleading with him, as Maureen only continued to stare, dumbfounded, at Brevan.

"Have you the room?" Genieva's father asked. "The house looks small from without."

"You and yar wife can stay in me sister's old bedroom. It's the nicest, it is. We've got a spare next to that one for the lass. Genieva and I have our own. Ya're welcome in me house . . . as long as ya accept that this is my house. Mine and Genieva's," Brevan answered.

"Oh please, Evert. She's our daughter," Genieva's mother whispered.

Genieva watched her father's face hopefully. After all, they were her family—for all their faults, she loved them. She could hope for nothing more from them than forgiveness and under-standing.

"Very well. We'll stay the day and one night," Evert Bankmans agreed. "But I've got to get back to Chicago immediately." Going to Genieva, he took her by the shoulders and glared harshly at her. "I'll accept this, Genieva, and deal with it the best I am capable. I don't, however, approve of what you've done."

"Choosing my own course, being that it was correct and legal, Father . . . was right for me. Brevan is more of a man than Andre Stewart could even fathom. I want a full life," Genieva explained.

"If you'll be excusin' me now," Brevan muttered, striding toward the front door—and, no doubt, escape. "I've got a full day's work to be finishin' in an hour's time before the sun sets itself." He let the screen door slam behind him as he left.

"Oh, yes," Brenna said, fairly leaping to her feet. "Travis and I have ever so much to do yet in the day, we do." Offering her hand to Genieva's mother, she quickly shook hands with the woman. As she took Travis's arm, leading him toward the door, she winked at Genieva.

"It was mighty nice meeting you folks," Travis said, shaking Evert's hand. He tipped his hat at Genieva before he and Brenna followed Brevan out of the house.

"He is magnificent!" Maureen sighed, walking to the window and watching Brevan saunter toward the barn.

"He is not a horse, Maury," Genieva reminded. "And he's married." For all the love Genieva held for her sister, she was not blinded by her sweet beauty. Maureen was an incurable flirt— even with men who weren't overpoweringly attractive the way Brevan was. She felt very uncomfortable suddenly being witness to her sister's obvious infatuation with Brevan.

"Well, I'm glad he's gone," Genieva's mother commented, putting an arm around Genieva's shoulder. "He's terribly large . . . and quite frightening. Is he as violent as he appears, Genieva? I've heard tell of the Irish temperament."

"He's no brute, Mother. He's an extraordinary man," Genieva replied—thoughtful.

"What next?" Brevan grumbled to himself as he stormed into the barn. "I've got me a whole crew of irritatin' relations now." As he began to toss the hay into the feeding troughs with a pitchfork, his mind repeated the conversation with the Bankmans.

He'd gone into the kitchen for a glass of milk that morning—wondering where Genieva had run off to, for she was nowhere to be found. As he sat in his house relaxing for a brief few moments in the day, there came a knock on the door, and he'd opened it to find Genieva's family staring at him—mouths gaping open in surprise.

Brevan had been instantly furious with his wife—for she had never made mention of her family to him. Furthermore, as her father began to relate the reason for their unexpected visit and Brevan learned that Genieva was to have wed some wilty, choirboy type in Chicago, he was more agitated. Yet he'd bound his temper and waited patiently for Genieva to return from wherever it was that she'd gone off to.

Brenna and Travis had arrived shortly after the Bankmans, and Brevan was forced to endure nearly an entire half an hour listening to their polite and insincere conversation. He spoke hardly a word himself—only listened as Genieva's babbling sister related the circumstances in Chicago that had apparently caused Genieva to flee.

When Genieva did return, looking at her family as if they were the angels of death sent to take her, Brevan learned all the more of Genieva's arranged marriage. It became clear to him then why such a completely adorable woman would accept a marriage and situation offered by a stranger living nearly as far away from Chicago as possible. This angered him even more—that a parent would force a child into such an unhappy life. Brevan knew that were he ever to have children, he would let them make their own path—prayerful and hoping they would be good and happy adults.

These thoughts brought his mind to settling on the farce he had concocted to convince Genieva's father of the seriousness of her having married. A child? Whatever had made him think of Genieva carrying his child? He surely never intended for her to do so. Never! Why, that would entail . . .

"Ya're losin' yar brain, ya are, Brevan McLean," he mumbled to himself. Still, an image of a small girl with his wife's color-shifting eyes and freckled nose kept presenting itself to his mind's eye.

He paused in pitching the hay. Leaning on the fork's handle, he thought once again of Genieva's eyes. He chuckled at the thought of the deep brown hue they assumed when her temper was provoked—of the near emerald green shade they blazed each time her jealous nature was uncovered. He winced as he thought of the grayish blue tint clouding her eyes each time she felt pain or deep sorrow. He inwardly chastised himself, knowing that at times he had been the cause of this color manifesting itself. An arrogant smile spread across his face then, as he remembered vividly the violet color her eyes had sparkled the few times he had held her

in his arms and kissed her. Definitely the violet—
that was certainly his favorite color of Genieva's
eyes.

He felt his masculine pride welling in his chest
as he thought then of the way Genieva's body
had melted to his when he'd taken her in his
arms to defend her only moments before.
Chuckling, he resumed his efforts in the barn,
mumbling under his breath, "Well, at the least
their bein' here should provide some entertainin'
situations."

It was late afternoon before Brevan entered the
house again. Genieva had endured several more
arguments with her father and endless other
comments from her sister about Brevan's profound good looks. Thus, she was immensely
relieved to see him walk into the kitchen—for
his entrance ended all conversation.

He smiled at Maury and her mother and went
to where Genieva had three loaves of bread
dough rising on the stovetop.

Genieva saw Brevan approach the loaves and,
going to stand next to him, warned, "Just one
pinch." Genieva had learned that not only did
Brevan dip his fingers into cake batters and
cookie doughs—he was destructive to bread
loaves as well. There were many times she would
come in to check on the rising bread only to
find it looking like a hen had been pecking at it.

"One pinch?" he asked, raising his eyebrows in daring.

"One pinch, Brevan," Genieva repeated. To her horror, he shrugged his shoulders and quickly pinched her smartly on the seat of her skirt. "Of the bread dough, Brevan!" Genieva scolded. "Of the dough!" He shrugged and winked slyly at her before pinching off a large piece of dough from one of the loaves and walking casually to the other side of the room.

"Oh, my! Oh, dear," Abigail gasped, as she began to swoon and fan herself once more. Genieva looked to her sister. Maureen was simply crimson with delight at what she had just witnessed. Genieva bit her lip to hide the amused smile forming on her own face. The expressions of her family, save the angry one of her father, were completely amusing.

"Would yar sister be wantin' to help me milk the cows then, Genieva?" Brevan asked. "It would seem they missed bein' milked this mornin'."

"No, I don't think that would be . . ." Genieva began. She did not want her flirtatious sister too close to Brevan.

"Oh, I'd love to!" Maury exclaimed.

"Oh, my dear, no," Abigail objected, fanning rapidly. "Don't let her do it, Evert."

"Let her go, Abigail. We don't want Maureen bolting from her responsibilities," Evert said pointedly to Genieva.

Maury giggled and linked her arm through Brevan's, leading him toward the front door. "I've never been on a farm before, Brevan," she told him, flashing a dazzling smile.

"Really now?" Brevan asked as they left.

Genieva went to the window and watched them for a moment. After putting the loaves of bread to bake in the oven, she excused herself and left the house, making her way toward the barn. As she approached, she could hear Maury talking to Brevan, and she quickened her step, for she recognized the intonation in her sister's voice at once.

"I mean . . . after all, Brevan, you are . . . how can I put this tactfully?" Maury flirted. "You are amazingly handsome, you know."

"Am I now?" Brevan asked.

"It turns a girl's knees to jelly just looking at you!"

Enraged, Genieva opened the barn door and stepped in to see Brevan sitting on the stool milking one of the cows. Maury was bent over him, leaning as close to his face as she could conceivably be—trying to appear interested in the milking process.

"Are you quite finished, Brevan?" Genieva asked, trying her best not to snap out the question. "Dinner's nearly ready."

"Oh, Nieva," Maury giggled, "do you actually do this most of the time?"

"Yes, Maury. Milking has to be done every day. Why don't you go in and ask Mother to check my bread for me?"

Maury smiled at Genieva and nodded. She was nearly to the house when Brevan stood up from the milking. Instantly, Genieva glared at him, turning briskly on her heels and heading for the house.

"Here now, lass," Brevan said, catching hold of her arm and turning her to face him, "there's nothin' to be gettin' yar skirt all wrinkled about."

As Genieva looked up at him, the emerald green of her eyes caused his eyebrows to arch in surprise. "Flirting! Shamelessly flirting with my own sister! And in the barn of all places!" she shouted in a whisper, glancing around to be certain no one was about.

"Me? Flirtin' with that wee, silly lass?" Brevan defended. He chuckled, amused. He continued, "Genieva McLean, I would no more flirt with yar shallow-minded sister than I would a dead woman!"

"I heard you," Genieva argued.

"Ya heard her, Genieva. Not me. Think back on it now," Brevan reminded.

Genieva continued to breathe angrily—now humiliation accompanied her irritation—for she realized he was correct. Brevan had said nothing improper to Maureen.

"She's a watchin' us now, she is," he whispered then.

"Where?" Genieva asked, turning to look around.

"Aaahhh! Don't look about, lass. We'll let her think she's not bein' seen. And we'll teach the bitter pill a lesson, too, we will," Brevan whispered as he pulled Genieva's body snugly against his own.

"What . . . what do you mean?" Genieva stammered—thoroughly unnerved by the sensation of astounding elation that traveled through her body at his touch.

"Don't be lookin' like ya're not wantin' me attentions, lass. She'll be on to ya then," Brevan whispered as he pulled her even tighter against his body. "Let yar arms go 'round me shoulders," he instructed. As Genieva did let her trembling hands lock at the back of his neck, Brevan said, "Ya see now, that be lookin' a bit more believable."

Genieva drew in a nervous breath as Brevan, pulling her hair to one side, let his mouth hover teasingly over her neck just below her ear.

She flinched as his warm breath tickled her neck torturously, and he whispered, "Relax, Genieva. I'm not about to do anythin' too . . . familiar out here in the broad, bright daylight." Genieva's insides began to quiver as his unshaven chin pushed the collar of her shirtwaist down—his lips planting a moist, lingering kiss at the back of her neck.

"Why didn't ya tell me about your family before?" he asked, holding Genieva's neck in one hand—letting his thumb caress her throat.

As Genieva's eyes lifted to meet his, Brevan was momentarily distracted as he watched their very shading fade from green—gradually assuming a violet hue. He smiled, pleased in the knowledge that he alone had caused the tinted transformation.

"I-I . . ." Genieva stammered, for she was completely preoccupied by his gorgeous face before her. "It wasn't important," she finished as every segment of her body wished only that he would grant her the ecstasy of his kiss.

Brevan's index finger softly rested against Genieva's lower lip for a moment before he proceeded to trace the soft outline of her delicate mouth with his thumb.

"Ah, but it was, lass. I might have been better prepared to meet them had I known they existed, ya see."

As Genieva gazed into the tantalizing blue of the Irishman's eyes, her breath quickened at the remembrance of the mouth-watering taste of his kiss. He was toying with her again. No matter what his motive this time—whether he meant to simply mock her or to truly remove all doubt from Maureen's mind of their relationship—he was taunting her.

Abruptly, Genieva took Brevan's delicious face between her hands, pulling his head toward hers as she issued a firm kiss. The blissful physical connection lasted longer than she had intended— for the feel of his mouth to hers was not something easily sacrificed. After a few moments, she did release him, stepping back. Upon seeing the satisfied grin spreading across Brevan's face as he looked at her, however, she was embarrassed and wanted only to escape him.

She tugged at the waist of her blouse, straightened her posture, and said, "There now. She's seen us. Maureen should have no doubt now who you belong . . . where she can't . . ."

"Whose territory she's tresspassin' on, ya're tryin' to say," he chuckled.

"Yes. Yes, exactly." Straightening her collar, Genieva turned to leave, adding, "Now, if you'll excuse me, Brevan. I've dinner to attend to." She felt the fiery blush on her face and scolded herself for allowing it. But as she took her first step toward the house, Brevan caught her arm in one powerful hand, rather mercilessly yanking her around to face him.

"Now, lass," he began, gathering Genieva into his arms again. "Do ya really believe she'll be thinkin' that's proof of a passion between us?"

"Of course!" Genieva defended herself. "I've never in my life . . . she knows I would never . . . I mean . . ." she stammered.

"Give yarself up to me for one wee bit of a minute, Genieva," Brevan whispered. Genieva found it difficult to breathe—breathless in his arms. "'Twill be a heavenly surrender, and I'll give yar sister a show she won't soon forget, I will." As his head descended toward hers, he added, "Ya'll not soon forget it either."

"Please, Brevan. Don't . . ." she breathed as his lips gently pressed hers.

Instantly, Genieva melted into Brevan's arms—his lips hovered just above hers for a moment. "'Please, Brevan' will do, Genieva," he whispered just before his mouth locked with hers in an uncompromising, sincere, and ardent exchange.

For those following few moments of nearly fatal, ecstatic delirium, Genieva was entirely unaware of anything else existing in the world. She heard nothing save the mad beating of her own heart—the quiet rhythm of Brevan's breathing. The sweet and often powerful fragrance of the honeysuckle growing on the outer wall of the barn was replaced in her senses by the subtle yet masculine scent of Brevan's shaving soap, still lingering on his face. She could feel only his arms as they held her next to his solid, capable body—his mouth moist, hot, and demanding on her own. Over and over, her heart and mind silently agreed—shouting to her inwardly—reminding her painfully again how deeply and completely she loved this man. Moments like these with Brevan made it difficult for Genieva to push that fact to the back of her mind. She winced as the knowledge of his not returning the cherished emotion upon her renewed itself in her heart and mind as well.

Brevan ended it then, placing one last lingering kiss on Genieva's forehead. As Genieva abruptly pushed herself back from him, she fancied she was swaying unsteadily for a moment and could not bring herself to look up at him.

"There. The lass should know for sure and for certain where her place be now," Brevan said—his voice low and unusual sounding.

"Yes. Yes," Genieva agreed, nodding as she turned to leave.

"Ya may be wantin' to change me bed sheets, Genieva," Brevan added. "Unless ya're not mindin' sleepin' in them after I've been in them by meself near to a week."

Genieva stopped—turned to look at him. "What?" she asked.

"Still . . . now that I'm thinkin' about it again . . . I'd be offended if ya did, I would." As Genieva's mouth dropped open in sudden realization, Brevan chuckled. "Ya've got the look of havin' seen the screamin' banshee, Genieva. I've no intention of sleepin' in the barn like the stock. And bein' the perfect gentleman that I am . . . I don't expect you to."

"But I . . ." Genieva began.

"And bein' that yar entire family needs lodgin' for the night, that leaves one choice, it does."

"But I . . ." she stammered.

"Ya're right, lass. After yar kissin' me like you just did . . . I'm a wee bit worried that ya'll try to take advantage of the situation this evenin'."

"Me?"

"Yet, I think ya be disciplined enough to keep yar hands to yarself, aren't ya, lass?"

Genieva could only stand staring at his attractive face—his mischievous grin. He was right. They would have to share his room. *His bed,* she thought, swallowing hard.

"Go on with ya now, Genieva. It's gettin' late, and I'm hungry, I am."

Chapter Ten

"You mean, your father and I must share one bed?" Abigail inquired of her daughter. Genieva had shown her father and mother into her room following a late supper.

"We only have three bedrooms, Mother," Genieva explained. "Maureen needs one, and I . . ." She stumbled over the words. "Brevan and I need ours."

"There's only one bed in their room, too, Mother. I looked," Maureen whispered to her mother. Genieva sighed with exasperation as her mother instantly began blushing crimson.

"Well . . . when in heathen country . . . do as the heathens do, I suppose," her mother sighed.

Genieva grinned and shook her head. "Come on, Maury. I'll tuck you in as well," she said, leading her sister to the spare bedroom.

"Doesn't he simply smother you at night, Nieva?" Maureen asked, dropping her voice in a tone of conspiracy.

"Whatever are you going on about now, Maury?" Genieva sighed. She was tired and a bit weary of dealing with her sister's trivial and endless questioning.

"What I mean is . . . that's a small bed in your room, and Brevan is such a large man. It seems to me that . . ."

"Here's your room, Maury. Just go to sleep," Genieva interrupted, her patience spent.

"But . . ."

"Good night, Maury," Genieva said. She closed the door—putting an end to her sister's curious chatter.

She was tired as she entered Brevan's room and startled when he unexpectedly spoke from behind her. He stood in the doorway, smiling at her—a rather amused expression across his handsome face.

"Have ya got the meddlin' in-laws all tucked in for the night then, lass?" he asked, grinning with understanding. He had unbuttoned his shirt and was awkwardly attempting to change the bandage on his knife wound. Genieva was suddenly worried over not having attended to it sooner.

"Yes," she answered, moving to assist him. "I don't remember them being so . . . so . . . irritating."

"They're in a strange environment, Genieva," he explained as she secured the fresh bandage over the wound. "And tryin' to accept a strange situation, they are." Brevan covered his mouth as he yawned, stretched, and stripped off his shirt.

"I'll um . . . I'll just rest on the sofa awhile," Genieva nervously stammered.

Yet as she started to move past him, he caught hold of her arm.

Lowering his voice, he said, "And undo the

vision I've been slavin' meself all day to create? Never." He pointed to his bed. "You'll be sleepin' there, ya will. I'll stretch out on the floor next to ya."

"Oh, no. I couldn't possibly . . . you need your rest and . . ." she began.

"Get to bed, lass. I'm worn to the core today," Brevan interrupted as he sat on the side of the bed. He removed his boots, letting them drop to the floor.

Unexpectedly, he took hold of Genieva's arm and, laying back on the bed, pulled her down beside him.

"Brevan!" Genieva exclaimed in a whisper. He rolled toward her, gathering her in a tight embrace. She immediately understood his actions as she heard Maureen's voice from the open doorway.

"Excuse me, Nieva," her sister called—feigning innocence. "Do you have an extra blanket somewhere near? Oh my, pardon me, will you?" Maureen said—her eyes nearly bugging out of her head as she stared at Genieva and Brevan.

"Here," Brevan said, sitting up and tossing the girl the quilt lying across the foot of his bed. "Ya can have this one. We'll not be needin' it." Then he stood and strode to the door. Closing it before Maureen's astonished face, he added, "Good night, lassie."

When Brevan returned to his bed and took his

pillow from it, Genieva asked, "Why do you work so hard at continuing this farce?"

Brevan threw another quilt to the floor, tossed the pillow on top of it, and lay down. He stretched his long body the length of the makeshift bed.

"It boils me blood that they're so puffed up and snobbish, it does."

Genieva looked away, muttering, "I'm sorry."

"It's no fault of yars. I've no doubt it took a fair amount of courage to leave like ya did. And it makes me angry that they drove ya to it."

"I'm weak, I suppose. It was my duty after all," Genieva sighed.

"It was not, lass. Everyone should have the right to choose their own path as an adult." Obviously wanting an end to their conversation, he added, "Good night then, Genieva."

"Good night, Brevan."

The hours passed slowly—for Genieva found sleep elusive. Her mind and senses were alive with the memory of Brevan's kiss earlier in the day. The marvelous sensation of being held in his arms still permeated her body—she ached to be held by him again.

Yet in the darkness, her fearful memories of her meeting with Cruz on the path home from Lita's house began to haunt her as well. She would have to tell Brevan about it. But when? Not with her family under his roof to witness every fearful and threatening word. Her thoughts wandered to her family, and she smiled—amused at the way her mother had nearly swooned each time Brevan entered the room muttering something insinuative. She covered her mouth, stifling a giggle as she recalled the incident at dinner.

Abigail had asked for someone to pass the butter.

"Let me do that for ya, Mother Bankmans," Brevan had offered. Then, taking a knife in his right hand, he reached around her mother, letting his arm rest around her rather plump form, and sliced a bit of the butter from the mold. He continued to hold her mother at his side as he buttered her bread for her, saying, "I can spread it on thicker than any man." Her mother had nearly fainted dead away, and Maury was again crimson with delight at her mother's blushing. Her father had not been amused, and that in itself was amusing to Genieva.

Turning to her side, she leaned over the side of the bed and stared at the man sleeping on the floor next to her. He was resting on his back, his arms raised and hands tucked firmly beneath his head. His feet were crossed and his hair tousled and mussed looking. He certainly was a beautiful sight to behold. In that quiet moment as she studied him, Genieva suddenly owned more patience with her sister's endless questions about Brevan.

Suddenly, the need to touch him was just too much to deny. Carefully, Genieva let her hand move from the bed and to his hair, stroking it softly and relishing the feel of it between her fingers. Her great fatigue left her reflexes too relaxed, and when Brevan suddenly caught hold of her hand, she was unable to retrieve it at once.

He did not open his eyes, simply pressed the palm of her hand firmly against his chest, holding it in place with his own. He seemed to be asleep. Even when Genieva whispered his name several times, he did not stir. Slowly, she pulled her hand from beneath his. He did not wake, only turned to his side, his back toward her now.

He's so strong, she thought. Not once had he mentioned his fresh wound—not once throughout the entire day. In those only quiet moments she'd had all day, Genieva was again reminded of the danger her Brevan was in. Cruz had inflicted a brutal wound to him the night before—and Brevan had retaliated. Cruz would be hungering for vengeance. A vision of Cruz standing before her on the pathway home that morning leapt to Genieva's mind. His threats had been lewd to say the least. What would she have done if Joaquin had not been near? She would've been ruined—ruined as Amy Wilburn had been.

The need to be near Brevan was heightening, and she again reached down, lightly caressing his shoulder. Just touching him comforted her. She wondered what it would be like to touch him whenever she needed to—to kiss him whenever she wanted to. Would it be too wonderful to hear him whisper in her ear that he loved her? So wonderful that it would cause her to be deafened to any other word spoken?

"Do ya want me in the bed with ya, Genieva?" Brevan grumbled. "For I'm certainly gettin' no sleep down here with ya pawin' at me every livin' minute."

"No," she assured him, snatching her hand from his shoulder. He began to chuckle then, and she watched him roll over onto his back once more. His eyes were moist with amusement when he looked at her.

He chuckled and whispered, "I thought yar mother would faint dead away right there at the supper table this evenin'."

Genieva grinned, delighted that he too was thinking of the incident.

"Yes," Genieva giggled softly. She covered her mouth with one hand for a moment, trying to keep from making too much noise. "But it was a terrible thing to do to her, Brevan," she whispered—an attempt at an obligatory scolding.

"Aye. That it was," he chuckled. Genieva was startled as his pillow hit her square in the face before he tucked it beneath his head once more. "Now off to sleep with ya, lass. I'll not be worth a nickel in the mornin'."

Genieva set a plate heaped with bacon and eggs on the table before Maureen.

"Is he already up and out?" Maureen asked, looking about.

"He goes out before light, Maureen. He's a hard worker," Genieva confirmed.

Lowering her voice, Maureen asked, "Is . . . is he simply delicious, Nieva?"

"What do you mean?" Genieva asked—though she knew exactly what her sister intimated. It irritated her that her sister was forever preoccupied with men.

"I mean," Maureen began, sighing and closing her eyes—a dreamy smile plastered across her pretty face, "when he kisses you, Nieva. Is it . . . is it just delicious?"

"For pity's sake, Maureen. That's not a question you ask someone," Genieva scolded.

"Oh, but you're not someone, Nieva. You're my sister. And I think Brevan McLean is the most attractive and desirable man I have ever seen." Genieva set a glass of milk before Maureen. She drew in a deep breath—attempting to settle her irritation with her sister. "I mean," Maureen continued, "how do you keep your hands off of him? If I were you, I'd be in his arms twenty-four hours a day!"

Genieva sighed, entirely exasperated. "There's work to do here, Maureen. Grow up a bit, will you?"

"No need to get so testy, Nieva. I was only asking."

"Just eat your breakfast, Maury." Genieva was quickly remembering another reason she'd found for escaping her family. Though she loved her sister, she'd forgotten what an agonizing nuisance she could be at times.

Leaning against the sink as she watched her sister eat, she shoved the last bite of her own bread and jam into her mouth. The screen door opened, and Brevan entered the house. Genieva rolled her eyes in frustration as her sister immediately leapt from her chair to greet Brevan.

"Good morning, brother-in-law," Maureen chirped.

"Good mornin' then, Maureen," Brevan said before going to the sink and washing his hands under the pump.

"Would you like to join me for breakfast?" Maureen cooed.

"I had me breakfast before the sun was up today, but thank ya for the invitation." As Genieva watched in astonishment, Brevan reached over one shoulder, pulling his shirt off over his head and tossing it to the floor. "Those bloomin' pigeons have nested on the barn roof again, Genieva. Little plums aimed their bums right at me when I came out of the barn this mornin'," he growled. He soaked a cloth under the pump and wrung it out. Handing it to Genieva, he asked, "Will ya be a saint, Genieva, and wipe me back clean of whatever might have soaked through me shirt?"

Taking the cloth he offered, Genieva bit her lip to stop the triumphant grin threatening to control her expression. She had seen the widening of her sister's eyes as she ogled Brevan when he removed his shirt—her gaping mouth when he'd handed her the cloth.

"There," Genieva said, dropping the soiled cloth into the sink. "I'll get you a clean shirt," she offered.

"No need of it. It's warm enough to go without today, it is," Brevan assured her. Genieva felt her heart begin to race wildly as Brevan looked at her, grinning and winking. "I see ya've been into Brenna's strawberry jam again," he said, placing a hand on either side of Genieva—forcing her to lean back against the sink.

Self-consciously licking one corner of her mouth, Genieva admitted, "Yes." As Brevan slowly leaned closer to her, she whispered, "Brevan?"

"Ya've missed a dab there, Genieva," he mumbled as his mouth descended upon the opposite corner of her own. As a reflex, her hands went to his shoulders. She pushed gently at him, but he was undaunted. Genieva's heart began to hammer furiously within her chest as his mouth affixed moist, teasing kisses to the particular area of her face. Raising his head from hers for a moment, he ceremoniously moistened his lips and moaned, "Mmmmmm. My mistake, Genieva. 'Tis the cherry jelly ya've been into."

"Brevan," Genieva whispered, shaking her head as his descended once more. But as his mouth took hers, this time in a ravenously passionate kiss, all thoughts of deterring him were obliterated as the taste and feel of him consumed her senses. Brevan gathered Genieva fiercely into his arms, pulling her tightly against him as her own arms slipped around his body. Not even the sound of her mother's horrified gasp upon entering the room and catching sight of them could distract her—for she was lost in the moist, sweet flavor of his mouth as they kissed.

"Genieva Loretta Bankmans!" her mother exclaimed. "Evert! Oh, Evert! Look at that!"

As Brevan's mouth worked, enkindling Genieva's to meet his demanding, passionate kiss, Maureen's words kept echoing through Genieva's mind. "When he kisses you, Nieva . . . Is it . . . is it just delicious?" It was delicious! So profoundly delicious that Genieva thought she might never quench her thirst for it!

"Genieva!" her mother screeched once more. "Stop that at once! Such behavior . . . and in front of your sweet, innocent sister! For pity's sake, cover your eyes, Maureen."

The piercing sound of her mother's dramatics intruded upon the luscious kiss. Genieva pulled her lips from Brevan's, feeling ashamed somehow for having reveled in his kiss so deeply. She guiltily cast her gaze downward, feeling her mother's disapproving stare from across the room. Yet Brevan took her chin firmly in one hand, raising her face toward his. His piercing gaze was fixated on hers—though he spoke to her mother.

"Ya'll be excusin' me, Mrs. Bankmans . . . but I wasn't finished kissin' me wife," he rather growled. With one last lingering, fiercely applied kiss, he rendered Genieva weak and helpless once more. He released her, squinting a wink of triumph at her just before he turned away.

As she noted her mother's expression at having witnessed Brevan bare from the waist up, Genieva bit her lip to conceal the delighted grin begging to spread across her face. She stifled a giggle when Abigail began fanning herself rapidly with one hand—the other dramatically clutching her bosom.

"Such heathenism!" Abigail gasped.

Brevan only smiled as he moved past Genieva's mother, brushing her arm slightly with his bare chest as he went.

"Forgive me then, mother-in-law. As ya can see, I've me work to do, I have," he said.

"Evert! Oh, catch me, Evert," Abigail whimpered, swaying back and forth slightly.| "I'm going this time. I'm going!"

"Mercy on me, Abigail. Have mercy. He's simply a boy," Genieva's father sighed with ripe irritation.

"Ha!" Abigail exclaimed, fanning herself more rapidly, yet straightening. "That is no mere boy, Evert. And he's a beast to boot!"

"He seems to treat our daughter well, Abigail," her father corrected as he went to stand before Genieva. Taking both her hands in his, he said to her, "I forgive you, Genieva. It shall take me some time to accept this situation, perhaps . . . but I have forgiven you."

Genieva forced a smile—though she felt little like accepting his apology.

"Then . . . I forgive you, Father," she said.

"For what?" her father shouted with offended indignation. "I've done nothing to . . ."

"Mercy, Evert," her mother interrupted. "What's done is done. Let's get on with our lives. And let's get back to some semblance of civilization. Mercy," she sighed. "Squeaky beds, bare men, public displays of affection. I'm near to smothering in rural life." She fanned herself dramatically, and Genieva smiled. For all her petty ways, she loved her mother and ever found her theatrical reactions entertaining.

After Genieva had served her family a hearty farm-sized breakfast, she stood with Brevan on the front porch waving as Evert, Abigail, and Maureen Bankmans rode away in their rented wagon.

"We'll visit, Genieva," her father had promised. "We love you, and we want to visit again. Though not for long, mind you."

Maureen waved frantically from the wagon

as it lurched away, calling, "Write to me, Nieva!"

"I will. You, too," Genieva called in return. She was surprised by the small pang of regret she felt at seeing them leave—for she did love them—no matter how shallow they were.

"Don't lose complete sight of propriety, darling!" her mother called, waving the handkerchief she'd been using to dab at her eyes. "Remember, I raised you to be a lady."

Genieva nodded and waved.

Her mother began weeping profusely as Brevan called out, "Don't worry, Mother. I'll look after her, I will."

As Genieva watched the wagon move further and further away, a great and lonely anxiety began to settle in her bosom. Her family had found her—they had forgiven her, and they had gone. Things would return to their normal routine, and Brevan would no longer feel obligated to help create the illusion of a man and woman excessively in love.

"Well, it's off to the orchard, I am," Brevan said. He turned and began striding away.

Genieva resolutely folded her arms across her chest and ventured, "I thank you for that, Brevan."

He paused, turning to look at her. "For what are ya thankin' me, lass?"

Genieva looked away for a moment—struggling to control her emotions.

"F-for pretending," was all she could say. When

he only stood looking at her, she added, "I know it was a great sacrifice for you. Spending a night on the floor alone constitutes a gallant act . . . and your being wounded to boot. I-I just wanted to thank you. I had no right whatsoever to ask you to pretend . . ."

"Ya didn't ask me, lass," he interrupted. He returned to her, took her shoulders firmly in hand, and said, "They're lookin' back, Genieva. One last performance for yar mother this be." Genieva's heart swelled as his delicious kiss was hers one last time.

As he pulled her into his arms and against his powerful body, she relinquished all her resolve to resist him—entirely surrendered to the need to receive and respond to his masterful affections. His kiss was long, deep, and driven. When he released her, she stood weakened, shy, and unable to look at him.

"I'll be in for lunch at noon, Genieva," he said. He turned and left her then.

Turning to throw one final wave to her departing family, Genieva saw that the wagon was no longer in sight. In fact, her common sense told her it had most likely been some time since her father would've turned the wagon north. It would've been impossible for her family to have seen Brevan kissing her.

Quickly, she looked to Brevan. He paused, smiling victoriously. Arching one handsome brow, he chuckled before continuing toward the orchards. Genieva bit her lip, delighted as she realized the kiss they had only just shared had not been for her family's benefit.

As she went about her chores later in the day, Genieva found herself preoccupied with thinking on what had transpired over the last two days. She and Brevan had gone from lugging pail after endless pail of water to the plants to dancing in the rain. Brevan had been injured when Cruz had stabbed him. Genieva's family had found her, and things had been somewhat mended between them all. Furthermore, she had spent a night in the same room with Brevan and been favored with his affections. She shook her head, wondering in that moment at the drastic change of venue her life had taken. If only Brevan could truly care for her, she knew she would be the happiest woman alive.

Genieva glanced up—watched a wagon pull up in front of the house. She recognized Mrs. Wilburn as the woman nearly leapt down from it.

Running up the front porch steps, Mrs. Wilburn cried, "Is anyone home? Mr. McLean? Are you there?" Genieva set the bag of chicken feed down on top of a barrel sitting nearby and hurried toward the house. She stepped up behind Mrs. Wilburn in time to see Brevan answer the door as he stuffed a piece of bread and jam into his mouth.

"Mrs. Wilburn?" he greeted, his voice muffled by the food he fought to chew and swallow quickly.

"Oh, Mr. McLean!" the woman began. Genieva could see she was frantic—for her face was tear-stained, and her hands mercilessly wrung her apron. "I'm sorry to bother you . . . but is . . . is Mrs. McLean . . . your brother's wife . . . would she happen to be here with you?"

"Lita?" Brevan asked. "No. I've no notion as to where she is if she's not at her house."

"What is it?" Genieva asked, stepping up onto the porch. Mrs. Wilburn whirled about to meet her.

"It's my Amy," she stammered, tears spilling from her eyes. "Her time has come, and we're all alone, you know. I was hopin' that Mrs. McLean would come home with me and help us."

Genieva smiled at the distraught woman. "I'll come with you. Just let me grab a few things. Don't worry."

The woman's relieved smile was pitiful somehow. Genieva knew Mrs. Wilburn was frightened and alone.

"I'll wait for you out here," Mrs. Wilburn said, going back to the wagon. "Thank you, Mr. McLean," she added nervously.

Genieva pushed by Brevan as she entered the

house, but he caught her arm and turned her to face him. "Ya've got yar responsibilities here, ya have," he growled.

"Have some compassion, Brevan," Genieva scolded.

He followed her into her bedroom as she removed her apron and asked, "Why would she be lookin' for Lita's help anyway?"

"Lita's a compassionate woman. She probably felt she could trust Lita to help her," Genieva answered.

"There's somethin' ya're keepin' from me, lass. What is it?"

Genieva did not turn to face him—for she feared he would see the guilt on her face—the profound guilt washing over her at not having told him the entire truth about the day in the orchard with Cruz, Lita, and Joaquin. Furthermore, she had told him nothing whatsoever about her more recent encounter with Cruz.

As the guilt of withholding the truth from him continued to gnaw at her heart, she mumbled, "I have to hurry, Brevan. The girl must be terribly frightened." Quickly Genieva turned, pushing past him once more. Brevan caught her by the shoulders and stayed her, however.

"Tell me what it is, Genieva. I'll not let ya go to that lass 'til I know why ya pity her so."

"I pity her because she's a poor young girl who may not be at any fault in finding herself in this condition," Genieva explained. She felt tears welling in her eyes.

"What do ya mean? Of course she's at least at some fault of it."

"I-I don't think so," Genieva mumbled, looking away from him.

"Tell it to me now, Genieva. What is it ya're not wantin' me to know? I'll not let ya go to her until ya've told me the truth of it."

Genieva looked up into Brevan's angry expression. He would be furious, she knew—furious at her for withholding the truth from him and furious at the truth itself. "You won't let me go anyway when I tell you."

"Tell it now, Genieva. That lass is waitin' for yar help. I promise I'll let ya go no matter what ya reveal to me now."

Swallowing hard, she whispered, "Amy's . . . Amy's . . . it's Cruz Archuleta's baby, Brevan."

Brevan's hands slid from Genieva's shoulder. He looked at her in horrified disbelief. "And ya think he . . ."

"Don't speak of it aloud, Brevan," Genieva cried, covering his mouth with her hands. "I can't bear to think of it, let alone hear it said." She could not tell him more of Cruz. She could never tell him that Cruz had struck her, thrown Lita to the ground, and threatened them both—she could not tell him of his lecherous threats to her on the path home from Brian's house. In that moment, she realized for certain that Brevan would see reason then to go looking for a fight with Cruz Archuleta. And Cruz would win, because he was a coward and would not meet Brevan alone.

"B-but Lita says Joaquin has feelings for the Wilburn lass," Brevan whispered.

"He does. Cruz Archuleta is a monster! Now let me go to her. You promised me," Genieva cried. She turned, running out the door—wiping tears of fear, anger, and frustration from her cheeks.

The sun had gone down hours before as Genieva bathed the new baby in the warmed water at the sink in the Wilburn kitchen. It was a healthy and very large, squirming boy she held in her arms as she walked back into Amy's bedroom to give the infant to its mother.

"What will you name him, Amy?" Genieva asked as she handed the bundle to the tired girl lying in the bed.

"Marcus," Amy whispered in a reply. "He was my brother who was lost as a baby."

"Your husband is here, Mrs. McLean," Mrs. Wilburn announced softly from the doorway. As Genieva turned and began to leave, Mrs. Wilburn caught her hands. As tears filled her eyes, she whispered, "Thank you, Genieva. Thank you for your pity on us."

Genieva swallowed the hard lump of pity in her throat and said, "You should let people know that Amy was guiltless in this matter, Mrs. Wilburn."

The woman only looked away, shaking her head.

"They would never believe me," she said. "People like to think the worst. They like to have the hushed gossip sessions and point their fingers at someone's problems . . . problems more obvious than their own."

Genieva nodded, for she knew the woman was right. As she entered the kitchen, she saw Brevan standing with his back to her, looking out into the night through the open door. He turned when Mrs. Wilburn cleared her throat, and his eyes seemed to bore directly into Genieva's soul.

"Will ya be needin' anythin' further, Mrs. Wilburn?" he asked. "Before I'm takin' Genieva home? Can I do anythin' for ya then?"

Mrs. Wilburn shook her head and put a tired hand to her forehead. "You've been kind to let her come, Mr. McLean. I know you must resent us for . . . for people accusing you of . . . but I want you to know that we never implied . . ."

"I know that, ma'am. I'm holdin' no grudge. I just know me wife is tired and needs to be home restin'."

"Yes, of course. Thank you both."

Brevan helped Genieva into the wagon before climbing up next to her. "It's near to midnight, lass," he scolded. "I was wonderin' when to come and get ya. Ya never said how long ya'd be."

"One never knows how long this will take, Brevan," Genieva sighed. She was so tired. The past twelve or more hours had drained her both physically and emotionally. It was no easy thing to watch a woman endure the pain of bearing a child. She closed her eyes for a moment, inhaling deeply of the fresh night air.

Just as Brevan readied to urge the team onward, a man on horseback emerged from the darkness. Genieva gasped as she recognized Joaquin. She looked to Brevan, whose chest immediately began to rise and fall with the labored breathing of barely restrained fury. Quickly, she put a hand on his thigh and squeezed hard enough that his attention was drawn to her instead.

"Judge not, Brevan," she whispered.

"What are ya wantin' here?" Brevan growled, looking to Joaquin once more.

"I've been waiting out here every night for a week to make sure things went well when . . . when . . ." Joaquin stammered.

"Things are fine," Genieva told him. "Amy is fine . . . and the baby."

Joaquin shook his head sorrowfully.

"Ya're more of a man than I, Joaquin," Brevan growled. "Or less of it . . . for I'd have killed a man for less than what yar brother did here."

The deep brown of Joaquin's eyes narrowed as he glared at Brevan and said, "Even if it was your hermano . . . your brother that did it?"

Brevan looked to Genieva for a moment—his eyes burning with fury as he answered Joaquin's question. "I fear that I would. Even if it was me own brother." He snapped the lines, sending the team bolting past Joaquin.

"He has a kind heart, Brevan," Genieva said when they'd nearly reached their own home. "He's torn. Torn between family and himself."

"Makes no difference, Genieva. He knows right from wrong. He should do right and leave the wrong behind him, family or not," Brevan growled. "Lita has done as much."

Lita, Lita, Lita! It seemed everyone was forever praising Lita! She was a good woman—a good, kind, and beautiful woman—but Genieva was tired, and her temper was about to get the best of her once more.

"Oh, that reminds me," she began casually as Brevan helped her down from the wagon. "Juan Miguel thinks that you fathered Lita's baby. And I think that's the only reason you're still alive. For . . . although Juan Miguel means only to intimidate you . . . Cruz means to do otherwise."

"What?" Brevan roared.

"Yes. It was yesterday morning that I found out. But with my family showing up on the door-step and this going on . . . I completely forgot to mention it to you," she said sassily. She stomped off toward the house then. When she entered it, she turned to look back at him, and the great

256

weight of the guilt she felt collided with her heart as she saw the look on his face. Brevan stood shaking his head—an expression of ignorant disbelief on his handsome face.

"Why?" he asked, looking to her. "Why is it that everyone brands me with bein' unchaste? Brands me with corruptin' and carousin'. And now . . . now . . ." He shook his head and chuckled—unable to comprehend it all.

"Lita fears for you, Brevan. It's why she won't speak to her father of the truth," Genieva said, going to stand before him.

"And Brian?" he asked. "Does he agree with her method of protectin' me?"

"H-he didn't know until I did. But it's kept him safe as well, for Juan Miguel . . . or rather Cruz . . . for I believe it is Cruz that means you harm . . . he's confused as to which of you to destroy first," Genieva explained.

"Ya've kept all this from me? Ya've known about Amy Wilburn? Lita lettin' her family think . . . about Juan Miguel and Cruz? And ya've not told me a shred of it until now? Why do ya find it necessary to lie to me, Genieva?" he shouted at her.

"I've not lied to you. I've simply not told you things. And you've done the same to me! What do you expect when you've done the same to me?" she cried. "Do unto others . . ."

"Oh, don't be throwin' the scriptures at me, lass! It's well I know them."

Genieva could only stare at Brevan as he groaned—then began to laugh. "I've done nothin'!" he shouted at the stars, putting an angry fist to his forehead. "I've done nothin' to provoke any of this! I simply live on this earth!" He strode to Genieva, took her shoulders in his powerful hands as he chuckled with disbelief. "Nothin'! I've done nothin'. Ya tell me what I've done to earn this!" Frowning, he shouted, "Why is this all comin' down on me own head? The Archuleta family thirstin' for me blood to be spilled on the ground? Why? The entire town blamin' me for poor Amy Wilburn? Why? And now this. Lita usin' a lie to keep me and Brian safe? Why would she do a thing like that? Ya tell that to me, lass!"

"Because she loves you, Brevan!" Genieva cried in a whisper. "Everyone loves you, and they don't want to see you harmed. Brian either! They would, any one of them, Brenna, Travis, Brian, Lita . . . they would do anything to protect you! So would I! Don't you see? You've always been the protector. You don't recognize it when the danger is aimed in your direction."

Brevan released her. He straightened his shoulders—a gesture of defiance.

"I am their protector and yars . . . as well as me own. I won't hide behind Lita's apron. She'll tell her father and brothers the truth of it . . . or I will. She'll tell them the truth and remove Brian and herself from danger, she will. Cruz will

258

find that I am not so easily exterminated." He paused, still glaring, but looking toward the barn now as he spoke. "Now, off to bed, Genieva. Ya've got a long day ahead of ya."

Not knowing what else to do, Genieva turned from him and did as she was told.

Moments after laying her tear-streaked face against her pillow, however, she heard something—a noise from outside. Quietly, she rose from her bed and walked to her window, peering out into the darkness. Click. Click. Click. It sounded like something striking metal, and as she strained her eyes through the dark, she could see Brevan sitting on the ground, his back against the barn. Click. Click. Click. She watched as Brevan picked up several pebbles lying about on the ground around him—tossing each one at the metal band of the rain barrel sitting some distance away. Click. Click. Click. Genieva crept back into her bed. Several minutes later, the noise stopped, and she heard Brevan enter the house. She heard the pump at the sink, the scrape of a chair leg on the floor, and then the heavy tread of his boots as he started down the hallway.

Opening one eye ever so slightly, she peered through her long eyelashes—watched as he stopped in her doorway. He stood still, seeming to study her for a moment. She struggled in keeping her breathing slow—appearing to be asleep. He simply stood there.

Why didn't he go? she wondered. He reached back and took hold of his shirt, stripping it off over his head. Still, he stood looking at her. *Please,* she silently pleaded with him. *Please just go to bed!* Her heart began to hammer as he walked forward and hunkered down at the side of her bed, staring directly into her face.

"Ya're wide awake, ya are," he whispered. "Open yar eyes and look at me, Genieva." With a heavy sigh, she did as he demanded. "I'm sorry," he said as she stared at him. "I should've told ya meself the truth about Lita and her family. I should not have kept it from ya so long."

Genieva swallowed, searching for the courage to speak. "It's all right. I understand," she whispered.

"And ya shouldn't have kept yar knowledge from me either. Am I right?" he asked.

"You *are* right," she agreed. Sensing his next question—for it was as if she could hear his thoughts before his lips spoke them—she held her breath.

"Have ya anythin' else that needs confessin', lass? Let's hang our laundry out for each other here and now. I'm askin' ya . . . with a promise that I won't act on anythin' ya don't think I should."

Genieva's heart beat so furiously she felt it might leap from her chest and into the open air at any moment. She couldn't lie to him. She couldn't keep the truth from him any longer, and she knew it had been wrong to do so in the first place. Now it would be worse—for she knew his anger would be all the more stoked when he learned she'd withheld the knowledge of her experiences from him. Still, only the truth would serve her now.

Genieva sat up and drew her knees to her chest. She swallowed the hard lump of trepidation in her throat and began, "In the orchard . . . the day Lita and I talked with Joaquin . . ." Brevan closed his eyes for a moment, inhaling deeply to ready himself. "Cruz was there first. He came upon Lita and me as we were walking. He was so rough with her, and I was frightened for her. H-he . . . grabbed me by the hair and tried to . . ." As Brevan suddenly jumped to his feet, she reached out, taking hold of his hand to stay him. "Lita interfered, and he threw her down. It angered me so that I said some things to him and provoked him, and . . . and . . . I didn't fall in the woodpile that day, Brevan. Cruz struck me because I spit in his face."

"He struck ya?" Brevan shouted, pulling his hand from hers. "He dared to touch ya . . . to lay a hand of violence against ya?" His eyes were blazing with fury. "I'll kill the devil, and I'll not wait another moment!"

Frantic, Genieva reached out, taking hold of his arm as firmly as she could to stop him—for she knew he meant to kill Cruz. "Wait, Brevan! Don't. You promised me," Genieva reminded.

"You've kept somethin' the like of this from me, Genieva? Why? Why would ya keep this from me?" he demanded.

"He wanted me to tell you! He wanted to draw you out . . . to make you mad so that you'd confront him so he could . . ."

"Draw me into a trap and be rid of me like I was a skunk in his cabbage?" he finished.

Genieva could only nod. "It will all come together horribly one day, Brevan. Juan Miguel is greedy, and he wants this land. I believe . . . though he meant at the time to sacrifice her . . . I believe he wants Lita back as well." Throwing aside her covers, she stood before Brevan as he simply dropped his head for a moment and sighed. "And . . . and . . ." she stammered.

Looking to her once more, an expression of extreme dread on his face, he prodded, "There's more ya haven't told me, isn't there, lass?"

"Coming home from Brian and Lita's," Genieva began, "the day my family arrived, I was coming home along the path, and . . . and Cruz . . ." Her words were lost as a flame of anger leapt again to Brevan's eyes.

"Come now, Genieva. Let it all be told," he growled.

"Cruz . . . he threatened me. He thinks that Lita and Brian's baby is yours, and he threatened to . . .

oh, Brevan!" she cried then, burying her face in her hands. "He's done no less to poor Amy Wilburn than he intended to do to me!" Looking up at him, shame washing over her for not having told him the truth at once, she added, "If it had not been for Joaquin's intervention . . . I don't know if I could've . . ."

Genieva gasped—covered her ears with her trembling hands as Brevan reached over, then, picking up the washbasin sitting on a table nearby. Raising the basin above his head, he threw it to the floor. The sound of the porcelain shattering as it hit the floor was deafening, and tears burst from Genieva's eyes. Finally, she found the courage to look up into his angry and tortured expression. Brevan was looking about, as if searching for some other poor thing to smash.

"I'm sorry, Brevan," Genieva sobbed. "I know I should've told you right away. B-but . . . it's what Cruz wants, and I don't want you hurt. I thought it better to keep silent. Everyone told me I should and . . ."

"Who?" he shouted. "Who told ya to keep the truth from me, Genieva?"

"Lita. Lita and Joaquin . . . for they both know what Cruz is capable of and don't want to see you . . ."

"I'm no slinkin' slug, Genieva. I'll not stand here and let Cruz get away with . . ."

"You promised me, Brevan!" Genieva cried,

taking hold of his powerful arm once more. "You promised me that you wouldn't act if I didn't think you should. Remember, you promised me!"

Brevan's chest rose and fell with his angered breathing as he glared down at her. "Cruz Archuleta has dared to touch ya . . . to harm ya and to think of . . . how can I let that go, Genieva? It's a man I am! Not a weasel! I can't just . . ."

"You can. You promised me. If you break your promise to me now . . . how will I ever find the courage to tell you things I should in the future? Promise me you won't act like a madman, Brevan. Promise." Genieva released his arm— let her eyes plead with them.

Brevan gazed into the stormy blue of Genieva's eyes—the blue telling him her soul was grieving. As he gazed into their pleading color, visions of Cruz Archuleta laying his hands on her flashed in his mind. How could he stand firm? How could he not act? But he had promised the lass. He had promised, and he would not damage her trust in him.

With an angry, defeated sigh, he growled, " 'Tis tired I am. More tired than I've ever been. I promised not to act on whatever it was ya were to tell me, lass. And though me mind and heart and soul tell me to mount me horse and hunt the blackguard and his family down . . . I'll wait. No doubt he'll come for me soon enough. But ya must promise me, Genieva . . . never to keep a thing from me again."

Genieva nodded. "I won't. I promise it to you," she whispered. She wondered—should she tell him? Should she tell him now, as he stood, tired from work and life—should she tell him she had fallen in love with him—that he was life to her— that without him she would shrivel up and die? Without Brevan, Genieva knew she would become nothing—die for lack of his sunshine smile—his precious scent—his quenching kiss.

"All right then. We'll both to bed. It's behind in me chores, I am. And I need yar help more tomorrow since ya were gone today. I'll be up all the earlier in the mornin' . . . for I need to visit with me brother first thing."

Brevan turned, storming out of the room. When he'd gone, and she heard the violent slam of his bedroom door, Genieva let the tears run freely down her cheeks. The tears were not accompanied by loud sobbing but simply streamed profusely in silence as her mind accepted that Brevan would be in more danger than ever now. She knew he meant to visit Brian the following morning in order that he might tell Lita to speak to her family concerning her baby. Then Cruz would have no reason to dally about going after Brevan finally—and fatally.

Chapter Eleven

Strangely, as the summer weeks wore on, Genieva began to worry a bit less with each passing day. Not only was Brevan safe and unharmed by mid-August but there had been no more threats from the Archuletas. Genieva had seen Cruz several times, just beyond the orchards, but he had never approached her or Brevan. She wondered at the reason—for she knew how completely he hated Brevan and how carnally he felt toward her. Yet he stayed at a distance, and she could only assume his father had forbidden him to interfere with them again. She surmised Joaquin must've indeed been wrong about his brother. Cruz must still hold some respect for his father's wishes. It could be the only explanation.

Joaquin had made some peace with himself as well. Genieva saw him several times during her occasional visits to check on Mrs. Wilburn, Amy, and baby Marcus. Mrs. Wilburn seemed to have eased some of the inner pain once so apparent on her features before the baby had been born. Amy was radiant—seemed hopeful once again.

Lita and Brenna both anticipated the arrival of their babies. Even though a great sadness would sometimes overwhelm Genieva in wondering whether she would ever bear children of her own, she harbored a great happiness for each of them.

Genieva had never known work as hard as harvesting the corn had been. She'd never imagined what the growers went through to produce the fine ears of yellow sweetness the kitchen help had bought at the markets. She'd always simply eaten it and never given a thought to where it came from—until now.

Harvesting the corn took insight, hard work, and a bit of luck. She had been so fearful in early summer—wondering whether or not Brevan's crops would live through the lack of moisture. She'd prayed daily for rain, and when it had come at last, it was the most beautiful sight, sound, and scent on earth. Still, the two days the corn sat in piles after being harvested were the most unnerving. Brevan had explained that were the rains to come before he got the crop sheltered or preferably to town to sell, the entire crop would be lost because of the rain, and not for lack of it.

"How can you stand it? How can we keep from losing our minds over worry?" she had asked him at dinner the night before he would take the corn to town.

Brevan shrugged as he took an overly large bite of mashed potatoes. "I don't know," he mumbled with his mouth full. "Ya can't be worryin' yarself sick, Genieva. If we lose the crop . . . we'll go from there. But we won't lose it . . . I know."

"The clouds are dark and thick tonight, Brevan. It may rain," she commented. She, for one, was nearly ill with worry. It was funny though—she didn't worry about the loss of profit should they lose the corn—she was worried because she feared it would harmfully affect Brevan.

"It won't be rainin' tonight, lass. I promise ya that," he said. Wiping his mouth, he pushed his chair back from the table. "To bed with ya now, Genieva. We go to town early in the mornin'." He left the house to check on the stock then, and she was alone.

Genieva was tired. Her body was tired, and her mind was tired. She fancied even her very soul was tired. The thought entered her mind that she wished she were heavy with expecting a child. Then she wouldn't have to work so hard. She envied Lita in that moment, and not only because her condition confined her from such hard work. Lita and Brenna didn't work as hard as Genieva did anyway. Well, at least not at the same chores. They sewed and mended, washed and cleaned house. They canned the food ripening in the garden and entertained their tired husbands with interesting conversation and affectionate flirting. Genieva envied their callings in life compared with her own. As she sat, rather depressed, her hands came to rest across her belly as they often did. As often was the consequence, her mind rushed back to the moments weeks before when

268

Brevan had held her tightly against his strong form. She thought of him pressing his own hand to her tummy—implying to her father that she carried his child. So many times since then she had wished it were true. She could think of no greater joy than to have a baby of her own—a baby who was part of Brevan. At least a part of him would love her then—and she would have something to rain her own love on.

Shaking her head to dispel thoughts of the impossible, Genieva rose from the table. After having washed the dishes, she retired to her bed.

Upon awaking the next morning, she was unable to remember having changed to her night-dress—for the extremeness of her fatigue the night before had been unparalleled.

As the team of horses labored to pull the large, heavy wagon laden with corn, Genieva covered her mouth as she yawned. The sunrise was indeed beautiful that morning—pinks and blues rivaling heaven itself.

"Clear and lovely skies we have this mornin', lass," Brevan said, inhaling deeply of the fresh morning air. "I'm glad ya chose to come to town with me, Genieva. It will do ya good to get away. And we'll get a good price for this corn, I know. 'Tis some of the best I've ever seen! And it's due to the diligence of the planter," he chuckled, winking at her. Genieva smiled, too—dazzled by his happy countenance and profound good looks. His undue cheerfulness left Genieva feeling deliciously warm inside.

She still felt tired, and her arms still ached from the harvesting two days earlier. Still, as they rode on, Brevan seeming to talk endlessly about the upcoming apple harvest and how plentiful the apples would be, Genieva's own discomforts were lost amid her attention to his charming ways.

"Ya see, 'tis a good life out here, it is," he said just before they entered town. "Ya're not lackin' for anythin' ya left back in Chicago, now are ya?"

"No," Genieva admitted. She had left no great love of her life back in Chicago. The love of her life was here—sitting next to her—traveling into town to sell his corn. No, she lacked nothing— missed nothing of Chicago. At least here she was in love—whether or not it was returned upon her.

Helping her down from the wagon, Brevan grinned.

"There now, lass. You go on into the store and pick up whatever it is ya're needin'. I'll be back within thirty minutes with a bundle of cash the like ya've never seen!" With a quick wink, he leapt back into his seat and urged the team on.

"Genieva!" Mrs. Fenton cried, nearly flying from the store and out to meet Genieva. "How wonderful to have you for a visit! I was telling Mary Clawson just yesterday . . . I said, 'Mary, you mark my words . . . Brevan McLean will be in town before the week's end with the best load of sweet corn of the year!' And I hoped you would come! It's been so long since you've been in for a visit." Putting a friendly arm around Genieva's waist, she led her into the store. "How's Lita? She should be about ready to burst by now."

Genieva giggled and nodded. "Yes, I think she's quite ready for the baby to come, Lilly. The summer heat has been very hard on her." ·

"Brenna was in . . . oh, maybe two weeks back. She's looking healthy and rosy with her baby on the way, too."

"Yes. It's so fun to have two babies to look forward to in the family." Genieva braced herself—for she sensed what was next.

"Well, just think of all the more fun it would be to have three on the way, eh?" Lilly Fenton winked slyly at Genieva. Genieva only smiled sweetly. She released the woman, going to stand before the bolts of fabric on a table just inside the store. "Patience, my dear, patience. Your day will come." Genieva closed her eyes for a moment, nearly unable to endure the powerful aching in her heart.

"We're completely out of cinnamon, Lilly. Nutmeg too. I hope you have some in," Genieva said, redirecting the conversation.

"Oh my, yes! Plenty, Genieva. Plenty. What else, dear?"

"I've a list. Just let me . . ." Genieva fumbled

271

around in her handbag for her list. She looked up as she heard Amy Wilburn squeal in delight.

"Genieva! Hello!" Amy greeted happily.

"Amy!" Genieva exclaimed, drawing her list from her bag as the girl approached. "You look wonderful. And look at Marcus!" Genieva could not believe how the baby had grown. "He's ready for school nearly!"

"He has grown, hasn't he?" Amy said, holding the baby up proudly for Genieva to see. "Mother," the girl called over her shoulder, "it's Genieva. She's in town."

Mrs. Wilburn entered the store—her face lighting up at seeing Genieva. "Mrs. McLean! It's been some time since I've seen you in town."

"Yes," Genieva admitted. "We've been so busy . . . the corn crop and everything."

"The man works you like a mule, I hear," Jenny Evans intruded as she too entered the store.

Genieva's heart sank instantly. She could tell by the irritated expressions on Amy's and her mother's faces that they were not pleased either.

"Brevan and I work together on the farm, Jenny. Someday, when you eventually marry, you'll understand that more completely," Genieva told the snip, flashing a false, but very friendly looking smile.

Mrs. Fenton was unable to entirely suppress her snicker, and Jenny's glare shot daggers at the woman. "Mother has a list for you to fill, Mrs.

Fenton," Jenny announced, holding out a piece of paper to the woman.

"As soon as I've finished filling Mrs. McLean's, Jenny," Lilly told her, taking Genieva's list from her hand.

Genieva was surprised when Amy suddenly leaned forward and whispered, "Joaquin has been to call three evenings this week, Genieva."

Genieva's eyes widened with delight. "How wonderful, Amy," she whispered in response. "Does he . . . does he like little Marcus?" she asked in a tentative whisper.

"I think so," Amy beamed. "I think he's forgiven me . . ."

"He had nothing to forgive you for, Amy," Genieva reminded.

Amy nodded. "I think . . . I think he's found his peace. He blamed himself, you see, Genieva."

Yes. Genieva understood. Joaquin had felt as if he had failed his Amy in not having been able to protect her. Perhaps that was one reason he had been at hand to protect Genieva when she needed protection. Joaquin knew Cruz's intentions toward Brevan and toward Genieva. No doubt Joaquin had promised not to let any other young woman suffer the same fate as Amy.

"I hear the McLeans are just bursting with expectant mothers," Jenny interrupted. Genieva looked to her. It was obvious the girl was miffed at being excluded from the conversation.

"Yes. We're growing in generations," Genieva replied.

"And how does Brevan feel about your inability to provide him with a son . . . to further the McLean name?"

Amy's and Mrs. Wilburn's mouths both gaped open in astonishment as Mrs. Fenton erupted, "You do beat all, Jennifer Evans. What a question! To utter such a thing in public . . . I can't believe what flies off that sharp tongue of yours sometimes."

"Come now, Mrs. Fenton. Would you pretend that you haven't already asked her the same thing?"

"I most certainly did not, and if you had any manners at all . . ."

"Brevan does not beat me because I am not expectant, Jenny, if that's what you mean," Genieva said calmly—though her stomach burned with angered indignation at such a question. "I know that because you could never capture his attentions, you like to imagine he is some frightening, merciless brute. But he is far from it and is a great deal more patient than most men, I assure you."

Snatching the list from Jenny's hand, Mrs. Fenton said, "On second thought, I think I will attend to your list first. Then you can be on your way."

Jenny smiled malignantly and went to look at

the few pieces of jewelry on display in a nearby curio cabinet.

"She's unbelievable," Amy whispered.

"Pay her no mind, Genieva," Mrs. Wilburn added. "She's just insanely jealous. She used to chase Brevan around like a motherless kitten."

Genieva nodded, but it was still taking every ounce of control she had not to simply slap the snip hard across the face. It was as if the young woman sensed Genieva's thoughts were often occupied with despairing in the knowledge of being childless.

"Ah, look at the lovely ladies about today!" Brevan flattered as he stepped into the store. Genieva was awash with relief at the sight of the handsome man before her. "Mrs. Wilburn, hello," he greeted, shaking the woman's hand. "And Amy and the little laddie," he said, shaking Amy's. "My dear Mrs. Fenton," he greeted, going to the woman and bowing low. "And even Miss Jennifer Evans," and he shook her hand as well. Genieva was astounded at the obvious blush blazoned across Jenny's face as she smiled up at him. "I've a few things to add to me wife's list, I do, Mrs. Fenton," Brevan announced as he leaned casually on the counter. Mrs. Fenton handed Genieva's list to him, and, taking a pencil from the woman's ear, he scribbled quickly on the paper. Then, turning to Genieva, he raised an eyebrow and smiled as he walked slowly to her. "I told ya, I did. Ya remember that I told ya I'd be sellin' that corn for a good price, Genieva?"

"Yes. You did tell me, and I never doubted you," Genieva agreed.

"Well, my plum . . . ya've no idea!" He took her hands, holding them tightly against his chest. "It's the harvestin' time of year, lass, and it's me favorite."

"I'm fast realizing that," she said. Oh, it was truly magnificent to feel his hands holding her own. Brevan cocked his head slightly—his eyebrows drawing together in a curious frown. "Ya're not yarself," he said in a lowered voice.

"I'm fine," Genieva assured him—unconvincingly. She couldn't help but quickly glance past him at Jenny—Jenny who stood watching them. She knew Jenny would only be reassured at seeing Brevan and Genieva together. She knew she would see through their farce. Yet she didn't see Mrs. Wilburn indicate to Brevan with a nod in Jenny's direction that Jenny was the cause of his wife's discomfort.

Brevan started to turn and look in the direction Mrs. Wilburn nodded. He stopped, however, remembering then that Jenny Evans stood behind him. With an instant understanding of the situation, he pitied Genieva, knowing full well Jenny Evans must've been taunting his young wife somehow. It angered him—infuriated him.

The little banshee! Jenny had endlessly hounded him before he'd married Genieva. In fact, the complete and unwanted attention he had received from the girl had often kept him from town in the past. Apparently, she'd now turned to irritating his wife. He would not stand for it! Not today.

"Ya're a liar, Genieva McLean," he said. Turning to Jenny and Mrs. Fenton, he added, "But don't ya worry, Lilly . . . Jenny. I know how to make her day bright and beautiful once more." Genieva gasped, caught completely unaware as Brevan suddenly pulled her snugly against him, wrapping her securely in his powerful arms. "Pucker up, me lassie. I've far too much excitement in me today to leave ya be for long." Genieva's senses were completely lost—lost to Brevan's delicious kiss. His kiss was firm, thorough, and she realized it had been far too long since she had reveled in the feel and taste of it.

Her heavenly euphoria was interrupted, however, when Jenny exclaimed from behind Brevan, "Well, what public indecency!" Putting a small hand to Brevan's roughly shaven cheek, Genieva attempted to break their kiss. Still, he only released her long enough to push her hand away from his face as he continued in his endeavor. "If I wanted to witness this kind of lewd behavior . . . I'd loiter in the saloon where it should be kept," Jenny spat.

Brevan broke from Genieva, shaking his head with satisfaction. Moistening his lips as if having just enjoyed some delicious dessert, he turned to Jenny and said, "You'll find nothin' in the saloon the likes of what's between Genieva and me, Miss Evans. But if ya're more comfortable in that atmosphere over there . . . well then . . ."

"I'll be back later for my mother's order, Mrs. Fenton!" Jenny spat. "The air is far too stifling in here at this moment." With a face crimson with humiliation and anger, the girl stormed out of the store.

As soon as she was out of distance to hear what was said, Mrs. Fenton, Amy, and her mother broke into peels of giggles. Genieva looked to Brevan, seeing his smile fade as he turned from her and walked toward the door.

"That girl gives me a pain in me stomach," he mumbled. Then to Mrs. Fenton he added, "I'll be back to collect the items on that list, I will. And me wife along with them, Lilly." Without another word or glance to Genieva, he left.

"How do!" Mrs. Fenton exclaimed. "That husband of yours, dear! He doesn't take anybody's guff!"

"Now I've ruined his happy day," Genieva mumbled as she watched him stride across the street to the blacksmith's building.

"What are you going on about?" Mrs. Fenton asked, coming to stand beside Genieva.

Genieva watched as Brevan stood across the street speaking with Mr. Clawson. "Did you see his face when he came in here, Lilly? The happiest I've seen him since the rains came in July," she said.

"He was as giddy as all get out, wasn't he?" Lilly agreed.

"And look at him now. He's irritated. Completely," Genieva pointed out.

"Well . . . yes. But by her . . . not anything you did," Mrs. Fenton assured her.

"Come on," Amy offered, tugging at Genieva's sleeve. "Let's you and I go for a little walk while Mrs. Fenton gets your things together."

"No, I . . ." Genieva began.

"It will do you good. Fresh air always brightens the mood after a minute spent in the company of Jenny Evans."

As Amy talked of her baby and Joaquin, Genieva tried to listen. Yet her mind, in all honesty, was still back in the store—in Brevan's arms. As she thought over the incident, she did begin to feel better, for in an odd way Brevan had championed her—come to her rescue. He must've somehow sensed the tension Genieva felt in Jenny's presence, and he'd dispelled any doubt the irritating young woman might have concerning the sincerity of their relationship.

"You're right, Amy," she said when Amy finally drew a breath and paused in her babble. "I do feel better."

"Good. I told you. We're almost back to the store, and look . . . Brevan's loading your things into the wagon already," Amy observed.

Yet as Genieva looked in the direction of the wagon, she gasped when Cruz Archuleta suddenly appeared before her. He had simply stepped out of the alley and into their path. Genieva looked quickly to Amy, who clutched the baby tightly to her bosom, hatefully glaring at the man.

"Hola, señora, señorita" he greeted, boasting a broad and sickening smile. "My two favorite ladies."

"Move aside, sir," Genieva demanded, attempting to appear calm.

Cruz chuckled, amused at her boldness. "I move aside for no one," he reminded her.

"You'll move aside for us or regret it for the rest of your life," Genieva stated. She wanted to scream, to cry out for Brevan's help. Yet she remained outwardly unruffled—for she suspected screaming was what Cruz wanted. She would not endanger her husband. She only hoped she could remove Cruz from their presence before Brevan came out of the store once more.

"Do not threaten me, mí amor," Cruz growled. Reaching out, he grasped Genieva's chin tightly in one hand. "I no fear you or your ugly husband."

"You are afraid of him. That's why you try to frighten me instead of threatening him face to face. You're nothing but a coward." She pushed his hand from her face and stood glaring up at him. Genieva sensed Amy could only watch in terrorized bewilderment. She was too frightened to act on her own and go for help. "Now, let us pass."

Cruz shrugged and moved to one side, motioning for Amy to move on. Amy moved past him, hurrying to the store. Yet as Genieva made to move past him, he caught her tightly—one arm around her neck and his hand over her mouth as he pulled her into the alley. Genieva tried to scream, but his hand was secure over her mouth, and he slammed her small frame against the outer wall of a building.

"I see why the idioto married you," Cruz growled—his face so close to Genieva's that the stench of his breath caused her stomach to churn. Wantonly, he chuckled. "You make a man loco . . . and I think it's time Brevan McLean shared his good luck with others." Genieva tried to struggle even harder, for she knew all too well what he intended. "It will be better for both of us if you do not cry out," he threatened as he released his fierce hold over her mouth. Still, the second he released her, she did cry out.

"Brevan!" she screamed only to feel the stinging pain as Cruz slapped her soundly across one cheek. It shocked her into silence for a moment— but only a moment, and she began her struggling anew. "Brevan!" she screamed again. Genieva moved her head from side to side as Cruz attempted to take hold of her mouth with his. When he took hold of her hair just above her forehead, slamming her head back against the wall, it sent pain and bright lights shooting every direction in her mind. Her head ached with the intense pain of the blow.

"Call for him again, and I'll rip the hair from your head," he growled.

A moment before his wet, stench-ridden kiss would've attacked her own pretty mouth, Genieva saw Brevan step up behind the man. Brevan took hold of Cruz's hair, causing the villain such surprise as to release his hold on Genieva. The moment she was free of him, Brevan, still gripping the degenerate's hair, pulled back powerfully, sending the man stumbling to the ground to land flat on his back.

"Brevan," Genieva breathed as she reached out for him. Her relief was short-lived, however, for Cruz rebounded instantly, reaching up and swiping Brevan's feet out from under him. The two men were rolling about on the ground, slamming each other's heads against whatever building, rock, or object was at hand—throwing already bloodied fists at each other's faces. Genieva screamed as Brevan dealt a particularly brutal blow to Cruz's head, and it did indeed seem to scatter his wits for a moment. It was long enough for Brevan to stand. His breathing was labored as he wiped the blood from his lip, glaring down at the devil at his feet.

"Get up, Cruz. Ándele," a voice ordered from the alley behind Brevan. Genieva turned. Three other men approached, and Genieva knew fear as she had never known it. She recognized only one of the men. He had been the man who had accompanied Cruz and Joaquin when she and Brevan had been watering the crops months earlier. She remembered Cruz referring to this man as his brother Mateo. The other two men were Mexican as well, and Genieva knew her worst fears were being realized—Cruz had used her to provoke Brevan into a trap.

Cruz chuckled as he slowly stood up. "Where will you run now, hombre?" he mocked.

Brevan turned to face Cruz once more, growling, "Why run from you? I'd have more reason to run from me grandmother." Swiftly, the sole of Brevan's large boot met squarely with Cruz's face, sending his arms flailing, and Cruz fell to the ground once more. As Brevan turned to face the other three men, Genieva knew he would not back down from them.

Panic began to burn within Genieva, and in desperation she stepped in front of him protectively. "Move aside, Genieva!" Brevan demanded, pushing her aside. She only stepped in front of him once more.

"Hide behind your wife's skirts, McLean. It won't stop us," the familiar-looking man threatened. As Genieva felt Brevan's hands on her shoulders, no doubt intending to move her again, she turned and fastened her arms tightly about his waist.

"Let me alone, Genieva!" Brevan commanded as he tried to detach his wife from his body.

"No!" she cried.

"Move the woman, McLean. She's in our way," the leader threatened.

"Genieva!" Brevan bellowed. "You'll not dare to touch her, Mateo!" Brevan's strength was a hundred times Genieva's, and he managed to detach her and push her aside just before Cruz's brother Mateo lunged at him with a knife.

Genieva saw Cruz was trying to stand. Quickly, she picked up a nearby board, hitting him solidly on the back of the head. He fell, dazed, and she ran into the street screaming, "Help me! Help!"

She saw Amy down the street talking to Mr. Clawson—pointing in her direction. Mr. Clawson dropped the large tool in his hand and started toward her. Two other men from a building across the street were nearing as well, and from her right she saw Joaquin intent on her as he ran toward her. Frantic, she turned back toward Brevan— saw him catch Mateo's wrist, halting the knife the villain held in midair. Brevan's knee met the man's waist, rendering him breathless, and Brevan sent him tumbling to the ground.

Mr. Clawson and the other two men began shouting as they hurried toward Genieva. Their angry threats caused enough intimidation to send the two remaining to retreating.

"Get up, Mateo," Cruz growled, raising himself to his hands and knees and spitting blood from his mouth. "You are only a coward if you lay there," he spat.

Genieva gasped as Cruz reached down and pulled a long knife from his boot. He stood, glaring at Brevan.

"Leave here, Cruz."

Genieva turned to see that it was Joaquin who had reached them first. "Go home, Mateo."

Cruz turned, spitting on the ground before his brother. "Joaquin," he panted. "Finish the Irish idioto," he ordered.

Genieva looked to Joaquin. Brevan was still standing, but had been badly beaten by the men. Joaquin was fresh, and should he choose finally to side with his family and attack Brevan . . .

"No. McLean has done nothing, Cruz. Papá is wrong . . . you are wrong to attack him," Joaquin said.

"Coward!" Cruz shouted. "When Papá hears of this, he will no longer call you son."

Genieva could see the obvious pain in Joaquin's eyes as he said, "Tell Juan Miguel that I no longer call him father. And I no longer call you hermano, Cruz." He looked to Mateo and urged, "Don't do this thing, Mateo. It is wrong."

Mateo spit on the ground ceremoniously and shouted, "Go away, you coward. Show your face no more on Archuleta lands."

"You Archuleta boys go home!" Mr. Clawson ordered as he came to stand beside Brevan. "You've caused enough trouble today." Cruz and Mateo walked past Brevan and down the alley. "And tell your father he's no longer welcome in my business!" Mr. Clawson called after them.

"I thank you, Ralph, for comin' to me aid," Brevan panted, shaking the man's hand. "Hoof, Tandy," he said, nodding his thanks at the other two men. Going to Joaquin, he offered his hand, and when the man took it tentatively, he assured him, "It was a hard thing to do, Joaquin. But it was the right thing, it was."

Joaquin nodded, and it was obvious that he was still uncertain of his choice. "Please," he began. "Please let me know when Lita's baby is come."

Brevan nodded and wiped at the blood that still trickled from the corner of his mouth. Then he turned his attention to Genieva, and she saw the anger in his eyes. "Never," he said, shaking an index finger at her. "Never interfere. Ya could've been hurt badly."

"You could've been killed badly," Genieva argued.

Mr. Clawson chuckled, and as he turned he said, "I'll leave this fight to you alone, McLean. And I wouldn't be as confident of victory if I were you."

Again Brevan wiped the blood from his mouth, wiping it carelessly on his trousers. "We'll discuss this further in private, we will," he muttered, taking Genieva's hand and pulling her toward the wagon, which still stood in front of the store.

Mrs. Fenton gasped when she saw Brevan's condition as he forcefully boosted Genieva up into the wagon. "Are you certain you are well, Brevan? The doctor is just around the corner and . . ."

"I'm fine, Lilly. Just need to get Genieva home now. I thank ya for everythin'. Have a nice day," he said, smiling pleasantly at the woman. Amy and Mrs. Wilburn stood staring—mouths agape in awe. Amy offered a friendly wave to Genieva as the wagon lurched forward.

"I can take care of meself and of you, Genieva! I don't need ya steppin' between me and me trouble," Brevan scolded once they were well on their way.

"They meant to kill you!" Genieva reminded him, brushing a tear of frustration and residual fear from her cheek.

"That they did. But they wouldn't mind riddin' themselves of me wife in the process," he grumbled. He inhaled a deep breath. "I should've killed Cruz anyway just for layin' his filthy hands on ya." After a moment, he chuckled—quite unexpectedly. "Still, it's flattered I am . . . that ya would try to protect me as ya did."

"This won't be the last time they try to kill you, Brevan. Cruz is . . ."

"We'll talk no more of it today, lass. It's determined I am . . . to enjoy our good fortune of the day."

"But . . ."

"No more of it, Genieva," he ordered. Sighing and smiling with contentment, he handed the lines to her. "You drive them," he said. He leaned back, stretching his arms wide before tucking his hands at the back of his head. "I want to enjoy the ride."

Genieva was unsettled—frustrated. Fear and anger simultaneously welled up inside her. She pulled the team to a halt abruptly, jumped down from the wagon, and began walking.

"What are ya doin', lass? We've got to get home. The day is far from over, and I've . . ." Brevan called after her.

Genieva kept walking, shaking her head as she raised one hand in the air to indicate to him she would not listen. Her body began to quiver with anxiety as her feet carried her to no particular destination. The tears were flowing freely down her cheeks, and she did not try to stifle them—for they gave her much needed release of powerful and conflicting emotions.

"Genieva, for pity's sake, lass . . ." Brevan grumbled from behind her. She quickened her step, knowing he was directly at her heels. " 'Twas a scuffle. A wee wrestlin' match that . . ."

Turning to face him, she cried, "A scuffle? A scuffle? Do you really think me so dimwitted, Brevan?" His eyebrows rose in surprise as she continued her verbal scolding. "They meant to kill you!" she said. "Do you understand that? They meant to kill you. Leave you dead in the alley, with me standing there having watched! It's not something I can dismiss . . . simply sigh and forget just because you've sold your corn for a good price today. Unlike you . . . there are more important things to me on this earth than the crops . . . than the farm for that matter."

"Come, Genieva. Get back into the wagon and let's be for home. It's early in the day . . ." he demanded, pointing to where the team stood, careless of what their masters were doing.

"I'm walking. I can't sit still in that wagon after what just happened," Genieva argued, turning from him and walking away once more.

"You'll get in that wagon, lass, or I'll pick ya up and drop ya there meself," Brevan growled.

Genieva turned toward him, her defiance complete. "You will?" she dared.

"I will . . . and don't ya dare to doubt it," he assured her.

"You? Pick me up and dump me in the wagon? In your condition?" Brazenly she returned to where he stood—the buttons from his shirt flying every direction as she ripped the garment open and inspected his torso. The painful-looking bruises, purpling and bluing on either side of his rib cage, indicated to Genieva at once that if his ribs had escaped breaking, they were bruised to an agonizing pain in the least.

Pointing to his chest indicating her suspicions had been confirmed, she said, "I doubt you can even walk without it paining you, Brevan. Look at this!" Again she motioned to the bruising at his ribs. She took his hands in hers—holding his bruised and bloodied knuckles up to his face for his own observation. "You see this?" she asked. She dropped his hands and touched his swollen jaw with her fingers. Letting them travel gently to the corner of his mouth where a streak of blood was drying, she dabbed at the sticky mess. Holding her own blood-stained fingers up for his inspection, she said, "Don't threaten me with physical superiority today, Brevan McLean. You're not up to following through with such intimidations." The sight of him standing before her bleeding and bruised was overwhelming, and she turned from him as her tears fell more excessively than ever.

In the next instant, she felt herself being turned and hoisted into the air. As her mid-section came down roughly on his shoulder, she whined, "Put me down! Put me down, Brevan!" Still, as he strode angrily back to the wagon, she knew he intended to make good his threats.

"I've had enough of it this day, lass! You've tried your hardest to ruin me joy in me good fortune. Sulkin' in the store with Mrs. Fenton when Jenny Evans was givin' ya the screws . . . pickin' a fight with Cruz Archuleta in the alley there in front of the entire population of the town!"

"Me?" Genieva exclaimed. "I did no such . . ."

"I'll not have it, do ya hear me?" Brevan muttered as he sat Genieva solidly on the wagon seat once more. "Ya glue yar bum to that spot, and don't dare to move until we're home again."

"Don't bully me, Brevan. I'm upset and . . ." Genieva began.

"I'll bully ya anytime when it's the only way to get some sense into that skull of yars," he interrupted. Wincing at the obvious pain caused him simply by climbing up beside her, he said, "And I'm well aware ya're upset, lass. But stewin' on it only serves to make yar mind less and less at ease. Look at me," he added, gathering the lines in his hand. "There I am . . . just loadin' our things into the wagon. And what happens? Amy Wilburn comes a runnin' into the store like the bloomin' banshee itself is at her heels, screechin' about Cruz snatchin' ya into an alley. I run out there and find me wife pinned against the wall and that slimy, sick scoundrel droolin' over ya like ya were roast lamb on the Sunday table!" He shook an index finger at her as he continued, "Ya think that didn't upset me? Ya think I wasn't all churnin' and burnin' inside with the agonizin' anger of a crazy man?" Genieva snapped at his scolding finger with her teeth, but he pulled it away quickly enough that it wasn't trapped. "But it's a fine, beautiful day, and we've had good fortune. It's over. What's done is done, and we can't change it. And . . . considerin' I have been nearly beat about like an egg in a bowl, I think I deserve to have ya respectin' me wishes! And I'm wishin' to put it behind me and enjoy me day!"

Genieva brushed the tears from her cheeks with the back of her hand and straightened in her seat. "If that's what you want then," she agreed curtly.

"That's what I want," he affirmed.

They were each silent on the way home.

As soon as the wagon halted before the barn, however, Brevan spoke. "Now . . . there's no need to be gettin' Brian and Travis all nervous about this . . ."

Genieva had seen how Brevan's body had begun to stiffen from the soreness he was beginning to feel. Thus, once he'd begun to climb down from the wagon, she swiftly leapt from it. Hitching up her skirts, she began to run headlong in the direction of Brian and Lita's farm. Brian at least must be told. Someone had to help her protect Brevan! He certainly didn't plan on protecting himself very well.

"Genieva!" Brevan shouted after her, "Ya get yar bum back to this house! Genieva!" But she knew he was too sore to keep up with her when she had such a good head start. Even were he to take out after her in the wagon, she could still outmaneuver him and avoid being captured again. Memories of her encounter with Cruz between Brevan's farm and Brian's pricked her mind, but still she ran on. Panting and gasping for breath, she arrived at Brian's farm to find him and Lita in the house enjoying an early lunch.

"Híjole!" Lita exclaimed as Genieva burst in upon them. "What has happened to you?"

Brian was on his feet at once asking, "What is it, Genieva?"

"In town . . . just this morning . . ." Genieva panted. "Cruz . . . he dragged me into an alley, and when . . . when Brevan came . . . he . . . there were others waiting. Oh, Brian!" she pleaded, "You've got to make him understand how serious this is! They tried to kill him!" Lita immediately buried her face in her hands and began to weep. "I'm sorry, Lita," Genieva apologized. "But . . . but Brevan's chasing me. He didn't want me to tell Brian . . . yet you had to know, Brian! Someone's got to help to protect him from . . ."

"Get back in the wagon, Genieva," Brevan ordered from the doorway then. "I swear ya're like bein' shackled to a toddler's tantrum, ya are."

"Oh, Brevan!" Lita cried upon seeing Brevan's bruised and bloodied condition.

"Ya've got to be more watchful, Brevan," Brian muttered, inspecting his brother. "They mean to kill ya, and they'll do it if ya fight them alone."

"He laid his filthy hands on Genieva, he did!" Brevan explained.

Lita gasped, suddenly doubling over.

Genieva was immediately at her side. "He didn't harm me, Lita. I'm fine. Don't worry. I . . . I had to tell Brian, though. I had to . . ." she stammered.

"I'm all right, Genieva," Lita said, exhaling a heavy sigh. "Do not worry for me. I'm fine. I'm only sorry that mí familia is so . . . so evil!"

As the tears of hurt and humiliation flooded Lita's cheeks, Genieva dropped to her knees next to her friend. "Joaquin was there, Lita. He helped us. He denounced your father and brothers and helped us."

The joy in Lita's eyes was apparent. "Oh, mí amor. Mí hermano! Joaquin is a good man, Genieva."

"Yes. He is, and I know how hard it was for him."

"Get in the bloomin' wagon, Genieva," Brevan sighed with a tone of complete impatience.

"Good girl, Genieva," Brian said, taking Genieva's hand and pulling her to her feet. "Ya know Brevan won't ask for help to . . . well, to save his life." Genieva nodded—though she was suddenly overcome with fatigue. "I'll talk to Travis, and we'll be more watchful from now on. And you," he said, pointing to his brother as he spoke, "quit playin' the hero. Ya'll get yarself killed."

Brevan sighed—defeated somehow. He nodded, admitting, "It was bad today, brother Brian. It could've been a lot worse, too, I suppose." Turning to Genieva, he begged, "Please get into the wagon, lass. I'm done in with chasin' ya down today."

Lita squeezed Genieva's hand with encouragement as Genieva smiled and turned to go. She felt guilty for upsetting Lita when the time of her baby's birth was so near, but she feared for Brevan, knowing it had been more than necessary to have informed Brian.

Quickly, she left the house, Brevan hot at her heels, and climbed into the wagon.

Once they were on their way again she ventured, "I'm sorry, Brevan, but you take your strength and weaknesses for granted. Juan Miguel or Cruz . . . you're never watchful of trouble."

"Yes I am. I'm more observant than ya credit me, lass," he defended.

"You flatter yourself."

"I don't," he corrected her. "I knew ya were upset when I first came into the store after sellin' the corn, I did. I knew Jenny Evans had been twistin' yar pride."

Genieva breathed a heavy sigh at the remembrance of the taunting she had endured at Jenny's hand. "You've no idea the things she says," she mumbled.

"I've more idea than ya think. She's been accusin' ya of not bein' able to keep me at home, as she puts it, since that first day we went to town together months back. I've no doubt that today the subject she used to undo your corset strings was in the way of the babies comin' to everyone in me family except me." Genieva looked at him. "And more than that . . . yar pride allows her to get the best of ya, it does."

Genieva was silently fuming! Still, she delivered her rebuttal as calmly as possible. "And your pride puts your life in danger."

He nodded. "Maybe so. So when ya've mastered yar own, ya can preach to me about mine." He sighed and asked, "Now . . . are ya or are ya not interested in the price I got for the corn?"

Genieva looked at him, feeling her heart and temper soften. He had tried so hard during the morning to enjoy his accomplishment, his success. Yet, time after time, mostly because of her, he had been unable to do so.

"I am," she said.

Chapter Twelve

Brevan explained there would be perhaps one or two weeks from the time the corn was sold before the pears and apples were ready for picking to begin. One week had already passed. The bruises on Brevan's body were fading to a yellowish-green hue, and Lita was feeling better and more energetic than she had in some time. It had taken quite a lot of self-control and patience for Genieva to calmly go about her daily chores. She found herself constantly looking over her shoulder and wondering at Brevan's where-abouts. Still, her evening swims in the pond helped to relax her tired body and mind, and she continued to enjoy them at the end of each day.

One evening, nearly two weeks after the incident in town with Cruz, Genieva was floating in the pond, when she was suddenly startled as something fell into the water near her. By the size of the splash the object had made, Genieva knew at once it could not have simply been a fish breaking the surface. She treaded the water as she looked about, and an overwhelming sensation of impending doom caused her body to feel cold—for she saw an apple bobbing up and down in the water near her. The trees from the orchard were far too distant for the apple to have simply fallen into the pond. Someone had thrown it there. Furthermore, her instincts instructed her that it had not been a friend who had done so.

She glanced quickly about but could see nothing. The sun had begun to set, and the fuzzy colors of dusk made it hard to see clearly in any direction. Genieva began to swim toward shore. Yet as Cruz stepped from the orchard, bathed in the purple light of early evening, she was still too far from shore for her feet to touch ground.

Cruz chuckled as he hunkered down on the pond's shore, taking a large bite of an apple before tossing it into the water as well.

"Hola, hermosa," he chuckled. "You look good in the water, señora."

Genieva did not even consider trying to avoid a confrontation with Cruz by talking sense to him.

Instantly, she began to scream, "Brevan! Brevan, come quickly!"

"I have been watching you swim for some days now, señora. It gives me much pleasure. And now when I come to speak with you at last . . . what do you do? You call for your hombre to come swim with you instead of me," Cruz chuckled.

"Leave now, you . . . you snake! Brevan!" Genieva cried as she turned and began swimming to the opposite shore. She heard the screen door to the house slam shut, and she turned to glare at Cruz. "He's coming. You'd better leave if you value your filthy life."

Cruz stood, a triumphant smile on his face. "You are lucky that mí padre has forbidden me to kill your hombre, niña. I would slice his throat open before your eyes now if it weren't for that." As quickly as he had appeared, he was gone, vanishing into the hazy light of dusk.

"It's Cruz!" Genieva panted, swimming to shore as Brevan sprinted toward her. "He was here! Only a moment ago!"

Brevan looked about, straining his eyes through the fading light. "I'll not be findin' him now. He knew I was near at hand," he mumbled. "Are ya well then, lass?" he questioned, taking hold of her hand and helping her out of the water. She nodded as she gasped for breath and pushed her wet hair back from her face. Brevan grasped Genieva's shoulders, frantically searching her eyes. As his eyes traveled the length of her body, examining her for sign of injury, he asked, "Are ya sure, lass? Ya're not holdin' anythin' from me, are ya?"

"No, no, he didn't come into the water." She drew in another deep breath and collapsed into the security of Brevan's embrace. "Juan Miguel has forbidden Cruz to kill you, but I'm afraid his pride will get the better of his loyalty to his father. You're still in great danger, Brevan."

Brevan held her tightly against him. The warmth of his breath on her hair helped to quell the chill spreading over her body—the chill borne of being wet in the evening air and from fear.

"I'll be fine, Genieva," he soothed. "But no more evenin' swims for ya, lass. Ya'd best get inside or ya'll catch yar death. I want one more look about."

"No, Brevan, it's too . . ."

"I told ya, I'll be fine, lass. I've got to be certain he's no longer about. Off with ya now," he said as he gathered her clothes and thrust them into her arms. She didn't even scold him for the gentle pat he bestowed on the seat of her bloomers—for she knew it was his reassurance to her that all would be well. And besides, she adored the teasing attention from him.

The following afternoon, Lita entered the house—her eyes bright with happiness.

"Buenas tardes, Genieva!" she greeted.

Genieva and Brevan had agreed not to tell Lita of Cruz's visit to the pond the previous evening. The time for her baby to come was too near, and they feared upsetting her. So Genieva smiled happily at her friend as if there were nothing at all amiss.

"Lita!" Genieva exclaimed. "Don't tell me you walked all the way over here."

"I needed the air and the walking. I could sit still no more today," Lita explained.

"Well, have a chair, for pity's sake. You shouldn't be out like this. Does Brian know you're over here?" Genieva asked. Lita's face was too rosy and her breathing too quick it seemed.

"No, he's gone to town for some things, and I can't go now, you know," Lita sighed. "Brenna is feeling so sick, and Travis is out in the orchards. I knew you would be in this time of day. It is near time for Brevan to come in for lunch, yes?"

"Yes. And my duties seem too tedious today. I had to do something else for a change, and you will be glad. Look," Genieva said, holding out a plate of cookies to her friend. "You've come over on the right afternoon."

Lita giggled and took two cookies. "Oh, it is too uncomfortable to sit. Will you walk with me in the orchard?"

"I-I don't think you should be up so much, Lita," Genieva argued.

"It's not comfortable to sit today, Genieva. I . . ." The cookies fell from Lita's hand as she doubled over clutching her stomach.

"Lita!" Genieva gasped.

"Something . . . something is wrong . . ." Lita moaned.

As fate would have it, Brevan entered the

house at that very moment. Frowning, he began to scold, "Lita. Brian would nag ya blue if he knew you were . . ." Yet, upon seeing her obvious discomfort, asked, "What's the matter?"

"It's the baby," Lita answered as her face grimaced in pain. "I think . . . I think . . ."

"I think you'd better help me get her into the spare room, Brevan," Genieva interrupted. "Then, as quickly as you can . . . go to town and fetch Brian home."

"Yes, yes. I'll fetch Brian," Brevan mumbled as he gently gathered Lita into his arms, cradling her carefully as he carried her to the spare room. Genieva sensed his instant and complete uneasiness. She frowned—he looked entirely undone!

"Gently, gently," Genieva reminded him as he placed Lita on the bed. "Now, before you go for Brian, fetch me some towels and put the kettle on the stove."

"Mmm hmm," Brevan mumbled, nodding. Yet, he only stood staring at Lita—her face constricted with pain.

"Now, Brevan! Go!" Genieva ordered, pointing to the kitchen.

"Yes, yes," Brevan agreed as he turned and left.

"His face was as white as the snow," Lita groaned as she almost laughed. The pain had passed for a moment, and she tried to breathe slowly and deeply.

"He's out of his element here," Genieva commented, taking extra pillows from the nearby trunk and placing them at Lita's back. "I'll get a cool cloth for your forehead." But as she turned to fetch the item, Lita caught her hand and stayed her.

"I'm . . . I'm . . ." she whispered. "Very much fear is in me, Genieva."

Genieva forced a smile and squeezed Lita's hand with encouragement. "I've helped with birthing more times than most girls my age have, Lita. Everything will be fine."

Still, by the time Brevan returned with Brian nearly two hours later, Genieva was frightened. Lita's pain seemed more intense than the other women she'd attended. Furthermore, Lita was a beloved friend—a sister. This too was heightening Genieva's own anxiety.

"Thank goodness you've come, Brian," Genieva sighed as Brian entered the room. The man went straight to his wife, kneeling beside her and taking her hand in his own.

Brevan started to enter the room after him. Yet, Genieva saw the color drain from his face once more, and he slowly backed away. Snatching the cloth from Lita's forehead, Genieva tossed it to Brevan. He caught it—though obviously startled.

"Soak it with cool water again, Brevan, and

wring it out well," she ordered. He nodded and swallowed hard. Genieva needed him. She knew his strength and control would return once he was involved, and she needed his—for hers was beginning to fade, and she knew she would need her wits about her.

"I've never in me life seen the like of it," Brevan stammered as Genieva approached him in the orchard late that evening.

"I know," she sighed. "Isn't it . . . well it's . . . we've witnessed a true miracle. It was beautiful!"

"What?" Brevan breathed. A deep frown furrowed his handsome brow as he ran his fingers through his hair. "Beautiful?"

"Yes. Lita's strength . . . the baby . . . Brian's concern and tenderness. Oh, Brevan, it was so . . . so . . ." Genieva struggled for words to describe the miracle she had just witnessed. She had seen children brought into the world many times, but each time it amazed and astounded her.

"It was torturous!" Brevan growled. Genieva looked up at him—startled at the unsettling tone of his voice. "I can't even be imaginin' such pain! Such loss of blood and strain on a body."

"It's the way babies are born, Brevan. Everyday . . . everywhere. What did you think . . . ?"

"I never imagined it was the like of what me

own eyes just witnessed, I didn't," he answered. The fear and anger in his voice was alarming—leaving Genieva speechless. She had never seen Brevan McLean frightened by anything—but witnessing the pain and effort of childbirth had truly dealt the man an unsettling realization. She'd noticed his initial nervousness, but when Lita began pushing the baby from her body, he had once again become the impenetrable wall of strength she had always known him to be. It was, after all, he who had settled Lita when she had begun to panic at the most crucial moments before the baby was delivered. It had been he, Brevan, who had kept his brother calm when watching his wife's agony had nearly become too much for the man to endure.

"They're both fine, Brevan. Lita . . . the baby. They both . . ."

"She could've died, Genieva!" he exclaimed, taking hold of her shoulders and looking desperately into her eyes. "She would've left Brian alone and broken in the world. He loves her more than his own life, he does."

"And so do you," Genieva muttered as understanding struck at her heart.

Brevan released Genieva's shoulders and straightened. "Of course I love her. She's family. Me own sister in a manner. I'd never want to have to bury her, and I'd not wish to watch Brian suffer either."

"But it's the way children are brought into the world, Brevan. Didn't you look at the baby? The sweet bundle of innocence that Brian and Lita will love more than life? She'll bring to them more joy than . . ." But she paused when she realized her words meant nothing to him.

"And now," he grumbled. "Now I've got to stand by and watch Brenna go through the like." He looked down at Genieva again. "I could never put a woman through such agony."

"Well, then," Genieva spat as tears brimmed in her bluish eyes. "It's a good thing you've married for practical reasons, isn't it? Since you've no great love or desire for your own wife, you'll not have to worry about losing your personal workhorse . . . your slave . . . to childbirth." She turned to leave, brushing a tear from her cheek. She glanced back at him, adding, "But because of your selfishness in not wanting to deal with the realities of life, you've stripped me of my heart's desire to have children of my own!"

"Genieva," Brevan began.

"It's not your fault, Brevan . . . and I'm wrong to blame you. I married you for selfish reasons as well," she sobbed as she ran from him and toward the far end of the orchard.

Genieva was angry—angry with Brevan for being human and having fears—angry with him for not loving her and returning to her everything she felt for him. Still, she was more angry with herself—for confessing to him her desire to have children. How could she have let her guard down so easily? She sniffled and straightened as she walked. After all, she reminded herself, she had come here to escape marrying Andre—to escape the stifling city life she had grown to loathe. She really had no right to expect anything from Brevan other than providing her with shelter and nourishment. But even so, she thought as her shoulders drooped once more, she was in love with the man. And that was something she hadn't planned. She had planned to love him. She had even loved him before she had arrived. But she hadn't planned to fall so completely in love with him that everything else she had planned was thrown to the wind. Yes—Genieva had quickly learned a harsh life's lesson—when a woman was hopelessly and entirely in love with her husband, nothing else in the world mattered or seemed important if he didn't love her in return. She had learned maternal instincts were strong and natural in such a circumstance, and the realization of never being able to nurture such strong instincts was a dismal and despairing prospect. Of course, it was only Brevan's children she desired to have—to hold and to love. She knew no other man on earth could've evoked such binding, unbreakable, and concentrated feelings.

"Genieva." Brevan's voice from behind her startled her, interrupting Genieva's thoughts. He took her hand and tugged at it, attempting to get her to face him. But she was humiliated at having had yet another emotional demonstration before him and would not look at him. "I'm sorry," he continued. "I've ruined the moment for ya, I have. And I had not the right to do that." Genieva closed her eyes, squeezing the tears from them in an effort to stop further moisture from releasing itself. "It's tired ya be . . . always tired. It causes ya to lose patience with me frailties. That's all. In the mornin' things will seem less bleak."

"You do *not* understand," she mumbled. "You'll never understand."

"I do understand. I understand better than ya . . ."

"No. You don't," she argued, finally turning to look at him. "You're a man. Men don't feel things the way women do. They don't need the same things women need. Please don't insult me and think me ignorant enough to believe that you understand what I'm feeling."

She watched as his jaw clenched, as he struggled to remain calm. He inhaled a deep breath and said, "Very well. I admit it. Perhaps I don't understand women and their needs. But don't boast such understandin' and superior intelligence, Genieva. Men feel things too. Men have wants and needs. And believe me, if ya had any knowledge whatsoever of the feelin's, the wantin's, and the needs of the man standin' before ya now . . . ya would not be so quick to judge as ya have been."

Genieva blushed. She had been judgmental, but her temper was provoked at his superior attitude. "I know you better than you think," she began curtly. "You feel almost nothing—joy, fear, or sorrow—unless it's connected with your precious land and crops. You want nothing more than to have the best crops and make the most profit on them. And you don't need anything. You don't need anything other than the satisfaction your work and your land gives you."

Brevan's eyes narrowed—his teeth ground almost audibly. Yet he simply said, "Ya're tired. Ya're tired, and it often makes ya cruel. I've learned that much about ya, I have. And it's a thousand times more than ya've learned about me." Dropping her hand, he turned to leave.

Genieva dropped to her knees, burying her face in her hands. Looking up to see him striding away from her, and overwhelmed with feelings of defeat, she pleaded, "Please, Brevan. Just one day. I just need one day to . . . one day of . . ."

He stopped, obviously sensing her sudden humility, and turned toward her. When her pause was not broken, he urged, "One day. What are ya talkin' about, Genieva?"

Genieva cast a shame-filled gaze to the ground

as she continued, "I just need a day . . . a regular, normal day . . . a day when I can forget I'm only here to work for you. Just one day to forget this marriage is a farce." Sitting down in the grass like a wilting flower, she added, "I need a day of make-believe, Brevan. I promise . . . I swear to you that day after tomorrow I'll work hard for you. I'll not complain or whine. But tomorrow . . . please. Just let me have tomorrow to remember who I am . . . to forget that I'll never have . . . let me have tomorrow to tend to Lita and not have to worry about finishing my chores."

Brevan sighed—his eyes narrowing as he looked away for a moment.

"I was afraid it would become too bleak for ya, I was," he mumbled. "Ya're young, and yar heart still has the needs and desires of youth, it has. I knew this would come, but I chose ya just the same. An older woman would've . . ."

"An older woman would not have worked as hard for you as I do," Genieva spat at him suddenly.

"I'm no slave master, Genieva!" he defended himself. He moved toward her—towering over her.

"You're close enough to it, Brevan! And you do it to try to block out the reality that you're young enough as well. Only you've managed to bury your heart and pretend you need nothing but this land and hard work!"

310

"That is all I need," he growled. "Ya told me so yar ownself just a moment ago."

"You're a liar." Sighing heavily and shaking her head, she mumbled, "I've not the energy or the desire to argue with you tonight, Brevan."

"I'm not a liar, Genieva! If ya were a man, I'd knock ya flat out for callin' me such," he growled. "But I'll be givin' ya pardon for I know ya're tired, mind and body." Taking a deep breath and releasing it slowly, he seemed to have calmed his temper when he continued, "Rest then tomorrow, lass. Ya work like a horse, and I'll not deny that. But I'll be remindin' ya of somethin', I will. Ya married me, Genieva McLean. And when ya did, everythin' of mine became yars, too. This land, this house, everything. And if we want to go on livin' here and on the land we love, we have to work at it hard . . . every day. So, ya take yar day of rest, forgettin' that ya work for me, as ya put it, and pretend that ours is a common marital relationship." He turned to leave once more. He paused, looking back at her. His eyes narrowed and he leveled an index finger at her. "But I'll tell ya this . . . if ya're wantin' to act like any other married couple . . . then be prepared to carry the pretense to the letter, lass."

"Wh-what do you mean?" Genieva asked as an odd, thrilling sort of warmth ran through her.

"I mean to say that a husband has the right to

311

expect certain attentions from his wife, he does. Ya have yar day of common marriage. I'll give ya that. But I'll have me night of it!"

Kicking a wind-fallen apple that lay on the ground before him, he left—having ruined all hope Genieva had harbored of her day of rest being free from worry.

When Genieva entered the house some thirty minutes later, it was to find Travis and Brenna sitting at the kitchen table with Brian.

"Genieva!" Brenna exclaimed, fairly leaping to her feet and smiling brightly. "The baby is beautiful! Isn't she just the livin' princess?" Genieva smiled and nodded.

"You look done in, Genieva," Travis noted. "You must be tired."

Brenna nodded and going to Genieva, put an arm about her shoulders. "Ya rest awhile. I'm here now, and I can look after Lita and the baby."

"Oh, no. No, I'm fine. I want to . . ." Genieva began.

"No. I'll not have it. Lita's me own sister too. And I've missed all the excitement, I have," Brenna argued, directing Genieva toward her bedroom.

"You need your rest, too, Brenna," Genieva reminded, even though every thread of her tired body and mind begged for respite.

"I'm fine. You rest. Lita will need us tomorrow."

It was some hours into the late of the night when Genieva was awakened by the baby crying. Neglecting to take her wrap with her, she went to Lita's room. Brenna looked overly tired as she held the fussing baby.

"Oh, Genieva," Brenna sighed, relieved. "Lita is so tired, and the baby has just been fed. But . . . I can hardly keep me own eyes open a moment longer. I guess I'm not the strong woman ya are."

Genieva shook her head, smiling. "Your own baby needs you to rest, Brenna. That's why you're so tired. I feel much better now. I'll take the baby. You go lay down in my bed."

"I'm sorry, Genieva," Brenna apologized. The dark circles under Brenna's eyes were evidence of the young woman's intense need for rest.

"None of that. Go. I'll be fine."

"Thank you, Brenna," Lita whispered, reaching up and squeezing Brenna's hand. "Genieva is right. You need your rest."

Brenna nodded and left—though somewhat unwillingly.

As he entered the house after having walked nearly the entire boundary of his lands trying to dispel his frustrations, Brevan paused just out-side the door to the spare room.

"I'll stay here, Lita," Genieva soothed with kind

encouragement. "You need to rest. I'll rock the baby."

"Oh, Genieva," Lita sighed. "Isn't she bonita?"

"Oh, so very beautiful, Lita! She's the most perfect baby I've ever seen," Genieva assured her.

Lita laughed quietly. "You say that now, Genieva. But wait until you and Brevan have your first niña. Then you will say your own is the most wonderful . . . what's the matter, Genieva? Why the tears?"

Brevan winced at the pang in his heart for Genieva's sake. He continued to listen as Genieva answered, "I'm just tired, Lita. Only tired. And the baby is so beautiful. It's like having a tiny angel in my arms."

"Don't worry, mí amiga. You'll have your own niños and niñas some day. I know you will."

"You get some sleep, Lita," Genieva said, changing the subject abruptly. "You'll need it, 'cause I'm certain the baby will be raising the roof again in a while wanting to be fed."

"Ah, Brevan. Come in, come in!" Lita called as Brevan stepped into the room. "Oh, Brevan . . . come see the baby. Is she not the most beautiful thing you have ever seen?"

Brevan walked to stand beside Genieva, not missing the way she stiffened at his approach. He gazed down curiously at the woman who lay in the bed, and the child nestled snugly against Genieva.

"Are ya well then, Lita?" he asked.

"I'm fine, Brevan. Now . . . you take the baby. She es su sobrina, no? Your niece." Taking the small bundle from Genieva, Lita nodded to Brevan, gesturing he should take the baby.

"Oh, no," he argued, shaking his head even as his powerful hands supported the baby carefully. "I'm too clumsy, Lita, I am. And well ya know it."

But Lita ignored him—only smiled lovingly at him. "You see, Brevan. Mí hijíta . . . she likes you. She knows a handsome man when she sees one already."

Brevan stared at the tiny human fitting so perfectly in the crook of his arm. Carefully, he took one small hand in his, studying the tiny, petal-soft fingers. He chuckled when the dark-haired infant yawned widely, boasting a healthy tongue and set of tonsils.

"She's beautiful, Lita. She looks just like ya. Rare beauty she is," Brevan's low voice admitted humbly.

"Thank you, hermano," Lita whispered, gazing lovingly at the baby as Brevan returned the child to her mother's arms. "Now, you make sure Genieva gets to sleep soon, Brevan. She's tired."

Brevan looked down at Genieva, kneeling on the floor beside the bed. Dark circles of fatigue shadowed her pretty face below her eyes. Even the smile complementing her lovely lips looked less than bright.

"I will," he assured his sister-in-law before leaving.

Once in his room Brevan, tired as he was, found it impossible to sleep. His mind relived the birth of Lita and Brian's daughter over and over—the incredible pain that was so evident on the woman's face—the fear and concern radiating from his brother as he watched his beloved wife endure what must be endured. He had seen cows, horses, and all manner of stock give birth his entire life. But it was all too different when it was a human being—someone you loved.

He closed his eyes, trying to block from his vision the expression of despair and hopelessness he had seen on Genieva's face in the orchard. She was lonely, he knew. It was why she longed so for children. His guilt in having treated her so cruelly when he had known she only lashed out at him in frustration caused his stomach to churn. He should've been patient. He should've let her say whatever it took for her to ease her frustration, and he should've stood silent as she did so. But he'd faltered and threatened her in order to avoid defeat. He remembered vividly the expression of utter shock, complete embarrassment, and fear vivid on her face when he had told her that he would expect his night with her.

• • •

Creeping quietly into the front of the house, Genieva cradled the baby close to her bosom and sat down in the rocking chair near the front door. It was an unusually warm evening, so the door had been left open to provide some circulation of fresh air in the house. Genieva awkwardly scooted the chair around to face the open door. She smiled at the feel of the tiny baby against her body, coupled with the sweet, intoxicating aroma of the ripened pears and apples in the orchards.

"Have they named you yet, sweet pea?" she whispered quietly as the baby began to settle down. Bending her head, she kissed the soft, fuzzy head in her arms and smiled. How wonderful it would be to have a baby around to cuddle, she thought. Trying to suppress a yawn, she ignored her own great fatigue. As her feet pushed against the cool, wooden floor to rock the chair, she was haunted by the angry words she'd spoken to Brevan. She scolded herself inwardly. Why? Why did she always let her tired state get the better of her senses? He'd followed her into the orchard to try to soothe her. And she had repaid him with unfounded accusations and bickering.

She stopped rocking for a moment as she remembered the last words he had spoken to her that evening in the orchard, "Ya have ya're

317

day of common marriage. I'll give ya that. But I'll have me night of it!" Had he truly meant what her mind was interpreting his words to imply? Surely not. He had only been provoked by her verbal cruelty and had responded in defense of himself. What else could she have expected? She nodded, assuring herself Brevan had only spoken out of anger.

Sometime later, his mind still plagued with the anxiety caused by the baby's birth and his confrontation with Genieva, Brevan rose from his bed and wandered down the hall to Lita's room. She was there sleeping soundly—peacefully— and he was relieved for her. Brian had told him how hard it had been for Lita to rest during the last weeks before the baby was due. He was glad Lita had finally found her rest.

The baby wasn't with her mother, nor was Genieva. Frowning, Brevan wandered to the front of the house. There, he found himself witness to something that touched the deepest part of his soul. At first he thought he was dreaming the scene before him—for it was so naturally beautiful to him that it did indeed seem surreal. But as he approached—Genieva asleep in the rocking chair, the tiny dark-haired baby resting comfortably on her chest and in her embrace— he knew he was awake and the only witness to a rare, sweet moment in time.

Quietly he whispered, "Genieva, go to bed." When she did not stir, he reached out, taking a strand of her hair between his fingers. Tugging gently on the soft lock, he repeated, "Genieva . . . go to bed."

Opening her eyes slightly for just a moment, Genieva envisioned Brevan's handsome face before her own. Smiling happily, she closed her eyes once more so the dream might continue.

"Come along, Genieva," his voice echoed through her mind. "It's late. Ya need yar rest as well, ya do."

"Yes," she whispered out loud in her dream.

"Give the baby up to me," Brevan's voice whispered again, and Genieva sensed the bundle of warmth being taken from her arms. It seemed only moments later she imagined herself being gathered from the chair—held securely against Brevan's body. She let her hands caress the warm, smooth skin of his shoulders as he carried her—her face pressed gently against his shoulder.

"Mmmmm," she whispered with a contented sigh. "You smell so good."

The scent of his skin was indeed pleasant, no matter how faint. She was vaguely aware of her feet dropping to the floor for a moment—heard the soft rustling of bed covers being arranged. She was lifted again. The softness of pillows and quilts sent the dream of Brevan fleeting as she began to slip into a deeper slumber.

"Don't end," she whispered, reaching out and catching hold of her dream-induced-Brevan's hand, thus stopping the mirage from leaving her. "Hold me in your arms, Brevan," she whispered. "Hold me in your arms like he never will." She felt the warmth and power of the dream's arms envelop her. Again the scent of Brevan filled Genieva's lungs as she snuggled against the body of the dream. "It makes me so happy when you visit my dreams, Brevan. You always love me in my dreams."

As Brevan let his head fall to his pillow, he marveled at the things Genieva was speaking to him in her dreams. As he held her securely in his arms, her soft cheek pressed tenderly against his shoulder, he could not fathom he'd actually heard her correctly.

She's tired, he thought. *Completely delirious.* It would be unwise to take heed of anything she said in such a state.

Chapter Thirteen

It was the sun through the window and the enticing aroma of frying bacon that awakened Genieva the next morning. Rolling over to look out the window, she stretched her arms above her head and sighed with contentment. The wonderful dreams she'd dreamt during the night had dispelled her fears and anxieties. In the brilliant morning light she was renewed—felt thoroughly rested.

Yet as her eye caught sight of the white flannel underwear strewn across the washbasin on the table next to her bed, Genieva sat upright. Looking around, she gasped, realizing she was in Brevan's room—in Brevan's bed! Quickly, she threw back the covers, snatching a small afghan from the foot of the bed and wrapping it securely around herself before walking down the hall and into the kitchen. There at the table sat Brian and Brevan—both drinking tall glasses of milk as they waited for Brenna to pile their plates high with breakfast foods.

"Good mornin' to ya, Genieva," Brian greeted.

Genieva could only nod in response as she looked to Brevan with uncertainty.

He nodded to her and mumbled, "Good mornin', lass," as he did every other morning. There was nothing different in his manner to indicate he was disturbed in any way at her having been in his bed. "Did ya sleep well then?" he asked as Brenna set a plate heaping with good things before him.

"Ya look far fresher than ya did when I last saw ya in the midnight, ya do," Brenna confirmed.

"I-I . . . yes. I feel much better," Genieva stammered.

"Brian and I will take care of the chorin' on both properties today, Genieva," Brevan said—pointedly. "I've not forgotten I promised ya this day free to be with Lita and the baby. Have you?" He arched a knowing and reminding eyebrow, and Genieva swallowed the lump in her throat.

"No. I remember," she agreed.

"Very well. I'm certain Brenna plans on cacklin' like an old mother hen around here all day as well . . . so enjoy yar day, lass. I'll be seein' ya this evenin', I will," he said, a sly smile spreading across his face.

Genieva was completely rattled. Frantic, she looked about for something to divert her nervous thoughts and was thankful when Brenna spoke next.

"Lita and the baby are restin' just now. Here. Sit down and have a bite with these two hogs, Genieva."

Genieva tentatively sat down. As Brevan went about eating his breakfast as if it were any other day, she could only assume that everything was normal.

Throughout the entire meal, Brian bragged endlessly about the baby. Brenna and Genieva exchanged understanding glances, and Brevan chuckled—nodding in agreement each time his brother boasted of the baby's unique beauty and Lita's profound endurance.

When the two men had finished their meal, Brian stood, patting his stomach in a gesture of satisfaction.

"Ya're still a fine cook, ya are, Brenna," he complimented. Brevan nodded in agreement and winked at Genieva. "I'm off to check on me family before we go out to chores, brother Brevan."

"Ya do that, Brian. I'll wait for ya in the orchard," Brevan chuckled. Pushing his plate aside, he leaned forward, placing his mouth just next to Genieva's ear. "It's sorry I am . . . that I quarreled with ya last night, lass."

"I apologize as well," Genieva whispered— deliciously unsettled by his nearness—by the warmth of his breath on her neck. It was disconcerting to have Brenna there when Brevan was making peace between them. "You do realize," she continued, "that I was just so tired that I . . ."

"I do," he acknowledged. She flinched, delighted as he placed a quick kiss on her neck. "Make sure she gets enough rest today, Brenna," Brevan instructed as he rose from his chair. "I don't want her completely droppin' dead . . . especially not tonight."

Genieva slightly shook her head in disbelief as he winked at her before leaving.

As she gazed after him, Brenna said, "He's sure a pleased and pretty pup this mornin'. I guess sleepin' in the rocker didn't harm him after all."

"What?" Genieva asked. "In the rocker?"

"He was asleep in the rocker like the baby he held this mornin' when I got up, Genieva. I guess he rocked the baby while Lita slept after ya turned in again."

Genieva sighed, greatly consoled. For a few moments, she'd feared perhaps her heavenly dream of Brevan during the night had held more reality than she dared to imagine. It had, after all, felt so real—so warm and fragrant. But if Brenna found Brevan asleep in the rocker—he must've spent the night in it. Genieva was saddened that she had missed the opportunity to see Brevan caring for the baby.

"We have named her Carmelle, Genieva," Lita explained when Genieva had dressed and gone in to check on the young mother and new baby. "Brian wanted that her name should be Carmelita, after me. But I think that is, how you say . . . confusing? So, we have named her Carmelle."

"It's a beautiful name, Lita. I couldn't think of a more fitting one," Genieva said, smiling.

"Carmelle Esperanza McLean. That is mí hijíta's name," Lita sighed, gazing lovingly into the baby's face. "Esperanza was my mother's name, Genieva."

Lita's smile faded as she looked up to Genieva—her lovely eyes filling with moisture. "I am sorry to you, Genieva," she said unexpectedly. "I am sorry my family would cause you such worry . . . that a man I used to call hermano would try to harm you . . . try to kill Brevan."

Genieva frowned, shaking her head as she moved a lock of hair from Lita's cheek. "Don't worry about that now, Lita. We'll be fine."

"I am sorry, Genieva. You must know that I am. I must have your forgiveness," Lita pleaded, tears trickling down her cheeks.

Genieva leaned forward—embracing her friend. "You have nothing to apologize for, Lita. You've done nothing to harm anyone."

"Still, I am ashamed of what they do," Lita sighed. "Brian promised to bring us home just before supper, Genieva. Could you fix enough for you and Brevan to share with us tonight?"

"What a silly question, Lita," Genieva scolded, winking at her friend. "Of course. I will send you home with a warm and hearty meal."

Throughout the remaining morning hours, Genieva and Brenna talked with Lita, or with each other, and cared for the new baby. It had been so long since Genieva had giggled with her sisters-in-law—she could hardly remember the last time. While Lita rested before lunch, Brenna and Genieva sat at the table chatting over a glass of cordial.

"Tell me something of Brevan's youth, Brenna," Genieva asked in a moment of contented curiosity. "Was he always so . . . such a . . ."

"He always worked hard, he did," Brenna sighed. She rolled her eyes to emphasize the heavy sigh of annoyance she exhaled. "When we were but wee things he bossed Brian and me around durin' chores, and, oh, he paid for it at times! For we played the practical jokes of the little people on him, we did." Brenna giggled at the memory. "But, oh, he was fun! A fun and lovin' brother, as well. He played with us often and always protected us from harm."

Genieva smiled. She tried to imagine Brevan as a child—carefree, laughing, and exuberant.

"Give me a story of him, Brenna. Something silly and fun. Not so serious as life is now," she pleaded.

Brenna smiled. Her eyes narrowed and she gazed at the ceiling for a moment. "Let me think," she began, "a silly story of brother Brevan." After a few moments she smiled and leaned forward, dropping her voice in a conspiratorial manner. "He'd hang me from the nearest tree if he knew I was tellin' ya this, he would," she began.

"Then tell it quick," Genieva giggled.

"We had a cousin back in Ireland. Sean McLean was his name. Oh, I had the biggest infatuation with him for years and years. He was the tallest young man I've ever in me life seen—taller even than Brevan. It was six feet and six inches that he stood," Brenna spun the yarn. Genieva raised her eyebrows, impressed by the height of the man. "Oh, and it was handsome he was. Like a prince ya'd see in yar dreams. Well, Sean was seven or maybe eight years older than Brevan, and Brevan thought the world lived and died at Sean McLean's feet. He was a good man, our cousin Sean, and Brevan was right to admire him. Whenever Sean was up to visit, Brevan followed after him like a motherless pup, he did. He watched everythin' Sean did and memorized the way he did it. He hung on every word spoken by our cousin and believed Sean knew all things there was to know." Dropping her voice once more, Brenna grinned with mischief and continued, "When Brevan was . . . oh, about ten, I guess, Sean came to help our father on the farm one summer. I was in heaven, ya see . . . Sean there to pine away after every moment. I was so young. Anyway, I guess the story goes that one mornin' late in the summer, Brevan was pesterin' Sean near to dyin' with questions. 'How did ya learn to sit a horse so well?' he asked Sean. 'How did ya get yar muscles so large? How did ya grow so tall, cousin Sean?' he asked. Our cousin Sean had a lot of good qualities . . . and one of them was a wit and sense of humor . . . the kind that is rare among most people. 'Tall, is it?' he asked Brevan. 'Yes, I've grown tall, cousin Brevan, and because ya're me favorite of the cousins, I'll tell ya me secret of it.'" Brenna giggled for a moment—wiped the excess moisture of mirth from her eyes. "Can ya just see little Brevan McLean . . . eyes wide with wonder and excited beyond breathin' at the prospect of learnin' such a secret?" she giggled.

Genieva bit her lip as a delighted smile spread across her face. In her mind's eye she could well imagine it—and it was wondrous!

"So . . . cousin Sean says, 'The secret to growin' tall, cousin Brevan . . . to growin' tall and straight like the man ya see before ya is,' Sean whispered into Brevan's ear, 'first thing in the mornin' . . . and I mean first thing so the dew is still in the grasses . . . ya walk out to the fields, ya do, and ya find the freshest, warmest pile of cow dung that ya can. 'Tis best if the steam's still a risin' from it into the mornin' air.'" Genieva's eyes widened in disbelief, and she giggled, unbelieving, as Brenna paused to stifle her own giggles. "Then cousin Sean says, 'When ya find the ripe pile . . . the freshest, warmest, and deepest one of the mornin' . . . ya jump quick, landin' both yar feet square in its center, Brevan McLean! Ya stand there, cousin. Ya stand there 'til yar legs are achin' so that ya think they might fail ya . . . and ya chant, *grow . . . grow . . . grow.*' "

Genieva burst into laughter. "Oh, no . . . no, Brenna," she gasped, unable to control her giggling.

Brenna laughed so hard her breath had gone from her and she was having trouble inhaling another. Pounding the table several times with her palm, she mouthed, "Wait, wait." At last having drawn breath and settled her laughter, she continued. "And so, Genieva, the very next afternoon, Dad comes to lunch and asks Mother if she's seen Brevan all the mornin'. Mother worried, of course, because she hadn't seen one snitch of the lad since first light. We all were terribly worried, and so we set out, cousin Sean, Mother, Dad, Brian, and me, to find brother Brevan. And do ya know where we found him, Genieva?" Brenna asked, breaking into riotous laughter once more. "We found him in the west field . . . standin' in a soggy cow pile that entirely drowned his feet and ankles, sayin', 'Grow . . . grow . . . grow.' "

Genieva squealed as her laughter became uncontrollable. Brenna's forehead hit the table-top soundly as she let it fall there, no longer able to keep from howling either. Genieva had never in her life laughed so hard or so thoroughly, and when, after several minutes, she and Brenna were able to draw breath again without bursting into cackles, she sighed—contented. More relaxed and happy than she had been for some time—she smiled.

"It's a lie, Brenna. It has to be! Surely Brevan was never so naïve. Even as a child," Genieva giggled. Her ribcage was aching from the exercise of their laughter.

"It's the livin' truth, Genieva. As I sit here before ya, it's the truth," Brenna assured her, dabbing at her joyful tears with her apron.

"Thank you," Genieva whispered, taking Brenna's hand and giving it an affectionate squeeze. "Thank you for giving me this."

Brenna smiled and nodded. Both women startled—looked to the front door as there came a knock. Genieva released one last amused giggle as she stood and went to the door.

She felt her face drain of color—gasped as she saw standing before her Juan Miguel Archuleta.

She started to close the door, barring him from entering, but the man pushed his way into the house saying, "Por favor. I've only come to see mí hijíta . . . and mí nieta."

Genieva looked to Brenna. Yet Brenna only shook her head, uncertain herself as to what action to take.

"Brevan won't want you here. If he finds you here . . ." Genieva began. "You have harassed my husband horribly and tried to . . . at least, your son has tried to kill him! I'll not let you into his home!" she said—for her uncertainty had only been for a moment. She realized this man, Lita's father or not, was Brevan's enemy—her enemy. "If you try to come in any farther . . ."

"I only want to see Lita. Is she well? Is the bebé well? She is my daughter," the man pleaded.

"And Brevan McLean is my husband, Mr. Archuleta."

Juan Miguel scowled. He ceremoniously spit on the floor at Genieva's feet. Provoked by his disrespect, Genieva slapped him soundly across the face.

"Get out of my house!" she shouted. "Don't you ever dare to venture this close again, or you'll be fertilizing my flower bed!" Before he could react, she reached out, shoving him hard in the chest. As he stumbled backward, she closed the door and bolted it. "The rifle, Brenna!" she shouted. "Quickly!"

Brenna dashed to the rack in the hallway and retrieved the large gun hanging there. Genieva watched as Juan Miguel shouted in Spanish, storming down the porch. He mounted his horse, spurring it into a mad gallop through the orchard and out of sight.

Breathing a heavy sigh, Genieva tightly wrung the folds of her apron as her tension and fear began to subside.

"My heart's pounding so hard it pains me," she said to Brenna. Looking to her friend, she asked, "Was I wrong to refuse him? After all, she is his daughter."

Brenna shook her head emphatically and confirmed, "No. He means Brevan harm. And you. It would've been dangerous to all of us to let him in."

Genieva nodded. She knew she had done the right thing. For all she knew, the man may have meant Lita and the baby harm as well.

It was only moments later when the sound of heavy boots tromping across the front porch caused both women to leap to their feet once again—hearts thumping frantically. Someone pushed against the door—began beating furiously on it.

When Genieva heard Brevan's angry voice from the other side shout, "Open this bloomin' door, Genieva," she sighed and released the bolt. Brian and Brevan poured into the room together, and Brenna gasped as she saw the blood at Brian's temple.

"Brevan!" Genieva exclaimed. He held his left wrist tightly with his right hand. As Brian worked the pump at the sink, Brevan held his hands and wrists beneath the cool water. "What . . . what . . . ?" Genieva stammered, unable to complete the sentence—for once again she was witness to Brevan's blood being spilt, and it frightened her.

"Cruz," Brian answered. "Cruz, Mateo, and their slitherin' friends came upon us in the west orchard. But we gave them cause to think twice before tryin' to thwart the McLeans again, eh brother Brevan?"

Brevan nodded and continued to squeeze his wrist. Genieva rushed to where the two men stood. Brevan's shirt was soaked with blood at the right shoulder and stomach.

"What's this?" she asked as she quickly tore open the shirt to reveal a heinous, horizontal laceration across Brevan's belly.

"Ya're gonna send me to debtor's prison over replacin' the button's on me shirts, lass," Brevan growled, glaring down at her. "It's not as bad as it looks, that one," he assured her, looking down at his stomach. Genieva gently pulled the cloth from Brevan's shoulder to reveal yet another cut. "Nor that one, neither," Brevan grumbled as he continued to give his wrist his attention.

"It must've been planned, Brian. For Juan Miguel was here only moments ago," Brenna confessed then.

"What?" Brevan shouted. "In me own house? Ya let him enter me own house?"

"He forced his entrance," Genieva corrected as she dabbed at his stomach wound with her apron. She wasn't as convinced of its insignificance as was Brevan. "I sent him away."

"What did he want?" Brian asked.

"He said he wanted to see Lita and the baby," Brenna answered. "But I think he meant us all harm."

Brian and Brevan shared an understanding look, and Brevan said, "It's comin' to a peak now, it is." Brian nodded. "We'll all have to be more careful and watchful than ever before," Brevan added. Reaching down and tugging brutally at Genieva's apron strings, he untied the apron, pulled it from her waist, and wrapped it haphazardly about his wrist. "Ya take Lita to Brenna and Travis's, Brian. She can't be left alone, and I think they mean the least harm to them. Take her now, for I'm sure they're no longer about at this moment. But they soon may be."

"Ya're right. I'll take her now. Help me, Brenna. We need to make her comfortable," Brian ordered as he left and went to the back of the house.

"Ya should go as well," Brevan said to Genieva—looking down at his buttonless shirt—trying to figure a way to hold it together. "'Tis safer the more of ya that are together, it is."

"Absolutely not!" Genieva retorted. "I'm staying here! I'll not leave when . . ."

"You'll go! I said ya will, so ya will!" Brevan shouted, taking her shoulders firmly between his hands.

Genieva wriggled free of his grasp and argued, "I won't go. You can drag me there, but I'll only come back. My place is here."

Brevan sighed with irritation. Putting his fists squarely on his hips, he let his head drop forward as he said, "Fine. Ya're right. Ya're a wee little rat, and ya'll have yar way about it. I know that well enough."

"What are we going to do, Brevan?" Genieva asked then. "What? They're too devious, and we have too much work to do here to be constantly watchful and inside."

Brevan raised his head and looked at her. He seemed defeated somehow, and his arms dropped to his sides.

"We go on about it, Genieva. We go on about it. When it peaks, we'll be ready, and we'll prevail." He paused when she looked unconvinced. "We'll prevail because we're right, and they're wrong, lass. Good is on our side."

"Good doesn't always conquer," she reminded him.

"It will here. I promise ya that."

After Brian had taken Lita and Brenna home, the remaining daylight hours seemed long, lonely, and anxious. Brevan insisted Genieva have the rest of the day to do as she pleased. Yet she was too insecure to venture too far from the house—and far too worried about Brevan being out alone on the farm to occupy her mind with anything else. She tried to busy herself by straightening the spare room and washing the bedding used the day before during Lita's childbirth. Still, she felt nervous when she was out hanging the sheets on the line. She found herself constantly glancing over her shoulder—expecting to see one of the Archuletas or their vaqueros there.

As the sun began to set and Brevan had still not returned home for dinner, Genieva's worst fears began to heighten. She paced the floor anxiously, wringing her apron and trying to calm herself.

What a barrage of emotions Genieva experienced during the past two days. As she ventured out onto the front porch, watching the sun setting over the west orchard before her, she thought of the varied and extreme feelings that had churned within her recently. So many of them were odd and uncomfortable combinations—anger accompanied elation—envy shared joy—fear coupled with delight. Sighing heavily, she closed her eyes for a moment, reflecting on how fatiguing, how absolutely fatiguing it had all been. Her body was tired—her arms ached—her mind was dizzy—her legs were weak. She wondered if she could endure such fatigue for the many years and years to come.

When, at last, she opened her eyes, she gasped at what they beheld. Just in the brief moments since she had been reflecting with them closed, the skies had changed. Instead of the familiar shade of blue, white clouds drifting here and there, the sky blazed pink—the clouds boasting shades of purple the like she had never seen! The pink was a pink of such brilliance she could not compare it to anything immediately! The purples were the softest yet brightest lavenders and violets, rivaling the flowers of springtime.

"'Tis truly one of heaven's miracles, it is," Brevan's voice said.

Genieva tore her gaze from the nature's painting before her to see him standing off to one side of the porch. She'd been so enthralled by the spectacle in the heavens, she hadn't even heard his approach.

"I know that ya miss it often for the sake of gettin' me dinner on the table in a timely way," he admitted, walking to stand directly next to her before returning his attention to the skies. "I've wronged ya there, I have."

"It's no fault of yours," she defended him. "I've chosen to do that . . . to prepare dinner at that time. But I'm sad if I've been missing this all along."

"It's not always this perfect. But there are times when it takes yar breath away and helps ya to forget all else in the world," he noted.

Within minutes, the sun had dropped just enough to fade the colors, and darkness began to replace them.

"You'd miss it if you blinked," Genieva whispered. The fragrance of ripened apples floated on the soft breezes, and she inhaled deeply—their sweet perfume bathing her senses. She was reminded of another coveted scent, and she looked quickly to Brevan. His attention was still captured by the scene being played out in the heavens. She was glad, for it gave her several moments of freedom to stare at him without worry of being caught at it. She thought back on her dreams of the night before. What a wonderful dream it had been. She remembered vividly the scent of his skin as she had lain in his arms. If only the security and bliss she had experienced in those dreams could be real. If only.

"Did ya enjoy yar day of . . . normality?" he asked, without looking to her.

"Yes. Yes and no. This morning was wonderful! Such a fun time spent visiting with Lita and Brenna. But after Juan Miguel and . . ." Genieva's voice was lost as another thought entered her mind. Surely he did not mean to bring up in conversation their argument of the previous night—their argument ending in his threatening to . . .

"We mustn't let the unpleasant events of today ruin our remainin' evenin' hours together," Brevan mumbled.

Brevan struggled to keep an amused smile from spreading across his face. Genieva's eyes, though wide with understanding and apprehension, were quickly turning from their docile hazel color to the soft amethyst color he preferred. He thought for a moment that perhaps the purples of sunset's clouds had sifted themselves into her lovely eyes. He was determined to play this out. It was time he put Genieva where she belonged— really belonged.

"Let's to supper then, lass," Brevan said, motioning for Genieva to precede him in reentering the house.

All through supper Genieva's senses whirled. Her mind fought to devise ways of removing herself from the situation at hand. Silently, she tried to convince herself Brevan meant nothing by his remarks on the porch. She, being so terribly attracted to him and so hopelessly lost in her love for him, had simply misinterpreted his meaning. But as he looked up from his soup, winking at her, her nerves scattered to every venue but that of calm. Genieva looked away— tried to ignore the thrill washing over her at his flirtatious gesture. Quickly, she finished her meal and washed her own dishes and utensils. As she was putting her bowl in the cupboard, Brevan approached, placing his own dishes in the sink.

"Well, I'll . . . I'll um . . . get these done and turn in. Back to life as usual tomorrow. I'm sure I'll be all the further behind because of these past two days and . . ." Genieva babbled nervously. But when Brevan took her hands in his own, a knowing smile on his handsome face, she knew she was undone. She knew that no matter what his intention, whether he was teasing her or whether he was serious in his inference, she knew she had no power to resist him.

"We had an agreement, we did," he said, lowering his voice as he gazed into her eyes. "Ya've had yar day. I'll have me night, Genieva."

Reaching over his shoulders, he grasped the back of his shirt, stripping it from his body and over his head, as was his predictable habit each evening. Yet this time, instead of tossing it haphazardly into the basket at the foot of his bed, he simply laid it on the counter next to the sink. Taking Genieva's hands once more, he placed her palms on the warm flesh of his chest.

"I-I had better check those cuts you got today, Brevan. They might . . . they might . . ." Her words were lost as he bent and placed a soft kiss on her left cheek.

"Me wounds are fine, lass," he whispered.

"Brevan," she said, swallowing the lump of anxiety forming in her throat. "You don't really mean to . . . to . . ."

"To what, Genieva?" he asked. His quiet chuckle revealed he knew full well what she meant. Abruptly, she pulled her hands from his body, turned, and walked quickly toward her room.

"I'll be up all the earlier, Brevan. You've made your point, and I'll not ask for another day off any time soon," she called over her shoulder. Once inside her room, she shut her door, only to have him open it immediately, enter, and close it slowly behind himself. There was no light save that of the moon shining through her open windows, for she had not yet turned up the lantern at her bedside. The lace curtains adorning the window blew softly in the apple-scented breeze that wafted through the room. Reaching down, Brevan turned up the lamp sitting on the table next to the head of Genieva's bed.

"So ya're runnin' from me then?" he asked, grinning with delicious mischief. "You'll not pay the debt ya owe me for lettin' ya have yar day of rest?"

"Y-you don't really want me to anyway, Brevan," Genieva said. "And anyway . . . I spent half the day waiting on Lita and the baby and the other half worrying about the Archuletas showing up at any moment."

"Did ya milk the cows this mornin', lass?" he asked as he slowly approached. Genieva's legs were already braced against the side of her bed. There was no escaping him short of bolting out the open window.

"Well, no, but . . ." she began.

"Did ya pick the ripe vegetables in the garden today, Genieva?"

"No. I . . ."

"Did ya feed the chickens or mend me shirts—the ones ya've been poppin' the buttons off—or brush down me horses or water the stock or . . ."

"No!" she exclaimed. "No. You know I didn't."

"Then ya've had yar day, lass. And the sun has set. The night is upon ya now," breathtaking Brevan McLean mumbled in a low, alluring voice. Reaching out, he gathered Genieva into his arms, pulling her body flush with his own as his mouth took hers in a scalding, commanding kiss. At the first touch of his lips to hers, Genieva melted against him—like butter in a hot cast-iron skillet. The scent of his skin filled her mind—the feel of it beneath her palms causing goose bumps to ripple over her body, as she let her hands slide up over his shoulders to return his embrace.

He was like a necessary nourishment to her—a nectar—like tasting the beauty the sunset had painted across the evening skies! Brevan was the wonderment of her existence—her own allotment of heaven! And there was more. As his kiss intensified—as it favored her cheeks, neck, and mouth once more—she sensed he yet held himself in careful resistance. His threat had been just that, a threat. Somehow the sudden thought saddened Genieva, and she pushed herself from him, sitting down solidly on her bed.

"Let's stop this foolishness," she mumbled, restraining tears of hurt—for in those blessed brief moments, she had thought that he really did love her somehow. Or at least found her attractive—attractive enough to deem her worthy of his true affections.

Brevan sighed. Hunkering down before her, he took her hands in his. When she tried to pull them from his grasp, he tightened his grip.

"I can't fool ya for long, lass . . . can I?" he said. Chuckling, he continued, "Ya know me well enough, ya do. Well enough to know I'd never force ya to do anythin' ya didn't want to do of yar own free will and decision. No matter what me own desires might be."

Genieva looked to him quickly and asked, "What?"

Standing, he plopped himself abruptly down on the bed next to her. Lying back, he tucked his hands behind his head and explained, "I've wronged ya, Genieva, and I'm admittin' it to ya here and now. It's wrong I've been, to work ya like a jenny, expectin' ya to do the chorin' that Brian and me used to split when he was here." He sat up and looked at her. His expression changed—softened with humility. "But I'm repentin', and things are goin' to be of a difference now."

"What?" Genieva asked again. Her mind was still buzzing from his previous remarks. She wasn't sure what his implications now were.

"I'm tellin' ya that yar duties are changin', lass . . . for the better. I do need help with certain things on the farm. It's hard for me to get out and milk the cows mornin' and evenin' with everythin' else tuggin' at me. And the chickens . . . if ya could still see yar way to tendin' them and gatherin' the eggs. And I won't lie to ya about the orchards . . . when the pears and apples need pickin', it'll take both of us and then some hired boys from town to get the job done. But ya're me wife, not me slave, and the terrible pace ya've been keepin' up needs to slow down. I realized it for sure and for certain last night when ya snapped at me so."

"I'm sorry about that. I was just . . ."

"Very, very tired," he finished for her. "I know that. And it's me own fault, it is. I . . . I . . ." he stammered, looking away. "I don't fear much in this world, but I do fear distraction, Genieva. It's a life's load of work on this farm that I have, and I admit to ya here and now . . . ya distract me. I think I worked ya so hard on purpose to make certain the both of us were so tired and testy at night that there would be no liveliness left for . . . any other . . . activities."

Genieva's mouth dropped open in astonishment at what he had just confessed to her. She turned to stare at him. Brevan looked back to her, having sensed her staring, and said, "Well, it's a man I be, Genieva McLean! As regular a man as any other, and ya are a great deal better lookin' than I had expected. It's only natural that I should find ya . . . distractin'."

"It's why you wanted an older wife. You wanted a plump, perhaps unattractive woman that wouldn't tempt your . . ." she began, but Brevan's hand covered her mouth quickly, and he shook his head.

"Don't speak of it. 'Twas a shallow and selfish thing to do, and I would like to put it as far behind me as I can," he explained.

". . . masculine needs," Genieva finished, pushing his hand from her mouth.

"Needs have nothin' to do with it, lass," he corrected. "A man needs to work, to succeed at somethin'. If he can keep busy doin' such things, the other needs can be put aside. But put the cute lass before him and in his path every day, and it's distractin' to him. And no amount of hard work keeps his mind and body from thinkin' on the feel of her form in his arms and the taste of her mouth to his."

"But . . . it's only *me* you have here, Brevan. Surely I don't cause . . ."

"I've confessed all I mean to confess to ya this night, Genieva," Brevan interrupted, standing and looking down at her. "I've done a great wrong to ya, and I ask yar forgiveness with a promise to change me ways about it. Ya'll still have to do the work of a farmer's wife . . . the work Brenna and Lita do . . . but no more. From now on, I hope ya won't be so tired that ya fly at me as ya did last night. At least, not as often."

Genieva giggled, and when he looked at her—puzzled—she explained, "You were just battling with me last night then. You had me fooled, Brevan. I truly thought you intended . . . that just moments ago you were thinking of . . ."

The serious expression on his face caused her to pause.

"When I said it to ya last evenin', I did mean it, Genieva. I meant to have ya here and now. But me mind has settled durin' the day, and I realized the error of me ways in workin' ya so hard. So I've let ya escape me . . . this time."

He left the room, closing the door behind him, only to return a moment later, walk to her open window, and slam it firmly shut, securing the latch. "Ya'll sleep with that window closed from now on, ya will. We can't ignore the danger any longer." He did leave then—for good.

Genieva lay awake for a long time. Her mind and emotions were whirling with activity as they reviewed over and over the things he had said to her. Could it be true? Could he really find her attractive? Enough so that he'd felt the need to find ways of occupying himself, and her, in order to avoid giving in to his desires? And would she really be able to live the life of a wife where chores were concerned, instead of that of a hired hand? At last, she fell into a deep slumber, remembering the taste of his mouth when he'd kissed her and the wondrous feel of his arms about her body.

It seemed the nightmare was reality, and she woke. Sitting upright and panting, she felt the cool beads of perspiration on her face mingling with the hot tears stinging her tired eyes. The nightmare was gone the moment she sat up, but the anxiety lingered, and she had to reassure herself of his well-being.

Tossing her blanket aside, Genieva fled from her room and down the hall to Brevan's. Bursting in upon him, she sighed with relief as he sat up in his bed and grumbled, "What devil's chasin' ya in here at this hour, lass?"

Genieva closed her eyes for a moment—let her hands press firmly against her bosom in an effort to still the frantic, frightened pounding of her heart.

"I-I only had a nightmare, and it seemed so real. I had to be certain that you were . . ."

"I've been lyin' here for hours, me eyes glued to the roof for lack of bein' able to sleep, Genieva," he said, propping himself up on one elbow. "The situation is serious with the

Archuletas, lass. Juan Miguel and his boys mean me harm. They mean it for you too, for they don't want me to have a child that might inherit me property." He motioned with one hand for her to approach him. Pulling his sheet aside, he patted the mattress next to him. Genieva's mouth dropped open at his inference.

"Oh, no. That's not necessary. I . . ." she stammered.

"It is for me, lass. Ya'll sleep here where I can know ya're safe. And furthermore, ya won't be needin' to leap up from yar bed, runnin' through the house like a madwoman to check on me because of yar bloomin' nightmares."

"It wouldn't be proper, Brevan," Genieva whispered, glancing about the room as if expecting to find spectators hidden in every corner.

Brevan chuckled. "It's right, ya are. There's not one married couple, not one wed man and woman in the world who would consider sharin' the same bed, now is there?"

"It's different, and you know it," Genieva scolded, irritated at his sarcasm.

"Yes. It is. Now settle yarself in here with me, lass. I'm tired, and if ya make me get up and put ya here meself, I might take to snappin' at ya the way ya do to me at times." He patted the mattress again.

Inhaling deeply and summoning all the courage

within her, Genieva let her feet carry her to Brevan's bed. She sat down tentatively on the edge of it.

"There now," he sighed as he turned from her, punching his pillow several times before laying his head on it finally. "It's off to sleep with ya now, lass." Genieva still waited several moments, trying to find the courage to lie down next to him. "Genieva," Brevan growled. Quickly, she lay down, pulling the sheet protectively to her chin.

The overwhelming need to ask her question caused her heart to continue to pound furiously in her chest. She needed to hear it from him. He'd nearly said as much earlier that night in her bedroom. He'd implied it, but not said it as she needed to hear it. Her heightened anxiety and worry compelled her to ask him—straight and honest.

"Brevan," Genieva whispered timidly.

"Hhmm?" he mumbled.

"Is it truly all right that I'm not what you hoped for?" she asked, unable to force her voice beyond a whisper. "I know someone more experienced and older perhaps would've done better for you . . . in all respects. Are you . . . will you truly be happy in life having settled on me?"

Brevan raised his head. Frowning, he turned over, propping himself up on one elbow again.

Genieva looked away from him—afraid to see the answer in his eyes were it there. He was silent for several moments, and she began to feel ashamed at even venturing to put the question to him. Still, she needed to know. She needed to hear from his own mouth that he was satisfied with her—that perhaps there was a chance of his truly loving her one day. Not just be agitated by his physical desires for her.

"No one else would've been for me, Genieva. You are everythin' and all I wanted in a wife and so much more. For you and I, Genieva . . ." he lowered his voice and watched with delight as her eyes widened at his next utterance. "You and I are lovers as well, we are."

"I can't believe you'd mock me so," she whispered, looking away from him in an effort to hide the tears in her eyes.

"I do not mock ya, lass," Brevan whispered tenderly. Reaching out, he turned her to face him, brushing a tear from her temple with the back of his hand. "Think on it a moment. You and I *are* lovers, Genieva. It has been such since the first letters we wrote, it has."

Genieva closed her eyes, sending more tears trickling from the corners of them to moisten the pillow beneath her head. "Ya dare not deny it, for I see it in the lavender flavor of yar eyes each time I touch ya or am near to ya as I am now. And I taste it on yar lips and mouth when I lose me sense and take me pleasure in them." He took her face gently between his hands, turning her to look at him again. "I'll put an end to yar feverish doubtin', Genieva McLean. But I may raise a greater fever in ya the like ya've never imagined."

Genieva closed her eyes as Brevan's delicious mouth blessed her own with a coveted kiss. His kiss was laced with so much restrained passion, she could only guess at what the liberation of its full potency would generate. And his words held true—for the unendurable doubts in her fevered mind ceased as their affectionate exchange intensified. Gradually, Brevan seemed to untether his own restraints. As he let his body cover hers, Genieva became the enraptured recipient of his kiss in its full, unshackled, amorous fervor. His emotion spoke to her soul, and she knew, though he had not uttered it literally, that she owned his heart. He kissed her cheek lingeringly, brushing the remaining tears from her face as he at last spoke the assurance she'd so yearned to hear for such a long, long time.

"It's love that I have for ya, Genieva. The owerful, eternal kind of love that a man has for a woman who makes him want to live his life for nothin' else . . . for no other reason but the fact that he has her," he whispered. "I love ya, I do."

Genieva smiled as a final teardrop streaked her tender temple. "I love you, Brevan," she told him, thrilling at the gratified smile spreading across his handsome face.

"Ya've said it to me then," he whispered. "And now ya're mine, are ya? Now? This night? Entirely?" he asked, still hesitant.

"Entirely yours, Brevan," she assured him, reaching up to place a small hand against his unshaven face.

He smiled once more as his gaze fell to her mouth. Letting his thumb trace the pretty outline of her lips, he repeated, "Entirely mine," before lavishing her again with passionate, fevered kisses accompanying the profound, shared love they surrendered to then in each other's arms.

Chapter Fourteen

The winsome song of the meadowlarks lifted Genieva from her deep, contented slumber. The warmth of an early autumn morning met her as she slowly opened her eyes to the bright sunshine already streaming through the open window. The sun's light, coupled with the soft billows of the lace curtains at the window, painted lovely shadows on the walls.

She was not surprised to find Brevan had already left their bed to begin his day—for he was not one to oversleep. She was, however, delightedly astonished to find the largest, reddest, and shiniest apple she had ever in her life seen lying on the pillow next to hers. A small bouquet of wild daisies accompanied it, and she smiled, elated by the tender thoughtfulness of her husband.

Sitting up, she took the delicate flowers in one hand, brushing them lovingly across her cheek as she bit into the juicy sweetness of the apple. Her gaze fell then to the bed, and she placed a hand to her bosom, gasping as she realized the tattered quilt that was Brevan's usual and familiar bed covering had been replaced— replaced by the lovely quilt the women of the town had labored over months before beneath the fragrant blossoms now bearing abundant fruit in the orchard.

It was too much—too sweet and tender—too loving. Genieva tossed the covers aside and dashed down the hall to her room. She dressed quickly—though she was irritated with the time it took to lace her boots—for she must find Brevan at once. She must let him know what his attention to her morning waking had meant to her. As she tied the last bow of her boot securely, she heard heavy footsteps enter through the front door.

Dashing into the kitchen, the daisies and apple core firmly in hand, she called, "Oh, Brevan! You're so . . ." The words caught in her throat, however. For before her, in her very own kitchen, stood Cruz Archuleta. His nauseating smile curled his lips as he studied her from head to toe. The young man she recognized as his brother Mateo entered the house behind him, accompanied by two other vaqueros. Genieva was immediately aware that Mateo seemed uncertain, hesitant. When he removed his hat politely and nodded at her, she shook her head in wonderment—for it was only then she knew his age to be no more than sixteen.

Looking to Cruz defiantly, though her fears were mounting, Genieva ordered, "Get out of this house." But Cruz only chuckled. He knew all too well her extreme disadvantage.

"Where is your hombre, Mrs. McLean?" he asked, taking a step toward her.

"He's just outside. He's no doubt heard you approach, and if you value your life, you had better leave," Genieva answered, trying to sound as confident in Brevan's supposed nearness as she could.

"He is not too near," Cruz corrected her. "He is out in the orchard. I know. We watched him leave this morning, just a time ago. We waited until he was far enough from you." Cruz walked to where Genieva stood, stopping so close to her she could smell his reeking breath, already heavy with the stench of liquor even so early in the day. "Him. This Brevan McLean. He is a coward. He should not have such a woman as you. He is not man enough for you. I am right, yes?"

"No," Genieva growled. "If he finds you here . . . if you touch me . . . he'll kill you. I'm warning you for the last time to leave this house."

The brutal force of the back of Cruz's hand as he struck Genieva violently sent her plunging to the floor. She watched as her precious flowers and apple remains flew from her hands to scatter across the floor. She lay for several moments in shock before dabbing with her fingers at the cut Cruz's rough knuckles had left across her soft cheek. Looking up at him, she knew complete and frightful dread. As his smile broadened, she again understood his intention—absolutely understood it.

"Don't you dare to touch me," Genieva warned through clenched teeth. But the villain only laughed as he reached down, taking hold of the front of her bodice and pulling her to her feet once more.

"Touch you?" he mocked. "I'll do more than touch you, señora!" Genieva gasped as another painful blow was dealt to the other side of her face.

"What are you doing, Cruz?" Mateo exclaimed.

Cruz looked over his shoulder for an instant. He growled, "I was right, Mateo. She is here. Alone."

Genieva, though aching from the abuse dealt her by Cruz, did not miss the opportunity allotted her and, summoning all her strength, shoved Cruz, causing him to lose his balance and stumble backward. He caught hold of her wrist, however, and she was unable to pull free of him.

"Mateo," Cruz mumbled as he pulled Genieva's body flush with his own, "she is bonita, no?"

"Cruz," Mateo began, his insecurity and hesitation all the more apparent, "Cruz, let's go. Ven conmigo."

Cruz only chuckled. Taking hold of Genieva's chin tightly, his fingers tortured the wound at her cheek as they squeezed it mercilessly. Genieva cried out as Cruz forced her to the floor, pressing her bleeding cheek to the wood planks.

"Let the hombre see *that* when he comes back, mí amigos! It is good, Mateo, no?" The two vaqueros chuckled. Yet when there came no reply from his brother, Cruz stood, releasing Genieva for a moment and turning to face his sibling. "Answer me when I talk to you, hermano! It will make him loco with anger, Mateo! It is good, no?" Genieva's fingers again went to her wounded cheek, pressing on it in a pointless effort to stop the throbbing pain there. She drew her fingers from her face, studying for a moment her own blood, moist and red on them.

Then, seeing perhaps one last opportunity, Genieva reached out, taking hold of Cruz's boots and pulling at them as hard as she could. Her efforts were successful, and Cruz lost his footing, falling against his brother for a moment before ending on the floor. With only moments to act, Genieva dashed into her room, slammed the door shut, and dropped the heavy bolting board across it. Almost immediately, Cruz began shouting angrily in his native language as he pounded on the door. Knowing it would be a matter of mere moments before he broke the door down, Genieva rushed to the window. Struggling for a moment to release the latch, she opened the window and, wriggling through it, plummeted to the ground outside.

She knew Cruz would think of the window, perhaps deciding to enter her room by way of it.

Thus, without pause, she ran—ran toward the orchards, knowing Brevan would be there—ever her safety.

"You will not escape me!" Cruz shouted as he struggled to follow her through the open window. But the window was small, and it was not as simple for his bulky form to slip through it. "Ándele! Get her!" he ordered over his shoulder.

As Genieva reached the orchard and began calling Brevan's name, she heard the angry pounding of horse hooves and knew that Cruz would overtake her quickly.

"Brevan!" she screamed desperately as she ran between the trees, slipping once on a wind-fallen apple. "Brevan!" She paused for a moment, looking about frantically. But her protector was nowhere within her vision. He did not answer her call for him. Brevan was not in the orchard. As she looked back to see Cruz astride his horse—the others behind him, fighting at the tree branches hanging low and heavy with fruit—she realized that were she to escape, it would be her own doing.

The orchards and wind-fallen fruit indeed helped to slow the approach of Cruz and his accomplices. Staying close to the trees, for Cruz had not yet caught sight of her, Genieva made her way through the orchard and into the open. Pausing for only a moment to think, she remembered the rocky, hilled area to the north of the property. She had been there only once—on a day when she had needed to chase down a young calf that had strayed. But it was rocky and full of concealing crevasses, impossible to traverse on a horse or any means other than on foot. Hoping the orchards would continue to irritate and confuse the men for a time, she ran on. Her lungs burned—her legs ached with the strain of the sprint—but still she ran. As she neared the edge of the rocky hills, she could again hear the mad pounding of horses' hooves and the angry shouting of Cruz. Looking over her shoulder only once before leaping atop the first large rock, she felt tears finally begin to flood her cheeks. She knew all too well what her fate would be if the man who hated her husband so were to capture her. Quickly she began to climb among and over the large rocks in her path.

"The horses will not follow," she heard Mateo shout to his brother. But she knew that Cruz would. She only hoped she could hide herself from his sight quickly and well. It was her only chance of escape—of eluding a morbid fate. But Cruz, unhampered by bulky skirts and petticoats, was able to climb more nimbly and quickly. Genieva screamed as she felt his hand take hold of her ankle. Kicking at him with her free foot, the heel of her boot hit him squarely in the nose. It administered enough pain to him to cause him to release her ankle. As she neared the top of the first hill, the realization struck her that she had never viewed the other side of the formation. What if there were no more rocks to hide among? No more chances of escape? As she reached the summit, she cried out in frustration— for the hill did, indeed, flatten out for some distance before dropping off again.

"I'll kill you when I'm done with you!" Cruz shouted from behind her.

Genieva looked back to see him scrambling up the rocks toward her, his nose bleeding profusely. With no other path before her, she pushed on, running across the summit. Suddenly, there was a thunderous crashing as Genieva felt the ground give way beneath her. Her body was wracked with pain, and darkness enveloped her. Genieva had fallen, and fallen far. As she pressed her hands to her temples to lessen the mad pounding in her head, she looked up to see sunlight streaming through an opening some twelve feet above her. Her left hip throbbed fiercely. She sensed that, miraculously, nothing was broken. She looked up once more to the sunlight entering through the opening above. As she had feared, Cruz now loomed above her, blocking most of the sun's light, peering down into the darkness. He uttered something she couldn't understand, and then Mateo joined him in looking into the pit.

"Is she down there?" Mateo asked.

"It is too dark to see clearly. But I think she is there, sí," Cruz answered his brother. Genieva sat very still. The pit was too dark and deep for them to see her clearly, but she knew she mustn't move.

"I'll go for rope," one of the vaqueros offered.

"No!" Cruz shouted. "McLean will be back too soon. We leave her. If she is dead . . . she is dead. It is a long fall to the bottom, but such a strong woman would not be killed by such a simple fall. She lives . . . We will return for her. Vamos."

"But what if she climbs out?" one of the men asked.

Cruz chuckled. "She won't. It is a good prison down there, and no one will think to look here for her. We'll come back when there is the darkness of night." Raising his voice, he shouted into the pit, "Do you hear me, niña? You have nothing to fear. I will come back for you later!"

"We cannot leave without finding out if she is hurt or . . ." Mateo began.

"We will leave!" Cruz shouted. "The woman has caused enough trouble for me. And I know this way . . . if I cannot have her . . . well, then neither can McLean."

"Cruz," Mateo argued. "You said we were only going to frighten McLean. You said nothing about harming the woman, but now I know you want to . . ."

"Cállate!" Cruz shouted. "And you will say nothing to Papá about this! Do you hear me, hermano? Nothing!"

They were gone quickly, and Genieva was left

alone—safe for the moment. Her eyes adjusted to the darkness within her prison, and she began to look about, gasping when she saw the dead and rotted carcass of an animal lying only a few feet away. Judging from the skull and length of the leg bones, she surmised it had been a cow. She pitied the animal for the suffering it may have endured if the fall had not killed it.

The ground was damp, and the musty smell of the enclosure tickled Genieva's nostrils, causing her to sneeze several times in succession. There were masses of spiderwebs everywhere and insects of every sort caught fatally in them. As she looked about, Genieva noticed that large wooden beams lined the sides of the pit and ceiling around the hole through which she had fallen. Common sense told her she had fallen into an old mining shaft of some kind. Yet seeing no other beams of light before or after her as she peered into the endless darkness, she knew it would be pointless to try to venture in either direction without a lantern.

Genieva was sore from her fall, and when she stood, she felt the full force of the pounding her body had taken from her plummet—for her tender limbs, bones, and muscles ached the like they never had before. Looking up into the bright sunlight, she wondered, should she cry out? Would anyone hear her? Or would her pleadings for help only serve to draw Cruz back, intent on finishing his purpose concerning her? She decided to wait. Surely Brevan would notice her missing when he came home midday to find no lunch and no wife awaiting him. She would wait. Brevan would come. Seeking out a dry area, she found a large rock near to the beam of light radiating from the opening overhead. Carefully, she sat down and tried not to think of the dead animal next to her. How had the cow fallen through? There were no other visible signs of an opening above her. She shivered, for the dampness caused the air in the shaft to be cold as well.

As Brevan mounted the stairs to the front porch, a frown puckered his brow. He could not smell any inviting scents coming from the house to indicate Genieva was preparing a midday meal. Furthermore, the front door was still closed. Genieva always opened the front door upon rising in the morning. Brevan knew how she longed for the morning breezes in the kitchen. He thought that maybe she still slept. But until midday?

He pushed the front door open, and his gaze was immediately drawn to the floor near the hallway. An overpowering sensation of dread filled him as he gazed at the apple core and the wilted daisies. There was blood on the floor—smeared blood. On closer inspection he saw several drops of blood staining the floor nearby as well. Panic as he had never imagined caused his hands to begin trembling as, looking up and into Genieva's room, he saw the door was hanging by only the bottom hinge—the top and second having been broken. A moment before he entered the room, his attention was arrested by the fingerprints on the door. Small, blood-embossed fingerprints—he knew they were Genieva's. The window in her room, which he had closed and latched himself the night before, stood open, the breezes billowing the curtains. Rushing back outside, he saw the hoof prints in the dirt. He swore under his breath—scolding himself for not having noticed them before. He ran around to the side of the house and saw Genieva's small boot prints in the earth beneath her bedroom window. They led in the direction of the orchard, and he followed. But the moist ground between the apple and pear trees only told him that Archuleta horses had been there. The wind-fallen fruit was smashed into the grassy earth, and there would be no tracking anyone through it.

Brevan's breathing quickened as his fists clenched with fury and overwhelming worry. He ran a hand through his hair. He had to think—to act rationally. And so, running back to the barn and wasting no time in saddling, he mounted a barebacked horse. He would ride to Travis and Brenna's home.

"They've taken her, I tell ya!" Brevan shouted as Brenna and Lita both burst into tears. Brian and

Travis could only stare at him, stunned momentarily. "In the least of it they have taken her!"

"This has gone on long enough!" Brian bellowed then. "We must go to Juan Miguel. He has her. He wants you to come . . . but we'll go together. We three, we will. And we'll get her back, Brevan."

"To think what they may have done to her, Brian," Brevan breathed. Lita sobbed bitterly.

"Brian," Travis said then. "You take Lita and the baby and Brenna into town. I'll go with Brevan. Tell Sheriff Dawson what's happened. I only hope he's back from Santa Fe by now."

"Where's me wife, Archuleta?" Brevan growled. He dismounted his horse and began striding angrily toward Juan Miguel. Cruz stepped in front of his father, however, and Brevan stopped his advance, glaring hatefully at the filthy villain before him.

"What's this? Why do you put your dirty feet on our land, McLean?" Cruz asked.

Inhaling deeply, Brevan delivered a powerful fist to Cruz's midsection, sending him crumpling to the ground and gasping for breath.

"What is the meaning of this, Señor McLean? You come onto my land and attack my son?" Juan Miguel raged as he moved toward Brevan.

Facing Juan Miguel, Brevan repeated his question. "Where is my wife? What have ya done

365

with her? Believe me when I tell ya that if that maggot-infested son of yars has laid one finger on her, I'll kill every member of yar family that I find here!"

Juan Miguel patted Mateo reassuringly on the back as the young man came to stand beside his father. Turning to Cruz, he asked, "Cruz, do you know anything about Señor McLean's esposa?"

Cruz pulled himself to his feet and shook his head, feigning innocence. He moved to stand face to face with Brevan and spat, "I have no idea where your esposa is, McLean. And if I did, I would not tell you, for the look of fear on your face is enough to give me pleasure for years to come."

Brevan's massive chest rose and fell with barely restrained vengeance. He closed his eyes for a moment, fighting for self-control. He had to stay calm. He couldn't kill the man until he had found Genieva—else he may never find her. He looked to Mateo for a moment. The expression of guilt blazoned on the young man's face was his undoing.

"'Twas Archuleta horses that trampled me orchards," he addressed Juan Miguel, though he glared intently at Mateo. "Four of them. I'll give ya one guess who rode them in."

"I hate you, McLean," Juan Miguel growled. He spit on the ground at Brevan's feet and said, "I want your lands, but I do not have your wife.

I would not harm your woman. I do not need to use a woman to get what I want."

"Even if I believed ya," Brevan growled, "I know Cruz has the devil in him and that he has threatened Genieva many times since she first arrived here. He has taken her!" he shouted. "He has taken her, and it is on yar head that I place the blame, for the deviled demon in him was begat by you!" Turning back to Cruz, Brevan clutched the fabric of the front of his shirt. "Tell me!" he shouted. "Tell me where she is!"

"I am so sorry, hombre, I cannot tell you," Cruz said, an evil smile on his face as he shook his head. "I don't know where your little niña is. Perhaps she has gone to a better man. A man who . . ." His words were cut short by Brevan's powerful fist meeting squarely with his nose.

Rushing forward, two vaqueros took hold of Brevan's arms, pulling him backward and away from Cruz. But Travis raised his rifle, aiming it squarely at Juan Miguel's head.

"You let him be, Archuleta. Or I'll put a bullet in that ugly mug of yours," Travis growled.

Juan Miguel ordered the men to release Brevan. He frowned as he addressed Cruz, "I said nothing about harming the woman, Cruz. Do you know where she is? I am beginning to wonder if there is some truth to what your hermano Joaquin has told me."

Cruz chuckled and dabbed at his bloodied nose

with his shirt. "I have no hermano Joaquin, Papá. I have no interest in the señora. McLean has lost her somewhere and blames me."

Juan Miguel looked to Mateo, who immediately lowered his gaze. Though he still seemed uncertain, Juan Miguel insisted, "Cruz says he has not seen your esposa. He is my son. I stand by him."

Brevan laughed once—a disbelieving laugh of being awed by the man's feigned stupidity. "He stalks women and violates them, and ya stand by him? If ya deny what he is, Juan Miguel, then ya're truly a demon with him."

Juan Miguel stood silent for a moment. He looked to Cruz, who nodded reassuringly at him. "Get off my land," Juan Miguel growled then, reaching to his back and producing a pistol. "You will not come here and accuse my son of such deeds!"

Brevan wanted to lunge at him—pound him into the earth with his own fists. But the thought of Genieva stopped him. He must find her. He had no doubt Cruz and Mateo knew where she was, but he was beginning to see that perhaps Juan Miguel was earnest in not knowing of her whereabouts. He seemed truly unnerved by Brevan's accusations. Brevan knew he must remain unharmed—stay strong for Genieva. If harm came to him, he knew harm would come to her. More than he feared already had.

"We'll go," Brevan agreed. "We'll go for now. But know this, Juan Miguel . . . me wife's blood is spilled in me own house. Her footprints and the shoe prints of Archuleta horses are trailed to me orchards. She has disappeared, and yar son is responsible for it. I will find her. I will find her, and then I will find you and yar criminal sons. And when I do, ya'll wish the screechin' banshee had found ya first!"

As they turned to leave, Brevan mumbled, "We must look for her, Travis. Genieva is not there. Juan Miguel would know it, and it was not on his face. Still, the younger son, Mateo . . . he knows. I am certain he knows what happened. We'll go back to the orchard and look. The trail has to go somewhere. She has to be somewhere."

Brevan was physically ill with worry—his mind conjuring too many horrid fates that his beautiful Genieva may have endured. He felt a hot stinging as the moisture rose to his eyes, and he coughed to fight its release.

"Genieva," he muttered as the fear in him rose to a level he thought might render him helpless should he give in to it.

They searched. Brian arrived from town after having left the women and the baby with Mrs. Fenton. And they searched. Sheriff Dawson was still away, and the one deputy that the town owned had gone to confront the Archuletas himself.

"We can't see anymore, Brevan," Brian repeated again some hours after the sun had set. "We can't see."

Brevan shook his head, clenched his jaw, and pointed an angry index finger at his brother. "Were it Lita or Brenna, I would do no less, Brian. We'll look. We'll look until we drop dead from it."

"Brevan," Brian said calmly. "I only suggest we be goin' back to the house for some lanterns. We can't see where we ride in the dark, and it will do Genieva no good if we injure ourselves."

Travis put a quieting hand on Brevan's shoulder. "He's right, Brevan. We need light. We'll look. We'll look until we find her, but we need light."

The house was dark as they approached it—for there was no beloved wife at home to have lit the lanterns as the sun had set.

As they neared, the hair on Brevan's arms and legs and the back of his neck prickled as Brian mumbled, "Oh, preserve us! The pond. In the pond, Brevan."

Swallowing hard, Brevan slowly turned to look at the pond as they neared. The moonlight shone through a break in the clouds—he felt his heart nearly stop as his eyes fell on the white object floating in the pond. It was motionless. It was Genieva! The white of her petticoats and blouse billowing up from the water's surface was all too vivid in the moonlight.

Leaping from his horse and shouting in anguish, Brevan ran headlong into the water, swimming frantically toward her. Gasping for air and choking on the agony in his throat, he reached out, taking hold of the white fabric and pulling Genieva's body toward him.

"We wanted to be sure you found . . . something, McLean," Cruz's voice said from the darkness. Brevan tore at the fabric then to reveal only a large log beneath it. Swimming vigorously to the opposite shore, he ran at the villain, but Cruz spurred his horse, and Brevan stumbled to the ground.

"Where is she?" Brevan shouted angrily at the villain as he stood, spitting water from his mouth and wiping it from his eyes.

Brevan had felt relief when he had realized it was only a log floating in the water—relief that weakened his body for a moment. He stood still, nearly gasping for breath as Mateo rode up beside Cruz.

"Well, she's not in the pond," Cruz chuckled.

Ignoring the villain's insanity-laced sarcasm, Brevan looked up to Mateo. "Ya're a good boy, Mateo. Like Joaquin," Brevan panted as he labored to catch his breath. "Tell me where she is, lad."

Mateo looked to Cruz and then to Brevan and back. He shook his head, shrugging his shoulders in defeat.

"She has left you, McLean. Left you for a real man!" Cruz shouted. The sound of Brian's rifle shattered the night air, and Cruz clutched his grazed leg.

"Wait!" Brevan shouted. "They know where she is, Brian. Wait!" But Cruz was provoked, and Mateo obviously unsettled.

"I spit on your name, McLean. And I spit on your esposa! Mí padre is a fool! This land . . . it's all he wants. But me . . . I am smart. I want much more. I want the lands, I want you dead, and I want your esposa. Sí, I know where she is, McLean. She is nowhere." Then shouting, "Apúrate, Mateo!" he rode away.

Mateo's horse stomped the ground anxiously, but the young man paused. Just before following his brother into the darkness, he said in a lowered voice, "The rocky hills to the north. A pit. She's fallen there. I do not know if she lives." Then he rode away, following his brother.

Frantically, Brevan mounted his horse as Brian and Travis joined him with it. "The old mine!" he urged them as he dug his heels brutally into his horse—heading to the house for lanterns.

The moist, confined air with its odor of molds and moss was causing Genieva's stomach to sour. She had tried to stay calm—tried not to panic during the day while the sun still shone down through the opening above her. But the sun

372

had set hours before, and she now sat in complete darkness—praying that the moon would rise high enough at any moment to allow some hint of light into her prison. When the sun had set, it had also taken what little warmth had been given her, and now she was chilled and wet as she sat—in the dark and so very frightened. The cold, merciless anxiety devised by anticipation overwhelmed her. Night had come. And with it, would Cruz? Would Cruz keep good his threats to return for her? And what then? She knew all too well what he meant to do to her.

"Brevan," Genieva whispered aloud. "Please find me, Brevan." And she thought of him again, as she had all through the day and evening. What inexplicable joy she had known the previous night when she had realized he did, indeed, love her. When he had confessed his love aloud as she gazed into the deep blue of his eyes, she had thought for a moment she was dreaming—but she hadn't been dreaming—it was true. She'd realized then, too, that it had not been a dream she had experienced the night previous to that one—the night following the birth of Lita's baby. When he had gathered her into his arms, telling her of his love for her, she'd realized that the smell of him, the feel of his powerful arms around her, the smooth surface of his skin were too familiar to have only been dreamt of before. She remembered at that moment that he had carried her to bed—

held her warmly in his embrace through the night. And all the time she thought she had dreamt it.

And now—oh how she ached for Brevan's strength again—longed for the security that only he could provide for her. She thought of the soft feel of his hair between her fingers—the feel of his whiskery face beneath her palms. She broke into goose bumps at the memory of the warm, sweet taste of his mouth when he kissed her. She thought of him dancing about in the rain weeks earlier—like a king of the little people happy in his trickery. She thought of him covered in cake batter—standing angry before her one moment and chuckling as he dragged her into the pond the next. She thought of him championing her before her father—his capable hand pressing firmly against her belly—and she smiled then, knowing that someday she would carry his child there. She thought of the story Brenna had told her about Brevan and his desire to grow tall and strong. He was tall and very, very strong, and she smiled at the thought of him up to his ankles in fresh cow manure. Yet in the next instant, her delight quickly changed to sobbing as tears of fear and despair flooded her cheeks. *She* was safe for the moment. Certainly she was imprisoned in a lightless cell of mildew and death, but she was safe. Was he? She had tried to fight thoughts of harm coming to Brevan—for hours she'd fought them. But now, fatigue and despair won out, and she cried for him. Cried for him to help her, yes, but cried more over the anxiety of not knowing whether or not Cruz had murdered her husband in the hours since she had fallen.

Then, as if heaven itself had understood her fears, she heard him calling from above, "Genieva? Genieva? Do ya see anythin', lads?"

"Brevan!" she cried, standing and looking toward the opening overhead.

"Genieva, where are ya, lass?"

"Brevan, down here." Instantly a lantern appeared through the opening. She prayed thankfully and silently as it then illuminated the rugged features of her husband's face.

"Are ya well, lass?" he asked. Without waiting for an answer, he said, "Brian, fetch the rope from yar saddle! Quickly, lad! Ya wait there, Genieva. I'll be down in a minute. Ya just wait right there."

Genieva laughed and smiled through her tears of relief. "Where would I go, Brevan?"

"Ya weigh more than ol' Aunt Tilly, ya do, Brevan," Brian grunted as he and Travis lowered Brevan into the old mine shaft.

"Quit yar squawkin', and get me down there to her, Brian," Brevan scolded.

Before his feet were on the ground, Brevan reached for Genieva, pulling her tightly into his powerful embrace and against his invincible body. "Genieva," he whispered into her hair. "Genieva, Genieva, Genieva."

"I was beginning to . . ." she sobbed against him.

"To doubt me?" he finished.

"No. Never to doubt you," she corrected. "To doubt that you were safe. How did you find me?" she asked then.

"Mateo. I think there is some streak of conscience in a few members of that family, at least," he explained. Brevan tilted Genieva's face up in order to clearly see the wound at her cheek. "Are ya hurt otherwise?" he asked.

"I think I'll have a nasty bruise on my hip, and every bone in me aches. But otherwise . . ." Genieva began to answer.

"Ya fell in here before . . . before Cruz laid his hands on ya and . . ."

"I did. Thank the heavens. I fell instead of his catching me," Genieva assured him, touched deeply by the expression of intense concern on his face—the excess moisture in his eyes.

Taking her face between his hands, Brevan whispered, "I thought . . . I thought . . ." Without finishing what he had begun to tell her, however, he wiped the tears from her cheeks with his thumbs—kissing her mouth tenderly. As Brevan let his forehead rest on Genieva's for a moment, the love she felt for him swelled so profoundly that she could not endure it, and she favored him with a fully fierce and fervent kiss. Again Genieva experienced Brevan's kiss unleashed—

powerfully impassioned—and she marveled at its addictive essence.

"Ya're far too warm, ya are," he said, breaking from her suddenly. "Quickly, Brian! She's fevered."

" 'Twas the dampness and cold," Brian told Brevan some time later as they watched Genieva resting quietly at last. "But I'll wager she'll be fine when mornin' comes. Then we should take her into town to be safe with Brenna, Lita, and the baby."

Brevan nodded, caressing Genieva's cheek one last time with the back of his hand before rising and following Brian out of the room.

When he'd closed the door securely, Brian said, " 'Tis quite the turnabout ya've made where she's concerned in the last twenty-four hours." Brevan scowled at his brother, but Brian only chuckled and added, "Ya've admitted to yarself that ya love her finally. I thought ya'd never give in to it, Brevan."

Brevan nodded, placing a hand on his brother's shoulder. "Ya were right all the time, brother Brian. I thought she saw me only as a way to escape whatever it was she was runnin' from. And then she saw me as her taskmaster. I-I think I feared she would reject me as her friend and as her lover. She's so headstrong and proper . . . and I'm so headstrong and improper."

"A match made in heaven, brother Brevan," Brian chuckled. "A true and heavenly match."

"Travis," Brevan greeted as he entered the kitchen. "I thank ya, too, I do. Brother," and he shook the man's extended hand.

"I'm only glad that we found her. That we found her well and alive," Travis sighed. "But now one of us should be getting into town. Brenna and Lita will be sick with worry."

"You go, Brian," Brevan suggested. "Ya'll be wantin' to check on yar family. Travis can stay here with me, and we'll meet ya in the mornin'. Did ya find out when Sheriff Dawson will be back?"

"Tomorrow evenin', I was told," Brian answered. "We'll get help then, and Cruz will be run off for good."

"Run off? Runnin' him off won't be payment enough for what he's done to me wife, Brian," Brevan growled. "He's an animal and deserves less mercy than hangin', he does."

Brian nodded. "Juan Miguel is blind to his son's evil deeds."

"That he is. I've little compassion for his blindness . . . for he chooses to blind himself."

Travis had offered to keep first watch. Yet when Brevan woke and raised his head from the table where he'd fallen asleep in his chair to be greeted by the first rays of sunshine and the rooster's crow, he knew something was wrong. Travis should've awakened him long before daylight. Picking up his rifle, he slowly opened the front door. He saw Travis lying on the porch, apparently unconscious, as he felt the whip tighten about his throat. It choked him brutally, and Brevan dropped the rifle as his hands went to the mean strip of leather threatening to strangle the life from him. Brevan recognized Cruz's voice—chuckling at his ear as he held the whip tightly around his throat.

"Enough, McLean," Cruz growled. "This ends, now!" He shouted an angry order in Spanish. Mateo stood to one side as two other men loomed before Brevan. The triumphant grins apparent on the vaqueros' faces angered Brevan further, causing the Irishman's temper to flare more furiously than ever.

Genieva startled from her restful sleep when she heard a loud clatter from outside on the porch. When it was followed immediately by an angry, "Ándele!" she knew Cruz was in the house. Quickly she rolled from the bed and scooted beneath it the instant before the door to the bedroom burst open. She watched as two sets of boots stood just inside the room, the men obviously searching for her.

"Mateo!" came Cruz's angry voice again, "Apúrate! Apúrate!" Genieva clamped her hand tightly over her mouth as she watched one of the men kneel down on the floor. They would find her! She could only watch, paralyzed with horror, as the quilt hanging from the bed was raised and the face of Mateo Archuleta appeared before her.

His eyes were intent upon Genieva, but his expression uncertain.

"She is not here, hermano!" he shouted, letting the quilt fall once more and leaving her safe in her hiding. The two men left the room, and Genieva exhaled. She waited until she heard the heavy tread of their boots leave the porch. Carefully, she crept from beneath the bed and into the kitchen.

She gasped, horrified, as she looked out the kitchen window to see Cruz and two other men dragging Brevan toward the orchard, Mateo following. Brevan's neck was encircled by the lashing leather of a whip, and she knew Cruz meant to kill him. She heard moaning and peered out the front door to see Travis lying on the porch.

"Travis!" she called in a whisper. "Where's Brian, Travis?" But he was unconscious once more and unable to respond.

Burying her face in her hands, she fought to win control of the fear gripping her. They would kill Brevan! She knew they would. She was his only chance at escaping. Taking a deep breath, |she watched as the men entered the orchard. Quickly, she slipped out of the house, hiding behind anything concealing in her path and making her way to the orchards. When she found them, her heart begged her to scream as she heard the brutal snap of the whip as it tore into Brevan's flesh. They had tied him between two trees, stretching his arms out painfully on either side of him—each arm tied to a tree parallel with another. His shirt had been stripped from his body. The lash met with the bareness of his flesh.

The repeat of another lashing caused Genieva to flinch—to nearly cry out. Two more strikes, and Genieva could bear it no longer. Cruz was chuckling lowly—speaking to his men as he pulled the weapon back and readied to administer another painful lash.

"Cruz," Mateo interrupted. It was obvious he feared Cruz. Still, Genieva sensed his young conscience was stronger than his fear for a moment. "I have to speak. It is wrong. This . . . what you do. Papá gave McLean the land."

"Cállate!" Cruz shouted. "I care nothing for mí padre's land, coward! But McLean has made a fool of Papá. He has made a fool of me! Are you like Joaquin? Do you want to leave me? Leave the family?"

"No, mí hermano. No. But this . . . it is wrong. And what you did to McLean's wife. It is more wrong."

"What are you talking about, Mateo? Cruz told me he did nothing!" Juan Miguel suddenly appeared from the opposite side of the orchard.

Both men stood silent for a moment as Cruz whipped Brevan again.

"He did, Papá. He tried to get her . . . to violate her . . . only yesterday. It is why McLean came to our land. I-I told McLean where the woman was because I was afraid she might die where we left her." Juan Miguel took Mateo firmly by the shoulders. The look on his face was that of disbelief. "It is true what Joaquin told of his amor, Amy Wilburn. It was Cruz, Papá."

Juan Miguel lowered his head in defeat. "It is as I feared then. I heard the horses leaving, and I followed you here." Looking up at Cruz, he continued, "I don't want to believe these things about you, Cruz, but how can I doubt when it is before my eyes?" Turning his attention to the two vaqueros who had accompanied Cruz, Juan Miguel ordered, "Leave here! You have betrayed me! I pay your wages, but no more. I will not pay men who disobey my orders. Never show your faces on my lands again!" The men nodded, turned, and simply rode away.

"Your lands will only return to you when McLean is dead, Papá," Cruz argued.

Seeing that Cruz and the others were distracted, Genieva rushed from the tree that had concealed her. Running to Brevan, she threw herself against him a moment before the lash of the whip struck her own back, causing her breath to abandon her lungs. Never had she known such pain! Yet, somehow, she managed to remain standing. She would protect Brevan from another stinging lash—protect him as long as she could.

"Híjole, Cruz! Stop! You are an animal to whip a woman!" Juan Miguel shouted, grabbing his son's arm.

Cruz wrenched his arm from his father's grasp and laughed. "Ella es tan dulce . . . she is so sweet to try and protect him. But I don't mind whipping a woman, especially her!"

"Let go, Genieva," Brevan panted. "Run. Run for a horse!"

"No," she gasped. Then, sliding her hands from his back to his stomach, she reached quickly into his trouser's front pocket, retrieving the pocket-knife she knew he kept there.

"No, Cruz!" Mateo shouted as the man readied to strike again. The back of Cruz's hand met violently with his brother's face, knocking Mateo to the ground. Genieva nearly dropped the knife as the pain of another whip's lash cut into the flesh of her own back. Trembling, she raised the knife to the rope binding Brevan's right arm, anchoring his strength to the tree. With every shred left of her own strength, she cut it. Though beaten and bleeding profusely, Brevan acted quickly. Snatching the knife from Genieva's hand and pushing her to the safety of the ground, he cut the rope binding his left arm and turned to face Cruz. Genieva looked up to see the powerful man that was her husband shake his head and point an index finger at Cruz.

"You'll die now," Brevan growled.

Genieva looked to Juan Miguel and Mateo, letting her eyes plead with them. They seemed stunned by Cruz's actions, unable to react. Their disbelief, their inability to comprehend, was manifest in their eyes and expressions.

"Idioto! It will be you that dies now! Like a coward in front of your wife!" Cruz threatened, a triumphant smile spreading across his face. "There are three of us and only one Brevan McLean."

"No, Cruz, you are only one. You are not my son," Juan Miguel said in bitter despair. "You face McLean alone."

Cruz drew back his whip, sending it violently at Brevan. Brevan caught the lash in his hand as he allowed it to wrap painfully around his arm. With the intense, concentrated strength of his strong body, Brevan ripped the whip from Cruz's hand, tossing it the ground.

Genieva tried to stand, but the wounds on her back weakened her. She could only watch helplessly as Cruz lunged forward, knocking Brevan to the ground with the force of his fury.

"You bleed like a butchered cow, McLean," Cruz growled as he labored to wrestle Brevan to a disadvantage. Brevan gave no response but kicked the villain fiercely in his midsection, rendering him immobile for a moment.

"Cruz," Juan Miguel began, helping Genieva to stand. He seemed to be unaware of the brutal battle taking place between his son and Brevan—a vicious match of possible death. "Did Cruz try to . . . ?"

"His intentions were vile," Genieva sobbed bitterly. She was frantic! Brevan was near to being murdered, and Juan Miguel stood questioning her as if nothing were amiss at all. "He's ruined at least one woman, and he meant to do no less to me!"

"Why? Why would he . . . ?" Juan Miguel said, shaking his head.

"Why not?" Genieva cried. "You've sent him to hurt and harass Brevan. Why do you think him incapable of violating women? He is what you raised him to be!"

Juan Miguel shook his head as he looked to Cruz, who was struggling to stand. "No. I did not raise him to murder men or to harm women."

"I am your son, Papá. Your only true son," Cruz growled.

Genieva rushed to Brevan—for the blood streaming from the wounds on his back was profuse in the least.

"Joaquin," Cruz sneered, "he is a coward. And Mateo is the same. I am the only son you have that you can be proud to call son."

Lunging unexpectedly once more, Cruz grabbed Genieva's shoulders, throwing her to the ground before drawing a knife from his belt and cutting Brevan severely across the chest. Brevan responded by kicking Cruz's hand, sending the weapon through the air, and it disappeared in the grass.

Genieva screamed as a brutal series of fist-blows were dealt between the men. It was a horrid sight, and she looked to Juan Miguel.

"Stop him! Stop him! Cruz . . . he means to kill him!" she cried.

"He has the eyes of a devil, Papá," Mateo mumbled. "El diablo. I see the evil in him clearly now."

Juan Miguel still stood silent—making no move to assist either his son or Brevan. As if unable to comprehend his own actions, or those of Cruz, he turned and began walking away.

"Stop him!" Genieva pleaded with the man. Juan Miguel suddenly appeared older—weaker than a moment before. "You're the only one who can stop your son!"

"He is no son of mine. I-I . . ."

"Cruz!"

Genieva looked to see Brian and Joaquin approaching.

"Brian! Stop them!" she cried out. Looking back, she saw Brevan lose his footing—stumble backward as Cruz dealt a particularly lethal blow to his jaw. "Brian!"

"Cruz! Stop, or I'll kill you," Joaquin shouted.

Cruz turned. He looked to his brother a moment before Brevan hurled his body at him, sending Cruz plummeting to the ground. Brian ran to where his brother wrestled with the villain on the ground. Taking hold of him firmly, Brian pulled Brevan from Cruz. Joaquin reached down and took hold of Cruz's collar, pulling him to his feet.

"I should let McLean kill you for what you have done. You deserve no mercy for it," Joaquin growled.

Cruz, gasping for breath, only smiled, spit blood from his mouth, and laughed. Brevan pulled himself from Brian's grasp and stumbled to Genieva. Helping her to her feet, he gathered her into his arms, pressing her pain-stricken body gently against his own in a careful embrace. His breathing was labored, and he swayed slightly from side to side.

"Genieva," he whispered. "Ya shouldn't have . . . look at ya, lass." Brevan's face constricted with the guilt and anxiety he was feeling at Genieva's being beaten. She knew he felt her pain worse than he did his own, and she shook her head, reassuring him of her well-being.

Angrily, Brevan shouted at Juan Miguel, "Ya gave the land to me mother! Of yar own free will, Archuleta! That land I would've given back to ya, and well ya know it's the truth. But ya wanted everythin'! Me own lands, me brother's, and me sister's. Ours was not yars to have!"

Juan Miguel turned to face him.

Slowly, he nodded, saying, "Sí. You are right. I see now the evil in my soul, and I ask your forgiveness. I ask your wife's forgiveness. I ask forgiveness from my daughter and my true sons," the man confessed, looking from Mateo to Joaquin.

"I am your true son!" Cruz shouted. Reaching out, he drew a knife from Mateo's belt and raised it high above his head as he charged toward Brevan. "You will have your lands, Papá! I am Cruz Mondragon Archuleta! Your son!" he shouted.

Genieva heard the other blade slicing the air a moment before it embedded itself deep in Cruz's chest. He stopped—dropped his weapon as he took hold of the knife protruding from his own body. Pulling it from his chest, he looked up to Joaquin. Joaquin closed his eyes for a moment before facing Cruz—Cruz—his brother—his brother who would die from the knife thrown by his own brother's hand.

"Joaquin?" Cruz choked. "Mí hermano. You . . . you are my brother."

"And I pray for mercy on your soul, mí hermano," Joaquin whispered as Cruz fell to the ground. Cruz's evil was ended.

"I never meant to kill you, McLean," Juan Miguel muttered, kneeling beside his dead son. "I only meant to . . ."

"Ya've lost far more than a man should, Juan Miguel," Brevan breathed. "I can pity ya now for that reason. Take the sons ya have left and change yar ways, man."

Juan Miguel looked up to Brevan and nodded. "I will plague you no longer, Brevan McLean. No longer." He stroked Cruz's hair gently, and his anguish shown plainly on his face. "I have done you a large wrong, McLean. I am sorry, too, for Cruz. H-he . . ." The old man could say no more to Brevan. He simply sat staring at his dead child. "Oh, niño. Mí hijíto."

Brian took one of Brevan's arms from around Genieva, placing it about his own shoulders, helping to support him. "Ya're losin' face in me eyes, big brother. I've never seen ya so close in a fight."

Brevan smiled at his brother's ability to lighten the weight of his pain. He turned to Joaquin and offered, "I thank ya for me life."

Joaquin was pale, and Genieva pitied him. Evil or not, it could be no easy thing to kill one's own brother. It would haunt his mind forever.

"I have married mí amor yesterday," Joaquin stated. "I am taking Amy to Santa Fe to live. It is how I knew you were in trouble . . . for I was in town when Brian came to Lita last night. I knew Cruz would . . . I knew he would . . ." Joaquin was unable to finish. He asked simply, "You will let us visit Lita again before we go?"

Brevan frowned. "Me? Of course. But that is not for me to decide," he answered gesturing to Brian.

"Lita would have it no other way," Brian assured the man, offering a forgiving grin. Joaquin nodded.

"Travis!" Genieva exclaimed then, as she saw her brother-in-law wandering into the orchard before them. He held a hand to his head but seemed well otherwise.

"Help us above!" Travis exclaimed upon seeing Brevan's condition. "I-I'm sorry, Brevan," he apologized, shaking his head. "I . . . didn't see . . . they came from behind me and . . ."

Brevan put a hand on the man's shoulder. "It's none of it yar fault, Travis. None of it at all."

Genieva looked back to Juan Miguel and Mateo. They struggled to lift Cruz's body from the grass where it lay. Joaquin went to them, and Genieva watched as Juan Miguel placed a reassuring hand on Joaquin's shoulder. Joaquin bent, lifting Cruz slowly from the grass, cradling him in his arms. Brevan's gaze followed Genieva's, and they watched as the Archuletas left solemnly.

Brevan sighed. "He's . . . it's finished now," he said.

He gently turned Genieva's face to his own. Tenderly caressing her cheek with the back of his hand, he whispered, "Ya've given me life again, and in so many ways, Genieva. I thank ya for them all, lass."

Epilogue

The months had passed quickly since Cruz Archuleta had died in the orchard—and with them came a healing of wounds, both physical and emotional, for Brevan and Genieva. The apples and pears had been plentiful—as was the work. The first snows had arrived and with them Brenna and Travis's son, Sean.

Genieva sat contentedly in a chair, listening to Brenna and Lita dote on their perfect children. She looked to where Brevan sat before the fire talking with Brian and Travis. Her joy was manifest across her face in the form of a smile as she watched the men chuckle at something amusing in their conversation. Brevan seemed to sense her gaze upon him. He looked to her briefly, winking merrily. The familiar warmth that permeated her being at his attentions spread throughout her as a warm, comforting bliss.

Genieva's happiness was complete. Never had she imagined such a wonderful man—such a wonderful life could be hers. In that moment, the knowledge was overpowering, and she rose, taking her shawl from its hook behind the door and walking out onto the front porch.

The air was cold and very, very still. The frost gently floated through the night sky—sifting softly to the ground—dusting the surface of the newly fallen snow—as if a million tiny slivers of glass shimmered in the moonlight.

"It's too cold for ya to be out here without yar coat, lass," Brevan said from behind her.

The sound of his voice warmed Genieva far better than a thick, woolen coat ever could. His arms encircling her body from behind caused her to shiver with the thrill of being in his embrace.

" 'Tis a beauty of a Christmas Eve, it is," he commented. His breath in her hair was comforting, and she let her head fall back against his shoulder. He bent and whispered in her ear, "I love ya, Genieva McLean. Ya're the beauty and rapture of me life, lass. Did I live before I had ya?"

Genieva closed her eyes—content to stay in his arms forever.

"Did I breathe before I had *you?*" she whispered. Then, taking one of his hands in her own, she slowly slid it from its place at her waist, resting it squarely on her abdomen. She pressed his hand firmly against the place and softly said, "I have a special Christmas present for you, my love."

"Ya do? And what might that be, me lassie?" he asked.

"It's something you have to wait awhile to enjoy," she whispered as she caressed the back of his powerful hand lying gently on her belly.

"What is it?" he chuckled.

"Well . . ." she began, "it's either a boy or a girl."

As he turned her body in his arms, her heart knew pure delight—for the expression on his face told her his feelings—even before he spoke the words.

"Truly?" he asked, his face beaming with pride and joy. Genieva nodded, and he gathered her fully into his embrace. "Did I live before I had ya, lass?" he asked before pressing his lips to hers in a gentle kiss.

"Did I breathe before I had you, Brevan McLean?" she repeated.

Brevan brushed several snowflakes from Genieva's lovely, freckled face—gazing down into her amethyst eyes.

Smiling, he answered, "I don't know, lass. But I'm yar breath now. And you are breath . . . you are life to me."

And the kiss that Brevan had gifted to Genieva as her own so many months before was hers once more—warm, impassioned, deliciously moist, and filled with the heavenly promise of everlasting love.

Author's Note

I cannot believe that it has been ten years since *The Heavenly Surrender* was first published! Furthermore, I can't believe it's been even longer than that since I wrote it. And I certainly can't believe that it continues to be a "reader favorite" after all this time—but it does. Thank you, thank you for allowing Brevan and Genieva to linger in your heart the way they have lingered in mine.

I thought it might be fun to include a few little morsels of insight and history where the story of Brevan and Genieva McLean is concerned—a privileged glimpse at the things and people that inspired me while I was writing it. So what do you say? Are you game for a little meandering through my mind?

I've come to enjoy writing my Author's Notes. I find that I discover the most interesting things about myself and the venues of inspiration along which I travel during my writing processes. Sometimes I don't even realize certain things were inspired by my personal experience until I sit down to reflect about a book. Yet *The Heavenly Surrender* has always cached sources of scenes, scenarios, and personal experience for me.

Let's begin with this—*The Heavenly Surrender* was actually my first novel-length book. Before writing it, I found I usually grew impatient with a story—that I didn't have the attention span to write more than 30,000 words or so. Books like *The Unobtainable One*, *The General's Ambition*, *Indebted Deliverance*, *The Foundling* (you currently know that story as *Desert Fire*), *To Echo the Past*, *Divine Deception*, and *Sudden Storms* were all novella-length and represented my novice years of writing—the ones I used to cut my teeth on, so to speak. However, when I began to write *The Heavenly Surrender*, something changed: I wanted the story to linger— to last longer—and so it did!

Let's begin our amble through *The Heavenly Surrender* with a little insight into Genieva. I think Genieva was the very first of my characters in whom I allowed a smidgen of myself to be manifest via her physical appearance. I mean, we all know that when we read a book, we tend to place ourselves in the main character's shoes— to commiserate with her or him, right? But this is the first time I actually allowed the heroine to own a physical characteristic I own—freckles!

At the time I was writing *The Heavenly Surrender*, my youngest son was just a toddler— and wildly adorable! With black hair, light blue-green eyes, and a smattering of freckles that a body couldn't help but smile over, he was just too cute for words! The little freckles on his nose and cheeks just made everyone want to smooch them! People were always complimenting his freckles—though he wasn't sold on the fact that they were cute. Well, this is something I shared with him—and empathy for being noticed for one's freckles as a child. It's also something I share with Genieva.

As a little girl, I had freckles too. Though not nearly as adorable as my son's, I was forever being told how cute they were. Of course, like almost every other child in the world with freckles, I didn't think they were cute at all! Not one iota! Adults always told me how cute they were—but boys at school teased me incessantly. Add to that a little ditty my dad used to sing to me—a song about freckles, which included a comma that my dad would intentionally misplace in order to change the meaning of a certain lyric—and I was thoroughly a freckle hater. The song lyric went thus: "She's got freckles on her, but she's cute!" Dad was forever singing it this way: "She's got freckles on her butt, she's cute!" First, I most certainly did not have freckles on my you-know-what! Second, it just used to make me mad, and then Dad would laugh (actually, roar with laughter) at my irritated indignation! Needless to say, my freckles weren't my favorite thing as a child.

However, as I grew up, I realized that freckles weren't all that common. Furthermore, older boys began telling me my freckles were cute—

though not in the same manner in which my dad used to sing about them. Therefore, I eventually came to terms with my freckles. I even grew up enough to think the "freckles on her butt" thing was clever. (I recently found the real song—it's called "The Freckle Song"—and in the real song, the girl is "nice" instead of "cute." Just a note of trivia for your own useless trivia archives.)

Anyway, Genieva has freckles—I mean, she really has them. You do understand that to an author, all her characters are real people, right? Thus, I can tell you with full assurance that Genieva has freckles. It's something she and I share—perhaps via lineage and genetics—who knows! Regardless as to why we share this little pigment anomaly, Genieva and I both discovered that lethally handsome men like her Brevan (and my husband, Kevin) actually like freckles! (Hmm . . . Brevan? Kevin? Do you sense a little similarity there?)

Let us move on to Brevan for a moment. And what better place to begin than his name, right? So many friends and readers have written to me asking about the origin of Brevan's name. However, I don't think it was until a couple of years ago when someone asked me for the etymology of "Brevan" that I remembered where my brain had pulled it from.

I knew that I had named Brevan from a combination of my husband's name, Kevin, and the name Bevan. As you know, my husband's name fits him perfectly—*Kevin: an Irish or Gaelic name meaning "beautiful at birth, handsome, beloved."* See what I mean? Perfect for my Kevin! I liked the name Bevan because it sounded like Kevin, but it just wasn't, you know, cool enough for the character living in my mind. So, I started doodling on a piece of paper and eventually came up with Brevan! Interestingly enough, if you search on the internet for the meaning of the name Brevan—or look through any name books—you can't find any etymology for it! I suppose I should go onto one of the name sites and plop in my own two cents of where it originated. If you search for the name Brevan, only one thing comes up—one man with the name. Thus, I didn't really have an answer for the person who had asked me for the meaning of the name—and she was planning to name her new baby son Brevan! In the end, I simply told her my tale—the way I had contrived the name for the hero of *The Heavenly Surrender*—then added that she could always tell her son that he was just like Rake Locker, the hero in *The Time of Aspen Falls*—that he was named after a handsome, heroic character in a romance novel his mother had once read!

Speaking of Brevan—we cannot discuss Brevan McLean without making reference to his alluring Irish accent, now can we? Seriously, it's delicious the way he talks—don't you think? The fact of the matter is that I was a little nervous about it—about writing in dialect like that. But it's how Brevan talks—so what's a girl to do? In my mind, as the dialogue proceeded, Brevan's thick, delicious Irish accent just could not be slighted—I had to include it! And I'm glad I did! It was the only way to be true to Brevan and his siblings—to their heritage and all they worked so hard to hang on to.

Writing dialogue in dialect? Most authors don't do it—most editors would probably tell you it's suicide for a book. But you know me—I always have to be true to myself, and Brevan's accent is a very important part of who he is. And besides, authors and poets of long ago used to write in dialect, and their readers read it—so I figured we're all as smart as anybody else, even if we do use one third of the vocabulary used two hundred years ago. James Whitcomb Riley wrote in dialect. He was famous for it! Joel Chandler Harris did as well—and who doesn't *love* to read Uncle Remus? Elizabeth Gaskell also implemented dialect—as did many, many others! So, I tossed caution to the wind and went with my heart. I'm so glad I did!

As I said, I think Brevan's Irish accent only lends to his charisma and magnetism. Proof of that: A few weeks after having first read *The Heavenly Surrender*, a dear friend of mine (who shall remain anonymous for obvious reasons) called me up and said, "I had the most *wonderful* dream last night! I was on an airplane, sitting next to Brevan McLean! He was *so* gorgeous! And his accent . . . was too fabulous! And his kissing skills . . . whoa, baby!" Thus, I figured if my friends were dreaming about Brevan, writing in dialect must be okay (whew!).

Now, let's take a moment and talk about Cruz—the icky, rotten villain in *The Heavenly Surrender*. He's a creep! And I have to tell you—it took a lot of courage for me to write about his, shall we say, "immoral antics." If you think about it, the context of what Cruz did to Amy Wilburn, and threatened to do to Genieva, was horrifying! But it's what he did—and who he was. I actually struggled a little with revealing all this in the book. As you may recall, *The Heavenly Surrender* was first written when I was still only giving my stories to close friends and family. As it was my goal to write clean, uplifting romance stories, having to refer to Cruz's past actions and intentions was difficult for me—not because I couldn't write it but because I didn't want to freak my friends out. Therefore, I let one other of my closest friends, Karen, read *The Heavenly Surrender* as I wrote it. My friend Sandy was already reading it and giving me the thumbs up—but I felt I needed another reaction to Cruz.

What's funny about letting Karen read *The Heavenly Surrender* is that, having not grown up in New Mexico the way I did, she applied a little phonics as she read the book. It wasn't until well into the book (when it's finally revealed what really happened to Amy Wilburn) that Karen called me up one day and said, "I hate Cruz!" Of course, the funny part isn't that she hated Cruz—the funny part is that instead of calling him Cruz—pronounced "Cruise"—she referred to him as Cruz—pronounced like *crud,* "Cruhz." The moment she said it, I burst into laughter! It seemed so appropriate that she should rhyme his name with "crud." I loved it! From then on, Karen and I always referred to him as Cruddy Cruhz.

Anyway, back to Cruz, the villainous violator of a woman's virtue (I can never say the "R" word for that). It was a little nerve-wracking for me—having a villain who had actually violated a woman's virtue, as opposed to just threatening to do it. But that's what he did—he was that evil. (We can talk about him in the past context because Joaquin killed him, of course. By the way, I knew a boy in high school named Joaquin. He was such a nice boy.) Therefore, I had to tell the truth. And so I took a chance and wrote the book the way I wanted to write it—even where Cruddy Cruz was concerned. You may think I'm an idiot for this, but it was a big leap for me— entirely liberating, of course—but a big leap. I finally felt like I was telling the whole story for once—the good, the bad, and the very ugly.

You know how random my thoughts can be—how they can stray to another path very quickly. Well, it just happened! Thus, I'm going to jump over to something else I wanted to tell you that you might not already know: I almost deleted the famous "cake batter" scene from *The Heavenly Surrender*! I know! Can you even believe it? What was I thinking? I must've lost my ever-loving mind for a minute! After I'd finished writing the "cake batter, pond, kissing" scene, I thought, "Oh everyone is going to think that's soooo corny!" Therefore, for a few brief moments, I considered deleting it and starting over where Brevan and Genieva's first kiss was concerned. But (and I mean a super-big BUT), again that's what actually happened in their story! So, I left it—worried about it a ton—but left it in, again trying to stay true to myself and my characters. In the end, I'm certainly glad I didn't delete it! The "Brevan and Genieva cake batter, pond, kissing" scene still ranks at the top of the list when friends and readers tell me what their favorite moments in my books are (another big "whew!").

Which then leads me to this: sometimes Brevan gets a bad rap at first—that he's mean and uncaring and stuff. However, those of us who truly know him—see deep into his soul—

understand him (that would be you and I, of course)—know that his gruffness, his standoffish harsh manner, is simply his defense mechanism. Naturally, that all comes out later—but it always bothers me when someone misjudges my Brevan. I feel that, in truth, there are a lot of people who are misjudged because of their outward appearances. I think a lot of people don't wear their heart on their sleeve so that others won't know their true pain. I think the same is true with people who often put on a gruff, unapproachable vibe—it's their way of protecting themselves from pain. In other words, if no one gets close to them, they can't be hurt. That's Brevan. Sure, he was worried about losing his farm and stuff—but at his core, it was his fear of not just being distracted by Genieva but of loving her and knowing pain because of it. I'm glad *you* understand him.

(Oops! My brain just took another detour!) "But what about the plowing accident?" you may be asking yourself. "Was it based on a real event? Or is it purely fictionalized?" The answer is this: it has been changed, but the accident that inspired it was real!

Wayne States is my maternal grandfather and one of my very favorite people in life! He also quite often serves as profound inspiration for some of the characteristics and life experiences of the cowboy/rancher/horse breeder heroes in my books. I remember so many heroic things about him—the way his big ol' leathery hands would hold the steering wheel as he drove his pickup—the way he'd go out into the garage, find a black widow spider, and just smash it—"pop!"—between his thumb and forefinger. He did the same thing with a bumble bee once! I remember riding with him in his pickup when all of a sudden I started to panic because there was a bumble bee buzzing around on the front windshield. My grandpa simply reached up and smashed it with his big ol' leathery thumb! It was awesome!

Grandpa intrigued me in so many ways! He had a sort of Sam Elliott-type voice. In fact, every time I hear Sam Elliott, I think of my grandpa! As a small child, I was utterly mesmerized by the way he would alternately flex his biceps. I have a perfect vision in my mind of my grandpa sitting in the big leather rocking chair we owned (which had once been his), wearing his signature white sleeveless undershirt, with a regular undershirt over it—his hands tucked up behind his head—alternately flexing his biceps. I had never seen such skills! It was wonderful!

I remember my grandpa dancing a jig sort of dance in the kitchen of his house when I was older. I used to sleep in the bedroom just below the kitchen when I was visiting—and by about six a.m., he would begin to grow impatient with waiting for me to get up. Thus, he would start stomping around doing a jig on the kitchen floor and singing "Cigareets and Whusky and Wild, Wild Women" to wake me up. It was wonderful!

I remember his laughter—it's so clear in my mind! I especially remember the way he'd go, "Oh ho ho ho!" with a simultaneous smile and frown on his face whenever I hurt myself. It was a sort of amused hysteria he owned. He was concerned for me, of course—but it made him chuckle too. How do I know it was an amused hysteria? Because my mother and I both have it too! I don't know if it's a learned response or a genetic one, but my mom and I will both do that same thing if a child has just softly fallen down or bumped its head. It's weird, but it reminds me of my grandpa, so it's okay!

Well, when my grandpa was twelve, his father sent him out to a field with a team of horses and a disk harrow. It's kind of hard to describe what a disk harrow is. The best I can do is to say it was a now-antique piece of farming equipment. The driver sat on a metal seat above a line of disks that basically broke up the ground (plowed it) when the team pulled it. From his seat on the harrow, the driver would control the team with the lines the same way a wagon was driven (sort of). Grandpa was disking when the disks hit a bump in the field (probably a big clod of dirt or roots). The bump caused the harrow to pitch him forward instead of backward, and he fell in front of the disks. The team pulled the disk harrow over my grandpa's shoulder and back. Many farmers were killed or terribly mangled by similar accidents. Whether because the dirt was extremely soft or simply because he fell to the outer edge of the disk harrow, my grandpa was badly wounded but survived.

My mother described the scar left on her father's (my grandpa's) back: "Dad had a long scar on his back from his right shoulder blade, downward at sort of a slant, to the center of his back. The scar was half an inch or more wide and very, very long." I remember seeing the scar when I was a kid—and believe me, it was mighty impressive! My grandpa was funny about the scar too. Having a great sense of humor as he did, my grandpa always told people that a drunk had stabbed him with a broken beer bottle and that was how he received the scar. In fact, my mom was a teenager or older before she finally heard the truth. I think the real story is more impressive myself.

The song "Will There be Sagebrush in Heaven?" by the Sons of the Pioneers always reminds me of my grandpa. I think he would've asked the question and hoped there would be. (Personally, I can't imagine heaven without it!) Wayne States rode rodeo into his sixties, always loved horses and livestock, ate green onions right out of the ground without even washing them off, and when it was time for him to ride through that beautiful sagebrush in heaven, he went as he should have—literally dropped in the saddle.

When Grandpa was sixty-nine, he was helping to move some cattle on another ranch. The other rider with him rode ahead of the herd to open a fence, leaving Grandpa to close the fence at the rear of the herd. When the herd passed but Grandpa wasn't with them, the other rider rode back and found my grandpa lying on the ground next to his horse. The left ventricle of his heart had "burst," and he was dead. As devastated as I was by the unexpected and heartbreaking loss of my beloved grandpa, it always comforted me to know that he dropped in the saddle. It was exactly as he would have wanted to leave this earth— riding a horse and driving cattle (heavy sigh . . .). I miss my grandpa every day of my life.

So, there you have the story behind the inspiration for Brevan's plowing accident. As I'm writing this, I remembered that Brevan's dancing the jig in the rain was also inspired by my grandpa and his "wake up" jigs. I'm sure there are many other moments inspired by my grandpa—too many to list, I'm certain.

Speaking of scars—Brevan *really* gets banged up in this book, doesn't he? I've been asked why on several occasions. And the best answer I can give is this: because chicks dig scars! Further- more, we girls love a man who can take a brutal punch, then lay a villain out with one punch in return, right? Additionally, heroes (true heroes) always, always defend a woman's virtue against villains, protect and care for her, would take a bullet and die for the woman they love. Thus, how can a man like that *not* have scars? To me, scars are evidence of life lived—strength and endurance—experience. And in the end, I'll just say it again: we chicks dig scars! Simple question—simple answer.

You know, there is another little incident in *The Heavenly Surrender* inspired by something someone once related to me: the story Brenna tells Genieva of Brevan as a child, standing in the fresh manure pile in order to try and make himself grow tall. My friend Nan has a son (Terry) who, as a little boy, admired one of his cousins—everything about his cousin—especially his height. One day, Terry asked his cousin how he'd managed to get so tall. That's the moment the tall cousin told Terry that all he had to do was go out in the pasture one morning, find a fresh, steaming cow pie, stand in the middle of it, and chant, "Grow! Grow! Grow!"

Well, one morning when Nan couldn't find Terry and was beginning to worry, everyone went looking for the little tawny-haired boy. Where did they find him? Way out in the pasture—standing in the middle of a pile of cow manure, chanting, "Grow! Grow! Grow!" to himself! And you wanna know something? I think it worked! Terry's very, very tall! I thought the story was hilarious, of course, and asked Nan and Terry if I could use it in a book. They laughed and laughed and gladly gave me permission. Thus, Brevan had a similar experience to Terry's as a child. I love it!

Certainly, the most difficult part of *The Heavenly Surrender* for me to write was the (nervously, clearing my throat here) . . . the, um . . . (as I refer to it) the "consummation scene." It's not that I thought I couldn't write it; it was, again, my fear of writing about it delicately. You know? I almost chickened out at one point. But my friend assured me that I couldn't skew the story line. That was what happened, and it needed to be affirmed to the reader. Thus, I hitched up my petticoats and sat down in my computer chair (which at the time was a large white storage bucket) and began to write the "consummation scene" of *The Heavenly Surrender*.

To this day, it remains one of the hardest things for me to have written. Not because it's so detailed but because I wanted it to be just right. After having spent literally three hours on the same paragraph, I took a break and called another friend—you know her—Barbara. She's my "says it like it is" friend. Yet she knew I was delicate as far as the stress of writing my first "consummation scene" was concerned. So she proceeded with caution.

Her first suggestion was this: "Why don't you just put a lot of blank lines with a caption that says, 'fill in per individual preference or experience'?" Of course that immediately cracked me up to gut-busting laughter—sort of de-stressed me—and I was able to finish up the "consummation scene" between Brevan and Genieva.

In the end, it turned out quite harmless and vague. In fact, another friend wasn't even sure the marriage had been "consummated" after she'd read the paragraph! It's funny now because I wouldn't blink about the same situation these days. But it sure was stressful for me way back then. How funny—I'm such a goofball some-times.

Well, I'm sure that by now you're worn out from my babbling, right? Still, I enjoyed reminiscing about a few things that inspired me while I was writing *The Heavenly Surrender*. I really hope you did too and that you'll savor the story of Brevan and Genieva all the more now. It's a story that lingers in my heart as well as my mind because of my family history stories and heartfelt moments sifted through it. So here's wishing you lavender and pink sunsets, sweet fragrant sagebrush, romantic kisses in the rain, the comforting smell of horsehair and saddle leather, and everything else that makes life a *heavenly surrender!*

~Marcia Lynn McClure

The Heavenly Surrender
Trivia Snippets

Snippet #1—I *love* squeaky screen doors! My grandparents (on both sides of my family) always had squeaky screen doors, and I guess that's what makes the sound so beautiful to me. The houses I grew up in had them too, and I miss them so much. It's rare to hear one anymore—another simple pleasure lost to the past. When everything is really quiet—if I close my eyes and listen really hard—I can almost hear those old screen doors squeaking open as my grandma (or mom) steps out onto the old porch—smiling and holding a mixing bowl in one hand (the inside all drizzled with cake batter), holding a spatula in the other, and asking me if I want to "lick the bowl."

Snippet #2—At one point in *The Heavenly Surrender*, Brevan grumbles, "Ya're starin' at me like I've some creepin' crud about me," to Genieva. It's a very trivial little snippet indeed, but "creeping crud" is a phrase my mom used to always use. Let's say she had a little chapped spot on her arm or something—you know, a little dry skin that often appears in the winter. She'd say something like, "Oh, I wish this would clear up. I look like I've got the creeping crud!" I always loved that! Oft she would switch it for "ghastly disease" (for example, "I look like I've got some ghastly disease!"). Both of those terms are forever imbedded in my vocabulary, and I found "creepin' crud" worked very well for Brevan's dialect.

Snippet #3—Brevan is one of my heroes who takes off his shirt one of the same ways that my husband, Kevin, does—in one swift, muscle-displaying motion! Kevin has two ways of doing this. One is just like Brevan—by reaching back and taking hold of the back of his shirt and pulling it off over his head in one swift (again), muscle-displaying motion. The other way is by reaching over with his right hand, taking hold of the bottom of his left sleeve, and then stripping his shirt off (left to right) over his head. A couple of years after I had written *The Heavenly Surrender*, I was approached by this huge, hulking, muscle-bound ex-Marine whose wife had been reading my books. He was quite an intimidating presence. He looks at me and says, "I told my wife she can't read your books anymore." With chattering teeth, I squeaked, "Why is that?" He looked at me a moment, frowning, then said, "Last night she told me I take my shirt off wrong!" The response that silently echoed through my mind was, "Well then, you'd better work on it." However, I simply squeaked, "Sorry," and hurried off. The wife of the huge, hulking, muscle-bound ex-Marine later assured me that her husband was only teasing me (even though she really *had* told him he took his shirt off the wrong way the night before). Still, I wasn't so convinced and simply avoided him as often as possible after that.

About the Author

Marcia Lynn McClure's intoxicating succession of novels, novellas, and e-books—including *A Crimson Frost*, *The Visions of Ransom Lake*, *The Bewitching of Amoretta Ipswich* and *Midnight Masquerade*—has established her as one of the most favored and engaging authors of true romance. Her unprecedented forte in weaving captivating stories of western, medieval, regency, and contemporary amour void of brusque intimacy has earned her the title "The Queen of Kissing."

Marcia, who was born in Albuquerque, New Mexico, has spent her life intrigued with people, history, love, and romance. A wife, mother, grandmother, family historian, poet, and author, Marcia Lynn McClure spins her tales of splendor for the sake of offering respite through the beauty, mirth, and delight of a worthwhile and wonderful story.

Center Point Large Print
600 Brooks Road / PO Box 1
Thorndike, ME 04986-0001 USA

(207) 568-3717

US & Canada:
1 800 929-9108
www.centerpointlargeprint.com